THE ADVERSARY

Remember Matt Boyer

The Slender Reed

Which Grain Will Grow

THE ADVERSARY

BY H. H. LYNDE

Random House, New York

c. 2

"Day of wrath! O day of mourning!
See fulfilled the prophet's warning . . ."

PART ONE

"*The sons of earth
are waking
To penitential tears.*"

Death was the adversary Mr. Bixby had
predicted: the world was to end on that
day. Many people in the California town
believed him, but some scoffed at the
prophecy.

CHAPTER 1

Norma awoke, suddenly, as though someone had spoken to her. But
it was still dark and she could hear no sounds in the house, as for a
moment she lay listening attentively . . . and then for another
moment . . . wondering what had been on her mind when she went
to sleep, that it could lurk there in the corner waiting for her,
already pressing upon her before she had even recognized it.

Well, what day was this? Wednesday. Yes. Now she remembered:
Wednesday, and the next would be (or would *not* be!) Thursday,
the twenty-second of March, the date for which these neighbors
of hers were tensely waiting in exaltation or dread. Poor, silly people,
Norma thought. As if there weren't already plenty of actual things
to apprehend without dreaming up something grotesque like this.
It was going to be a difficult day, trying to steer a tactful course
between the ones who believed, and the ones who didn't—and of
course those others who apparently hadn't heard a word of it. Like
Roger and Miriam (who had been visiting her for two weeks now).
But it was still hours away, and besides there was something else—
something very pleasant. Why should one think of the disagreeable
thing first, so that it got in the way, blotting out the sun before it
ever rose?

Joyce would be back. That was it, and far more important to her
than anything else, which was selfish of her, she thought, unashamed.
(But aren't we all?) It was absurd how she missed the child, even
on a ten days' visit; more now than she had when she was away in
school and college for months on end. Though she suspected the
reason for that was simply that one of these times when Joyce
went away—and probably quite soon now, if not with Jim, then
someone else—it would be for good. Bound to be, and exactly as any
mother would have wished it, she told herself. But that was the

3

day—not Thursday, as they said—when the world would come to an end for her . . . And thinking that, she *was* ashamed. Norma Collins was more tolerant toward others than toward herself. And to have entertained such a thought for even the instant that it took to flash through her mind—to have let out such a puny-hearted, puerile, self-pitying cry, silent though it was . . . she had really shocked herself.

Go away, thought. All thought . . . Be still, like the night, can't you? For it was still night, and Joyce was coming back tomorrow. Joyce, and joy, together. She could remember the first time she had said those two words together . . . Still lying in bed one morning before it was quite time to get up and the baby was making funny cheerful little noises to herself over in the corner, and Bart had gotten up and taken her out of the crib and brought her over to Norma: a big fat armful of her by that time, about two years old. Eighteen months? She must have been. And smiling fondly, letting her bounce and burble beside her on the bed, she had murmured, "Joyce . . . my joy-forever," but the last word so soft it was scarcely uttered, and the baby gave another bounce and gurgle and echoed only what her ear had caught. "Jo-ey?" she repeated experimentally. And Bart, standing above them, had laughed and said, "Well, there you are—that's her first nickname." But no one else had ever used it; just the two of them. They had waited a long time for her, after those two miscarriages of Norma's, and everything about this baby was unique, unprecedented in the world. Joey . . . Norma hugged it close, the memory, the nickname, the very thought of Joey to keep her warm in her single bed (and to protect her too, from other thoughts which never died). And turning, slept again.

While, at the opposite end of the house, Roger was still awake, and had been since four o'clock. Four-seventeen, to be exact, when he had turned on the bedside lamp and checked his watch once more. Easy to misread those little blobs in the dark. Though he could almost have set the damn watch by the time he woke up, every night; or morning, whichever one cared to call it. It was a routine with him now. As usual, he'd gotten up and put on the wool dressing gown lying nearby, and cinched the belt around

4

himself. The fact that this was southern California didn't mean that it was warm at four A.M. . . . . And then, purposefully, crossed the room to the cupboard door which stood ajar, and swung it back so that the shoe bag hanging against the other side was right at hand. There were two or three pairs stuck neatly in their separate pockets, and he reached for the left shoe of the black pair, which he had not had on since he left the city, and had no intention of wearing while he was down here. Putting his hand deep into the toe, he extracted a package of cigarettes, and a screw-top lid, about two and a half inches in diameter, which had once belonged to some glass jar. He had to go back into the shoe again for the paper packet of matches.

He lit his cigarette by the dresser, and took a long drag of satisfaction; pocketed the paper packages but kept the metal lid ready in his left hand as he started over to the window. Halfway there he was reminded that his feet were getting cold, and he turned back toward the bed and shuffled into the slippers lying there. Miriam was always at him to put on his slippers.

He went to the open window then, and stood there, drawing deep on his cigarette and looking out on the quiet world of hills. The moon was down, long since, but even with the light in the room behind him, he could see one long sloping line down into the ravine, and beyond, a fainter one where the farther slope appeared to join it. It was all gray-black, and very peaceful. The quiet and the peace were balm, and yet even as he took them into his soul, along with the forbidden smoke, he did not, could not, quite believe in them. Oh, they were real enough, here and now. This was a California hillside, after all, and this was also a period between wars—between major wars, let us say. But *he* knew that the sense of inner comfort, of peace and permanence which they gave, was false. He could never quite forget that, no matter how still the moment, or how remote in time it seemed from what he knew to be the actual date in the twentieth century. In the Year of Our Lord, he thought somberly. It was a wonder that anyone could still use that phrase, though he supposed that many did.

Nevertheless, he could enjoy the dim view and the lovely stillness,

5

and the smoke, in an objective kind of way. Like a connoisseur in certain rarities. He smoked the cigarette close to the end and put it out carefully in his tin bottle top, and carried it along with him as he started to prowl. He crossed the room again (large and well appointed it was, for a guest room, though he was scarcely aware of that, and it had never occurred to him that Norma had moved out of hers, to let him have it), gently unlatched the door which led out into the patio, and stepped outside.

Sometimes he prowled the length of the ambulatory, to the paved terrace outside the living room, where they all spent so much of the daytime. Sometimes he went out through the gate in the low wall on his right, to look across at those other hills to the east. But tonight he simply stood outside the door and looked around—and up. He could see the stars now; though they were, he thought, beginning to fade. He regarded them, but thought nothing else about them. You were supposed to have ponderous thoughts when you looked at the stars, but he did not. They were too far. Too far away. Roger Norbeck was a man still close to his own world: the other side of the world, quite frequently, but still *his* world. He'd been over and around a lot of it, when all was said and done. He stood there, letting a few minutes slip idly past him in the dark, almost tangible in their passage, yet not quite touching him. Until something else brushed by against his leg, and paused and brushed back again in reverse, with a soft insinuating pressure, and Roger gave a sharp grunt of annoyance. That cursed cat again; it thought he was a pal, no doubt, because they were fellow prowlers in the night. But Roger had no use for cats, and he didn't appreciate the attention. Damn near broke his neck over the brute a few nights back. So now he muttered, "Go on with you, Cleo—get out," and moved his foot firmly to one side and the cat with it, until it was well out of his way, and then he turned and went back into his room, closing the door as softly as he'd opened it, though he had little fear of disturbing anyone. His room was at the end of this wing, and Norma had suggested that Miriam and he have two rooms adjoining so that both could get all the rest they needed out of this visit. It was pretty decent of Norma to have them for a month.

6

She'd always been a good friend. Well—and he'd tried to be a pal too, when she'd needed one. Since 'way, 'way back . . . Since that time in L.A. when she'd had a job in—was it Wilner's—or Wilburn's—no, what was the name of that store? No matter. And Joyce was only five or six, blonde and fat, cute as a pup. And he was still in the advertising department on the paper. But advertising was not for Norbeck; not for the long run. (Propaganda, yes; advertising, no—and what was the difference might one ask, except the product that one tried to put across?) In any case, he'd left that department of his life a good way behind him, when he became a *news*paperman—in the most literal sense of that word.

So where was he now? On a hillside, with a bad pump. And from here on, climbing hills or stairs or anything that went up—walking too fast, working too hard, late hours—were all verboten. Drinking also except for those two per twenty-four hours, doled out like a prescription. Smoking—wenching, presumably? No, no, Norbeck, that was irrelevant and immaterial, now; all out. No strain, no excitement. And that was what he'd lived on all his life: tension, deadlines, even a spot of danger now and then. They'd talked some twaddle about a nearly normal life; didn't realize that what they'd left him with was for him a sort of human hibernation—temperature 'way subnormal. Oh well, he'd gotten used to the idea by now. But he wasn't sure that Miriam had. He paused for a second on his way back across the room, to consider the door which stood between them, not quite closed, at his request. Though for some reason *she* didn't like it left wide open; she made some excuse about the light shining into his room if she read late. And of course there was this other side of it . . . when he got up and paced around in the night. Not that he believed it would ever waken her. She slept so deeply, so sweetly. Sometimes he went in there and stood looking at her—as when the moon was late and high last week . . . At her dark hair spread out, and the blurred shadows of her arms and breast, and her face with just the dark arch of eyebrows marked against it.

(Miriam, my love. If you are still my love . . . oh, *not* unfaithful. God no, I don't mean that—how could I ever mean that? But it's not just a wife with a conscience that I need. And I'm not much of a husband these days; don't think I don't know it. Maybe, again, in time. But will you wait—can you last it out—your love, I mean? Will it dry up—or drain away in some subterranean channel? Or will *I* drive it away, in spite of myself? I have one hell of a disposition these days. And sometimes I can't *find* you when I want you, dammit. Oh sure, I always want you—always will I guess, somewhere in my blood—only I don't mean that now. And I don't know how women really feel about it in their hearts—or maybe in their minds. I don't think they ever let us know—except for the moment maybe, the one incandescent moment now and again.

But there are all those other hours . . . and days . . . and how they add up when one's ill, my dear—you'll never know, I hope. They always seemed too few, before—but I never knew there were so many hours in a day. A night. The hours of darkness, by day *or* night, when I have such need of you, even when I turn you away—can't you understand?)

No, he didn't think she did. And it seemed to him at times that even when awake, she was as unconscious of that longing which was a kind of emptiness in him, of that weariness which weighted down his legs and soul alike, as she was when she lay there drowned in sleep. He didn't go into her room tonight; his imagination passed easily through the three-inch crack between door edge and jamb, and saw her lying—on her side, with one bare arm bent in a long living arc, dusky against the dead whiteness of the sheet, the long shape of her slightly blurred by a thin covering of blanket. Though never blurred for him. But he left his imagination where it had strayed off into the other room, and went over to the window again, and pulled up the comfortable chair and sat down, a huddled shadow facing out into the night.

His attention was caught after a moment by a spark of light down below, which went out at once, and presently came on again a little farther to the left; a double spark, he saw now, so it must be a car just leaving the village and starting the snakelike climb between one hill and another before it would reach this level. It had vanished again as it wound around the base of one, and he watched

8

to see if it would appear in any other gap. It was unusual enough to see a car pass by here in the daytime, so he speculated idly as to who this could be, while his eyes searched the dark outline where one slope met another. Couldn't be young Joyce coming back at this hour—though now he thought of it, Norma had said the girl was returning from her visit in L.A. tomorrow (which was today of course) . . . And why the hell couldn't it, if somebody's driving her down after a party up there, say . . . What's four A.M. to kids of that age, anyway?

The headlights did not reappear. But then he thought he saw a sort of glow, or brightening—from the glare against a wall, maybe— and it would be just about where that next house was, a quarter of a mile or so below Norma's. In the daylight, you could barely make out a pink piece of house among its heavy shrubs and flowers. So that would be the temporary neighbor he'd heard her speak of casually; fellow who'd rented the place for some months past. Came down from the city just for week ends, she'd said . . . Yep, that must be it, because the glow had gone off now, abruptly, like the flick of a switch. And a minute later an oblong patch of light sprang out; an open doorway with an upright shadow crossing it for a couple of seconds, until the door closed up the blackness again. Oddly, it gave him the feeling of being shut out—because, he supposed, he had had a momentary sense of another human being, awake and alive with him in the world.

How idiotic can a man get in a lonesome moment? He thought fleetingly of Norma, who had known what one kind of loneliness meant; found himself wishing—with an intensity that was so like prayer that it amazed him—that he could find a way to talk to Norma. *Norma*, he said urgently, insistently, as if he could make her hear though his lips had shaped themselves around her name without a sound. He believed she was the sanest woman he knew; and there were things she would know, *as* a woman. About Miriam, perhaps. And some of the other answers that eluded him. Women seemed to be able to talk things out. He didn't know why. Depended more on advice, maybe? Something outside, or detached from themselves, though it was elementary that they took everything more personally. Yet they didn't have a man's fierce, protective sense of privacy. That deep-rooted, grim reserve, which would keep its problems, its independence of decision, and its deepest hurts to its own self, come hell or high water . . . Why, there was nothing he could talk to Norma about! What was the matter with him, anyway? Needed his head examined—more than an electro-cardiogram, no doubt.

He fished for the cigarettes and lit another, and felt the package growing thinner, flabbier between his fingers. Made a mental note that he must get hold of that fellow with the assorted eyes, and ask him to get some more before he ran out. He had only one more package cached away now; like an alcoholic with his bottles hidden here and there, he thought, and grinned to himself. Fact was, he'd been afraid he'd have the very devil of a time to get any up here on Norma's hillside, until he'd tumbled to the arrangement she had with this chap to pick up the mail and newspapers for her every morning, and sometimes bring along some extra supplies from the general store in the village. He was a sanctimonious old cove, though, and Roger hadn't too much hope of him as a conspirator at first. Didn't seem to smoke or drink, or even swear. Roger had been honest enough, himself: explained candidly that they'd cut off his smoking for his own good, but added that of course it was a lot of damn foolishness to think a pack or so of cigarettes a day (or night) were going to do him in—or even shorten up his precious life!

"And right you are, sir," the old boy had said, fixing the blue eye on him, with a strange exalted glint. "With only the ten days to go, anyhoo—why, a lot of dern foolishness, *as* you say! Happy to oblige, Mr. Norbeck, sir—and I'll just leave 'em outside the gate here, in under the hibiscus bush—eh? The wife wouldn't think of looking for them there, now would she?" And he winked the brown eye— the solemn one, and Roger made an idle guess that the other man once had a wife who pried and snooped, and that might be the reason why he'd been so ready to co-operate. Could be; or had the fellow thought, just to look at him, that Roger only had about ten days to live anyway and so absolved his own conscience of any responsibility? Not that it mattered, one way or another. Except that, turning it over in his mind again—why yes, if he himself believed his time was really up, he'd be a lot happier about the whole situation. Fact.

At first, when it was touch and go with him, that was the actual assumption (he'd seen it in Miriam's eyes, despite the doctors' cagey generalizations; her eyes, in which both fright and love were so clear —then). But then it had lengthened out again for him—the probability—the possible span of life. And here he was today. And— here was Miriam too. With all those months of care, and wear upon her patience; of wear in the sense of friction between two moving parts too closely linked together. What had she to look forward to, except more of the same, for an indefinite period? Not mere weeks and months, but years, quite possibly, if he were careful—and always assuming that the Russians and Chinese—and all others including ourselves—were careful too (which was a larger and far more unjustified inference than the first). Miriam was eight years younger than he, but she was *young*, and he was now an old man to all intents and purposes. Middle-aged in fact but old in actuality. And crotchety as hell, and he knew it, and didn't mean to be—and was, regardless.

The first couple of months had been the worst for him, personally, not only the physical inaction, but finding his horizon shrunk from the broad global one it had been, to a matter of what he could read in the papers. The discovery of the number of hours there are in a day—in every single separate day—as though one had never before learned to read the figures on a clock face, had never once noted that the progress of the earth around the sun was scarcely perceptible to the eye of an ordinary, average man. A discovery almost as startling as that of one's own mortality, when first glimpsed at close range! One got the idea eventually, but with him, it had taken a couple of months to percolate. Not that one went around bellyaching, meantime. Anybody took what came, with the best grace one could, outwardly, but it took a hell of a lot longer to accept, inwardly, than anybody realized.

So . . . he was used to it now. And he'd learned to read the clock, even to watching the second hand, because he could really see that move. And there were days now, and even some nights, when he could think in terms of years again; figured he might have time to accomplish something more. *He* might, personally—if the state of the world permitted. There was always that catch now, in everybody's calculations, and it came first—not second, whether one were old or young. But if he was to have that time, it would have to be paced out at this rate, at so many revolutions *less*, a minute, than a normal everyday life. And that's where Miriam came in, for she was tied down to his rate of speed. Slowed down to watching over and keeping step with a superannuated partner.

They ought to have had children, maybe, but there were a couple of unanswerable arguments against that. First—the life they were living then held little room for children; even less room in which to bring them up decently. Knocking around the world, never knowing how long they'd be in one place—having to be in two places at once, literally, if she couldn't follow him. So they'd wait awhile, that's what they'd said. Later, maybe . . . Well, it was later, all right, and the second argument, to him, was more unanswerable now than it had ever been. Why (it ran) bring children into this particular world at this period in its history?—between World Wars II—and III? (Or would we even know when III began?) To be blown off it again at any moment. Or worse, to be left, like the piteous fragments of humanity he'd seen: without home or parents, without food or shelter. Babies with old faces; faces that contained at once the blankness of innocent incomprehension—and the predatory cunning of animals . . . Like some he'd seen in Korea . . . And a few years earlier in Germany; in Poland . . . Oh, Jesus Christ, why go back over them? It was a damnable thing to bring new life into an erupting, decaying, disintegrating civilization. And that was one regret he needn't have on his conscience. Whether he lived two more years or ten, he wouldn't have to listen to the patter of little feet as they grew into Number 9 loafers, and sit here wondering how to teach them to find their way through a forest of buried mines which were the facts of life. Not sex, but Life, and its concomitants, disease and death.

At which point, having completed once more the circle which

he had traveled so frequently before, sometimes by day and sometimes at night, his thoughts shot off on one of those inconsequent tangents which probably keep most of us sane when our needles get stuck in the same groove for too long. His meager ash tray was getting dangerously full, and he'd better dispose of the evidence before it got scattered over the rug, and gave his guilt away next morning—no, today. Besides he was getting cold. He got up and shuffled carefully over to the bathroom, where he dumped the stubs into the toilet and watched them flush out of sight with a kind of furtive enjoyment. (A guy had to have some fun!) And he would now go back to bed and read for a while, and then doze off again most likely, and sleep heavily for a couple more hours, before another day arrived, with a line of days beyond that on the waiting list. Until something blew up; the world around him—or the heart inside him. (Which would it be? Place your bets, *messieurs et mesdames*.)

PART TWO

"Marching as to war . . ."

CHAPTER 2

He was a rather fat little man, the one who drove alone down the coast highway in the very small and early hours of that twenty-first of March. Yet despite his solid weight—and the laughter such a notion would undoubtedly have caused among his acquaintances—he had at times felt almost bodiless. A curious sensation, as though his whole person, this *thing*—this endomorphic thing—which he called Bixby, were merely an instrument or conductor through which some current was steadily flowing toward an impersonal, distant but eventual purpose. He had that feeling again tonight, distinctly. Disembodied, yet not in any way detached from the force which moved him.

In fact, it seemed to him that the car he drove was the nearest thing to a body which he possessed at the moment; a projection of his physical self, though it bore no possible resemblance to the latter. On second thought, it might be the flesh and bone which had become a projection of this metal power plant, humming along through the night; not the other way around. (Those two strong beams of light converging on the road ahead were the eyes of the machine, not his. They saw, where he could not. As for the brain guiding and co-ordinating, was that his? Or in its automatic responses and reflexes, was it not also just a part of the machine itself?) In any case, the destination was the same, and the main point and purpose of this trip through the anonymous dark was so small as to appear scarcely a pinpoint on the map of one lifetime. Demonstrably unimportant, compared to the larger affairs he was accustomed to dealing with . . . The people to whom he had said good night at two A.M. would certainly have thought so, being businessmen—like himself, though they were native, while he had drawn his growth from two different soils. Yet this man whom they knew as Bixby was not a whimsical man; far from it. He was practical beyond any degree which they could conceive.

The particular goal for which he had set out tonight was not far distant: some seventy-odd miles south and east of the metropolitan area of Los Angeles. But the evening meeting had lasted much longer than he expected. He might well have waited to drive down until the next day, which would be Wednesday, if he had not so firmly made up his mind to *be* there, right on the ground and ready to deal with anyone who cared to approach him. Therefore, regardless of the fact that early evening had become early morning instead, he had sat the meeting out, unhurried, until he could break away as unobtrusively as he did everything else. Bixby was patient, he was invariably pleasant, and his very plumpness gave him that well-cushioned look which made him appear comfortable, even when he was not.

He didn't mind driving in the dark. Day or night, it made little difference to him. He never drove fast. And never slept much, night or day. So now, alert and wide awake, he could look ahead, down the long highway which stretched for miles at a time, like a dark and empty tunnel between the occasional lights of trucks approaching (thundering past, impersonal as planets coming out of nowhere, and gone immediately). And again, between the few clustered lights of little towns, themselves dead worlds which one passed by as quickly. (With mind averted from the memory of little towns which once breathed softly elsewhere, in their troubled sleep.) Straight ahead of him, toward the morning and this rather peculiar business to be transacted in the back-country village which he had adopted temporarily. Since six months ago.

It had had a strange fascination for him from the first hint he'd had of it; not the village itself, but the curious obsession which had laid hold upon it. There was something here which was not exactly familiar to him but recognizable, in some evasive sense. These predictions of a day of reckoning, of final doom or everlasting glory, were as old as man, of course. A recurrent mental phenomenon which one had read of here and there, in other times, other lands—amazing, preposterous. Amusing, now, if one cared to laugh; if one's taste for macabre humor had not long since died. It seemed that man had always had a monstrous talent for frightening himself; because he had been so long conditioned to fear, perhaps. He was used to it; therefore, where there was no real terror—he invented it.

What puzzled Bixby most was to observe that such a state of hypnotic superstition could be generated, in this world of today—by nothing. That such a phenomenon could actually take place anywhere against the grim realities of this century! That, in short, any mere figment could become a fact, in anybody's mind. It was incredible today. Yet that point of incredibility was exactly where his mind, long since become a sort of bloodhound after its own relentless fashion, picked up the scent of that faintly familiar clue. The trail of something that smelled, ever so slightly, of a Thought planted along the way. It interested him profoundly to observe with what primitive simplicity it operated among persons such as these. It seemed that they were as susceptible to any sort of suggestion as if they had never been vaccinated by one evil rumor. (Did people never learn?)

It was because he had nearly perished of his own inoculation that he listened now, so intently, to what was said, and what was not said, and to the overtones which only the disciplined inner ear of a man like Bixby could hear. He asked himself questions, in the manner of a cross-examining lawyer. Where had this suggestion first come from? Who was the instrument lying at hand here—to pick it up and pass it on so skillfully, and unnoticed? And who, in the last analysis, stood to profit by it? That was the question which pricked and finally prodded his practical acumen into watchful observation, until the time for action might arrive. And that was possibly why he had reverted more than once to the recollection of a chance encounter of several months ago, along this same route, although somewhat farther inland.

He had been traveling in the opposite direction that evening—rather early evening it was—on his way back to the city, and it was not long after he'd left the village that, coming suddenly around a curve, his lights had picked up the tall shadow of a young man walking in the same direction. He was not in the habit of picking up strangers and would have gone on by, except that as he'd slowed a trifle, the fellow made a half-turn and paused (like a startled animal uncertain whether to bolt across the road or back into the bushes), so that Bixby slowed down a little more—and then he'd recognized the one they called "Young Mears." Not that he knew him to speak to, for he himself was almost a stranger in the village then. But he'd begun to place a few of the names and faces, and since he didn't wish to be unfriendly, he'd stopped and offered the chap a lift.

For a second, the other had seemed to be of two minds whether to accept it, but then he'd gotten in with a mutter of thanks, and that was all he'd had to say for a number of miles. He'd sat hunched slightly forward, smoking one cigarette after another, and Bixby could feel a sort of tension in him, and took pains to drive even more carefully than usual, thinking the young fellow probably nervous with an older man driving; they often were, he'd noticed. Though this Mears, in the couple of swift sidewise glances Bixby had taken, looked rather an old-young man: as many of them did, to be sure, who had been through war. The only thing Bixby could recall having heard about him was that he was Mrs. Mears' son —or was it grandson?—who came down from college to spend an occasional holiday with the old lady. (That's what the village inhabitants called her—the Old Lady, though Bixby, never having seen her, reflected that she was possibly only sixty, or even less, and younger than himself.)

In any case, in that just faintly illuminated gloom, with the dash lights turned low as Bixby preferred them, the young man gave more the impression of watchful weariness, than of any youthful ebullience or easy relaxation. There was a sharp-cut effect about the big high-angled nose, the noticeably large ears—both accented possibly by the very close-cut hair which those boys in the service seemed to cling to, even after they were out—so that one got the impression of already deep-cut lines in the face, which of course one couldn't actually see in that light. No doubt he was one of these young-old veterans, finishing late their long delayed educations.

But since Bixby had as great a distaste for asking questions as for answering them, he made none of the usual idle queries;

remarked only that it was a pleasant evening, adding casually that he rather enjoyed driving at night. To which the other grunted assent, after one sharp sidelong glance of his own, which the older man felt rather than saw. A surly youth, Bixby had decided, or else he was in some deep dark trouble of his own; woman trouble, probably! And thinking of the very limited choice in village belles, as far as he had observed, had given Bixby a faint momentary amusement to smile over privately . . . But it was such a pleasant little village in the hills, and the people were so friendly, even to an utter stranger (quite different from the closed faces and unuttered suspicions in some places that he'd known), and presently he had remarked just that.

"I discovered it myself, by chance entirely," he had added. "Driving over to the coast from 395 one day. And I stopped, and rented myself a house for a few months, to come down from Los Angeles for a little rest over the week ends."

He hardly knew why he'd added that, except with some thought of easing the other's stiff constraint. There was another grunt of acknowledgment, but he saw that the hunched and bony shoulder next him had moved farther back in his peripheral vision, relaxing against the back of the seat, apparently. And suddenly the grunt was followed by a chuckle. Yes, it had been unmistakably a chuckle.

"Oh yes, they're friendly enough. But they're crazy, all of 'em. Crazy with the heat."

"Crazy, you think so?" Bixby had said mildly.

"I know so. I don't know if they were already that way before they went back there to live and bake their brains out . . . or whether they got that way from living there. But they're nuts, all right."

"So," said Bixby.

"I'll tell you something: tell you what you're going to hear, if you keep going back there for the next few months. Maybe you won't hear it all at once, but little by little. The world is coming to an end, see?"

"Is that so?" Bixby had said politely.

"I mean —it's coming to an end on a particular date, next spring. The twenty-second of March. Remember that."

"Yes, yes. I must write that down," said Bixby quickly.

"That's what they'll tell you. I'm just giving you a little advance information! And furthermore—now listen carefully to this one— the people who expect to be saved will gather together on the top of a certain hill (it's the highest one around there, incidentally) during the night of the twenty-second, all dressed in white, and ready to take off sometime after midnight. The exact hour not specified —just to build up the suspense." He began to laugh again, not out, but in, so that he seemed to swallow the sounds he had emitted. While Bixby, his eyes fixed on the road ahead, was somewhat relieved to note that it was only a short distance farther before this road would join the main coast highway.

"That is very interesting," he said.

"Interesting, hell! It's fascinating. How far they'll go—and what they'll go for. I'd like to lay you a little bet on that . . . But I haven't told you the best of it yet. You'll be hearing it anyway— so I might as well . . ." Yes, he had sounded for a moment just a shade regretful, as though he'd have liked to keep to himself instead of sharing the next morsel. "Well, sir, the final touch will be that they must let go all their most precious worldly possessions. Not just that they can't take 'em with 'em, but that they must actually get rid of 'em. Their house and lot, say—their store—or cow—or car, or what have you. And not sell them, either, mind you, because then they'd have the money, instead. They have to give the things away, understand?"

"I don't—quite see," Bixby had said carefully, "how, if every-body is expecting to depart the earth at once (from one high point or another, I assume?)—how they can all divest themselves—"

"That's where it's going to be so damn funny, don't you see? When everybody tries to give away what he's got to somebody else . . . Only of course, they won't all believe it—so somebody'll gamble with the devil and come out 'way ahead of the game. Oh, *boy*, would I like to be there!"

And that was when Young Mears had gone into that long-drawn-out spasm of laughter . . . except that, strictly speaking, it was drawn in with his breath, in three or four short dry chuckles, which sounded a little like the panting of a dog, for a few seconds only,

22

though he continued to shake with it silently. A mannerism only, yet a rather unpleasant one, especially considering the subject which he appeared to find so amusing. Bixby had made no comment that time, for they were approaching the junction of the highway with the secondary road which he'd been following, and seeing that the gas station on the right was still open, he'd said only, "I think I will stop here for some gas." The laugh beside him stopped, or was choked off.

"Oh, you do, do you?" said the other—and that was all he'd said.

The car drew into the gateway between the pumps and the glassed-in office, and as Bixby turned his head toward the latter, looking past his companion, he was aware that the man had un-latched the other door—at least he was able to recall some such impression afterward. But the attendant meantime had come round to his own side of the car, and for a second or two he was engaged with instructions to fill the tank with Ethyl, and have a look at that left rear tire also, to see if it was soft . . . Only a couple of seconds—and when he turned back again, his passenger had slid out of the seat beside him, leaving the door ajar. He waited for the servicing to be completed, paid the man and waited for his change, then waited for a moment longer, expecting the young fellow to return from the rest room. Though why he should wait, he thought, when it would be much better to leave him behind . . . but then he thought better of that, too.

"Tell that fellow I'm ready to go on, if he wants a ride any farther, will you?" he said to the attendant, who looked surprised, as if he hadn't noticed Bixby's companion. And he still appeared surprised and a little puzzled also, when he came back.

"There's nobody in there, sir," he said.

"No—o?" said Bixby slowly.

"No, sir."

They looked at each other, and each turned to gaze around the bare illuminated lot. There was no one in sight, and no sign of any walking figure along the road in either direction, just a couple of cars which went by at high speed, not even pausing.

"These hitchhikers—" Bixby began by way of explanation, and

23

gave it up with a shrug of his plump shoulders. "Well, thanks," he said, starting his engine.

"Thank *you*, sir. Come in again."

Bixby had driven on, reflecting upon what a peculiar lad that Young Mears must be; though, in turn, the gas station man had plainly thought *he* was the peculiar character, imagining that he had had a traveling companion with him . . . And after that, he'd forgotten the incident, having many other things to think of. Though he'd remembered it again, in passing, as he passed that gas station when he went down the next time—and again forgotten it, since there was nothing to remind him when he went in to get his groceries in the village store, or went walking up or down the hill during the next couple of days. Young Mears was not around the village at that time.

It was not until some weeks later, that he had picked up the first intimation of this prediction: heard exactly the things which the young fellow had told him he would hear. The hints were dropped furtively at first, with a twist of smile at the corner of the mouth, a watchful look in the corner of the eye, to see how he would take it, and each one who mentioned it—privately, of course—said, Mind you, I don't take any stock in this, but that's what they're saying. And when he'd taken it quite simply and unsurprised (which was easy for him, since nothing could surprise or shock him any more) he was, little by little, trusted with the further details. Finally, even apologetically, consulted as a solid businessman, who would know what might be done about certain property, in case of certain things happening . . . A house and lot, a nine-year-old automobile, some bits of ancient, treasured jewelry. And he had listened earnestly, his brown eyes sad and serious; and remembering Young Mears again, and the cynical implications of his laughter during that first encounter, Bixby had conceived the idea which he had since, very quietly, put into operation. So whether the prophecy and all its trimmings had been born out of wedlock in some lonely nightmare . . . or purposely promulgated . . . whether there were—certain opportunists, say, in this back country, as there were elsewhere through the world—Bixby would be on hand, prepared to meet this three-way challenge, alone and silently. Tomorrow.

No, no—today. The day was coming closer. The penultimate day, as he called it to himself. And reaching an unobtrusive landmark on the highway (that same gas station, now on his left and unlighted at this hour, so that it scarcely showed, a skeletal ghost to point the way), the car turned leftward seemingly of its own volition, and he felt at once closer to his destination, though he had another twenty miles to go. This was the secondary road which took a slight tangent course off into the hills, but he was still traveling mainly south and only a little east, toward what—only a few miles in from the ocean—they called the "Back Country" down here. There was no traffic now. His own lights were the only ones left to bore through the darkness, and there were no towns either, only a few clumps of houses, entirely black. Even when he came finally to *his* village, there were but two spots of light to be seen: the first one at the near end of the main—and only—street, a dim and economical bulb showing from inside the closed gas station and store.

It was when he had gone through the center of town, about the length of four good city blocks, that he saw the other light shining out through a side window on old Mrs. Mears' fenced-in garden. The old lady didn't sleep much either, he reflected, for that certainly wouldn't be Young Mears burning the midnight oil, at so many hours past midnight. By this time Bixby had of course learned more about the boy—who was no more than that, and a quite unexceptional young man it seemed, well liked in the village and not considered at all peculiar. He had himself run across him in due course, several times in fact, on the street or in the store, and he had spoken to him and always found him civil enough, but there had never been any reference to or explanation of his vanishing act at the gas station. Bixby had had an impulse to ask him casually what had become of him that night, but for some undefined reason, he had let it go. It had occurred to him that the young fellow might not even have recognized him as the man who had given him a lift— and why should he? No doubt he often picked up rides in that way, going back and forth to college, and he (Bixby) was admittedly an inconspicuous person whom many people failed to remember. He would unquestionably have forgotten the incident, in its entirety, if it had not been for the faint rumbling which he heard each time he came down from the city, giving evidence of the increasing apprehension—the uneasy fear—still boiling underground, and still scheduled so precisely to erupt on the twenty-second of March. . . .

Well, it would seem that most of the inhabitants must have good consciences indeed, if they believed this thing, as he'd been told they did. He considered once more the possibility that they did not believe it at all; that they knew it for a hoax, or at best a yarn spun out of someone's fevered hallucination. Could be, possibly, that they enjoyed the sheer unholy excitement, rumbling through their rutted lives, like some emotional cathartic long overdue to cleanse their systems. Perhaps they even saw it as a colossal practical joke? For he had to confess to himself that the sense of humor of the native American still astonished him, quite often. In that case, of course, he would have wasted much thought on the possible developments of a situation which did not even exist.

But then, as the road left town, and began its gentle ascent, he saw still another light: a long bright crack outlining three sides of a window with its blind drawn down—just above and to the right of the road, in that shack set in its fifty-foot square of unrelieved pavement—like an ark adrift on black water—where Alfred lived. Alfred—what? He did not know the man's full name; only that he looked the image of an old-fashioned parson, but was actually a retired storekeeper, who lived alone, and did not like flowers, it was said—which was why he had surrounded himself with concrete. It was also said that he sometimes went on four-day benders. So Alfred's conscience was not so good, perhaps? Or else he was beginning to celebrate rather early, in preparation for—or fortification against—whatever was yet to come.

The road climbed quickly and wound between one hill and another, for half or three quarters of a mile, which the car took easily, without even getting short of breath . . . as he would have done, on foot. And he was suddenly there, turning sharp into the drive which was scarcely big enough for a turn-around, pointing the car's dark nose into the darker hole which was the garage. He gave a small sigh of relaxation and, turning off the switches, rolled out from under the wheel, his feet feeling for the floor, and then in turn feeling their way on through the doorway which was only a shade lighter than the cavelike dark behind him. There was no door to close, so he went without pause around the corner to his own front entrance. His own until April first, according to the lease.

There, his fingers sorting out the keys on his ring to find the right one, he turned his head, as from instinct or habit, to look up the hillside a little farther, where he could just distinguish one wing of the house above him, jutting out . . . The house of Mrs. Collins. And there to his surprise, still another light was shining, in the window of that end room which he knew (from respectful observation of the house when she was staying alone there) must be her own. Ah, he was sorry . . . For why should *she* lose sleep? One of the loveliest ladies he had ever met, and sensible too. Mrs. Norma Collins: the name suited her—Norma—though he had not dared to call her that, yet. Sometime, perhaps? If, indeed, he should renew this lease which was just now expiring. She was so friendly a neighbor; so kind. A woman, moreover, who woke in him an ache in some long atrophied nerve-ends, like the pain felt by an amputee in the hand or foot which he no longer has.

He did not like to think of her, awake and worrying, on this night. He had wondered if she felt alone, sometimes, in spite of the young daughter, and the friends who so often came to stay. He had sought for an excuse, more than once, to drop in and call on her—and it might be well for him to pay his respects while he was here this time. In fact, there might even be some of that same peculiar business for him to attend to, in that very house, before this day was over. Bixby well knew that the old servants, Joseph and Bertha, were not (could not be) what they said they were, but he suspected that that might make them even readier victims—a guilty conscience being the best breeding ground for apprehensions, real or false.

He turned his head back, finally, from looking at that dimly lighted square of window a quarter of a mile above him, and opened his front door and closed it—not quietly—and switched on his own light to see what time it was. Not much past four-thirty; he could

27

still get a few hours of sleep. Perhaps he was a little tired, after all, though not in the habit of considering the matter. He walked on heavily into the bedroom beyond, his boots sounding loud on the bare floor between the rugs, but there was no one to be disturbed. Bixby had no family.

CHAPTER 3

The patio was a pleasant place to breakfast, on warm days like these. It opened its arms out toward the east, so that it got full benefit of the morning sun before it grew too hot. Norma's house was built against one hillside and looked across the widening triangle between two others, to that slightly higher knoll beyond, which was most often known simply as the Hill. The nearby slopes were covered with chaparral, dull green and pungent in the heat, but the Hill itself was bare and smooth in outline, save for the one small weather-beaten oak on top, growing close to earth and rounded like an inverted shallow cup or a small parasol.

For most people it would be a tiresome trudge from the village to the top of that knoll; but from here, taking one's ease in Norma's patio, there was a feeling of nearness and intimacy in looking across from one hillside to the other. Wise visitors always took note and spoke fondly of that little oak tree, too, which seemed to belong intrinsically to her view; almost as much as the espaliered pear against the kitchen side of the house or the drooping pepper tree just outside the low patio wall, or the big hibiscus bush the other side of the gate and a few feet to the right. The house had been an oblong box when she found it: a compact story-and-a-half, lacking both comfort and imagination. But the wide ledge on which it had been firmly grounded was large enough to hold the two one-story wings which she had added, to make more rooms and form an open-ended patio. Someone had said the house made him think of a comfortable chair, upholstered in bougainvillaea, its back against the hill, and armrests extended forward in the sun. A chair to lean back and dream in, and forget the world. To which Norma herself had made no rejoinder, though she was delighted that people found it comfortable, and peaceful to stay in. She, for one, had done little dreaming there; only a good deal of thinking, which is not the same. She had learned not to try to see over the Hill, never to look very far ahead in time, except as it was necessary to plan for little Joyce—now grown four inches taller than herself.

Even this morning, when she came out into the patio, she had thought no further than what to have for luncheon. Half an hour before, when she had opened her eyes to broad daylight, she had almost forgotten her earlier awakening in the dark, and recalling, put it aside again, as one making a deliberate choice—to remember only that Joyce would be home in time for lunch and that Miss Amelia was coming to sew today. She had dressed briskly then, putting on a fresh but faded blue linen, which was becoming to her own fresh—but faded—coloring. Norma was not far short of fifty, but still comely in a natural, ungirdled sort of way. And as she conceded a quick dab of powder on her nose, and combed her thick soft hair (not blond, yet nearer fair than brown), she had begun thinking busily of what sort of lunch to give them all. Something hearty enough for Joyce and her young friend, but not too rich to tempt Roger off his narrow path . . .

So, as she stepped out through the living room doorway onto the paved apron of terrace outside, and found herself greeted by a sudden blast of song, she stopped short in genuine astonishment. The blaring tones were issuing from an open window on the far kitchen side of the patio, and they did not come from a radio, either. Bertha had a powerful voice when she let it go, and there was something explosive—yes, rather martial about her attack this morning. The waves of sound seemed to carry some significance, like banners of an army on the march. And that tune she was slaughtering on her way —what *was* it?—Norma asked herself.

Then of course it came to her, in a rush of almost embarrassed recognition, as when one has passed by one's clergyman on the street without giving any sign of knowing him. "Onward, Christian Soldiers" —*that* was it—though the words were hardly distinguishable, as

Bertha's words often were, and already the volume of sound had faded to a preoccupied hum as she went about whatever unseen work she had in hand. Norma smiled a little as she crossed the grass toward the glass-topped table, set for breakfast in the sun. Joseph was just emerging from the dining-room door at the other corner of the terrace, balancing a silver tray with glasses on it, and her smile reached over to greet him encouragingly. She always felt he needed encouragement, even in the carrying of a small tray.

"Good morning, Joseph."

Joseph never smiled, but his precise "Good day, madam" came back in quiet dignity, until all at once Bertha's song broke out again with new vigor, and his wizened face, without changing expression, seemed to shrivel still more. He, too, stopped short, and turned, as though he would retreat hastily and hush that unseemly noise, or at the very least, cover it by his retreat. But Mrs. Collins' voice checked him reassuringly.

"Oh, never mind—don't stop her! It sounds so cheerful," she said, and added, after a second, conversationally, almost with a touch of apology, "You know, I had almost forgotten what day it was, Joseph."

"It is—Wednesday, madam."

"No, no—I don't mean the day of the week. I meant the date."

He seemed to hesitate, then finally, unwillingly, "Yes, madam."

"So this would be the last day, wouldn't it?" she said thoughtfully, and paused, half waiting to see what he would say, but characteristically he said nothing. "And that," Norma concluded gently, "is why Bertha is so happy this morning . . ."

Joseph stood there impassively, looking down at the now empty tray in his hands. When he did speak again, at last, it was only as if in recognition that some reply was expected, just for the sake of civility, for he was invariably polite.

"Ah-h," he said. "Happy." And his tone was as noncommittal as the two words standing aloof, one from the other.

He certainly did not look happy himself, and Norma wondered, not for the first time, if he did or did not believe in this crazy notion. She wanted to ask him, directly, Tell me, Joseph, do you believe this thing they're saying in the village? You know it couldn't be . . . (But perhaps he thought it could. She didn't know why she instinctively gave him credit for having more sense than Bertha, just because he was sadder and more silent.) And she did know he would only answer, Yes, madam—or, No, madam. And neither one would tell her anything at all. So she released him, saying casually instead, "You might bring the coffee out now, Joseph. Mrs. Norbeck will be along directly, I'm sure. I heard her moving around in her room a few minutes ago."

He turned away quickly and no doubt thankfully, but he had taken only a couple of steps when she thought to add, over her shoulder, "By the way, has Mr. Norbeck had his tray yet?"

"No, madam."

"And Alfred," she pursued, patiently, "hasn't he come by yet, with the mail and newspapers?"

"No, madam," repeated Joseph, with equal patience.

"Oh dear!" she murmured, partly to herself this time. "I *do* hope Alfred is going to be all right, today."

There was no answer to that, and she shook her head as if to clear it of the forebodings which were beginning to gather again (an unseen army getting ready to march on her peaceful hillside) and pulled out her chair decisively. But before she could sit down, Bertha's song had taken off in full voice like a plane already in mid-air whose motors had stalled for a second and suddenly caught again. Norma glanced around and saw that Joseph was still standing there, and they gazed at each other across the several yards of green grass between them, as though rooted in the same ground; both listening as in a slightly hypnotized distress.

"Oh, Joseph—" Norma broke out of it impulsively, "I do hope Bertha isn't going to be too—disappointed." But that seemed to shock him.

"Madam!" he said. "Oh, madam—Bert'a is a *good* woman."

"Why, of course she is!" Norma exclaimed. "Yes, of course she is! All I meant was—I just hoped . . . Well, you see, I can't help hoping that she won't be *too* disappointed . . . if the world doesn't come to an end just yet."

"Yes, madam," Joseph said, very formally; and what that meant, she didn't know. It could have been No, madam, just as well, and meant as little, Norma thought. It was like a small door closing, and—as on the other side of it—she could hear his quick steps retreating into the house, and she sat down at last. She unfolded her napkin in her lap, and folded her hands on the edge of the table in front of her, and sat there waiting—somewhat resignedly now—for Miriam Norbeck to come out to breakfast . . . for Joseph to return with the coffee and toast . . . for this complicated cock-eyed day to begin, officially. And she looked across her peaceful patio, over the low wall to the hills beyond, frowning a little, this morning, at the view which she loved so much; at the Hill, especially, with its little knob of oak on top.

She couldn't have said why this business bothered her so. It was so foolish—childish, even—and it would all be over shortly, without one's lifting a hand to help or hinder it. It was one thing you couldn't do anything about. Day came, every day. It was one of the few things in life, perhaps the only one, which one could count on. Tomorrow would be another day, that was all. And there was certainly no sense of personal apprehension in Norma Collins. She was not easily given to superstition, or premonitions either. She did not believe in hunches, not even in her alleged "woman's intu-ition." Not any more. (The day Bart was killed, she had had no breath of fear, no shadow of warning in her heart.)

She had no idea where this preposterous notion had come from, but she'd been uncomfortable about it for quite a while. She was trying to recall now how long it had been since she'd heard the first intimations of it. A month or two certainly. Might have been longer. She probably hadn't heard about it at all until it was well started. And then thought nothing of it except as one of those absurd vagaries which people get hold of now and again—every few years, or decades—or which get hold of them. Like children building up an imaginary game until suddenly it becomes real, and scares the daylights out of them. In any case, when she did finally realize that this particular delusion had become actual, and all but the last accomplished fact to many of the people in the village,

32

it had already gone past the stage where you could argue with it. You were on one side or the other, and that was that. She didn't even know how many really believed in it. There were a few who just laughed, of course; and there were those others, who drew back and didn't care to discuss it with you, a little hurt by the laughter, perhaps, if they were aware of it, but in their belief they were superior to it, also. And superior to the non-believers. (Ah, they would see, those last . . . but they would see too late . . . Which would have been the ultimate in Last Laughs, Norma reflected dryly.)

Now that the deadline was practically here, one could only wait for the day to pass: the whole twenty-four hours of it. And then—what a relief, she thought—when another day had come and the sun was up and the birds were singing, as they were now, in a beautiful harmonic confusion, and everybody could look around and see that they were still here too! But would they laugh, in their relief—at themselves? Or at each other, slyly? What she was dreading was not the expected event but the unexpected aftermath, whatever it might be. Not only the emptiness of disillusion following on shock, and not just everyday unhappiness in contrast to eternal bliss, but a sort of naked exposure of each one's individual miseries as they had sought to throw them off. She was afraid that it would be a little as if they had cast off all their clothes, and then they would have to come back, shamefaced, and pick them up and put them on again . . . And go about afterwards, each one remembering his momentary nakedness before all the others.

When that time came, it would be better—kinder, even—not to have noticed, or seemed much aware of what went on before. And that was why she had ignored the whole thing as best she could; pretended not to hear the whispers or their sibilant echoes; played very dumb. (She'd *never* meant to mention it to Joseph, and already wondered why she had done so—and wished she hadn't!) The one person she had longed to talk it over with was Roger, who had seen for himself the effects of insidious rumor, and had strong views on mass hysteria, creeping or rampant. But of course that was different, vastly different. What he had seen was all too real, and this was not. This would be merely comic opera to Roger. Full of quaint characters, like little old Amelia Smedley, with that look of shy but incandescent hope in her near-sighted eyes, even as she stitched away against time, trying to finish up a dress, or shirt, or *"robe"* for someone, before the appointed hour. Or Alfred, with one slightly wild blue eye yoked to the other somber brown one, who with all his determined godliness, drove himself to drink—quite literally— every so often . . . Or like the emotional and unintelligible Bertha and the inarticulate, impassive Joseph, jealously guarding the wordless ghost who still haunted them both.

Norma gave a little jerk, involuntary but quickly stilled, finding that Joseph himself was there again, at her elbow. (And what are *you* so jumpy for this morning, Mrs. Collins? she ticked herself off rather sharply.) Aloud she murmured, "Thank you, Joseph," as he placed the coffee pot beside her, and the carefully wrapped toast rack in front of her place; heard his inevitable, scarcely audible "Yes, madam" and then his steps padding quietly away again, back to the kitchen, where a stentorian hush seemed to have fallen now. Norma fingered her glass of orange juice and reflected absently that Miriam was slow in coming out . . . but her mind went right back to the other matter.

No, these people were her *friends*, after all, and she couldn't bear to have them laughed at, even if they were absurd. And that was why she hadn't so much as mentioned this fantastic business to the Norbecks, though now she wished perversely that she had, because it was almost bound to come out somehow during the next twenty-four hours. An old joke has less latent mischief in it, once the surprise detonator has been removed. She began thinking how she could attempt this. And knew she was only fooling herself, since even a prediction of Judgment Day has a certain newsworthy quality, not to be sniffed at and passed up by an old nose like Roger's.

It was almost odd that they hadn't heard some whisper of it from someone, though of course they had been pretty well insulated from the village just because of the regimen of quiet prescribed for him. She knew that if they had heard anything at all, they'd have taken it up with her at once, tossed it in the air like puppies with a brand-new shoe to chew on, in full enjoyment of something so

34

delicious. Not that they'd laugh out loud; not before the others. Roger was kind at heart, and Miriam was tactful. But they would be vastly entertained, nevertheless. It really would have *made* their visit for them: a highlight to remember, something with which to regale their more sophisticated friends, for years to come. (That time we visited Norma out in California, remember?—and the whole blessed village dressed up in white robes and marched up the hill at midnight, singing at the top of its lungs . . . And then like the old nursery rhyme, came marching down again . . .) Well, that was exactly why she hadn't told them, because she didn't want anybody from outside, laughing as if they were at a play.

On the other hand, Roger and Miriam were her own personal friends, and Norma knew very well that they needed amusement; almost any kind of amusement. This was a painfully quiet visit for that pair. It had to be, for Roger's own good, since that was what they had come for—a few weeks of utter quiet on Norma's sunny hillside. Nevertheless, it was dull for Miriam, and Norma felt sometimes that Roger himself was bored to the soul. Or was he merely restless, deep within himself? Or preoccupied with his own inevitable adjustment? Something not right, at any rate, although his heart condition was supposed to be so much improved. Something in his look went to *her* heart, these days. She had known him for such a long time, long before he and Miriam were married. It might even be that something was not right between those two.

But that was a dishonest thought, not to be given houseroom for a moment. And hearing the light clap of a door closing, across the patio, Norma looked up with a distinct twinge of guilt, as if her thinking might be overheard. Miriam was crossing the grass now, her quick graceful stride accented by the narrow well-cut gray slacks which so well became her slender figure, and Norma called across, "Hello, dear—" putting a little extra something into her greeting; a more conscious warmth of cordiality perhaps.

CHAPTER 4

For twelve mornings now, the two women had sat like this and chatted alone together at the table in the corner of the terrace, while the sun grew steadily warmer, and the chat itself became each day a trifle more spasmodic. There were parts of their exchange which had become almost a routine, like a scene learned by heart. Such as Miriam's quick opening comment on the morning itself: "*Another* gorgeous day! Honestly, I can't quite believe it," she would exclaim. Spontaneously at first, and later in a sort of puzzled wonder, as one not used to seeing the sky so clear and blue, day after day.

And there was Norma's opening gambit as well: "Had a good night, you two?" Or—"Hope Roger slept well . . ." Or more simply, shifting from the polite sentiment of any conscientious hostess to the genuine concern of an old friend—"How's Roger feeling today?"

"Oh, not too bad," the other would reply. Or, "Oh yes, he really sleeps quite well, you know, for all he *thinks* he doesn't!" Smiling as she said it, to erase any faint smear of criticism left by the words themselves. As one wife to another, that was all. But Norma had not been a wife for nearly fifteen years, and was discovering that she had grown oddly detached from that conjugal viewpoint which pretends indulgence while actually indulging its own half-concealed resentments.

Today, when she asked, almost before she could stop herself, "How's Rog feeling this morning?"—Miriam had answered with a shrug, "Oh, all right, I suppose. About as usual." So Norma had picked up the coffee pot and let the subject drop, reminding herself *not* to ask that question at all tomorrow. It was tiresome of her, even if she did want to know. She could observe for herself how he felt when he came out later. She was sure—or almost sure—that he was better now than when he had arrived; another couple of weeks would do a great deal more for him, and that was all that mattered.

Meantime, she and Roger's wife lingered over their breakfast each morning, with every appearance of content and companionship. But conversation so often wilted at the bud; the small sprouts, which each one put forth tentatively, did not seem to grow between them. In these past twelve days, they had asked and answered one another's questions about mutual friends, had compared notes on trips and traveling in general; they had spoken of meals and diets, as women will, and inevitably turned to the fascinating topic of Bertha—and her Joseph—with housewifely appreciation of the woman's marvelous cooking, as of the quietly dedicated (if not exactly deft) manner in which her husband went about his duties as houseman.

There was one moment this morning when Norma caught her breath, as Bertha broke out in song again, and Miriam's head lifted and turned with a small jerk of astonishment, to look at her hostess, dark eyes deliberately widened in a kind of facial question mark. But when the unseen prima donna, as if recalling herself, quickly reduced her volume, Miriam and Norma exchanged a smile for a shrug, without further comment, both aware that the door in the dining-room corner had opened and closed, and that Joseph's footsteps, short and careful, were pacing along the paved terrace not far behind them. It was only after he had reached and rounded the other corner that Miriam glanced slightly sidewise to watch him proceeding toward Roger's door, on the far side of the patio, with Roger's breakfast tray in his hands.

She remarked then, idly, "He certainly never was a waiter before, any more than he was a butler! D'you notice how he always carries a tray in his two hands 'way out in front of him, as though scared to death of it?"

"Oh yes, that's true," Norma agreed. "In fact, he does everything that way. Very carefully, but not at all as if he were used to it. And I don't suppose he ever was."

"I wonder *what* he was," said Miriam speculatively. "You'd never even think he was a foreigner, would you? No accent, I mean, except for that very precise and careful way that he speaks."

"And his occasional peculiar twists of grammar," Norma added, smiling again, indulgently. "Almost as if he were *trying* to distort it."

"Whereas . . . Bertha's accent is so thick you can't understand it no matter how hard you try. At least *I* can't! And Rog says he never heard anything like it, in or from any country he's ever been in. I do wonder sometimes how you manage to communicate with her at all."

"Well, actually, she seems to understand *me* all right, even if I can't always make out what she's trying to say, herself."

"That's very odd," said Miriam, frowning, and Norma laughed. "Why—do you find me so difficult to understand?"

"No, you dope! What I mean is, a person trying to learn a strange language can usually get his meaning across to someone who's familiar with it, even if it's in a lame sort of pigeon English—or whatever—but it's apt to floor him when the native speaks to *him*, because it seems so much faster to follow."

"Well, I can't begin to explain Bertha's idiosyncrasies. She's probably a law unto herself. Like all genius."

"And she *is* that. I never in my life tasted such food as that woman concocts. Simply fabulous," said Miriam dreamily.

"I think she's preparing to outdo herself today. You know," Norma began, rather cautiously now, as though edging up to a plunge which she didn't really want to take, "I've been meaning to tell you something—" But there was a sudden loud clatter from the kitchen, a veritable cascade of tinware, with a rapid flow of exclamations following after, and then equally abrupt silence.

"Seems to be a little nervous about it," Miriam commented, and Norma tried again.

"That's what I was starting to explain. I really should have told you and Rog before, I suppose. You see, it's sort of a special day—"

But Bertha, no doubt recalling herself—in another sense—had now lifted up her voice to its highest pitch, as though she would drown out and wash away the very echo of her own imprecations. Norma gave up, for the time being.

Miriam remarked, with a faint shrug, "She seems to be a prima donna in more ways than one, but I suppose that's the privilege of genius too. Must take some coping with, my dear, though I must admit this is the first time I've heard her singing hymns at this hour."

"That," said Norma, a shade crossly now, "is not a hymn. *That* is 'God Bless America.' "

Miriam cocked her head a trifle to listen more critically, with a nod of amused appreciation, as she remarked, "Why yes, so it is! Shows how long since I've been in church. But the other was a hymn, surely. I can't be that benighted!"

Norma nodded in her turn. " 'Onward, Christian Soldiers,' " she murmured.

"Well, I suppose that's almost a natural progression in her mind," Miriam suggested. "I mean, 'God Bless America' must *be* a sort of hymn to her, don't you think? They must feel they were delivered out of hell, quite literally, those two . . . Was it Poland, by the way—or Czechoslovakia—I never quite got it straight."

"Neither did I," said Norma.

"Now, what do you mean by that?"

"I mean I don't know . . . And I don't care *where* they came from, poor dears. They were Displaced Persons, and that's all I know. They answered my advertisement in the L. A. *Times*, without any references—and they've been with me almost three years now."

"But, Norma," Miriam objected, looking puzzled, "D.P.'s had to be sponsored by someone in this country at first, didn't they? And then they were responsible to that person or group, and he responsible for them . . . I don't know just how it worked but—"

"Oh yes, I know all that. But apparently they'd been released from their obligation to whoever was responsible for them, by that time. Since then . . . Well, they never wanted to talk about anything that had happened before they came here, and I don't wonder . . . So we've just left it at that. And I think," she added warningly, "we'd better leave it at that, now—" with a faint inclination of her head to let the other know that Joseph had come out of Roger's door and was returning. Miriam nodded in quick comprehension, and then in a rather social tone she offered, "You were starting to tell me something about some celebration today."

"Yes. But I can't go into that just now, either," Norma answered quietly, as Joseph neared their corner of the terrace.

"Oh," said Miriam, looking blank. "I thought it was something about Joyce's coming back today . . . Sorry."

"No, it was *not*," Norma said a trifle shortly. It did seem as though everyone was bent on being perverse or obtuse or both this morning. And though she now heard Joseph close the door into the house, she did not particularly feel like taking up the job of explanation again. There was a slight interval of silence until, watching the other nibbling on a thin piece of unbuttered toast, she said impulsively, "*Please* have some conserve on that, won't you? It looks so dry and unappetizing that way."

"No, thanks, dear."

"You do watch your figure, don't you?" the older woman said, a trifle ruefully.

"Oh, I don't know. I don't need to, do you think?" Miriam had pushed her chair sidewise to the table as she sat toying with her last cup of black coffee, and now, uncrossing her knees, she glanced down at her neat legs extended straight before her.

"No, of course you don't. That's what makes it so irritating!" Norma laughed, then sighed good-naturedly and helped herself instead. "Oh well . . . I daresay that's one of the compensations for being a middle-aged widow. Nobody's going to mind how fat *I* get."

"As to that, I'm not at all sure Roger would mind, if *I* did," Miriam retorted.

"Well, of course not, silly! Not if we're going to be serious about it. After all, the eyes of love, and all that . . ."

"I didn't mean that."

"Oh?" said Norma, a shade warily.

"What I meant was, I doubted if he'd so much as notice."

Norma looked at her with troubled eyes. They were making a great many false starts this morning between them and this was still another line she didn't care to follow through. But after a moment she said gently, "Anybody—who's sick—or even tired—isn't always so observant, do you think?"

"How right you are, darling!" Miriam reached for a cigarette, her fourth since sitting down at the table. But though her tone was light, the pause which followed seemed to settle heavily between them. That was the trouble, Norma thought worriedly; this conversational balloon, which they kept trying to toss back and forth so airily, had lead in it. There might be dynamite as well, if they got too personal. But she couldn't just leave it there, a dud on the dining table. So presently, and quite casually, she said, "This is an awfully quiet visit for you, Miriam. I keep wishing there were something more amusing to offer, for your sake even more than for Roger's." Miriam shook her head quickly.

"Oh, mercy, no. It's been exactly what Rog wanted, to complete the cure. We couldn't have come at all, if there'd been anything much going on, you know. And," she added sincerely, if a little flatly, "it's been a heavenly rest for me, too."

"Yes, I do know you needed that. It's been a long and anxious time for you, my dear."

"Five months—almost," said Miriam, but absently now, not so much in reply to what the other had said as seeming to count them over to herself. (November—December—January—February . . .) Then, with a sort of controlled vehemence which made her words sound much more abrupt, "But one has to stop resting sometime, or it becomes a way of life, instead of a rest, doesn't it?" So the new topic had run right back to the same explosive fuse, though the line leading to it was partly hidden, while part of it had been uncovered.

"I do think he's better, you know," Norma said tentatively. "Better, even, than when he came up here, I mean."

"Of course he is! The trouble is, he won't admit it."

"But, Miriam—dear—he always says he's fine, whenever one asks him."

"Oh, certainly. The conversational front. A man's pride held up like a shield, or a screen, before even his best friends . . . if it *is* pride. But you know all the time that he doesn't believe what he's saying—don't you?—and would probably be a little hurt if you believed him! What *I* mean, Norma, is that he *will* not admit to himself that he's practically well again."

"You think that's true?" Norma asked doubtfully, thinking, was it true that he was practically well? But Miriam, whose viewpoint was already facing in another direction, saw the query only from that other angle, and answered it from there.

"Why . . . else," she said slowly, "does he hold back from *living?* From even trying to get back to a more normal life again?"

It was the frankest thing she'd said in all these days, and her dark gaze was straight and somber as she turned it on Norma.

"I—don't know, Miriam. Maybe he just isn't sure of himself yet? I think—sometimes—a person who's been ill for quite a long while, is almost afraid of getting out on a limb, where people may expect too much of him. More than he can quite manage." Miriam was silent. She had withdrawn her glance to the cigarette in her fingers, which she appeared to be studying curiously. "After all," Norma went on, but cautiously, suspecting that she might be getting out on a limb herself, "you two did lead a very intense and active life. Too tense for most of us, the way the world is now, but I think you really enjoyed it, even when the going got rough, and might have been awfully dangerous."

"Yes," Miriam admitted. "We both enjoyed it. It suited us. *Both* of us," she repeated. "Especially when he had a base somewhere so that I could go along."

"And it's hard to give up," Norma said. *Almost* as hard for you as it must be for him, she thought, but didn't say it. "Still," she said aloud, "it must have been that very sense of strain, and tension which seems to be part of a journalist's life nowadays—especially a top-flight one like Roger. It must have told on him. Not only worn him out at the time, but left him less vitality or energy to come back with."

"Well, that's all over now, at any rate," said Miriam bleakly. "For better or worse." Whatever she meant by that, she checked herself, or was checked by the automatic association of those words. "His career as an active correspondent is over; the doctors made that clear enough, from the start."

"I know," said Norma softly.

"But that doesn't mean," Miriam went on with a touch of crisp-ness, "that he can't go on *living*—in a different sort of way. The doctor himself said that, even though Rog's case was not one where the damage could ever be entirely repaired—not just scar tissue, something about a weakening of the heart muscle and enlargement of the heart, I think, though I'm never sure I understand their language—" She seemed to waver for a second, recognizing her own limitations, and then rushed on again to reach her point, as though driven toward it by some propulsive force within herself. "The doctors *said* he could go back to some lighter kind of work, without deadlines —or pressure. But Rog won't have any part of *that*. And yet—he's not quite forty-six, Norma! He should at least go back to a place where things are going on around him, even if he isn't quite in the swim himself. Keep in touch with his friends, so he won't stagnate . . . won't just sit there, brooding!" She broke off again and leaned forward to stub out her cigarette, with quick impatient little jabs in her saucer, though a large crystal ash tray lay a few inches beyond.

Norma waited a second, wondering if she hadn't better leave the whole thing right there, pick up the silver bell and ring it for Joseph to come to clear the table. But instead of the bell, another sound broke the momentary hush; not Bertha's strident tone this time, but the rude *blat* of an old-fashioned automobile horn (the bulb kind) which seemed to carry a certain personal impertinence in its blast. It came from off behind the kitchen wing, like an off-stage voice, and it spoke three times in short succession.

"Alfred!" The two women exclaimed in unison, trading glances which said, on Miriam's side, "Roger's newspapers"—and on Norma's, "The mail—" and she glanced at her watch mechanically, noting that Alfred was much later than usual, as well as louder with his horn. But her thoughts reverted obstinately to the point where they'd been interrupted: to the troubled wonder as to what lay behind this seething impatience of Miriam's. Unless, of course, it was just her own personal boredom. But she didn't believe that Miriam was as selfish as that. In many ways she liked the girl (she was still a girl to Norma—who was so close to fifty now that she could almost see herself as sliding down the other side). She had always felt that Miriam had exactly the qualities which Roger needed; had in fact liked her for Roger, whether or not she found much in common with

43

her, herself. She was what Norma thought of as a *clever* girl; too clever for her, in many ways. But there was something here which she did not understand, and it had nothing to do with cleverness; perhaps that was why she had felt less—well, less tolerant of her lately. She doubted now that there was anything helpful which she could do or say.

"I rather gathered," she said at last, reluctantly, almost against her better judgment, "that he had it in mind to write another book."

"Oh yes. He talks about it."

"Well, I—I suppose it takes quite a while to—sort of germinate, doesn't it?" Norma smiled at her own fumbling with an unfamiliar jargon, but Miriam shrugged her shoulders.

"He's *had* quite a while," she said.

"But isn't it the actual start on anything that takes the greatest effort?" Norma suggested. "Just getting into motion again, after the inertia of a long illness? And starting a book must be like starting up a locomotive—for a long run. He just hasn't quite got the—*steam* to put into it yet."

She smiled again, at her own rather inept metaphor, but Miriam appeared not to be going to answer that at all, which might be just as well: this was an impossible conversation. Far better to stick to small talk, superficialities. They weren't close enough to talk this way, and the gap was widening. But as she was beginning to feel for an exit line, looking for any graceful retreat, listening rather impatiently for Joseph—who *must* be coming out with the mail and the papers any second now—Miriam's reply to her last words came quite unexpectedly, in a low and level tone.

"He hasn't got the will," she said, and Norma sat still and shocked, her hand pausing even as it reached out for the little bell, then dropping like a shot bird, back to the table again. How can you defend a man, against his own wife? But on the other hand, how could you let a statement like that stand, in untrue testimony against a friend you've known for ten or fifteen years? (Fourteen years, it was.)

"I don't know much about these things," Norma said finally. "About books and writing, I mean, though of course Roger used to talk a lot about his old work—"

44

"Well then, one thing which you probably don't know, Norma, is that among writers, the fellow who talks about the book he's going to do is practically a byword. Rather a bad joke, in fact."

"Why?" said Norma, stopped short again in surprise.

"Because he never does it, that's all. He doesn't write; just takes it out in talk. And I might add that newspapermen are noted for this little failing. Oh, not if they start publishing soon enough—don't misunderstand me. There are a dozen you could mention offhand who have done some wonderful jobs. But there are so many others, especially among the older ones, who have let it go too long. They always *meant* to write a book, you see."

"But Roger did write a book—and publish it!" protested Norma. "And a best seller, at that. I don't know what you mean."

"I don't know if I can tell you," said Miriam. She was sitting with her knees crossed now, and her long fingers clasped around them, and there was a look of tension from the fingers all the way through the poised figure. "Don't think I've forgotten *Operation Lifeline*. The title's been extraordinarily apt—for us, as well as for its subject. But it's a queer thing, Norma . . ." She was frowning intently as she paused. "It's so very queer the way things work out. That book was published just as we were going abroad again, and we didn't know how long we would be away. So Rog left everything, with powers-of-attorney and so on, in the hands of Gil Perkins, the only man he knew in the investment business. And all the royalties that came in in that next year and a half—everything was invested for us, and apparently Gil knew what he was about. But there you are: if we'd been home, we'd have spent it, I suppose—or more likely tried to invest or speculate for ourselves, knowing as much about that kind of thing as a couple of jack rabbits . . . and we'd never have known where it went. Instead, it's grown, and we have the income to live on now. Rog had half a dozen kinds of insurance to cover his medical and hospital expenses, so we haven't had to touch the capital at all."

"What a mercy," Norma murmured, "that he didn't have to worry about all that."

"Oh, it's been a godsend, no less. *Operation Lifeline*," Miriam repeated again. "And yet . . . the strange part of it, the—irony of it

45

is, here we are with enough to live on if we're careful—especially if we settled somewhere away from the city like this—so Rog doesn't want *me* to get a job again. Though I sometimes think it would be much better if I did—" she interpolated in one swift breath.

"Would you *like* to?" Norma asked in wondering disbelief, as one whose years of job-holding had left no yearning to return to them.

"Yes, I would!" the other came back in a flash, yet flatly. "Why not? It was interesting. Full of challenge . . ." (As one who looked back on something which had been *fun*.) But question and answer both had been only sparks generated by Miriam's sudden vehemence; an interruption which flew off into space, as she went on swiftly with what she had begun to say. "As it is, Rog doesn't have to take that desk job, though it might be good for him, and he doesn't *have* to write that book . . ."

After a minute Norma asked, trying to get back on safer (more theoretical!) ground, "Is that the only reason writers write—to eat?"

"Well, no," conceded Miriam thoughtfully. "If it were, they'd get themselves an easier job, I guess . . . But it helps to keep them at it," she said, with a slight, knowing smile, "until it's gotten to be such a habit that they can't stop."

Unless their hearts give out, thought Norma; but she said, "I still don't understand quite what you meant when you spoke as though his other book didn't *count*, somehow."

"Because that wasn't a book in the sense I mean: it was already there, you might say, in the columns he'd done over that whole period; not quite literally perhaps, but almost. This would be a different kind of work, that's all—something he's never done before. And if he doesn't start soon, he never will. See?" said Miriam abruptly, with a pent-up impatience, as though she were explaining something to a rather dull pupil.

"I see," said Norma. Though what she thought she saw was a good deal more than what she heard in the words just spoken.

Miriam had gotten up from the table in one sudden motion, and standing there, she gave her body a little stretch, as though to free it from some invisible confinement. She looked down at Norma from that slight elevation—a graceful figure in her gray slacks and soft white blouse; an attractive woman—not beautiful, perhaps not even pretty, but still arresting, in some way, with her white skin and the dark hair which was very sleek and neat and had no touch of gray in it; with those expressive and sometimes stormy eyes, and an enigmatic mouth, carefully drawn in dark red lipstick. And Norma remembered how happy this girl had looked a few years ago, how proud and *right* she had appeared beside Roger, what an unusually well-matched pair the two had seemed together.

And on the rush of that recollection she spoke out once more, impulsively, "Oh, Miriam—Miriam, what *difference* does it make, really? He's already had a notable and successful career, and you've had wonderful fun together during that time. It's tragic, yes, of course it is, that he can't go on with it—still farther—but after all, he's made quite a good recovery so far, and isn't that all that really counts? You have enough to live on, and you have each other . . . So what does it matter, if he doesn't sit at a desk—or start a book at once—or ever, for that matter?" Miriam did not answer for the space of perhaps three seconds, as though she might have counted them off.

"Because, Norma, I don't think he will begin to live again—until he begins to work again. And by work, I mean write. Even if it's only rewrite. He's that kind of a guy, that's all. Meantime . . ." Her tone had been level, but on that word it fell off a half note, and then fell silent.

Meantime, thought Norma Collins, you have days and nights—even the possibility of years, ahead of you, together. What *is* the matter with you—can't you see what a little fool you are? You're thirty-seven or thirty-eight, and you haven't grown up yet. Why, my Joyce would have more sense at twenty . . . Or would she? No, I suppose we never do mature until or unless we're forced to—the hard way. We'd all remain children in a never-never land, if we were allowed to. We never learn, until it is too late . . .

Meantime, thought Miriam, turning away, taking a few aimless steps just to get away from the table . . . meantime, you'll go on thinking I'm an utter beast, a rotten selfish little beast, but you don't know what I'm fighting. All you can think of is that We Have Each Other—because you lost Bart suddenly, and had no second chance.

47

(Oh, yes, you've said that plainly enough, even when you were being most tactful!) But if Bart had been maimed in that accident instead of killed outright—if he'd lived on for years, a cripple, *then* you'd know better what I'm afraid of. You'd have some idea of what I'm talking about, though I can't *say* what I mean, and it comes out all distorted . . . And Rog puts his best foot forward for you, naturally. He doesn't take out his depression and every little irritation—on you. You don't see him sunk in that deadly apathy and inertia, as I do. Without a word to say to you for hours together. Not even hearing what you say. Not *seeing* you unless you use some ruse or trick to rouse him—some silly petty thing—and half the time that just annoys him again.

She stood looking off at the hills which seemed to hem her in, even here. In town, it had been the walls; up here, it was the hills. And she heard Norma saying, "Well—meantime . . ." picking up the word smoothly and casually, as if noticing it had fallen there between them—just as her ears picked up the sound of the dining-room door as it clicked again behind them—"meantime, here comes Joseph with the papers and the mail."

CHAPTER 5

Miriam turned back quickly to watch the little man advancing primly toward them, holding out a small packet of letters, like a shallow dish which might spill over, while under the other arm he hugged a half dozen sealed rolls of newspaper.

"Hello, Joseph," she said, and—"Good day, miss," he replied formally. He placed the letters on the table in front of Norma, and looked up at Miriam, sidewise, a little like a bird listening for a worm, she thought, restraining her facial muscles with a slight effort, as she strolled back and stood nearby, while Norma sorted the letters into two piles. For that matter, Miriam reflected, she herself was behaving rather like a bird waiting with her bill wide open for a crumb . . . or something—though she was not expecting anything of

48

interest in the mail. Not expecting anything at all, she thought impatiently; just One More Day. And she heard the conversation going on between the other two without really listening to it, quite without interest.

"Alfred was late this morning," Norma had observed as she picked up the letters.

"Yes, madam."

"He sounded rather exuberant, too, judging by the way he was blowing that horn." But her tone was regretful, and Joseph's rejoinder was solemn, when he had given the matter his full and serious consideration.

"Yes, madam. I suspect—he was."

Oh, really, thought Miriam—*really!* Who cared if Alfred's arrival was late or noisy? Time meant nothing up here anyway, and who was there to hear him? There was nothing to do but eat and sleep—oh, yes, and read the damn newspapers, of course. But who wanted to look at *them*, with the news getting worse every day, and the headlines growing taller and blacker, as if they had some dreadful inherent life of their own, like parasitic worms . . . Roger was the only one who was morbid enough to want to read them, headlines, fine print and all—which was, she supposed, why Norma made such a point of having them sent up promptly from the village. And why she and Joseph went on and on about it now, looking so earnest and shaking their heads over an hour's delay. But what of it? *So what?* Miriam felt like shouting at them, when she became aware of something different—irrelevant—in what Norma was saying, though there was no apparent transition or shift of direction.

". . . Too bad. And if he's starting in this early . . . Yes, I know, he won't show it for some time except by being so unnaturally happy . . . but then all of a sudden it'll catch up with him. And meantime he'll be driving up and down and around these curves like mad, all day." She had been holding one little bunch of letters in both hands, riffling the edges with her thumb, back and forth, until, noting the direction of Miriam's glance, she awoke to what she was doing. "I'm sorry, my dear! I wasn't thinking," and she handed over the envelopes addressed to Norbeck. But to Miriam, the conversation had begun to make a little sense, and she caught at it, as at some straw floating by.

"Don't tell me!" she exclaimed. "Not the pious Alfred—?"

Norma nodded ruefully.

"Never would have guessed it," said Miriam with a chuckle, which somehow released the tightness in her diaphragm. She was eager to welcome a touch of impious amusement on this sun-baked, almost too sterile hillside—with its isolation that was like a quarantine. But she realized that Joseph did not look amused; was in fact only waiting patiently to get her attention as he stood there with the bulky rolls of newspapers still in his arms.

"Shall I take—these in—to Mis—ter Norbeck?" he asked.

"Why yes, Joseph, thank you. And I'll bring the rest of the mail in presently."

"Very good, miss." He padded quietly away, cradling the burden of gloom which he carried most carefully. As if, thought Miriam, were he to drop one of those things it might explode at his very feet. Pleasant idea, on a nice sunny day . . . And once again she pulled her glance back to the letters, now in her own hands, which she began to sort out mechanically. Typewritten letters for Roger (tossing them down on the table), a note addressed to herself— pausing to look at it, until she saw that it was an invitation to some mammoth luncheon to be given for a well-known woman journalist . . . back in New York. Norma was looking through her own mail meanwhile, and thus preoccupied, when Joseph returned a moment or so later, they both failed to notice that he was there again until he gave his nervous little cough.

"I—beg your pardon." And since he had addressed neither one, they both looked up at him.

"Yes, Joseph?" said Norma.

"I was—to convey a message. From Alfred," he said reluctantly, and seemed to stick there.

"Yes, Joseph," Norma said again, patiently. "What was it?"

He coughed once more.

"He—ah—sent—the ladies—his compliments, madam. He wished you—both—a very good day. A *very good* day," the little man repeated

50

doggedly, and to Miriam there was something faintly, if satirically, ominous in the inflection of those two words. More like an admonition to be a Very Good Girl—than to have a good time, she thought, restraining a smile, as a bubble of mirth, like a very small balloon inside her, began to rise, lifting her up with it.

"Why, thank you, Joseph," Norma said gently, and Miriam laughed—laughed out that time, and reveled in the relief it gave her. She really couldn't help it.

"Now *I* think that was very nice of him. Especially to include me!" But she saw that Joseph still had not completed his stint, and paused, wondering what more could possibly follow.

"Alfred also sent word—to *Mis*ter Norbeck, which I—fear I forgot—to deliver," he said apologetically. "It does not appear—important—but perhaps—"

"I guess I can pass it on," said Miriam, still smiling. But when Joseph cleared his throat and brought it out, it was only some nonsense about telling Roger to be sure to notice the hibiscus bush out by the gate; that it was putting on the best show it ever had, or some such thing. Both women were watching him attentively now, the one with sympathy, and the other merely puzzled. Joseph himself appeared somewhat perplexed as he looked over at the bush in question which grew and bloomed, though not in any great profusion, just to the right of the patio wall.

"All right, Joseph, I'll tell him," said Miriam.

"Thank you, miss."

"Thank *you*, Joseph," Norma added softly, as he once more made his thankful retreat into the house.

"Poor little man," said Miriam. "He's so precise and conscientious, isn't he? I should think it would be a bit of a strain for you sometimes . . . between the two of them."

"Well, yes, perhaps it is," said Norma. And then, after a moment, thoughtfully, "I never knew Roger had such a passion for hibiscus."

"Well, he hasn't, of course. Rog hardly knows a lily from a rose. You know that!"

They both laughed then, feeling quite pleasantly drawn together for the moment, and Miriam added carelessly, "He was probably just being polite to Alfred, when the old boy was pointing out the beauties of nature to him."

"But Alfred doesn't like the beauties of—I mean—" said Norma, and broke off as Miriam gave her a small mischievous grin.

"Doesn't approve of nature you mean? I wouldn't wonder! He doesn't look as if he approved of anything. Oh well, it's nice to know he's human after all. You know," said Miriam, partly, yet only half, joking as she said it, "*I've* been a bit afraid of him, to tell the truth—with his stern and piercing look, and that forbidding manner . . . You can say as often as you please that he used to sell groceries, but I'll bet he was a preacher before that. In another life, maybe. He's got that look of hellfire in his eyes, like some old-time evangelist." Norma looked up at Miriam quite seriously.

"You know, that may be it," she said. "He may have some hellfire in his soul—poor man. Perhaps that's what he has to get away from, every so often."

"Might have a bit of that minister from *Rain* in him—remember?" the other suggested, but Norma shook her head decisively.

"Oh no, now you're going off on a flight of fancy. Poor old Alfred has never been known to cast so much as a wandering eye on women. In fact, he was devoted to his little wife, and just about crushed with despair when she died. I really thought he'd go out of his mind for a while."

"Oh well . . ." said Miriam, with a little yawn, already bored with the speculation she had raised. After all, Alfred was scarcely promising material for distraction. She began opening and glancing through a couple of notes which she still had in her hands. But they didn't hold her attention long either, and after a moment she tossed them back on the table and reached down to pick up her package of cigarettes again. She stood there by her chair as she lighted another, squinting thoughtfully through her own smoke, out toward the hills; stirred restlessly, stretched a little, looked back with tightening lips at Roger's mail, still waiting mutely to be taken in to him. And then she moved off deliberately, without it; across the grass, out to the middle of the patio where she could look out straight across the gap in the hills, to the farther one. The round, smooth one with its little button of an oak tree on top. It gave her a lift, somehow, that distant outlook. She thought it was the mere break in the hills which did it—giving positive proof that there was something beyond the ones which closed her in. She reflected that she'd like to walk up there some day, all the way up, so that she could see over and beyond it.

But she paused now, irresolute, as though pulled by magnets of equal force: in one direction the horizon, and in the other, her husband waiting for her in that room only a few yards away. She knew she ought to take his letters in to him; he had little enough to keep him interested, aside from the damned newspapers and the double-damned radio—and those were bad for him. They certainly didn't make him any happier. He was never "happy" any more, she thought resentfully, even accusingly. But then her attention (wavering like the needle on a compass which was itself being moved around by some careless hand) was caught from still another direction, by the sound of steps crunching on the roadway. And catching gratefully at any diversion at all, she watched a moment longer and was rewarded by the sight of Jim Mears' head—and presently his shoulders—rising gradually with the lift of the road, from left to right along the line of the wall. Like someone climbing a flight of stairs . . . but of course it was only because he was so tall that you could see him rising for so many seconds in a row.

Nice guy, young Jim, she mused. And young Joyce had better think twice before she let him get away. Though who was *she*, to be sure, to be critical of Joyce's evident yen for greener fields and wider horizons? To the girl, Jim was just the boy next door, no matter how tall and husky and likable he might be. So they were sisters under the skin, Miriam reminded herself irritably—and uneasily, denying the comparison in the same thought wave. For Roger was no boy-next-door, after all. He was the man in the same room; adjoining room here, thank God. They had been shut in too closely together, that was half the trouble. Shut into a box, with four walls and a ceiling—and no windows, she thought desperately. No windows to look out of mentally, except (you might say) onto the devastated wasteland which the world would be before too long, according to Roger Norbeck.

"Hi, Mrs. Norbeck," said Jim, outside the gate.

53

"Oh—Jim! Good morning." Miriam knew she sounded startled, as if she hadn't seen him coming, hadn't been looking right at him in fact, waiting for him to turn his head. (And why should she put on a pointless little act like that, for a mere child like Jim? Just to keep herself in practice, possibly?)

"And the top o' the mornin' to you, ma'am!" He said it with his pleasant grin, falling into what he called his gardener-handyman approach, in which he evidently found some childish entertainment —like a balancing act between his usefulness to Norma, his devotion to Joyce, and his own independent status as the grandson of a friend and neighbor. Everybody seemed to put on some kind of an act, consciously or not, Miriam decided with a certain resignation. But she picked up the cue about the morning automatically as she strolled over toward the gate. She had concluded also that Californians were obsessed by the weather, and one might as well humor them.

"It *is* tops, too," she agreed. "I never saw such days as you have up here. Each one seems to be better and brighter than the last!"

"Well, I'll tell you, ma'am, we sorta planned it that way. Saved the best one for the last. Like the icing on the cake, see?" (Whatever he meant by *that*, she thought.) But though his confidentially solemn tone suggested that it was intended for some kind of wisecrack, he didn't wait for her to get it. He must have seen that Norma was about to disappear into the house, for he raised his voice a trifle and threw it after her, deftly, like a lariat.

"Hi—Mom Collins! Isn't this the day that big blonde brat of yours gets back?"

That stopped her. She turned, almost at the doorstep, and looked back to answer indulgently, "Hello, Jim." And added, more noncommittally, "Yes. Today's the day—" And broke off again, as though halted by her own words that time.

"Big day all around, from what I hear," said Jim, still grinning. "Good thing she'll be back in time, eh?"

Miriam had turned a puzzled look from the young man at the gate over to Norma on the other side of her, who had started back toward them. It seemed to Miriam that all this made slightly less than sense. In fact, on second thought, everybody sounded a trifle wacky to her ear this morning—from Bertha's singing, to Joseph's cryptic mono-syllables, to Alfred's silly message . . . In any case, Jim appeared bent on making these very heavyweight jokes of his, whatever they were about, and Miriam, who still thought of herself as young, was faintly chagrined to find that the humor of the *very* young quite often nowa-days struck her as strangely obscure. Just not funny. Though even Norma, who was more used to them, was not smiling now as she approached.

She said, rather pointedly, to Jim, "It's always a big day for me, when Joyce gets back."

"Yeah," said Jim. "Yeah, I guess that's right." And went on a little awkwardly, as if to cover up a small error in taste. "Well, anyway—I was thinking—I might wash the car, to kinda dazzle her with, if you'd like me to drive you over to the junction. What's she coming down on—the three-forty or the noon bus?"

"Well, no, Jim. As a matter of fact, she's not coming down by train, or bus."

"Flying, driving, or walking?" he inquired politely.

"Driving, I believe."

"Don't say," said Jim. "What in?"

"I don't know, literally," said Norma, smiling. "She's coming down with some friend who has some business in San Diego, and I'm given to understand that we're putting him up overnight."

"Him," the boy repeated. "I see." He was still standing as before, looking over the gate at them, still wearing the same grin, though it had stiffened at the corners. "Well, whadd'ye know?" he said thoughtfully, as if to himself, but Norma answered, nevertheless, taking the question for her own.

"I don't know nothin'," she assured him, lightly.

"No more than me?"

"No more than you," she confirmed. "Just somebody from this last week-end party, I gathered. And a good chance to get a ride down."

"Sure," Jim agreed, with equal carelessness. "Oh, sure. The kid's just a hitchhiker at heart, that's all. Well, guess I might as well wash the car anyway, if you'd like to have it done."

"I would," said Norma. "It needs it."

"Besides, everything oughta be left real clean, you know, ma'am. No mud or fingerprints," he said, reverting—it seemed deliberately—to that hired-hand drawl of his and the heavy-handed humor which apparently went with it. And it might be just that combination which had worn Joyce down and driven her away so suddenly, Miriam thought . . . in which case, she could only sympathize, feeling once more the humorless weight which pressed upon her own spirit.

But then, abruptly, Jim dropped his load of facetiousness and added, as though reminded by what he himself had said, "Oh, say—by the way, I brought Miss Smedley up with me, but she had me let her out down below. Wanted to stop a minute at the Weber house, she said." He sounded uneasy. "I guess she'll be along any minute, now."

"All right, Jim. Thanks for bringing her up."

But there was something bothering him still, because he stood there frowning deeply. Finally, with a jerk of decision, he said, "You know that guy—?"

"Which guy?" Norma asked gently, with a smile of sympathy in her eyes; but as if he could read there the thought of Joyce's new escort, Jim cut her off rather curtly.

"No—not him. I mean this little fat guy, the one that's been renting the Weber place, this last five-six months."

"Why, of course," said Norma in surprise. "Mr. Bixby."

"Well—uh—you think he's all right, do you?"

"Why yes, Jim," she said again, still more surprised. "He seems a nice little man. We don't see much of him, of course. He just drops in very politely for a call now and then. Never encroaches, or anything like that—if that's what you mean."

"Naw—it's not what I mean," Jim said rudely. "Sure, he's polite enough. I mean—*all right*." He looked across at Norma fixedly, as if trying to convey some particular point. "Well, I *mean*—" He blurted out then, "There's Miss Smedley going in to see him this morning, for instance—"

"I didn't know he was down today. He doesn't generally come in the middle of the week."

"*I know he doesn't!*" Jim fairly shouted. "So there you are—and there she is—and anybody who knows her way around less than little old Amelia—"

"Why, Jim!" Norma exclaimed in utter astonishment, and Miriam echoed her, "Why, *Jim!*" with even more pointed emphasis and much more enjoyment. For even she knew Mr. Bixby by sight: that quiet, pudgy little man with the sad round face, who spent the week ends in that house a few hundred yards down the road from Norma's.

Norma said now, trying to straighten out the smile which kept encircling the corners of her mouth, "I must confess the idea never even occurred to me, Jim. That is, of Mr. Bixby as a wolf . . . in sheep's clothing—" And she almost giggled.

"In rabbit's fur, you mean!" put in Miriam. But Jim gave her a terrific glower from under his heavy brows.

"Aw, skip it," he said, turning his back on them in disgust, but with a certain dignity as well. "Wasn't what I was getting at." And he went off, with a mutter to himself that was like a growl of animal annoyance. Neither of them caught the words.

CHAPTER **6**

They stood together for a moment longer, watching in a sort of absent fascination as the wall—from right to left, now—rose like water, to his hips, his waist, and then his shoulders, so that by the time he reached the opposite end of it, only his long neck and large ears and nose still stood out above it—and finally, for that second before he disappeared from their sight, the dark close-cropped top of his head. They looked at each other then and exchanged a smile.

"I don't know what on earth he did mean," said Norma in a low tone, lest he could still hear her. "Jim is often cryptic, I must say, but—well, *you've* met Mr. Bixby, even if you haven't yet seen Miss Amelia!"

"Just the same, Jim thinks she isn't safe with him," said Miriam amusedly.

"But it's fantastic! Quite aside from Miss Amelia herself (and just wait till you do see *her*), to dream up dark suspicions about that comfortable, sensible little man, so anxious to be pleasant to everybody . . . And in the middle of the morning, too!" Norma finished helplessly.

"I'm beginning to suspect you have a lot of sinister characters around here," Miriam commented.

"Oh, rot. They're more simple than sinister, if you only knew it—" But Norma broke that off. "As for Jim, I don't know what's got into him."

"Maybe the lad is still in a state of shock," the other suggested. "Wolves on the brain, just at the moment."

"Well, yes, perhaps," said Norma, not literally agreeing with the notion but adapting it where it might fit in. "I know I gave him something of a jolt, when I said Joyce was coming down with this other man. But I thought it was only fair to give him some warning, before they both turned up."

"*I* thought he took it very well, for anybody who's as much smitten with your angel child as I take it he is."

"Yes," said Norma slowly, almost reluctantly. "Yes, I'm afraid— he is. He's always said Joyce was the only girl . . . just never seemed to look at another. Which is absurd, of course."

"You like him though, don't you? He certainly makes a point of that 'Mom Collins' line, I noticed."

"Oh well, that was just a joke when it started. You know the sort of thing. We were all having a Tom Collins one day, I forget who else was here at the time, but Jim had never had one, and he drank the whole thing without saying a word, and then all of a sudden announced solemnly that he thought he'd prefer a Mom Collins for everyday use. Just trying to be funny of course—but it seemed to stick, the way those silly tags do, sometimes . . . Unfortunately," she added.

"Why unfortunately, if you like him yourself? Or don't you?"

"Ye—es . . . yes, of course I like him." Norma said a bit irritably. "Jim's a dear, in many ways. But—they're infants, that's all."

"Oh, I don't know. They both look pretty well grown to me."

"Grown, yes—but not grown-up! And they were only sixteen or seventeen when they first met down here. Since then, they haven't even given each other a chance to know anybody else, either here or all through college. Imagine!"

"Nope," said Miriam. "I can't even imagine it. My God, at that age I thought I wasn't even having a passable time, if I didn't have about six or eight of them baying at my heels." An all too obvious comment passed through Norma's mind, which she discarded hastily, and pursued her own line of thought as though she'd scarcely heard the other.

"Trouble is, they have no perspective, yet. How could they? No comparisons to build on. And Jim," she said, more slowly, "hasn't a prospect in the world—unless perhaps his grandmother should die and leave him what little she has left."

"I wondered why you were taking it so seriously," Miriam remarked, not acidly, but shrewdly, and Norma retorted, "Well, why wouldn't I, for heaven's sake? Though I *didn't*, I assure you! Not for the first four years. I never dreamt of taking them seriously. This 'going steady,' as they call it, generally lasts a few weeks, or a few months at most. But not with those two. And now they're talking about getting married . . . Or they were," she corrected that, with an intonation of conscientious doubt.

"Everybody gets married right out of the cradle nowadays," said Miriam carelessly. "How old are they, anyway?"

"Not quite twenty-one. Both of them. Their birthdays are only a couple of months apart."

"My dear, they're generally veterans at that age, now!"

"Yes, I know. But that's another thing." Norma paused, frowning. "You see, he's still waiting around to be drafted. Just hasn't happened to be called up yet, though most of his friends have gone. He could have enlisted, of course. But he hasn't. And I don't know why, exactly . . ."

"Joyce?" suggested Miriam.

"I—don't know," admitted Norma, rather unhappily, now. "She doesn't talk to me as open-heartedly as she used to. I suppose I have been dragging my feet—though very carefully—trying not to let them notice, or think I was against them. Which I'm not!" she interrupted herself sharply, as though arguing the point with someone else, not Miriam. "But I couldn't let them go tobogganing into marriage practically from their teens, since I'm the only one to act as some kind of brake. His grandmother doesn't care . . . No, no, I don't mean that, exactly. She cares about Jim, I'm sure—though she's a rather austere and undemonstrative old lady. (You'll meet her today, by the way. She's coming up to tea.) But she simply takes a hands-off attitude with him, as though bending over backwards from influencing him in any way. About anything."

"Hasn't he any other family?"

"Not—quite his own," said Norma. "His parents were divorced, you see, and his mother remarried almost immediately, I gather. Jim doesn't seem to have any great sense of belonging, there. Though how his mother could ever let him feel that, I don't know. His father was killed in Korea. And Jim never mentions him. I don't think he was much good, from what I've heard, outside . . ."

"So you think Jim isn't much good either, is that it?" Miriam asked, and Norma turned her straight blue gaze to meet the other's speculative one.

"No, I can't believe that," she said honestly. "Because there's so much that's fine about him. And he's not lazy, though he seems to lack a sense of direction—or decision. I don't know. Maybe it goes back to this everlasting uncertainty—about war. Or possible war."

"Oh, let's say probable war," said Miriam with a sudden crisp hardening in her voice. "Let's be realistic by all means. Well, it's no worse for the young than for the rest of us, is it? In fact, we've already 'had it,' you might say. My generation—and yours too, of course. *They* may even be the lucky ones, not to have wasted so much time and anguish fighting off the inevitable, or sitting out the suspense between rounds. That is, if we're all going to be blown off the earth at the same time—any moment now." She broke off almost impatiently, as the other's troubled eyes continued to rest on her.

"Some will be left, they say," Norma reminded her, at last. "Besides, I think it does matter more about them—the young—if only because we have 'had it' in another sense. We've already had so much of the wonder and beauty of life. Our quota, probably."

"Oh yes?" said Miriam.

"Well, haven't we?" Norma pursued and the other gave a shrug.

"Oh yes," she conceded. "I daresay. However, we've seen more trouble too. So it cancels out. Anyway, I refuse to wring my hands over the next generation. Selfish of me, no doubt, but my hands are full already."

"Perhaps," said Norma, rather low, "when one has children, one may have more of a sense of continuity. One's anxiety is projected farther ahead—unavoidably. You just can't help wondering what your children will be doing—what they'll be up against, long after you're gone. Even speculating about what sort of children and grandchildren they will have . . ." She smiled, trying to lighten this strangely unreal conversation which had fallen on them, like a shadow over their idle personal talk. But Miriam cut in coldly, "And whether and how much the unborn generation will be affected by radioactivity, for instance."

"Oh, Miriam," breathed Norma, her voice dying in her throat.

"Sorry," the other said. "Don't mind me. That's the way Rog talks, you know, and I've been—contaminated myself, I guess. Anyway, I readily concede to being glad I'm not a parent—and that goes from any angle you care to look at it!" She flicked away her current cigarette on the grass, as if to close that subject also, though Norma wanted suddenly to add, You should have been . . . You would have grown up more fully yourself, if you had . . . (But of course that wasn't even true, because some of them didn't.) And yet the thought kept leading her a little farther, because that might be the very thing that was wrong with Miriam, whether she knew it or not: the running sap blocked off, the lifestream dammed—or damned, if you like—to stagnate, or dry up. A trite enough conclusion, but if it were true, then she had been tactless, Norma thought.

"I shouldn't have—put it that way, Miriam," she said in soft apology.

"What?"

"Well—about when one has, or hasn't children . . ."

Miriam's glance was merely amused; or so it seemed.

"Did you think you'd hurt my feelings, dear?"

"I hope not. I didn't mean to—but it was stupid of me, just the same."

"But I meant exactly what I said. I'm very glad I have no children," Miriam repeated, as though the other might be slightly deaf. "You can't believe that, can you?"

No, thought Norma, she did not believe it, and wasn't even sure whether Miriam believed what she had said, or was herself deceived. But meantime the two women, turning, had begun to move back across the grass toward the house, as if in tacit agreement to leave behind them one more byway which had proved a dead end. The breakfast table had been cleared of everything except for the two small packets of mail which still lay there on the glass top, like two islands on a flat sea, waiting separately to be rediscovered. But though she was gazing ahead, Miriam's mind swam backward again—away from them.

"So anyway," she said, "Jim's hanging around doing odd jobs and such, just to be near the beautiful blonde brat, as he fondly calls her . . . While she's gone off to have herself some fun! *I* don't see why you're worrying, dear. It's working out the way you want it to."

"I'm not sure what I want," said Norma, in a troubled tone, which was perplexed as well. "All I know is, it's *not* working out too happily between the two of them at present. For the first time in all these years they've been having misunderstandings—real ones, I'm afraid, not just little tiffs and spats."

"And when this invitation came, she went off practically on the next bus, to show him he wasn't indispensable," said Miriam lightly.

"Something like that. But now, I don't know whether she's bringing this other young man down as a further demonstration to Jim, or if she's really taken with him. I must say she sounded awfully pleased with herself on the phone, telling me about this 'older man.'"

"Older?"

"Around thirty," she said.

But Miriam did not laugh.

"Oh, God," she said irritably, "how young can they be, even at twenty!" They had reached the table now, and Miriam picked up her letters with a quick impatient snatch, juggling them in her fingers like a deck of cards, as if to straighten them into a nice even stack. And then, patently recalling herself from such illogical annoyance, "So that's all you know about the new heart throb, is it?"

"That's all. His age, and his name, which is Don something. I can't even remember the last name, now. By the way, I do hope Rog won't mind having a stranger lurking around. It's only for overnight, I believe."

"Why, of course not! What an idea. It'll be good for him. I only wonder if we aren't taking up too much room, Norma. With an extra guest, for instance?"

"Oh mercy, no. I always use that upstairs room in the old part of the house—over the living room, you know—for an overnight or week-end guest like this young man, anyway. Landon!" she said suddenly.

"*What?*" said Miriam blankly.

"No, Landis, that's it. Don Landis." But Miriam still looked so startled that she added in explanation, "I've been trying to remember the young man's last name, that's all. Not that they use 'em any more." But the other scarcely seemed to hear those last words; she was not listening now, unless it were to some echo in her own memory.

"Don—Landis," she repeated evenly, and—it seemed—rather vaguely, as in polite acknowledgment of an introduction; yet there was something in the very evenness of her voice, like a plate carefully balanced, which made Norma glance back at her.

"Do you know him?" she asked.

"No . . . No, I don't think so. The name sounded familiar, for a second. But we've met so many people here and there, you know. One can't remember half of them . . ." Her words trailed off, more vaguely than before, but her eyes had dropped to the handful of letters which she was still idly juggling. "I must take Rog's mail in to him," she said, as if the thought had just occurred to her.

"And *I* must tackle Bertha," said Norma cheerfully, quite aware of the procrastination they had both been indulging in, for entirely different reasons. And for another instant her twinkling glance offered to exchange smiles in recognition of that fact. But Miriam had separated her own notes from the envelopes with typewritten addresses, and her fingers were flipping through the latter once more, checking them over, half automatically it seemed, until at the bottom letter she paused, rereading the address, and then inserted a long red-nailed finger in the flap and tore it open. As she did so she looked up, and catching the reflection of amusement—like an afterglow—in the other's eyes, gave a small self-conscious laugh.

"Silly, isn't it? I never even think of looking for letters to myself among these typewritten things. I guess I forget that women are on a lot of . . . sucker lists, too."

The explanation hung on the air, a trifle awkwardly, but there was no one to notice, for Norma's practical mind had run ahead to face her immediate household problems. She was not even thinking of the younger woman now, and with an absent, "Well, see you later, dear—" she turned and was on her way into the house at last, while Miriam's eye went back quickly to the half-page letter which had been typed on a business letterhead.

CHAPTER 7

She had been standing in the same spot, motionless, for quite long enough to read the letter through; even to reread it twice over. But she was still engrossed when there came a clicking, rattling sound from the direction of the gate. Miriam raised her head sharply, and saw a face, with glasses, and an unfashionable sailor hat set straight above them, topping an oddly shaped figure which looked—what one could see of it over the low gate—as if it were dressed in brown wrapping paper.

"Come in!" she called, as she thrust her letter back in its envelope, folded it in half and slipped it into the pocket of her slacks. But her normally quick fingers had moved stiffly, as though not quite thawed from their frozen immobility of a moment before, and one of the other letters had fallen to the ground. She bent swiftly to retrieve it, and when she straightened up again she had also picked up her poise, so that she could smile as she looked across the patio and saw the same face still peering over the low redwood picket barrier, while the same sounds of ineffectual fumbling at the latch continued. She also saw that what she had taken to be the woman's shoulders were actually the corners of a large square parcel which she held clutched against her, and it *was* wrapped in brown paper.

"Oh, wait a minute, and I'll help you," Miriam said now, crossing the square of lawn between, with her swift graceful stride, and she added pleasantly as she opened the gate, "I didn't realize you had your hands so full."

"Oh, thank you—thank you very much," the little person said, apologetically, "I couldn't seem to undo the catch . . . I couldn't quite see the handle, you understand . . ." And Miriam observed as she moved in past her that she had not one, but two of those bulky parcels in her arms. No wonder she couldn't see what she was doing. And she was still an odd little figure behind that brown-paper front: small and thin, neatly dressed in a flowered but faded print—which had no shape, because *she* had none, Miriam thought, with a passing touch of pity. She wondered if she had ever been at all pretty, even when young, with that dark skin which now had the look of having weathered—not in the sun, but out of it, and the brown eyes which had a misty, near-sighted look behind her glasses.

"You do have a big load there. Let me take one of those, won't you?"

"Oh no!" the woman exclaimed, and seemed to embrace her armful more tightly, as in alarm that the other might try to take it from her, might even lay a hand on it. "I am Miss Smedley," she added formally.

"Yes, I rather thought—that is, I remembered Mrs. Collins' saying you were coming today . . . And I'm Mrs. Norbeck." They smiled at each other, Miss Smedley with a sort of prim timidity, and Miriam in what she hoped was a reassuring way; the little thing seemed so shy, so nervous. And as they walked back toward the house, Miriam offered, almost in spite of herself, "What a lovely day it's going to be, isn't it?"—feeling that any topic other than the weather might put the creature to sudden flight. Even her reaction to the weather proved somewhat surprising. She took in a great breath, lifting her chin and stretching her thin neck so that she seemed to grow another inch. Even her bundles appeared to swell with the same afflatus, and her pale eyes behind the glasses grew luminous as she answered.

"Oh, beautiful!" she said. "Beautiful—beautiful—just the way we expected it would be, isn't it? From sunup . . . to sunup, one last glory to carry with us to eternity!" Her voice quivered slightly, and Miriam wondered if she were quoting some line from an old song; or poetry, perhaps. She certainly hadn't expected such an ecstatic response to her commonplace remark, despite her previous recognition that the weather was not just an ordinary conversational stopgap out here, as it was in other parts of the world. Here, it seemed to be a continuing, living entity, no more to be ignored than another person in their midst. So Miriam agreed affably, "Yes, indeed," and added, smiling, "Though I must say, if it's fine from sunup to sundown, I'll be quite satisfied!" But she saw that her attempt to lighten up the subject had brought a cloud—of doubt, or mistrust, was it?—to the other's face. So again she added, rather hastily, "Well, I suppose you know just where to go—"

"You mean, at break of day?" said Miss Smedley, gently in her turn.

"Why—not exactly," Miriam said, wondering why *she* should be confused. "I just meant—now," she concluded simply, thinking that this was like one of those senseless conversations in a dream.

"Ah, but *now*—" Miss Smedley caught that up, brightening. "Now, the way is clear ahead, and so short that we can never lose it again." She looked so happy, having uttered this, that Miriam thought she'd better leave it at that. But the other continued to pursue whatever it was that she thought she meant. "Isn't that a lovely, comforting thought?" she asked shyly, but eagerly too.

"Yes indeed," said Miriam once more, inclining her head—almost by main force, as if she'd had to reach up and push it into the semblance of a nod with her own hand—and as she did so, discover-

66

ing those letters for Roger still in the other hand: a reminder and an avenue of escape. "I guess I'll have to take this mail in to my husband. He hasn't been too well," she explained, trying not to sound abrupt—not to startle the creature in any way, and found that Miss Smedley was positively beaming at her.

"Ah, but he will be now!" she almost sang. "Isn't that wonderful to think of, Mrs. Norbeck? And isn't it nice that his mail arrived in time? *I* sent several letters myself—all *air mail*, too—just to make sure, you know."

"Why yes, it—does help to speed it up," said Miriam idiotically. "Well, I—you will excuse me, won't you?" (Reminding herself to walk, not run, to the nearest exit; trying to contain, as in a separate compartment, the hysterical laughter which was ready to brim over—even while the rest of her was still parched for laughter.)

"Why, of course, dear. I'm just going to sit down here for a little tiny minute," said Miss Smedley, and lowered herself carefully onto a straight chair just under the wide eaves which shaded the flagstone terrace, still clasping those big bundles against her front, but still able to peer over them, out into the patio. "I do like to look up there—at the Hill," she confided softly.

"Yes, so do I," assented Miriam, thankful to be able to agree with something which sounded more rational. "And I'm sure Mrs. Collins will be back in a minute," she murmured, edging away now, definitely. "She just went in to confer with Bertha a few minutes ago."

"Oh yes," said Miss Smedley dreamily. "I won't interrupt them. I'm sure they have a *lot* to arrange for today . . ." though that last was said to no one in particular, and she seemed scarcely to notice that Mrs. Norbeck was already moving swiftly away.

Miriam went straight to Roger's outer door; actually, she thought, with a momentary flash of surprise, eager to reach him now: to have something amusing to tell him for a change. But when she went in, the room was empty and the sound of the shower told her where he was. He must have got tired of waiting for her (or more accurately, for his mail) and decided to get up. Well, she *had* been lingering out there longer than usual this morning; she knew that very well. In fact—be honest, Miriam—she'd been stretching out her attenuated

67

sense of freedom for just as long as she could find an excuse to do so.

And now she stood in the middle of the room, listening to the steady downpour of the water. (Rog always turned a shower on full, till it sounded like Niagara.) Looking at the covers on the bed, not thrown really open, but just halfway; in a mess as usual. The wallow of newspapers, half of them on the floor—but then in contrast, a neat sheaf of clippings precisely pinned together and placed on the bedside table with a paper knife to weight them down. It irritated her almost unbearably to have to read the papers, herself, with those great holes cut out of them, though—as he said—if there was anything she wanted, she had only to turn to the paragraphs he had already culled, which were there to refer to in the most convenient form. Of course it never occurred to him that she might just want to see some frivolous advertisement of a dress or a blouse on the back of one of those eternal everlasting political articles!

At one time, she had done all the clipping for him: items which he had marked with blue pencil, and some which she even thought he might have missed and for which he often commended her; he used to say she was as good a secretary as she was a wife. (Better, no doubt, since she had been a damned good secretary before she'd ever been a wife . . .) But he didn't say that any more. Now he was too impatient, because he was not busy himself; strange that he had been more patient, when he had less time. Now he wanted everything done at once, couldn't wait for her to finish up some laundering if he wanted her to type a business letter for him. And yet he took a perverse and dilatory satisfaction in all his careful reading, marking, cutting, filing . . . ("read, mark, learn and inwardly digest") thought Miriam, and to what end?—since the book he talked of writing was not intended to follow those factual lines anyway. She wondered sometimes whether his busy painstaking preoccupation was like the motion of a flywheel which kept on spinning for a while after the motor was cut off. Or was it more in the nature of perpetual motion which he subconsciously kept going, just to keep his mind turning over and over and hide from himself the fact that he would never, never—*never* write again. Not a book . . . Not anything. She didn't know. What she did know was

68

that as she stood listening to the pouring water which drowned out all other sound, it was once more as though she were drenched in the depression of these last months. The spark of amusement which she had brought in with her was already flickering damply; it would be entirely gone, she felt, if she tried to transmit it to Roger. He probably wouldn't think it funny, so why tell him? Why, she thought, even wait here until he came in? Ordinarily she would have stopped to tidy up the room; making the bed as she had done each day since they had been at Norma's, in a slight gesture of easing along the household routine. But she could come back and do that after he had finished dressing and gone outdoors. As the water went off, with the pained grunt of a suddenly closed valve (it was a wonder he didn't wrench off the handles of anything he touched nowadays!), the impulse of escape took hold of her again, and in the lull of silence accompanied only by the tapering-off sound of dripping, Miriam carefully laid Roger's letters on the chest at the foot of the bed, in plain view where he couldn't miss them, and slipped quietly into her adjoining room, pulling the door to, behind her—without quite latching it, for that might make a noise.

How silly of her, she thought. Nothing to do in here, for her own room was scrupulously neat, as she had left it when she went out to breakfast. Except perhaps . . . to empty out the waste basket, after she had added one scrap to the contents. Her hand went back to her pocket again, almost furtively, retrieving that typewritten letter, and she moved toward the dressing table where the basket stood half concealed. She paused there to consider it, simply as a piece of paper, now, not rereading it. How silly of *him*, she thought— to imagine that she would care to continue a momentary flirtation begun at a cocktail party. And rather crude and callous of him too, to take this way of following it up. Not that the letter said anything except that he was coming down this way, understood they would be fellow visitors, and so on—but it was plain enough what he expected her to read between the lines. A hint—a warning not to be surprised to see him—a faint insidious suggestion . . . Just what kind of woman did he take her for, anyway? As for Joyce—poor little Joyce—not dreaming she was being made use of; a little too young to recognize the easy technique of an "older man of almost thirty."

Miriam smiled a little wryly, as with quiet care she tore the letter into small bits, and dropped them into the basket. There! she told herself. At least she would make a point of not being anywhere around when they arrived. That should give *him* a hint that she wasn't interested. She would go off on a long walk, as she'd been wanting to. Even if it was getting warm now, it would do her good. Sweat out this restlessness, perhaps; wear down the seething nervous energy, in exercise which would tire her physically. That was it; she needed exercise . . . But still she stood before the table, regarding herself in the mirror, the erect and graceful figure in which she felt—not pride or conceit, but just a certain detached and justifiable satisfaction. Joyce was much prettier and much younger, but she felt no envy of her now; only this irrelevant compunction. For in spite of herself, and the way she meant to handle this situation, there was a little tremor of excitement inside her. (An irresistible quiver of response to the mere flattery of being pursued?) She could even see that the white silk of her blouse, where it lay on her breast, was lifting with a deeper, or quicker, breath than usual. And she met her own dark eyes in one searching, candid glance which said silently, You *are* being something of a bitch, aren't you, Miriam?

Well, she would change her shoes anyway, as an announcement of her intentions, to herself and others. She would be ready, then, to start off on her hike in the hills, just as soon as she had done Roger's room. So she turned to the cupboard and brought out a more serviceable pair, and as she sat down on the window seat to slip out of the light sandals she was wearing, she heard another flood of sound—not water this time, and not next door, but voices—no, just one voice full of exclamations and accents tumbling over each other, out in the patio. Bertha, she thought, smiling to herself.

"Ah-h, Miss Am-*eel*-ya!" she heard. "You kom, you kom like a leetle *an*gel already. And I'm so glod, so glod to see you thees day. Thees vonderfool day, eh?"

Well anyway, that's what it sounded like to Miriam. The woman talked more like a waterfall than any human being she had ever heard, though as Roger said, it might very well be the Falls of Zambesi, since no self-respecting North American cataract ever uttered sounds like that. What a thing to have to cope with her as Norma did, day after day; must be rather like a gush of warm soapsuds, that you'd have to keep rinsing away, to get anything clear. And how anyone ever found a chance to put in a reply was an interesting question also. No wonder Joseph was a silent man. In fact, Miriam caught herself glancing out the window as she straightened up again, just to check and see whether Miss Smedley was still there; and she was, indeed, smiling raptly if a trifle dazedly as Bertha's volubility poured over her. She had even relinquished one of the sacred brown-paper parcels to the other woman, and was, it appeared, being gently convoyed on the bubbling stream of talk over to the door which led into the dining room and kitchen quarters.

What a pair. And what on earth could those two have in common, anyway? Miriam shrugged to herself and gave it up, about to turn to the cupboard again to put away her sandals, when she noticed that Norma had come out of the house from another door, through the living room no doubt, and was standing there unseen by the others, as if loath to interrupt them; just rather worriedly regarding her two employees as they disappeared. That patio was like a sort of arena, Miriam thought; or let's just call it a stage (sounds less bloody, even if it's more banal) where the characters entered by one door and spoke some lines and made their exit through another. She was reflecting upon this in some amusement, beginning to see what people meant when they said they simply lived in their patios down here, and at the same time acutely aware of the small sounds of someone moving about now in the next room, and of her own dis-inclination to engage in any action in the wings—when suddenly she went to her own outer door and out upon the stage again, as though she had been waiting for her cue.

She said, strolling over to Norma, "My dear, I am simply fascinated by your sewing woman! I let her in at the gate a few minutes ago, and got embroiled in the most bewildering conversation with her."

"You did?" Norma looked up quickly, but she was not smiling. She did look worried, for a fact, thought Miriam as she answered gaily, "I certainly did! I began to wonder which of us was . . . Tell me, *is* there anything wrong, Norma? I mean . . ." She hesitated now, but the other didn't help her along.

"Just what do you mean?" she asked, after a small pause.

"Well, isn't she a little—off the beam?"

"No, I don't think so, if you mean more than just . . . Oh, she's an odd little character of course, the way lots of people are when they live alone for a long time. The way I'll be one of these days, no doubt," said Norma, smiling.

"Oh, rubbish. You! You're the most normal person I ever knew."

"Is that a compliment? I'm not quite sure."

"Why yes, I think it is," said Miriam in something like surprise, considering the point for a moment. And then, realizing that she was being deftly switched off on another track, she went back a step. "I didn't mean to criticize the poor little thing, Norma. I just couldn't seem to follow her, or understand what she was talking about."

Norma had seated herself on one of the padded redwood settees, and Miriam lit a cigarette. But she didn't sit down; there was a temporary look about them both, even as one of those little silences blew up like a stray breeze between them. Neither one of them wanted to get into another of those involved, indefinite conversations through which they had been twisting and turning earlier. Yet Norma heard herself asking, cautiously, "What *did* she say—do you remember?"

"Oh, I don't know, really. It was more an impression than the actual words, I guess. Seemed to follow after my unwary comment on the weather, as I remember it. She went off into a sort of poetic rhapsody about the beautiful—beautiful—be*auti*ful day—and one last glory to carry us to eternity, or something of the kind." Miriam laughed a little as the words came back to her. "I didn't know if she was quoting some old song of her girlhood—or what . . . Is she a sort of—religious fanatic?" she asked then, half curiously.

"Not—exactly. Not quite as you mean, I think." Norma gave a sigh, but it was indrawn, one of those long breaths to carry one over a slight rise ahead, and she looked up frankly to meet the other's puzzled glance. "I should have told you this before," she said, and paused, and Miriam waited. "In fact I tried a couple of times this morning, but I knew how it would sound, so—peculiar, to say the least. And I'm fond of these people around here, you know. I suppose I didn't want even you and Rog to laugh at them. I didn't want to laugh myself," she added ruefully.

"Do you mind telling me what *you're* talking about now?" inquired Miriam mildly.

"Sorry—I can't seem to get it out, can I?" And Norma did laugh then, apologetically. "Well, you see," she said, "this is it: they all think the world is going to come to an end . . ."

"I suppose it will, sometime . . . 'What goes up must come down,' so to speak . . . which is to say, all the lava and stuff we're told about will blow it apart again—or freeze up solid—or collide with the sun or something—if we don't blow it up ourselves, which possibility we've already mentioned this morning." Miriam's light tone turned very dry and she gave a careless wave of the hand with the cigarette in it—as if to push aside the smoke.

"Tomorrow," said Norma.

"What d'you mean, tomorrow?"

"I mean the world is coming to an end *tomorrow*. That is, sometime after midnight."

"Oh, Norma Collins!" said Miriam, beginning to laugh again, just as Norma had known she would, and the latter countered indignantly, "I didn't say *I* believed it, you idiot! I just said that's what these people around here have got into their heads. Miss Smedley for instance."

"Oh, so that's what she meant by that 'sunup to sunup' business! My dear, how absolutely marvelous! I never heard anything so—I can't help it, Norma—you *know* it's funny!"

"Of course I know it," retorted Norma rather crossly, "but it's pathetic too, when you know the people. It's just so ridiculous that you don't know whether to laugh or cry . . ." But they were both beginning to laugh by then, Norma still reluctantly, but Miriam was giggling like a schoolgirl, going off into new bursts every time she began to run down, and finally dropping down beside Norma on the settee from sheer weakness.

"Look, dear—we must be careful," the older woman cautioned.

"We *can't* hurt their feelings, you know, and Miss Smedley will be back again any moment, after she's finished trying on Bertha's robe."

"Her *robe?*" said Miriam suspiciously, catching her breath, and Norma began to giggle where the other had left off.

"Oh yes, that's part of it. They're all to be dressed in white robes—"

"With wings?"

"Well—no, I don't understand so. Maybe they expect those to be provided . . . I don't know how they expect to take off, otherwise."

"Did you say 'take off'?"

"From the Hill up there." Norma inclined her head in the direction of the smooth rolling curve of higher ground in the middle distance, outlined against the hot blue sky. "You see, they're supposed to go up to the highest hill and wait there—singing, I believe, and praying, until dawn, or until the exact moment arrives. The hour wasn't specified, I don't know why."

"Oh *no!* My dear, it's the most fantastic thing I ever heard of. You mean they actually believe that at a given moment—"

"That's right. Sometime before daybreak, on March twenty-second," said Norma firmly.

And they both began to laugh again, helplessly, until the sudden clap of a screen door closing caught them in mid-breath and stopped them short, with a look of guilt flashed between them. Norma turned her head very slightly, as if her neck had suddenly gone stiff, toward the kitchen corner of the patio, but Miriam had glanced the other way, and said quickly, "Oh, it's only Rog . . ." And then raised her voice with a new and genuine lilt in it. "Hi, darling!" she called. "Come on over—I've got the most wonderful news for you!"

He didn't look too receptive, thought Norma, as he walked toward them across the corner of lawn, his expression not only unsmiling, but closed and unresponsive, somehow. Perhaps he felt left out, if not exactly neglected, with the two of them giggling like fools out there . . . And as always, each time she saw him after an interim of hours, she was struck anew by the *spare* look he had these days. Roger had never been a heavy man, but he had been well muscled and well filled out for his height of five feet nine; had what was

74

generally called a stocky build, she supposed. Of course the doctors nowadays made a great point of paring down the pounds, when there was any trouble with the heart . . . Norma knew that; she just couldn't get quite used to its application with Roger, any more than she could get used to his colorless lips. No, not colorless either, because they were almost blue. A delicate mauve, as though he'd been licking one of those old indelible pencils.

"Hello, Rog," she said, with gentle warmth, and his lips smiled then, as he approached.

"Morning, Norma. Well?"—to Miriam—"What's up? What is this fabulous good news?"

"Wait till you hear!" she said, with relish. "It's marvelous, darling —really fabulous!" And she added, softly but distinctly, and with a certain impressiveness, "The world—is coming to an end, my good man—tomorrow. At daybreak, more or less."

"You don't say," he replied. "Well, I've been expecting it for some time. But I didn't expect they'd give us warning of the exact day and hour."

"No, but, Rog, we're not joking. That is—"

"Neither am I," he said drily, sitting down near them in a chair in the sun; but though he leaned his head back in a gesture of relaxation, letting the warmth beat down on his face, his expression was still somber. Miriam knew that expression well; it settled on him by the time he had finished the newspapers almost every day.

"Listen, you goat," she said impatiently. "You'd better stop looking at the world through a telescope for a minute, and begin to notice what's going on right around you. It's much more entertaining!"

"Oh, I wasn't deprecating present company, either," he said.

"The point is," Miriam insisted, "that the whole blessed village really believes this thing—that the world's coming to an end, tomorrow morning, on the dot! Isn't that priceless?"

"Not quite all of them," Norma put in conscientiously. "It's hard to tell, in some cases, just who does and who doesn't—"

Between them, they had finally secured Roger's full attention. He looked from one to the other with the old quizzical spark beginning to show in his eyes, while the smiling creases deepened at the corners of his mouth.

"Well, if you two aren't just cooking up a dish of slapstick—to jar a poor old hypochondriac out of his lethargy, you might at least tell him what it's all about."

"I *am* telling you, my pet. This darling little village back in the hills has got its mind made up that this is the end, period. The very last day there is—and there ain' gonna be no more!" Miriam was thoroughly enjoying herself now. "What's more, they've all got themselves lovely white robes for the occasion—in fact, Norma's own sewing woman is just delivering the latest models to Bertha and Joseph out in the kitchen. Did she bring yours too, dear? Or is that the little number that she's going to whip up for you today?" She had turned to Norma, who had been sternly declining to laugh, but now in spite of herself, something very like a chuckle got away from her, and Miriam paused to laugh with her at her own flippancy, the two of them together relishing this whole absurd business for a moment, while any critical edginess of the past hour was smoothed away between them. "And tonight, Rog," Miriam went on blithely, "they're all going to climb up to the top of the hill over there, singing hymns and things—and wait for the dawn to break—and the big take-off! Isn't it just the most enchanting thing you ever heard of? Do you suppose we could go along too?—Oh no, *you* shouldn't make the climb, dearest—but *I* could, and get an eyewitness report for you. *Think* what a scoop! END OF THE WORLD—AT PRECISELY FIVE FORTY-SIX, or whenever the sun rises around here . . . I'm sure I wouldn't know, not having come in with the milkman for so long now . . . The only trouble is," said Miriam, frowning intently, and pursing her lips to keep them in order, "I haven't got a *thing* to wear! Not all white, that is—except—oh yes, in my city suitcase— you know, Rog, the one we left in the closet, that I haven't opened since we've been here? I *do* have that white faille dinner dress, that I've been saving for some really big event . . . Only thing is, it's strapless and topless and all the rest—I don't know if that would meet with the regulations . . . Do you think it *would* do?" she asked Norma, big-eyed and innocent, tilting her head on an anxious, questioning slant.

76

"It's pretty damn low," said Roger.

And of course Norma had to laugh again with them both. What else could she do? "Idiots," she said indulgently.

The fact was, that she found she couldn't resent any of it, after all; not even on behalf of her own villagers—because Miriam was getting so much fun out of all this nonsense. She had seized on it as though fairly starved for a tidbit of amusement. (Which in itself was illuminating, wasn't it?) She was simply, as she had said, enchanted by the whole idea, as though a sort of carnival had been planned especially to top off their visit. As for Roger, his grin remained, etched in by the lines made long ago—when he had used it a lot more—though his voice was serious enough, as his wife paused and gave him a chance to put a word in.

"Kidding aside," he said to Norma, "is it a fact, that they've really bought up this notion wholesale?"

"I guess it is," she admitted apologetically.

"What started it, anyway? Who sold it to them?"

"That I don't know, Roger. I honestly don't, though I think someone brought it in from outside. Somebody who'd been off to the big city, maybe, or away visiting somewhere. Or they might have read it in a book, for all I know."

"Yes," said Miriam pertly. "I've noticed that people have the most amazing way of believing anything in print. I mean, if it's in print, it *must* be true, my dear!" she mimicked, but Norma passed that over.

"It could be just someone stopping for gas—and spreading the word, darn them!—as they drove through the village. Like pausing to pass on chicken pox," she said, with a tinge of resentment. "All I know, or feel sure of, is that they couldn't have made it all up themselves. Not these people who live right around here. But there are cults galore in California, you know. It seems to be a hothouse for them."

"*Is* it a religious thing?" asked Miriam again, but the other shook her head.

"I don't think so—exactly. Not in the regular sense, that is. Some of the ones I know—who seem—well, most convinced, say—don't even belong to the same faith or church. Any church, perhaps. All we have here is a little community meeting house where different ones, from different sects, alternate in conducting services. And I'm sure I haven't heard of any one of those who seems to be—sponsoring the idea." She shook her head again, because any terms one used to explain this phenomenon sounded so out of place. So *silly*.

"Oh, I daresay some self-appointed prophet must have got it started among a few susceptible souls," said Roger carelessly.

"They might even have got hold of one of those old prophecies that are always being dug up, mightn't they?" Norma said to Roger.

"Oh, sure. Sure. This isn't an uncommon one at all, you know. Must have been dozens or scores of times in history when somebody —somewhere—foretold the end of the world. I must look that up sometime, just for curiosity," he muttered thoughtfully, his passion for unearthing facts beginning to operate quite automatically. "Seems to me there was a really big to-do about fifty years ago. No, maybe it was further back, in the eighties—upstate in New York, wasn't it?" he asked himself, frowning.

"Well, anyway," said Miriam brightly, trying to snatch the silly subject away from him—and keep it silly—keep it light, like a bright-colored balloon to play with. But Roger went right on, pulling it down, anchoring it so he could examine it more closely.

"The day of judgment has an awful fascination for the superstitious mind," he resumed judiciously. "I suppose the idea of death and disaster, for the world, or for the individual, is always there and not too deeply buried in our primitive subconscious. Not so deeply as we like to think. So we ignore the well-reasoned warnings of our few real statesmen, and go into fits of irrational jitters over a flying saucer, or a pockmarked windshield—or some damn crystal-gazer's forecast."

"Look, dear," Miriam said, with a light, punctilious pretense at patience, "we're not talking about the beginning of World War III, see?"

"Aren't we?" said Roger. "I thought we were talking about the end of the world. They could be the same, you know."

"What we're talking about now—is *now*. Here, and now," said Miriam distinctly, as though calling someone back from a long way off. "That is, tomorrow, and this little village right below us, and the extraordinary delusion it's got. The funny little village, and the *funny* side of this illusion—can't you see. . . ?" But her voice broke, and the lilt had gone out of it now. The balloon had in some way been pricked.

"Yeah, I see—and I heard you the first time," said Roger, not too agreeably, so that Norma thought in distress, Oh, dear, that's what they do to each other, every time. Over everything. Over nothing. And she got up with decision.

"Well, children, personally I have a lot to do before the day of judgment." Roger looked up at her, smiling again at last.

"Why bother?" he said. "It's too late now, anyway."

"Oh, *God!*" said Miriam explosively, and she sprang up too, but not with Norma's deliberate decisiveness: more like a jet of water gushing forth irresistibly, and then for a moment standing poised on the very force of its own energy. "I am going to take a walk," she announced.

The other two looked at her, not in surprise but thoughtfully, as in appraisal of this new decision, Roger's head tilting back to regard her from where he remained seated.

"Okay," he said quietly—very quietly, now. "You don't have to make a declaration of independence about it, you know." And then, as if belatedly offering his contribution to her fun, which he had spoiled, he inquired, "Going to climb the Hill? Might be a good idea to reconnoiter up there—sort of case the joint. I mean, of course, the area for the take-off."

"I might," said Miriam crisply, not looking at him, but over to the Hill beyond, lifting her face to the sun, seeming almost to stand on tiptoe, though of course she was not. She was merely standing lightly erect, hands in pockets like a boy, her neatly shod feet firmly placed and ready to carry her away . . . away from here, and especially away from him, while Roger watched her, his eyes embracing her now, reflecting almost wistfully the picture he held of her, the color and shape of her. The reflection which would be left there on his retina, like a negative to be examined in his own inner dark room while he waited for her to come back.

79

But it was Norma who spoke up and said, "Just don't go too far."

"Oh yes, what time is lunch?" Miriam asked, brightly innocent. "Will Joyce and friend be down by then?"

"I expect so, but I don't really know. We won't wait for them if they're not here by one. I didn't mean that, anyway—I meant the sun. It's going to be hot, you know," said Norma warningly.

"Oh, but so nice and clear and dry! I love it."

"Watch out for snakes," said Roger suddenly, and Miriam looked at him that time. It was an oddly arrested look, as though questioning what (just *what*?) he meant by that. But after that one swift glance she turned away again, like a deaf person who had wondered if someone were addressing her, and decided not. She ignored the interjection as if indeed she hadn't heard it, and went on quickly, repeating her own last words for emphasis.

"I love it," she said. "And I feel as if I could tramp for miles and miles today. Well, dears . . . see you!" and she turned her back on them both and started straight off for the gate, with no more than a gay little wave of the hand.

"Miles to go, before I sleep," muttered Roger. He and Norma watched her cross the patio, go out through the little gate, and rapidly descend on the unseen road, until her head disappeared below the line of the wall, without so much as another backward look. "Mim . . . come back," he said. But it was not a call; he hadn't even raised his voice, and Norma knew that he was not aware that he had spoken those last words aloud.

CHAPTER 8

She had been on the point of going about her business, leaving him to sit there in the sun, as he often did for a good part of the morning. But now she couldn't go. She looked down at the jutting profile of his face, turned slightly away from her. Already forgetful of her presence, probably. He was absent so much of the time now; she wondered where he went.

"What did you mean, Rog, when you said, 'Miles to go, before I sleep'?" she asked softly.

"What?" He came back part way; thought a minute. "Oh yes, I guess I was quoting."

"Oh," she said.

"Those lines of Frost's . . .

> *The woods are lovely, dark and deep,*
> *But I have promises to keep,*
> *And miles to go before I sleep,*
> *And miles to go before I sleep . . .'* "

"Oh . . ." she repeated. And then, "Yes, it does seem like that sometimes, doesn't it?"

"I think so. Frequently."

"When one is awfully tired—" she murmured compassionately.

"Tired. Well, that's the alibi one uses, I suppose. When one's energy—or will—appears to have ebbed away, and there's no returning tide. And the job," he added grimly, "isn't done yet."

Norma stood for a moment, still watching his face attentively: a rough, seamy face, liberally freckled after these days in the sun; with sandy eyebrows and a rather high forehead, crossed by heavy horizontal furrows; with eyes that were green, and full of changing light, rather like water. It was a face that she had known long and well, yet seemed to be relearning now, and it came to her almost irrelevantly, that she was *very* fond of Roger. She didn't know exactly why, because he could often be quite as exasperating as he was likable. Must be just because he was such an old friend; though that didn't ring altogether true about someone she had scarcely seen during the last ten years, and she had to admit that his illness had changed him in some way. The way he seemed to think, for instance, even more than the way he looked. He was leaning forward now, elbows on knees, staring down at the grass between his feet, as into a deep pool, and she sat down again beside him unobtrusively. The things she had to do could wait a few minutes longer.

"This job," she began tentatively, "which you say is still undone. Did you mean—that book that you've been planning?"

He didn't answer at once, and when he did, it was not quite a reply to her question.

"I feel I've let Miriam down, of course."

"I don't see that," said Norma flatly.

"You don't. Well, let's say that my ability to make any sort of a life for her—has been considerably curtailed."

"But, Roger—"

"No use blinking the fact, Norma, that it would have been a lot better for her in the long run, if I'd gone right out—fast. So . . . There is the sense of a personal obligation, not paid up, while all the time one goes further and further into debt."

"Oh, that simply is not so!" Norma burst out, sitting up very straight, her blue eyes bright with something like anger. "Between two people who love each other! I never heard such nonsense. Debts and obligations . . . sounds like not 'supporting her in the style to which she's been accustomed'! No, no—I know you don't mean it in the usual financial sense. But it's nonsense just the same. As if she wouldn't a thousand times rather have you—*you!*—even if you were in a wheel chair or bed-ridden . . . Why, my dear, you do Miriam an injustice even to think such a thing!" (Or does he? she thought uneasily; wondering why she was so forcibly contradicting the very doubts which had arisen in her own mind. Maybe I'm the one who doesn't know what I'm talking about: all I know is what I would feel.)

"Oh sure," he said. "Of course. Let's—skip that part of it. I shouldn't have said what I . . ."

"No—and neither should I," she replied swiftly, and after one scarcely split second, he went on to answer the question which she had really asked.

"You were right—in a way, the first time. The book *is* there, waiting to be written—and all the time my hungry conscience keeps gnawing away."

"Hungry?" said Norma, puzzled, and he shot her a sidewise glance.

"Didn't you know a writer's conscience was always hungry? Not only the poor cuss himself—who may be starving. It keeps on nibbling and gnawing at his vitals, like the fox inside that Spartan kid's shirt,

82

remember? And this thing's been waiting for a hell of a long time, too."

"Has it?" she asked, not sure whether he meant the conscience or the book by now, but deciding quickly to settle on the latter. "Yes, I suppose the whole thing must have been building up in you all these years, almost like another collection of the things you had to say. The experiences you've had—things you've seen—people—places . . . I hadn't thought of it that way before. But now, with all those notes you've made—" She paused, terribly aware of what Miriam had said not an hour ago, and quite aware that he was looking up at her, out of the corner of his eye, and there was an odd gleam in it. Conscious also that she was venturing onto unfamiliar ground, as, at the same moment she observed Cleo approaching across the grass with a measured delicacy and dignity. Well, Norma thought, she had her own antennae, hadn't she?—like a cat's whiskers—to let her know how large or how small an opening she needed, to go on, even into strange territory? So she continued, a trifle ingenuously, "You know, Rog, I have a feeling that you've got this book all but written, and don't quite realize it yourself. I think I can understand how it looms over you like an impossible task, just to *begin* . . . Isn't it just a question of sorting and—sort of linking the notes up together, before it will be practically done?"

But Roger shook his head.

"Nope," he said. She was silent then, watching the cat come up from behind him, and with bland confidence, smooth herself from nose to flank against his leg. He looked down, pushed her aside with his foot, gently enough but definitely.

"You go away, Cleo," he said. "You know I'm no cat lover." So Cleopatra was also rebuffed, but her feelings appeared unruffled as she sat down a few feet away and started washing the lower portion of her left hind leg. And Norma reflected, with a sudden catch of inner amusement, like a stitch in her side, that neither the cat's nor her antennae were working very well that morning.

"Well, of course I don't know anything at all about writing books," she said cheerfully, but added with a small shrug, emulating the cat's impersonal disregard of slights, intentional or otherwise, "I'm sorry if I was stupid, Roger."

"Oh, bless your heart—you're not stupid, Norma. But writing's a funny business; everybody goes at it differently. Thing is, here—you got off on the wrong road. This—alleged—book of mine isn't quite the kind of book you had in mind. It's not a compilation of personal experiences or even personal opinions based on same, like the other one. Not even a memoir," he said drily.

"Oh," she said, once more, reflecting that that seemed to be her stock reply this morning.

"That's what you expected me to do, wasn't it? Of course. What anybody would expect a fellow like me to do. A journalist's report on his life and times while there's any life left in himself. "*Oh no*," he said again. And then, reluctantly, "It's—a novel, Norma."

"A novel!" she echoed, thunderstruck.

"That's right." He looked up at her almost sheepishly, and at that moment he reminded her of nothing so much as an awkward, overgrown schoolboy. As for what he said, she couldn't quite believe it.

"But—why?" she said at last, out of her bewilderment.

"Why? Well, I'll tell you. I seem to have reached a spot—maybe it's the dead center of the hurricane, the vacuum, the hole in the doughnut—I don't know—where I have no wish to make any more reports or summaries. Not even a final prophecy of doom if they don't take my advice on how to run the world. But, damn it all, I do have something that I'd like to say, if I can manage it. It has to do with *people*; individuals, and their separate, personal, strangely indestructible value in this cockeyed world. So a novel seems to be the best medium for putting it across. Not a romance, mind you; most readers seem to think that's all a novel's good for . . . My God!" he said, breaking off rather angrily. "Does one have to make an apology for putting what little one may know into imaginative, or story, form?"

"Of course not," she retorted. "You know I didn't mean my question to sound that way. I just naturally thought of the background of your work as—well, *facts*," she finished helplessly, wondering why he was looking at her that way, so intently.

84

"Facts," he said. "Solid facts. The very ground we stand on, eh? Well, nobody could tell you better than the boys in the press box— or broadcasting booth (same thing now, in effect)—just what can be done with those little cornerstones of our universe. However—" He gave his shoulders an impatient heave, like a big dog coming out of water. "That's not what we were talking about."

"No," said Norma firmly. "We were talking about your book. The novel."

"What I'm talking about now," he corrected her, "is fiction. Fiction has fallen on hard days, poor old girl."

"So much of it is such poor stuff now, don't you think?"

"Sure. Pure tripe," he agreed heartily. "I seldom read a novel myself."

"Well, that's what I thought!" she exclaimed inadvertently. She was growing more bewildered with every speech he uttered.

"Did you ever notice, Norma, how a lot of people seem to feel a little more virtuous for reading a piece of non-fiction?"

"Virtuous?" she repeated, in surprise. "No, I hadn't."

"It's true, my girl. They seem to think they're being more intellectual, even if it's only some half-baked inspirational eyewash, or the story of some fellow's setting up housekeeping in a tree, or on an ice floe, say—and not for any scientific purpose either. Hell, look at any best-seller list. There's as much tripe—or trivia—on the non-fiction side as there is on the other. Not all of it—don't think I've gone overboard on the other side of the boat—"

"But, Rog," said Norma weakly, "I think people feel they're learning something. That they—well, they haven't been quite wasting their time when they've been reading something that isn't—just imaginary. You've got to realize that."

"Sure," said Roger. "I do. But did *you* ever realize, Mrs. Collins, that notwithstanding all the great dialogues, the works of philosophy —history and science—religion . . . Still, of all that heritage of reading matter which has come down to us, that which was good enough to last (i.e., true enough, according to the standards of time itself), for man to keep and buckle to his soul throughout the ages— yeah, and *keep on reading*, now and then—" He paused, his look

85

searching her eyes, her face, not so much for agreement, she thought, as for simple comprehension, and then finished quite matter-of-factly. "That the great mass of it, the bulk of real treasure, was fiction, in one form or another? Epic poetry—plays—novels—even folk tales. Fiction," he said again, very softly, "which is man's own image, re-created by himself, according to the inner truths he's learned about himself. *I* say you can learn more about the human beings we are, and live with," said Roger flatly now, and bringing the flat of his hand down hard on the redwood chair-arm, "from a great novel, than you can from any history, or any number of tracts, scientific or otherwise . . . *If* it's good enough," he ended almost carelessly, leaning back, as with the beginning of weariness.

Norma sat very still, a little dazed by all this, not sure how much of it made sense. But more than that, she was amazed—transfixed—by the way Roger had come to life for that moment or two. She remembered Miriam's words, "He won't begin to live again—" and she saw clearly that it was the first time since he had been here, that he had been fully alive. If only, she thought, she could find some way to hold him from slipping back—some fixative of the spirit, if there was such a thing.

"I don't know whether I agree with you or not, Rog," she smiled. "You've said several things that had never occurred to me. I'll have to think about them."

"Look—I'm not setting myself up as any authority. You know me well enough for that, Norma! You asked me a couple of questions—I tried to answer them—honestly, for myself, that's all. Of course," he added, with a faint lighting up (like a reflection) of that earlier, slightly sheepish grin, "you gotta remember who's talking. Just one of the boys who still thinks he's got a novel in him . . . Poor deluded devil, and may God have mercy on his soul."

"Boys," he had said. "One of the boys." Just a part of the jargon they all used nowadays. But that's exactly what he was, in some inextinguishable part of him, she thought—and in a sense, found she loved him for it. While, at the same time, she was groping for something further. Had her finger all but *on* that thing which was much more important. Not just the small-boy in man, eternally

86

appealing to the maternal female. (If it were only that, why was it that the little-girl peeping out of the eyes of a middle-aged woman was always slightly revolting, like something which has begun to decay while still unripe?) But the boyishness in a man was not necessarily immaturity. It could be, rather, one of those "intimations of immortality"—the Glory and the Dream, and she saw suddenly that what she had taken for a mere adolescent ambition in Roger, a bright toy never quite relinquished when he put away childish things—was, or might be, something much more: the creative up-springing of everlasting life, perhaps . . .

"By the way," he added. "I didn't mean to suggest that *I* was the potential author of the Great American Myth—I mean, the Great American Novel. I'm not that far gone into my second childhood."

Norma shook her head and passed that over as a matter of course. She had known without his saying so that he was not so naïve as that. *That* would have been childish indeed, not boyish. And Roger was no child. Furthermore, she had in that moment or two thought so far beyond what he had last said, that she was wondering only if she could bring him along with her.

"You know, it's very odd," she said slowly, remembering Miriam's words an hour ago—forcing them back upon themselves, reversing their very meaning into an opposite, forward-moving channel, "odd, how things work out sometimes. Maybe this is the way you were meant to go, after all. And you might never have broken away from the other work, if you hadn't been ill!"

"No," he agreed. "I probably wouldn't have." But his voice was heavy again, with a sort of tolerant irony, or possibly fatigue. His expression had gone noncommittal, and the spark of light in his eyes had died out. Unreasonably, irrationally, she felt the sting of tears behind her own. She was getting nowhere, *nowhere*, after all this talk, all this listening. They'd gone around and around an empty circle and come out exactly where and what they were before: a moody man, once full of action and decision, now full of windy theories; a simple housewife, trying to deal with the vagaries of a sick man or a frustrated author (which was he, actually?) when she should be dealing with her cook, her seamstress, her odd-job man—who were at least all working toward the dawn of eternity. Or thought they were.

Roger was leaning back in his chair once more, with his legs stuck straight out in front of him, his head tipped forward toward his chest, as he looked out from under his sandy-colored brows, not off at the hills or the horizon, but at the cat a few feet away. Cleo had uncurled her tail and stood waving the tip of it thoughtfully as she in turn regarded him. Norma recognized that look of arrested poise, an expectant look, as though considering the next step, which she knew very well would be a leap into Roger's lap. But instead of warning him, she got up once more, decisively.

"I guess I'd better stick to housekeeping," she said, and he looked up at her, in mute compunction.

"Not much use, is it? Trying to explain one's own inner impasse at a time like this. Thanks for listening, anyway." She didn't know just what he meant by "a time like this," but that last—"thanks for listening"—went to her heart again.

"Why wouldn't I listen, for heaven's sake? We've been friends for a long time, haven't we, Rog? And suddenly, just in a few minutes I've begun to know you better than I have in all these years. It's like meeting somebody new, and rather wonderful—and finding it's the same old friend too. It makes me—realize," she said impulsively, obstinately, making one more try, "how awfully proud I'm going to be one day, to feel that that book was started right here, under my roof, on my hillside."

Dead silence, then. And then he laughed. "Good old Norma," he said. "My good old friend." Oh no, it was no use. It was like trying to move a dead weight, she thought; like trying to pry off its base some big, delicately balanced boulder, that would go roaring down the canyon, gathering speed and power, she was sure—if one could only get it started. If one could even find out what little ridge or pebble it might be that was holding it there . . . Or was it just apathy, inertia, when all was said and done? The dragging weight of a tired man, older than his years. "When all was said—and done." The words echoed back at her, from one corner of her mind to

88

another. She was wrong, and the Boy was gone, after all, she admitted to herself a little sadly. Even the cat had decided against him, it seemed, and was walking off to investigate some other business. At the same moment Norma saw Joseph approaching softly but purposefully from the dining-room corner, and she had better be gone, herself . . . But, "What *is* it, Roger?" she asked gently, looking down at him. "Why don't you—why can't you—make a start?"

To her utter consternation he leaned forward again, and put his hands up to cover his face. At first, she thought he had broken down in tears; then saw that it was his head he was gripping, as if to hold it together, the fingers digging into his scalp. And then just as abruptly, he dropped his hands, and sat looking at them, his large freckled hands, as they dangled between his knees. He lifted one, his right one, and turned it first one way—palm up—and then the other, as though to see whether the mechanism of joints was working.

"You see that?" he asked finally.

"Yes." (But she also saw Joseph, standing stock-still, and still yards away, and she looked up and met his apprehensive gaze, and shook her head ever so slightly.) "Yes," she said gently once more, returning her full attention to Roger.

"It's just as if it were paralyzed, Norma. I don't know how else to explain it to you. Don't think I don't know how all this looks and sounds to somebody else. Puling," he pronounced dispassionately but with great distinctness.

"Oh, Roger! What a word to use—" But he waved aside the interruption with the left hand, still studying the right one, as though for signs of leprosy.

"Here's a guy," he went on doggedly, "with a terrible unsatisfied compulsion to write something on his own. He's got plenty of material—too much—stuffed into his head. What's more, he's had a certain amount of leisure forced upon him. An unspecified term of leisure," he corrected carefully, and then seemed to snap that off and begin again. "This fellow even has a friend—who offers him her hillside, her house, her special corner of peace and quiet in which to work . . . Peace and quiet," he repeated grimly; and then he turned on Norma as though she were the accused. "So why in the name of all the furies doesn't he get going? That's what you ask, isn't it?"

"That isn't what I meant, Rog," she said, in deep distress, because it was what she had meant; thankful only that the perceptive Joseph had vanished even from the edge of her vision.

"Of course," said Roger, very reasonably now, as though arguing the other side of the case, "there's a certain amount of all this fiddle-faddle that goes with the business of writing anyway; certain amount of doodling held to be permissible, whether it takes the form of sharpening pencils or oiling up the typewriter, or just trimming your fingernails . . ." He examined his nails absently, and then locked his fingers together. "And beyond that again—a long way beyond that, Norma, there must always be the question in any writer's mind, when he's out on his own, not doing somebody else's assignment or—what amounts to the same thing—keeping the pot just barely boiling: *is this thing worth doing?* Not for posterity, mind you. Anybody who's consciously writing for posterity, or thinks he is, must have a head blown up with helium or something. Anyway, one has to figure without posterity these days—without even the normal life expectancy of an average book. Why, there may not be time to finish the first draft, my dear."

"But, Roger of *course* there is, if you don't try and rush it, set yourself a slower pace perhaps—"

"I didn't mean that," he put in mildly.

"And if you have the conviction that something's worth saying— and you implied you did have—"

"Yes," he said. "That's right. I have. And sometimes it seems quite clear—and almost possible. Until the newspapers come in again," he said, conclusively, as if that were the end of it.

"The—newspapers?" Norma repeated.

"Yes. The newspapers. With all the news. All pointing up one lead, to one main event. Even if it hasn't happened yet."

"I'm not sure I understand what you mean," she said cautiously.

"Why, the end of the world. Tomorrow at daybreak," he said, smiling, and though his tone was mildly derisive it was plain that in some special sense, he meant exactly what he said.

"So . . . that's it," breathed Norma.

"Yep, that's it."

"Oh, Roger, you don't *really* think—" Norma began, and stopped again. Not for lack of words, because he had practically put the thing in words himself, but because she discovered all at once that the question she had started to ask seemed just as fantastic to utter aloud as the one which she had found so difficult to ask of Joseph or Bertha. ("Do you really believe this thing they are saying, about the end of the world?") And for the first time it struck her that there was something, some faint disturbing resemblance between the two ideas, quite aside from the ironic figure of speech which he had twisted into a link: as though far back in their ancestry there might be some illicit relationship, unguessed at before now. It was so incongruous that she couldn't quite grasp it; so ludicrous that it was beyond laughter. Or was it ominous instead? Whatever the word for it, it had stopped her in mid-sentence, almost with her mouth open.

She stood looking down on his thick sandy thatch, roughed up where his fingers had clawed through it, surprised fleetingly to note how grizzled it was in the bright sunlight; she seemed to have been standing there for hours, constantly aware of the circling flow of life around them, sucking at her with its need of her on one side or the other. Reminding her with little noises to which her ears were painfully alert: the voices, the clatter, the whir of an egg beater in the kitchen, all ground to a stop now; the whining hum of the vacuum cleaner in the living and dining rooms, and intermittently the smaller hum of the sewing machine off in the other corner which was her present bedroom; the sound of steps, of running water, the metallic snip of shears outside the patio wall where Jim must have found some sort of job to do, while waiting to ask her about something. Oh yes, she'd seen his long face regarding her over the wall a while ago, evidently deciding not to interrupt this earnest conversation. And there was Joseph with his tentative approach and tactful disappearance. Even the cat was prowling over toward them once more, as if disapproving of this unusual mid-morning conference in the center of the patio, and bent on breaking it up. She knew that the sewing machine had been silent now for minutes—too many minutes—and she thought there was a shadow lurking behind the screen door to the living room the last time she had glanced that way . . . It was a swirl of quiet forces moving round and round them, gentle but persistent, centripetal, pressing in on her attention. Yet it was nothing but the ordinary domestic functioning of a house; a household. Nothing important.

It was Roger who needed help, or comfort, of some kind—and she didn't know how to give it to him. Looking at the familiar contour of that head, she wondered why she had never realized what a subtle form of suffering was going on inside it all the time. This paralysis of which he had spoken, this state of brooding immobility which she had seen for herself, was not a personal attitude as it appeared at first glance; to some degree, oh yes, inevitably, because Roger was a very human being—but it was wrapped round and augmented by this swollen, sensitive awareness of the outer world, which many years of "covering" it had made the very ache of it a part of his inner self. So, thought Norma, it was not self-pity. Nor was it any mere sense of his *own* futility or imminent extinction which hung over him; it was his world's unforeseeable, unplannable future over which he sat here yearning, day after day, worrying, helpless, as he would over the threatened future of his own child. (Lucky they *had* no child of their own, after all; she saw that now.)

And having seen so much, she said at last, "You really think we're all quite close to the edge of extinction, do you?"

"Doesn't everybody, who thinks at all?"

"I don't know, Rog. Probably we *don't* think—most of us, except when it's forced on us for a hair-raising week—or a month . . . We don't want to. We read these things, and hear about them, but they just don't seem possible—or else they're too awful to contemplate. But you—what you meant a minute ago was that it's the state of the world which makes any job you might start now—seem so futile?"

He threw back his head and opened his mouth to laugh again, but the laughter wouldn't come; it failed him, and he shook his head.

"That is the understatement of the twentieth century, my dear Mrs. Collins."

But Norma did not smile.

"I see," she said simply, and could find nothing more to say, that would be of any use to him. Make some ineptly bright protest against his grim exaggerations—when he might very well be right? She had never felt quite so inadequate as she did that moment; helpless to help a friend, even to offer a little comfort. The only thing she could think of doing was to touch that grizzled head with her fingers; to sit down on the broad arm of his chair perhaps, and lay an arm mutely across his shoulders, just for solace of a sort . . . And that would be a fine gesture, wouldn't it, if Miriam should come in the gate just then! Silly enough, goodness knows—but for that very reason, the more difficult to explain.

But Cleo, having no unselfish motives, had no such scruples either. She had come up from behind Roger's chair again and stroked herself against his leg, then turning with a flourish of her tail and a look of pleasure quite oblivious of their problems, prepared to repeat the smoothing gesture in reverse, when she saw that he had changed position, stretching his legs straight out in front of him now, lying back in the chair with his eyes closed, his hands and forearms inert on the armrests. Norma saw that the cat had assumed that same expectant, speculative look of poised, arrested motion, and at the same instant she heard a voice, restrained but distinctly plaintive.

"If I could see you for just a *little* minute, Mrs. Collins, please . . ."

"Yes, Miss Amelia, I'll be right in," she replied, without turning her head, still watching absently as the cat jumped, so that she saw Roger start a little and open his eyes as Cleo preened a bit and prepared to settle down on his stomach.

"Howd'ya like that?" he said indifferently, not even moving to dislodge the animal, his hands still lying slack on the chair arm. (As if paralyzed, he had said.)

"I'll have to go in," said Norma regretfully, because there was nothing she could say or do.

"Run along, child. You've let me talk half the morning away and your staff'll never get ready for the big event at this rate."

He looked up at her then, a dead-pan look, and she felt provoked with him again, and turned and left him there without another word. But as she reached the living-room door, she was reminded of something and turned back to call to him, a trifle satirically now.

"Oh, Rog, I forgot to tell you. Alfred left a special message for you, to look at the hibiscus outside the gate. Seems it's never been in finer shape or something—so if you can spare a few minutes to look at it . . ."

For a second he didn't answer, and then lazily, he said, "Okay . . . I'll give it the once-over after a while." He made her so *mad* . . . And yet she couldn't bear to leave him, somehow. He was sick, and old at forty-five. He was a Boy, with some unquenched ambition still . . . He was a hard-working, hard-headed reporter, not afraid to go anywhere to get the facts he was after, nor afraid to look them in the face. But he had stopped working and gone on thinking, and there was something corrosive in that disconnected process, which was eating away the human being inside that reporter. For another second, two seconds, she stood with the screen door open in her hand, looking back, wondering impatiently how long Miriam intended to be gone—though she could see how he must get on her nerves at times. She saw Roger raise one hand, finally; saw it settle gingerly down into the cat's fur, and she thought, A *cat* for comfort —and he doesn't even like cats much . . .

PART THREE

". . . the industrious sun
Already half his race hath run"

CHAPTER 9

Ordinarily, Jim went back to the village again around noon, and had his lunch at home with his grandmother. Except, that is, when—having run out of jobs to do for Mrs. Collins—he lingered on to play with Mrs. Collins' little girl, and would most likely be invited to have a snack with the family. Since Joyce had been away, however, there had been no point in that, and since Miss Amelia was working only the half day today, he had expected to scoop her up at twelve sharp, and drop her off on her own doorstep in about three minutes flat. Especially after he had acquired the information from Joseph that Miss Collins and her friend were liable to turn up in time for lunch. In a Cadillac convertible, no doubt; white, with pink leather upholstery; long, low and powerful. He'd better get his grandmother's 1937 Studebaker down the hill before something like *that* came snorting up to swipe it off a curve; or so he told himself as he sweated around the border of the driveway on hands and knees, trimming its green whiskers clean and close, like a six P.M. shave when a guy was taking his girl out to dance that evening.

But then, by golly, Miss Amelia, always so punctual, was not *ready* to go by twelve o'clock! But she would be—in just a Few Little Minutes, she called to him, when he went looking for her, peering through the screen door into the dimness of the house. If he wouldn't *mind* waiting? she added plaintively. So he'd waited nervously for fifteen minutes, which he considered more than a few. And then Mrs. Collins had come out and explained that Miss Smedley had been delayed for a while in her work that morning, and would he wait a little longer? And of course he'd never been able to refuse Mom Collins anything, because she was so darn decent to him. Which was more than he could say for her big blonde brat.

So Jim sat around and smoked; and stood around and watched,

while Joseph began to set the glass-topped table for luncheon out in the corner of the terrace. With five places. And then he spotted a few fresh weeds in the bed under the kitchen window and went in after them, and saw a few more farther along, and impatiently hauled off his flapping shirt again, and tossed it out on the grass, and went on working doggedly. Might just as well get 'em all while he was at it; everybody else was tidying up his bit of universe in readiness for the universal End, and this—today—was the end of something, for him; he was now gloomily convinced of that.

He was still on his knees, groveling and sweating, when he heard the car down below. Jim's ear was quick, especially for the sound of a motor, but the car was coming fast up the grade and before he could so much as rear up from a groveling even to a praying position, it was around the last sharp curve and spurting up into the driveway. Still unseen beyond the wall, but he didn't need to see it; he knew the sounds, and he knew Joyce's happy chuckling laugh too, and here was he, trapped in the flower bed.

He decided to stay right there, on hands and knees, with brown back and dirt-stained blue jeans turned toward the patio—crouching like an animal against its natural habitat, he thought, the humor of it not altogether escaping him. But he figured they would go right on into the house, and he would then clear out, and wait for Smedley in the jalopy. So he'd watched them, with his ears only, as they approached the gate, giggling away together while they fumbled with the latch, because both evidently had their hands full, then coming on into the patio, still full of chat and backchat. Jim reached for another weed, cautiously, so he wouldn't make a quick enough move to attract attention, but also so he wouldn't be caught in the attitude of a frozen rabbit, in case they did happen to look over his way. He could hear the fellow's polite comments on the house and the view and so on, and Joyce's offhand answer, and he judged from the direction of their voices that they'd almost reached the flagging of the terrace, when—bingo! there was the slap of the screen door and a glad cry from Mom Collins, coming *out*, not even giving them a chance to go in. And there were the greetings, and the introduction of this guy (name of Landis, Jim noted) and then more talk, talk, talk. And they must have dropped all their gear right there, while they went into the matter of the drive down, practically light by light, both red and green—and why they were late to lunch. Only Mom Collins reassured them that they weren't, because she'd planned for a late lunch, and she didn't think Miriam had come in from her walk yet, anyway . . .

At that point there was the sound of another door, and the hair on Jim's neck stiffened like a dog's, because if Miss Amelia came out now, he'd have to rise and show himself—but apparently it was only Joseph. He heard Mom Collins say, "Oh, thank you, Joseph. Just leave the big suitcase in the den for Miss Joyce, will you? And the other bag—that's yours, isn't it, Mr. Landis?—that goes upstairs." Letting old Joe carry his kit upstairs for him, thought Jim disgustedly; what kind of a . . . And then there was *another* door-clap, and that it seemed was Mr. Norbeck, and there were more introductions, and as far as Jim was concerned that really tore it, because next thing Mom Collins was saying something about a drink before lunch, and that meant they'd all settle down right then and there. So he'd better get the hell out of here, right here and now.

But as he started to rise, with quiet dignity, still in slow motion, so as not to catch the eye unnecessarily, he heard Joyce exclaim in pleased surprise, "Oh, Rog, don't tell me you two know each other?" —and then break off in a laugh, and Jim knew with a grim and sinking certainty that she was *not* laughing at that happy coincidence, but had just looked over in his direction. He had hoped that he could pick up his shirt and just stroll off—invisibly—to the gate, as any other workman around the place could have done without attracting any notice at all. But out of the corner of his eye he saw first one and then another of the group turn to look, and Mom Collins called cheerfully, "Why, Jim! I didn't know where you'd gone. Come over here." So he picked up his shirt, not bothering to put it on, and crossed the grass—still, he hoped, with a certain offhand nonchalance.

"Hi, Joyce," he said carelessly, and she, with the devil in her blue eye, looked from him to the stranger and said, beamingly, "This is our hired man, Don."

"Mr. Mears, Mr. Landis," her mother broke in quickly, and added, "I don't know what we'd do without Jim's friendly offices," as the fellow stuck out his hand democratically and said, "Glad to know you, Mears." But Jim didn't smile.

"Pleased to meetcha, sir," he said deliberately. And felt like the Hairy Ape in person, and sweaty to boot, dark brown and glistening in the sun, from brow to navel. True, everybody went shirtless nowadays, if the sun was out, or if he had a job to do, or without any excuse at all. Generally, in fact, there was a sneaking male pride to be found behind the open exhibition of a good torso and some well-browned muscles; but for the moment, Jim's physical vanity had gone into reverse. Even his hair was wet with sweat, and his face was probably dirty where he was apt to smear it with a careless hand—and he *knew* his hands were filthy and rather hoped he'd passed some dirt along with that handshake. Not that there was anything offensive about this Landis, even if he was clean—and reasonably well groomed, in a good tweed jacket and slacks with a neat sharp crease in them. He looked regular enough (though a lot too old for little Joyce), and Jim knew very well that he himself was being childish, but for the life of him he couldn't seem to help it, the way things had happened. And of course it was only about a second, during which the dirt he had (literally!) thrown into the gears seemed to slow things down, before Mom Collins had switched back smoothly into high, as she turned to Roger.

"Well, have you and Mr. Landis decided yet whether you do know each other?" she asked cheerfully.

"I don't know," said Roger, frowning. "I don't know where it was, but—"

"I think I do." The younger man was smiling with a disarming sort of frankness—which Jim, regarding it, instinctively distrusted. "I think it was some big shindig out in Bel Air last fall, though I can't say I even remember the name of our genial hosts. I remember you very well, but then you're a pretty well-known man, Mr. Norbeck."

Roger shook his head, obviously bothered. "Sorry," he said. "I used to be better at these things."

100

"Oh, you meet a lot of people," said Landis, passing it off.

"That may be, but I used to be better at remembering 'em too," said Roger almost grumpily.

"Well, we'll see what Miriam says about it," said Norma casually. "And meantime, how about that nice long drink before lunch? Jim, will you have one too?"

"No, ma'am. Not me, thanks," said Jim stiffly, still very much the hired man, though he had just exchanged a long cool stare with the daughter of the house. But Norma's eyes passed over him indulgently, and she said, "Joyce dear, go and tell Joseph, will you?"

Joyce had scarcely swung away—with a particular flirt of her full skirt, which Jim recognized as aimed at him—when there was a sharp click at the gate, metallic and arresting, so that they all turned to look. It was Miriam Norbeck of course, and a very neat entrance she made, Jim thought later, reflecting back on it. She swung the gate open, came through and pulled it to behind her, leaning back against it for a moment, as though to get her breath —though it made a nice pose for the audience out front—calling lazily to Joyce, "Hello, dear! Nice to see you back . . ." And then coming on toward them with that light graceful walk of hers, but moving more languidly than usual—or was it just more languorously? At any rate, they all stood watching her approach as though hypnotized by the pretty sight, except Joyce, who came back a few yards to meet her.

"*Missed* you!" said Miriam, touching her cheek to the other's. "*So* good to have you home again. And just see how much at home *I'm* getting, talking as if I were the one who lived here! Hope I'm not keeping you all waiting for lunch," she said to Norma, brightly apologetic. "Hello, dear." This—casually—to Roger, and smiling up at Jim, she went right on, "Jim, I think you and I are the only ones who know how hot it is out in that thar sun!"

Curiously, though she had called direct attention to his revolting condition, it soothed instead of smarted: made him feel virile and earthy in a *good* way again, even stretched a little bond between them as he saw that her hair looked a bit damp, too, where it curled around her temples, and there were tiny beads of moisture on her upper lip; and somehow, seeing how her breast rose and fell under that soft silk blouse, he got a sense of pulsing, bodily warmth, and —well, a kind of earthiness too, though not of garden soil, but human. Woman, maybe. It caught him by surprise, even as it made him feel better, because though he was well aware that Mrs. Norbeck was an attractive woman, she was also a middle-aged woman, and this thing, almost like an emanation, had never quite got through to him before. Though it passed, of course; it seemed to pass *him* by, almost as fast as he'd felt it; as, in fact, having greeted each of the others in turn, her eyes went on questioningly to the strange young man, pausing there for the introduction of this new arrival in the group.

Mom Collins said easily, "Miriam, this is Mr. Landis, who drove Joyce down from Los Angeles."

"How do you do, Mr. Landis." She had inclined her head slightly as her glance met his; not extending her hand—so his dropped quickly to his side again.

"Mrs. Norbeck," he acknowledged gravely. And then, looking over at Roger with a grin and a lift of his shoulders, "You see? She doesn't remember, either."

"Should I?" said Miriam quickly, her brows arching in a little smile of surprise, or apology—if apology were called for, while the others laughed comfortably, like a group watching some quiz program, a little smug in its advance knowledge of the right answer.

"That was a mean trick," said Norma. "They were trying you out."

For a moment there was a very odd expression in Miriam Norbeck's dark eyes as she looked from the others back to Landis; a watchful guarded look despite her wide-open gaze. Her lips parted a little and her breath was carefully indrawn, if not actually suspended, though no one could have noted that who was not watching her bosom rise and fall. As Jim was, and maybe the other men had been, too.

"Why, no, of course you shouldn't," Don Landis reassured her. "No reason at all." And Roger added carelessly, "We were just saying before you came back that we thought we'd run across each other somewhere. Landis here thinks it was at some brawl up in Bel Air last autumn. We thought maybe you'd remember."

"Why—yes," said Miriam, slowly. "Of course! At the Winchecks' house, wasn't it . . . ? Of *course* I remember you now! I think we even had quite a talk—about something—though I haven't the slightest idea what it was, now!" The light of recognition had come on gradually, like one of those lamps with increasing degrees of power as one turns the switch, and with it her whole face lightened, and relaxed also, and her eyes held a new sparkle as she laughed. "How could I be so stupid? But there were a lot of people there, you know, and we met so many . . . And of course seeing you up here, all of a sudden—so *unexpectedly*," she said, smiling and putting out her hand to him now, like a peace offering.

"Sure. Of course," said Mr. Landis, on a note of soothing unction.

Holy cats! Jim thought. You'd almost think the guy was purring. He didn't know what was the matter with them all, but this sounded like a lot of phony dialogue in one of those so-called society films. He couldn't see why they kept going on and on about it, and he didn't know why *he* had to stick around here listening to them. He had no part in it and wanted none. All he wanted was out— and that before Joyce came back again, with Joseph and the drinks and that look in her eye . . . hostile and inviting, taunting and impish—and still angry with him, too, just because he was made the way he was and couldn't help it. Jim looked sideways, cautiously, to see if she was coming, and saw somewhat to his further befuddlement, that Miss Smedley was standing over at the edge of the flagging, like a little monument of patience (as if she'd been waiting there for hours!) with her hands crossed in front of her, her old leather bag dangling from them, her sailor hat straight across her brows as usual, but her head tilted as she regarded them all with wistful benevolence. Holy cats, thought Jim again. Why couldn't she have come out fifteen minutes earlier?

It was not until they were both in the old Studebaker and already halfway down the hill, that he began to get a delayed and more objective reaction to the uncomfortable quarter of an hour just spent up there in the patio. They had all been uncomfortable for some reason or another; that was the thing that came home to him now. Mom Collins had been uneasy. And Miriam Norbeck had been putting on some kind of an act, if Jim had ever seen one. As for Joyce, damn the brat, Jim thought—and instantly took back the thought, because he loved that brat, no matter how she tried to needle him. There were two people in the world that Jim would give his eyes for. His grandmother was the other one, and between the two of them, they were slowly driving him nuts. Some day, he thought bitterly, maybe they'd realize that—by the time he was over on the other side of the globe in a foxhole made of ice and mud.

It was at that exact moment that Miss Amelia, sitting composedly beside him, spoke dreamily.

"Peace," she said, "perfect peace."

"What?" asked Jim, the word jerked out of him involuntarily, as his thoughts were jerked out of his own preoccupation.

"Why, I was just mentioning the lovely peacefulness of this Last Day." There was a reverent emphasis on the last two words which left no doubt about her meaning. *That* thing again . . .

"Oh yeah. Yeah, sure," Jim said, because he'd made up his mind weeks ago to go along with what anybody in the village said about it. You never knew who was going to jump in what direction in a crazy business like this, and there was no use arguing about it. And she gave him a shy and happy look now, in reward for his agreement.

"It's almost as if, already, we were being drawn up and out of our little selves," she murmured softly.

Jim wondered if Miss Amelia wrote poetry, secretly. She had the earmarks, though he'd never thought of it before. Funny how you could see somebody, year in, year out, and never even guess what went on under a ridiculous old-fashioned straw sailor like that. But he kept his eye on the road; they were practically there now, drawing up in front of the tidy little shack where Miss Amelia had lived ever since he could remember; since the first time he'd come down to spend his holidays at his grandmother's, and probably a long time before that. As far as he knew, Amelia Smedley had been born there, and lived there all her life. He stopped the car, but she didn't move.

"I feel so much happier about it, Jim, now I have everything arranged," she said confidentially, and she seemed to be looking at the little house—fondly, but with a certain detachment. The horrid suspicion which had come to him earlier that morning, when she'd asked to be dropped off to see that Mr. Bixby, returned to him suddenly and in force.

"Oh, look!" he began in protest. "You don't mean that old guy is taking over your—" He stopped short, clamping his mouth shut again. This was *none of his business*, he told himself. But she was nodding her head quietly, as though she understood his question perfectly, and that were answer enough. "You see," she explained simply, though regretfully, "they are not all coming with us . . . But that—is up to them, isn't it?"

The goofy thing about it was that though it made no sense at all, he seemed to get what she meant to convey. But when he made no answer, she added anxiously, "Jim—oh, Jim—*you're* coming up with us tonight, aren't you?"

"Oh . . . sure. Yeah, I guess so," he said uncomfortably. (What could a fellow say? What *do* you say to crazy people—you humor 'em, don't you?) And she was nodding happily again, so evidently that was the right reply.

"Of course you will," she said. "I knew you would. You see, I know you so much better than you probably realize—on account of him."

"*Him?*" said Jim, genuinely startled.

"Your father," she said quietly.

Oh well, one *said* "crazy," but that was just a figure of speech. To apply to people whose ideas you didn't share. But never before that minute had Jim Mears suspected that Miss Smedley was really off the beam. Odd, yes, and abnormally shy and sensitive; peculiar, sure —but half the village was peculiar. They *liked* being out of step; that's why they came here in the first place, or stayed on, once they got here. (Maybe that's why *he* liked it, huh?) But it was not the sudden apprehension of Miss Amelia's lunacy which set something prickling stiffly in him. It was that last phrase, those two words: "Your father." Two words which Jim never wanted to hear, linked together—and seldom did. But now Miss Amelia had turned in the seat to face him, with the misty unfocused look which her eyes had without her glasses.

"I'm going to tell you something, Jim. Something I haven't told anybody else in the world." (Oh, ye gods, he thought, in real alarm, but though he swallowed hastily, he couldn't get a word out.) "You see—" she went on with a little rush of breathlessness, "*he* was the first one to tell me . . . what was going to happen. Tonight, I mean. Nobody else knows, Jim, where the Word came from. But it was from Philip."

Jim looked at her in stupefaction, but steadily, trying to see past that slightly dazzled look in her eyes—as if they were full of watery sunlight or something; testing in his head the words his ears had certainly heard.

"When—was—this?" he asked finally, letting each word out carefully.

"Oh . . . months and months ago—in the autumn," she said. "There was plenty of time, you see. And it was better for it to come very gradually, a tiny hint here, and just a word somewhere else, as if one had read it perhaps—giving the truth time to grow and spread. Like a living plant."

He paid no attention to that last gush of rhetoric; he was thinking slowly, as though his brain could barely lift and turn this thing over, to look at the other side of it. "Months ago"—she'd said—"in the autumn"—which meant four or five months, maybe. But his father had been killed over four *years* ago, in Korea.

"I know it's hard to take in, Jim," she said, with evident sympathy for his difficulty. "But he was as clear—and real—as you are, this very minute. The only difference was that the sun wasn't bright, as it is now, because it was toward the end of the day and the days were getting shorter, too. It was rather beautiful . . ." Her voice was hushed, and she was not looking at him now, for which he was obscurely thankful. She sat with her hands clasped tightly on her knees, the old leather bag dangling from one bony wrist—and a tip of silver on the second finger of her right hand, he saw now, with a surprise that was of no consequence. Just a notation of the incongruous. One who took her glasses off and left her thimble on . . . And he had no doubt she expected to step off into eternity just that way.

"It wasn't dark at all. I don't mean that. Not even quite twilight. But I'd gone for a little walk up the canyon, and the sun had gone down behind the hill before I turned back. It was just at the edge of the eucalyptus grove, that I first saw him, though I didn't recognize him of course, till I came nearer. I had my glasses *on*, then," she said quickly, as if she had felt his thought, her glance swerving toward him for an instant, then away again, out through the windshield and down the road, of which she saw nothing. "But of course I wasn't expecting him . . . I've dreamed of him often, Jim, but I had never even dreamed I'd see him again—like that. It was strange, too, for I think he was almost as surprised to see *me*—though he must have been sent back for just that purpose. He looked—quite startled." And she looked tenderly indulgent as she admitted that, and added, "So perhaps they don't know quite where they are, at first. Anyway, there he was, half sitting and leaning against a rock, as though he were waiting for something. Or someone . . ."

Jim was sweating again, slightly, but this was a cold sweat in spite of the sun beating on them through the windshield as they sat there. He tried to think how he could stop her, how he could get her out of the car and into the house, without removing her bodily, or worse yet, hurting her feelings or driving her a little farther over the brink. But all he could do was sit there, with his big mitts lying stickily on the steering wheel in front of him.

"He looked a little older, Jim, and thin, and his temples were grayer than I remembered, even with that funny short haircut that I suppose they make all the soldiers wear—so that was the way it was when he was—killed. And so shabby too, as if he'd picked up some old shirt and trousers, any old place, just not to be in uniform, I suppose. I—I thought my heart would stop," she said, almost in a whisper, "when I saw that it was Philip there. But then I came straight on, and I said, 'Hello, Philip,' and he said, 'Why—Amelia! It's you.' That's exactly what he said . . ." She paused a moment, marveling at the significance of that.

"And then we began talking, about one thing and another, without any preliminaries at all. I mean, not the way the rest of us generally have to, to lead up to something. It was so natural, Jim. You see, I'll have to make a little confession. I've been a very *shy* woman, all my life."

He didn't know why that increased the feeling of queasy pressure in the pit of his stomach, but it did; her saying that, as if nobody had ever known. And she went right on, timidly and yet relentlessly.

"It had always been hard for me to talk to him, before—but now it was so easy. And he asked about people in the village—you and your grandmother first, of course . . . And I told him how terribly broken up she had been after his death, and never quite the same again, since. So stern and dry-eyed, as if she didn't dare unbend. And he was very quiet for a while, and finally said he didn't know whether she would see him now, or not. And I said, 'You mean, whether she *could* see you?' And he said yes, he guessed that was it. You could see that he was uneasy, sort of nervous and unhappy about it, whether he could even get *through* to her, I suppose. And then he said I'd better not mention to anyone that I had seen him, and when I protested that they would want to know how he was, and how he looked—" She stopped, and smiled to herself. But to Jim she said, "D'you know what he said next?"

"No," said Jim, and his voice came out in a rather hoarse croak.

"He said, 'They won't believe you, Amelia.' And I said, 'They won't be able to help believing me, because *I* will know I'm speaking the truth.' And he muttered something about yes, he supposed people would believe anything—if it was told them in a certain way. But he didn't want me to: he made quite a point of it. And then—he began to tell me, very slowly, and I remember how he watched me as if to see whether I would be capable of understanding—and believing—what he was here for . . . So that some of us, at least, would be ready, when the Day came. I've thought so often, since then, that that must be what so many others—over *there*—have tried to do, coming back here and there all over the world, to some little place they had known, just to see someone whom they felt was closely enough—attuned, to be able to see them, and prepare a few more in turn, for what was coming . . . I remember," Miss Amelia said steadily, "every single thing he said. Just how we should go up to the top of the Hill as the Hour came nearer. Even the white clothes we should wear. Leaving everything else behind, of course. I remember how he looked at me, so earnestly, so intently, when he explained about divesting ourselves of those possessions which we value most. That was important, Jim, because it's just as you and I said a little while ago, there are some who won't go with us tomorrow, because they aren't ready to give up things. Philip knew that, of course; he knew what people are, when it comes to their little worldly possessions."

Yeah, he ought to, Jim thought—and caught himself back hastily, in a sort of horror to find himself carrying on the smallest extension of these maudlin imaginings. He would be gibbering himself, in a minute. It was the weirdest thing he'd ever got into, this conversation, and at the same time it was the most horribly embarrassing—which was what took all the possible humor out of it. He might be able to laugh later on, but right now he felt sick at his stomach, and for the life of him he couldn't think of anything to say to stop her turning her soul inside out. And then with great thankfulness he heard her saying, "That was about all, really. It was beginning to get the least little bit dusk then, in the shade of the trees, and when he looked around, I had the feeling that he had to get back—somewhere, by a certain time perhaps. And I didn't want to have him—just disappear, Jim—I felt as though I couldn't bear that, so I said I must go on home myself. I wanted to touch him, Jim—just touch his shoulder, or his hand, you know . . . I loved him—always, my dear—you understand that now, don't you? And I wasn't sure if he had ever known it, himself. But of course I realized that I couldn't have felt even his sleeve, no matter how—material—it looked, and to have put my hand out and touched nothing—well, I felt I couldn't bear that either. So I said good-bye, and just turned and went home quickly and never even looked back again."

She'd stopped at last, but she continued to sit there as if she'd forgotten how to move. And suddenly it occurred to Jim that if he'd had the elementary manners his grandmother was always trying to din into him, and gotten out and gone around the car to open the door for her, he would have been saved all this. So he opened his own door now, and unfolded his length from under the wheel, and went around to open the other door, and she got out quite docilely. As simple as that. But she was looking up at him rather anxiously, as he closed the door with finality, and prepared to return to his own side.

"Thank you for taking me up there, and back, this morning," she said sweetly.

"Sure. Glad to," he said.

"And oh, Jim—you didn't mind my telling you all this, did you? We're so close to the end now and it did seem as though you were the one person who should know . . . You see, he was very stern about my not telling anyone I had seen him, or where the *word* had come from. I don't think I should tell your grandmother, though, if I were you. I *had* to tell you, that's all, because I was afraid you might not plan to come tonight. And because you're so like him. It catches me right in the heart, sometimes," she said, putting her hand up to touch her collarbone.

"Well," said Jim, unsmiling. "That's fine." (Yes, that was just dandy, because if there was one thing he hated being told more than any other, it was about that resemblance to his father.)

"Even your funny, sudden smile, when you've been very solemn," said Miss Amelia tremulously. "Even your *ears!*" she finished with a little sob, and she reached out and touched Jim's bare forearm timidly, with the tips of her dry fingers, which was more than she had ever dared with his father, alive or dead, and then she turned and fled down the path to her house. And Jim got into his grandmother's old crate, which made a convulsive leap away from the curb, like a runner from a standing start, and as it shot down the short remaining slope and on into the village, one thought kept on echoing, or exploding, like a backfire from the engine, or from his own mind —Tell my grandmother . . . *tell my grandmother!*

CHAPTER 10

Mrs. Mears was still sitting at the table, finishing her lunch, when Jim came into the dining room. He saw that she was smoking, which always surprised him a little, and presently he realized that her plate was empty, with knife and fork laid precisely across it, and from the mound of cigarette butts in the ash tray, it appeared that she must have finished her meal some time ago. He was surprised again, for his grandmother was a sparing person in all things, and chain smoking—which indicated a lack of discipline or severe self-control—was just the kind of thing she didn't do. So he knew she must be unusually disturbed about something.

"Hi, Gran," he said.

"Good afternoon," she replied imperturbably. "Have you had your lunch?"

"Nope. I got held up."

"I waited for half an hour or more, before I decided you weren't coming." It was a dispassionate statement, not a complaint, but he said, "I'm sorry," with a slight feeling of compunction, and added ruefully, "I just couldn't help it."

"Your plate is in the oven, but the heat's been turned off for quite a while."

"Oh, that's okay." He went on into the kitchen, and like the well-trained youngster who had been coming to visit his grandmother these many years, he automatically washed his hands at the sink before opening the oven and taking out a lukewarm plate with a large helping of beef stew upon it. When he went back to the table, she had put out her last cigarette and was still sitting there, motionless, erect. She was always erect, standing or sitting. He had never seen such a straight spine as his grandmother had, though he took that as much for granted as he did most other things about her: her frosty black eyes, her dry sense of humor, her clipped economical way of speaking. Her economical way about everything, for that matter, including the cheap cotton dresses she wore day in and day out, and the old things she hoarded, from better days. The only expensive-looking thing about her was her hair—which after all had not been bought. That was still thick and soft-looking, though it was the color called iron gray—except just where the middle parting reached the high hair line, like the prow of a boat, and on either side two small white waves rose slightly and curved apart to flow back smooth and straight over her ears and into the plain large knot at the back of her head. Probably she'd done her hair that same way since she was a girl.

But Jim was concentrating on the plate in front of him, and gave only an occasional automatic glance up in her direction, as if to check and see if she was still there. And it was only because she didn't ask a single leading question that after a couple of minutes he tossed off the information that it was on account of Miss Smedley that he'd been delayed. The old girl, he said, was only supposed to be working the half-day up there, but then she hadn't finished up whatever she was doing by noon, and Mrs. Collins had asked him to wait for her, so he'd been stuck with it.

"She isn't so old. Not sixty yet, I should think," said Mrs. Mears, and he threw her a look of amusement, as if she were trying to be funny intentionally. "Not that it matters," she added, "except that your stew is cold." She didn't remind him that it was only because she knew young Joyce was away that she had expected and waited for him today.

"It's good, anyway," said Jim.

"I suppose," his grandmother remarked, after a moment, "that Amelia was running up a *robe* for Mrs. Collins." It was just the very slight emphasis on the word which indicated the kind of garment to which she was referring. But Jim shot a beetling look of protest up from under his brows.

"Oh *gosh*, Gran! Mrs. *Collins*! She's got too much sense."

"Hm," said Mrs. Mears. Which Jim knew was not intended as any reflection on Mrs. Collins, but only implied that one needn't be too astonished at any moment to discover just who was sensible and who was not. It was typical of the day-to-day relation between him and his grandmother—a part of their mode of getting along together—that they had never openly discussed this business of the village delusion. Just dropped a casual reference to it now and then, assuming and accepting the fact that they both knew all about it and what *they* thought of it. Knowing her, he knew she couldn't have believed in it, and that was quite enough for him. He wished now that he hadn't even brought up the subject of Amelia Smedley. It set him thinking again, about her and her hallucinations, if that's

112

what one would call them. And he didn't want to think about her at all, for any pity that he might have felt for her had been shocked into revulsion. The mere fact that this dried-up little old thing had nursed a long unrequited love for his father did not seem pitiable so much as disgusting.

All Jim hoped was that his grandmother would never hear of any of it. (Tell his grandmother!—his mind backfired in one more explosive pop.) It wouldn't be from him she'd hear of it, that was for sure. He never talked about his father if he could help it, and certainly they never talked about him together. There were only two things which Jim felt he knew with any certainty, about his grandmother's feeling for her only son: first, that she'd adored him, as only a deeply reserved and dignified being can give devotion to one, or possibly two, in a whole lifetime; and second, she had been badly hurt by him. How Jim knew either of those things he couldn't have said, though the first must have been absorbed when he was pretty young.

He'd always been aware, without ever thinking where the knowledge came from, that his grandmother hadn't much use for his mother. From those earliest holidays which Jim had spent with the old lady, when—and because—his mother and father were "having trouble," the boy had known obscurely that his grandmother blamed his mother for it in some way; even though her criticism remained unspoken. It was only later, much later, that she must have recognized certain things about Philip Mears which could not be laid at the door of a marriage no longer in effect. Jim could remember something she had once said to him, blocking some kid whim of his, firmly and regretfully, and even then his instinct told him that the regret in her voice was not for him but for the other boy, long since grown up.

"I may have spoiled your father a little, Jim," she'd said. "But I'm not going to make that mistake with you." Which must have been a difficult admission for her to make, for Mrs. Mears was still a rather imperious person in those days; an almost regal figure in Jim's first memories, though oddly enough he'd never been afraid of her. It was long before his own memories began that she had been, according to old photographs, quite a beautiful woman. She had also been very well off at one time—for quite a long time after her husband's death; had traveled a lot, taking young Philip abroad for his vacations, summer after summer. But she'd always brought him home again for his schooling, and he'd been sent to the *best* schools, and got himself expelled from several of them. Jim knew now that that wasn't just on account of having been an indifferent student, like himself. He knew plenty about his father now.

Even as a kid, he'd begun to see him for what he was, more clearly than he ever saw his mother, whose image changed in shape and color, from the varying lights thrown upon her by other people. They thought he didn't know what went on around him, the rows and recriminations, the lulls which were uneasy at best. (How unconscious did they think a boy of ten or eleven could be, anyway?) To be sure, he didn't always know what the rows were *about*; it was the tense and sultry atmosphere which he felt in his bones (like a rheumatic old man!) before the storms blew up, or afterwards. He didn't know that Philip Mears was gambling and philandering. What he did know was that he was bone-selfish, and lazy too, not physically but as an offshoot of that immovable selfishness. He could be tireless enough on the golf course, and played a pretty, clean-swinging game too; was a keen hunter for all game and fowl (oh yes, and women too). An expert marksman in fact, though he had needed no small arms for the latter. He could, without moving a finger, be charming, and very good fun, when he felt like it. When it cost him no effort, in other words. He had so many qualities which made it easy to admire him, that Jim could almost understand why his grandmother had adored him (even why his mother had fallen in love with him, though he was not a handsome man) and why, when very small, he himself had looked up to him as quite a wonderful guy.

But there are things which one gets onto, even when too young to figure out what they mean. There was the way he would begin to show Jim how to do something—swing a golf club, say, or how to hold a gun—and then become impatient of his fumbling (no matter if the club was too long for him) and immediately lose interest: tell

114

him it was no use wasting time on *that*, because he'd never make a golfer anyway. Or conversely, if Jim showed a hint of promise or proficiency and tried to set himself up—in his own estimate, chiefly —with a bit of childish brag, his father would take the rifle out of his hands, fire a round of bull's-eyes without even seeming to take aim, and then cock his eyebrow at his son as though to say, "You think *you're* good, huh?"

What Jim had come to dread, however, more than anything else in his dealings with this unpredictable man, was his peculiar sense of humor. Not just the unerring way he had of poking so-called "fun" at something the boy was doing; something quite simple and serious perhaps, which had not seemed in the least ridiculous until his father turned up the silly side of it. There was also the *kind* of thing he'd laugh at, shaking in a spasm of those silent, indrawn chuckles—and then telling his wife and son they had no sense of humor . . . even if Jim had laughed uneasily, aware that there was something faintly, eerily funny there, though he couldn't seem to enjoy it much himself. And this was not just common ribaldry, which, if he'd gotten it at all, would have passed him by at that stage (and which, he guessed now, his mother probably *would* have laughed at), nor even childish practical jokes, which Jim could have enjoyed then, being still a child. No, the things which Philip Mears had thought the funniest had always had a touch of the fantastic about them, and to this day there was no other name Jim could put to them. But—he thought now, with sudden painful clarity—if his father had been in a position to observe from where he presently sat that Amelia Smedley thought she had met and communed with the spirit of her long cherished love—meaning him!—he would undoubtedly have thought it the most hilarious, delectably convulsing—absolutely the funniest damn joke, bar none, that he had ever heard.

And then to top it off would have been the knowledge which had come to Jim today, that of all the impossible possibilities in the village, it was Miss Amelia and no other who had planted the seed of this weird hysteria, now grown into a state of ripe emotional panic in some, a sort of self-hypnotized exaltation in others. Pretty hard to understand how anybody could have fallen for that thing, wherever it had started. It was beyond *him*, anyway, and as he shoveled the tepid stew into his hungry stomach, and added several slabs of bread and butter, and sluiced that down with three glasses of nice cold milk, he began to feel soothed and replenished and inclined to dismiss the whole crazy business, for a sort of Walpurgian phantasmagoria in the back hills . . . Boy, that was pretty good! Walpurgian phantasmagoria . . . He'd have to try that out on Joyce, he told himself, rather pleased with his garbled invention of such a rolling phrase—until it occurred to him with a jolt, which felt like a rock dropped in on top of the stew, that Joyce was practically out of his life now.

Nevertheless, his appetite jarred but not entirely appeased, he reached for a couple of bananas from the bowl in the center of the table, and cut himself a wedge of chocolate cake, thick enough to stand up on its base like a flatiron building. As he did so, he was aware that his grandmother was watching his motions, reflectively or absently, he didn't know which. And again, because she hadn't *asked* him anything, he offered another bit of news, as though it were an afterthought of no particular importance.

"Joyce got home today, by the way."

"By bus?" Mrs. Mears inquired, with some point, knowing that someone would have had to drive over to meet the girl.

"Oh, some Hollywood type drove her down."

"Well." It was a complete statement.

"Some guy who knows the Norbecks," Jim said, with a fine effect of carelessness, adding to himself—or thinks he does.

"Well," she said again. "That's nice. They'll be having a very pleasant little gathering up there tonight, then. To view the fireworks." Upon which, she rose with an air of calm conclusion, picked up the dishes at her end of the table, and went out with them to the kitchen, leaving Jim to muse on that last crack. Which, in turn, had left him with a sudden, sharply sketched outline of that small exclusive group up there tonight. Not out on the windswept Hill, but at home at the Collins house. It was a picture that he hadn't stopped to look at before, but he saw it now distinctly, as a scene framed in his own mind's eye. The patio, dark and oblong, like a pool, just faintly lighted by the glow from a few encircling windows. And those four or five—yes, *five*—chosen persons, comfortably relaxed after one of Bertha's sumptuous dinners. You couldn't often sit out in California after the sun went down—not at this time of year, even in the back country—but this was one of those brief spells which might come for a day, or several days, though slightly off-season, as if held in literal suspense by some charm for a specific purpose. And there, sitting cosily in the soft dusk, watching the stars, talking or not as they felt like it, waiting for the moon to come up over the Hill . . . were the Norbecks and Mom Collins—over *there*, in a loose clump of three. And over here, a little removed from the others, sitting closer together on that double redwood seat with its thick cushions to lean back on, was Joyce—and the other guy. Instead of him.

Jim had finished his lunch now, but he reached for a cigarette and lit it and sat with his shoulders hunched, looking down at the crumbs on his plate, adding a few ashes to them from time to time —a filthy habit, of which his grandmother had nearly broken him, though he didn't know he was reverting to it just then. He seemed, for the moment, to have bogged right down where he'd stopped and turned to face this thing that had happened to him and Joyce. It was not just a sick sinking of the heart which he felt, but more like a sinking into quicksand, because all at once there was nothing firm to stand on in that spot which he had thought was solid; rock bottom.

So—that was the way things went, he told himself reasonably. He wasn't the first guy whose girl had gone back on him. But it was the first time it had happened to *him*, and that was probably why it knocked him off his base. A guy was crazy to stick to one girl, going steady for four years. Ought to have played the field the way the rest of 'em did. Young and old. Philip Mears, for instance . . . Ah, but that was *it*. Anything to be different from his father, play it in reverse the whole way through. Though it had been fatally easy to go steady with one girl, when she was Joyce, who was everything he wanted.

For a moment, his thought hung suspended on a sharp conscious-ness of Joyce which was much more than a mental image of her, or even a clear visualization. He could so nearly see, and hear her—feel under his finger the fine blond down on her forearm, smell the fresh unperfumed, purely personal fragrance of her hair—that it was more like a materialization close beside him, until he jerked himself up and ground out his cigarette, and continued to sit there, glaring at the square of window opposite him.

She had a good head under that shiny hair, which latter was no Hollywood gold or platinum, but like a beautiful blond Cocker spaniel. She had *sense*, Joyce had—especially for a girl, and always seemed to understand the way he felt about things . . . until just this last month or two. Oh, they'd fought before, like maniacs; she could make him madder than anybody living, but their fights had never lasted any length of time before. Might be that they'd come to count too much on that, to take for granted that they'd always make up again, in nothing flat—a process so piercingly sweet in itself that maybe it was dangerous because they'd learned to bank on that and the inner knowledge that it brought them closer each time.

The point was, they had learned to count on each other beyond anyone else, and that to Jim seemed all-important, when everything else in the world was so damned uncertain. It might even be that it was more important to him than it was to her, because if he had a future at all, Joyce was *it*. He wasn't one of these guys with a career bug. Maybe he wasn't ambitious enough. But, so help him, he was *not* lazy, like his father. Earning a living was what a man did (if he wasn't a parasite or just plain garden lug—slug, maybe!) and Jim had perfect confidence that he could earn his keep, and Joyce's too. He was *not* afraid of work, though he preferred to have some point or purpose to it. He did know he liked to work with his hands; probably ought to've gone to a trade school instead of college; studying had always bored him, and right now there didn't seem to be much point in it since Joyce had graduated in February. She'd been a couple of semesters ahead of him right along, but he'd flunked a couple of courses along the way, which didn't seem too important at the time, only now of course it left him with a full year to go, and it was a sure bet that he'd be called up before that. Right now, he was in that spot where everything looked temporary. Everything except the way he felt about Joyce. And that's what he'd wanted to get settled—for life—when he'd followed her down here.

But that, right there, was where they'd hit that uncharted rock, plumb in the middle of their course; where Joyce had stopped understanding how he felt or even what he thought. They'd agreed a long time ago that they were going to get married. But now, when he wanted to go ahead before he got in the service, she'd gone indefinite on him; wouldn't commit herself. She'd say well, maybe— when you get in—or after you get through college—or decide to get another job until you're drafted. But she wouldn't say *which* she'd rather he'd do, and when he tried to get an answer out of her, all she'd say was that that was up to him to make his plans and then she'd see . . . Almost as if she were waiting for an out: if he said he was going to do one thing, then that would be the one she didn't want any part of. She couldn't seem to see there was no *point* in deciding now what he was going to do after a two-year hiatus. And she just didn't *get* this feeling he had about not wanting to press his luck; not force the fates which had given him a reprieve—this extra chance to fix up his personal life, make *sure* of something in it, for now—and later. She just looked thoughtful and remote when he tried to explain that to her.

Almost seemed she wouldn't understand. About his grandmother, for instance. Joyce knew all about his parents being divorced, naturally, and there were a lot of things she seemed to have guessed without being told in words of one syllable. How a kid can become a sort of no-man's-land with the battle ranging back and forth across him—though in his case, they didn't fight over him; he just *lived* out there, dug his own foxhole, pulled the barbed wire over him and peered out through it to see which side was winning! But there was more to it than that.

He'd been sorry for his mother to begin with, in a kid's instinctive way, just because she was easygoing and kind of pretty, and his father was a heel. But by the time he was thirteen, and had been sent away to one of the "good" schools in the East, and she'd come up for one of the official parental week ends (dressed to the teeth and too much make-up), he'd gone through one of those soul-searing adolescent awakenings to the fact that his mother didn't quite stack up along with the rest. That she was—let's face it—a bit common. His grandmother had come up from New York that time, a day later than his mother, but she'd saved the day in some way he couldn't quite explain: like a fort or tower so outstanding in the background that people didn't really notice the cheap little bungalow with too bright a coat of paint. His father *hadn't* come, and though he hated him for it, Jim knew why. And though he rallied around his mother with almost an excess of pride and ostentatious devotion, he was ashamed of her.

That shame had left a nasty little scar; long buried now, but still there in the sense that he'd never quite forgiven himself for being ashamed of her that time. It might even be the reason why he was rather aggressively snobbish in reverse, nowadays, with his Hired Hand Act, and all. And later, when the divorce had finally gone through, and he was supposed to spend six months with one and six with the other, he had put on a heck of a fuss to make it clear to everybody that he preferred to stay with his mother, thank you. They'd paid no attention to that, of course, though he was fourteen then and thought he ought to have the right to decide something about his own life. It had turned out to be a strictly technical decision, since the first period allotted to his father had proved not only disagreeable between the two of them, but highly inconvenient to the latter, interfering as it did with his current living arrangements with a lady named Louise. So Jim had taken off on his own steam, for his grandmother's place down there in the hills, where he had gone with his father once or twice before. Which is to say, he traveled by bus as far as his depleted spending money lasted, then by dint of hitchhiking. And those last twenty miles in from the coast highway he had walked.

It was only during the course of the last few—and longest—miles, when he was tired and very, very hungry, that he had begun to doubt his grandmother's welcome. But it seemed that nothing could surprise Mrs. Mears, not even the unheralded arrival from San Francisco, of her grandson—on foot. He had spent the remainder of that summer there; a thankful interim, with few questions asked and no arguments. Dry and hot, but peaceful, and surprisingly happy. And when his mother remarried that same fall, and promptly became pregnant, it had undoubtedly made it easier for her when Jim elected to spend a good part of his next—the Christmas—holidays with his grandmother also. He felt strangely at home with the old lady by then, and in due course the feeling had become the fact, as his ever-lengthening visits to his grandmother grew into an arrangement which nobody had signed but which everybody found most logical and satisfactory.

Not that he harbored any feeling of resentment against his mother and her new family; it was just that he had less feeling of any kind about her, as time went on. He didn't mind his stepfather at all—or the two kids for that matter. When he did come home, she made special efforts for him, but somehow, she was like an uneasy apprehensive hostess, self-conscious with her own son. And that was partly due to something else, that she couldn't help—and neither could Jim. That was his unfortunate resemblance to his father, which grew more marked as he approached a gangling sort of manhood. His long bony build, his long face with the well-cut aquiline nose; his dark skin and eyes—even those inescapable big ears. (Even his voice, which *he* couldn't hear, of course.) He knew that he looked like his father, and he resented that fact; but he also knew, or thought he knew, that that likeness was a surface one. He felt that his mother, of all people, should realize that, and perhaps she did. The trouble was that there were mannerisms which came out unconsciously, and those disturbed her more deeply than his outward appearance. There were ridiculous things, exasperating to Jim because he wasn't aware of them until something occurred— like the time he picked up a glass, just an ordinary tumbler, and found his mother's eyes fixed on his hand, and a little worried pucker between her brows.

"What's the matter *now?*" he had demanded, more belligerently than necessary, and even as she'd given her head a quick shake, he'd seen the tears come into her eyes.

"Oh nothing, Jimmie. It was just the way you held that glass, in your fingers . . ."

"How else would I hold it, for Pete's sake?"

"Well," she said, "when I pick up a glass—like this"—she showed him, cupping it in her whole hand—"I don't hold it in my *fingers*, the way you do." (And the way *he* always did, she implied.) "Oh, mercy to goodness—it just startled me, that's all. It doesn't *matter*."

But it did matter; not that small gesture, nor another one. But the fact that she was so everlastingly on the watch for anything he did that was like his father. So afraid that he would turn out like him, in more important ways. They were both too sensitive about it, of course, though in most practical respects she was a rather calm and adjustable person, and had in fact passed on something of the same quality to Jim. It would have helped if they could both have recognized that, but they couldn't.

So he had gone there less and less. And the infants grew so fast that they became, in no time at all, strange brats seemingly unrelated to him. And his mother grew much fatter, and her curly hair became grayer, so that he felt more surprise than anything else when he did see her now. Almost had to remind himself that that *was* his mother.

On the other hand, his grandmother was certainly not like a mother to him, and he was glad of it. She didn't expect too much, yet she never belittled him either. A negative influence, one might say, but she belonged to him. All she had done was to give him a place to live, and grow up, as she said herself, with her usual dry detachment. But Jim knew better. Just as he came to know, or suspect, in time, that Philip Mears had done something corrosive to her life, as he had begun to do to Jim's.

He used to turn up now and then, for a visit with his mother, and —ostensibly—to see his son, if the boy happened to be there. But he was quite as likely to come down during school terms when Jim was away, and though Mrs. Mears never mentioned his visits in her occasional brief letters to her grandson, Jim would know, when he came

122

home the next time, that his father had been there. Somebody in the village might speak of having seen him—but not necessarily, and still he would know. He told himself once that it was almost like a faint unpleasant smell that lingered, but that was just a savage fancy, and he knew it. Sometimes, for evidence, there was actually something missing, such as the beautiful antique highboy that Mrs. Mears had long treasured, but which she now admitted with stern indifference that she had sold. It took up too much room . . . So Jim would know that his father had been gambling again. He was fairly sure, as he grew old enough to figure his sums in that sort of human arithmetic, that the reduction in his grandmother's circumstances—from the early affluence which he had only heard of, through the more moderate but solid means which he had seen for himself, down to this retreat in the hills, with a trust company check arriving in the mail every month—he was pretty sure that each successive change had been brought about by those recurrent occasions when she had had to meet her son's debts.

Once, with the greatest difficulty, Jim had brought out a painful red-faced protest against her continuing to pay for his own education. "Look, Gran," he'd said awkwardly, "I can work my way through like a lot of other guys do . . . If there's any point in a dumb cluck like me going to college anyway—which I don't see, myself." To which she had replied austerely, "The money for your education has been put aside, Jim—where it cannot be touched, for *any other purpose* . . . So you may as well make use of it—if you care to." He got the impression as she said that, that she intended not only the plain inference that his father could not touch it, but that she had so arranged the matter that she herself could not use it; could not, in fact, be tempted by her own weakness for her own son.

Oh yes, *that* was plain enough too, when they were all together. Jim had seen his father's most charming, witty side, on some of those visits, though he remained uncharmed by it himself. He was immune by then. Yet he liked, at times, to listen to the other two talk— like two old cronies of the same age, exchanging reminiscences of the trips they'd taken to far parts of the world. Funny people they'd met, ridiculous things that had happened . . . Jim liked to hear his grandmother laugh, because it was such a young and pleasing sound; like a happy echo, sort of . . . So few people had a *good* laugh—neither too loud, or tittery—neither giggle nor hoot nor cackle. It seemed a pity for one like that to fall into disuse. But she never used it now.

Never, since the time he had come home four years before, in the break between exams and the spring semester. He had known at once that his father—that is, he *thought* at first that his father had been there, as on the other occasions when he'd had that feeling of a lingering presence, and seen the shadow in his grandmother's eyes, as though all light in them had retreated into their deep sockets. He had seen, too, that dark pinched look around her nostrils, where the lines had deepened noticeably, like someone suffering from some incurable disease. Only this time, she had spoken of Philip almost at once.

She told him one thing that he had already begun to suspect: that she had not heard from his father for many, many months previously. But the rest was so off-beat and out of character that Jim could never have conjured it up by himself. It seemed that Philip had—of all extraordinary things—enlisted in the Marines shortly after the outbreak of the war in Korea. It was a mighty peculiar thing for him to have done, since he was well over age and had never shown the least inclination toward such unnecessarily patriotic gestures. He had been just thirty-nine at the time of Pearl Harbor, but he'd been content to sit out that war in some civilian defense job. In fact, it was only in the recognition that it *was* a weird, fantastic move, that Jim found it possible to believe that his father had done such a thing. But no doubt his grandmother was not able to see it that way.

She had, she said bleakly, known nothing at all of his enlisting, or his going overseas: of where he was, or even if he was alive, until she had received the notification from the government that he had been killed in action. It was that notice which had come, during Jim's last absence. So it was that, rather than any physical visitation from his father, which had left that look on Gran's face. And Jim, trying stupidly to take in the thing which she was telling him, feeling nothing of personal grief but only a sort of wonder at this last bizarre excursion, could see even then that there was more suffering than sorrow in the old lady's eyes. Though the sorrow was there, plain to see, and cut very deep. It was Jim's first intimation that some grief cuts clean, while there are other sorrows which are poisoned, infected at their source. Whatever motive his father had had for going off that way, with an indifference amounting to contempt for the concern and distress which he was surely causing, the tables had been turned on him with ironic finality: the kind of grim joke he might have laughed at himself, perhaps. But the hurt he had left behind was the kind that never healed.

That was the thing which Jim felt about his grandmother, which he could never have explained to anyone else, not even Joyce. It was the thing which he was dumbly trying to make up to her for, in any way he could. It was one reason why he would not enlist voluntarily, himself, though she had never dropped so much as a hint to hold him back. When his draft call came through—okay, that was *it*—but he would not move ahead of it. There was even something of this same feeling involved in his coming back here now, to spend whatever free time he had left. He knew he'd never be free in the same way later on, even after he got out of the service—always provided he came back. He would be married (maybe!). Anyway, he'd be out in the world and really on his own. And there was one more thing . . . For if and when he did come back, Gran herself might not be there. He worried a good deal, silently, about how she would get along, all by herself, when he *had* to go. She was getting pretty old now, and he had a hunch that her heart wasn't too good, from something she'd mentioned, almost too casually, once, though that again was something she would never talk about—didn't know what *he* was talking about when he tried to edge up to it later on! So he was only guessing; could never make sure one way or the other. And all these things lay, not as a layer of sentiment on top of his tacit fondness for his grandmother and the knowledge of what she'd done for him, but underneath—the very foundation upon which he stood in his relationship with her.

CHAPTER 11

He was not even mulling that over as he sat there, hunched over the remains of his late lunch. He had no need to case a background which he already knew. It was there, and that was enough. He had gone only so far as the thought that there was a lot Joyce didn't understand, and apparently never would—and there he stopped, trying to adjust himself to that one fact, and its corollary, that Joyce was through with him. That he and Joyce were *through*. That she didn't have what it took to bridge that one invisible crevasse between them. That she was just so fed up with him now that she could go off and forget him for a couple of weeks, or forever. Take up with any old wolf like this Landis—and bring him back with the pleased look of a cat that had swallowed a whole aviary . . . And even try to humiliate Jim before him. He'd never thought she'd do a thing like that.

Jim was all jumbled up in his mental metaphors; his thinking —if it could be called that—was a confusion of childish hurt and masculine anger, and a maturer groping toward acceptance of a tactical defeat. But one thing he was not confused about was the course he was going to take for the remainder of this week. He was not going near the Collins place until it was over. Mom Collins —that is, *Mrs.* Collins—had tried to get him to say he'd be up again that afternoon—something about a drink or supper or something, he hadn't listened enough to find out what, because he knew she was only trying to cover up her daughter's callous flippancy with her own kindliness. He'd mumbled vaguely that he didn't think he could make it, thanks, and added something about his grandmother's expecting him to do something for her—and then he'd eased himself out rapidly, though he saw Mom Collins looked puzzled and was going to say more if he gave her the chance. He'd made his intention clear, anyway: that he was not coming back that day. But now, when the swing door opened from the kitchen, he straightened up guiltily as Mrs. Mears came in.

"Aw, Gran," he said. "I'm sorry."

"You *have* finished, haven't you?" she asked, in her level voice.

"Sure. I just forgot . . . Just sitting here like a bump," he muttered. "Got to thinking, I guess." He got up and helped her scoop up the rest of the things on the table, and followed her out to the kitchen.

"Want me to help?" he asked, watching her as she briskly scraped and dunked the dishes in the pan of suds she had left awaiting them.

"Oh no. They're nearly done." But still he lingered for a moment.

"Well, anything else you want me to do?"

"Why no, I don't think so. Except to be ready to take me up there about five."

"Up . . . where?"

She glanced up at him then. "Why, to Mrs. Collins'," she said, as though reminding him of some foregone agreement.

"*What?*"

"She invited me to tea today. High tea. Or cocktails—and a little supper, I daresay. I thought you knew that."

"Oh." He sounded stupid; was, in fact, stupefied. "You—want me to take you up there?"

"I certainly do. I have no intention of walking up that hill, too."

He couldn't seem to think what she meant by that "too"—still grappling as he was with this reversal of the course he had decided upon for himself. To go right back up there, this afternoon! Tail between his legs. Asking for more of the same. But if his grandmother wanted to be driven up there, he had to do it. He could let her out at the gate, of course. But then he'd have to go back for her later on. So if he didn't go in, it would just look as if he couldn't take it.

"Okay," he said, at last. She was moving around the kitchen, methodically putting things away, and as she turned from closing a cupboard door, she gave him a considering look, as if measuring the length of time it had taken him to answer. But she had no need to ask why the reply had come so slowly.

"I did tell you about it, Jim," she said. "I'm sorry if it doesn't —fit in."

"Oh, sure, sure. It's all right. I forgot, I guess. What time did you say?"

"Just before five, I should think."

"Okay," he said. But to himself he added, *Oh Brother!* And went on out, through the dining room and on into the small living room, where he came to a dead stop in the middle of the floor. And stood there, thinking. Until a look of grim decision, almost of satisfaction, came into his face and hardened there, and he took the few remaining strides down the short hallway to the door of his own room. Once there, he crossed directly to the closet, and thrashed around inside it in the dark, feeling for what he wanted, emerging presently with a coat and pair of trousers over his arm, which he rolled up in a tight ball. Next he went over to the chest of drawers and pulled out one and then another, pawing through pajamas, underwear and shirts until he came to one of the latter: white, with pleated front, and still folded, stiff and oblong, as it had come from the laundry. He examined it sharply before putting it back and opening the top drawer, where he pawed around again, finally extracting a somewhat stringy-looking black bow tie, which he regarded dubiously, before he thrust it into his pants pocket. With the bundle under his arm he wheeled back to the door and strode out to the living room again, straight on to the front door, pausing only long enough to shout over his shoulder, "Be back in plenty of time, Gran."

He scarcely looked at the old Studebaker as he passed it, but went on down the road, intent as a bird dog on his purpose. Saw Annie Fitch and Mrs. Heeney yakking away outside the so-called Barber and Beauty Shop, cut across to avoid them—and *then* saw old Alfred coming along on this side, and felt like ducking back again, for Alfred was a tiresome bore even when sober. But when they drew nearer to each other, it was Alfred who passed *him* by, without seeing him. Not weaving exactly, and not shambling, but plowing along step by step as though he were walking in blinding snow and had to feel his way, lifting and placing each foot with care, while he gazed straight ahead, his eyes blank of any recognition of passers-by or familiar landmarks either.

Poor old soak, Jim thought, though without any special pity. Dry as a bone for months at a time, but when he began again he got really saturated . . . The observation was detached, incurious, since Alfred's life was not in any way entwined with his own. Jim kept on now, toward his objective, which was Mattie Owen's house. And she was there in the side window at her ironing board, just as he expected, so he didn't bother to go to the door.

"Hi, Mattie," he said, coming up to lean an elbow on the window sill. "Could you do a quick job for me?"

"Hello, Jim." She looked up briefly, and kept on moving the iron back and forth—slide, slide and slam; there was a kind of rhythm in the motion of her fat red arm. Her voice was deep, and her arm was strong, and some people were more afraid of Mattie's small talk than of any buzz saw. She didn't answer his question at first, so that when she countered, "Whadd'ye mean, quick job?" it held more promise of refusal than responsiveness. "If you mean wash four-five pairs of them dirty blue jeans you got on now, the answer's no," she said. Jim grinned at her, and wiggled his big ears ingratiatingly—which always amused Mattie, though she pretended not to notice, now—and put his bundle on the window sill.

"Nope," he said. "No wash-ee. Just press-ee one coat and pants."

She finished the piece she was working on and stood the iron on end, reaching over for his bundle which she unrolled on her board.

"Pete's sake," she muttered. "Black pants with a *ribbon* down the side—you in a band or something?"

"Nope," he said again. "Dress pants. You know—for big occasions."

"And a *white* coat," she said, shaking it out and holding it up at arm's length, like something she didn't want to get too closely involved with—even while she regarded it with a certain grudging admiration; his white tux, the pride of his life at formals up at college.

"Oh yeah, and this too," he added, pulling out the stringy tie and handing it over to her. She looked straight over at him then.

"Say, Jim, the whole get-up's s'posed to be *white*, kid."

"Huh?" he said a trifle blankly, and then with another dawning grin, "Oh—h yeah. Well, never mind. It's the best I can do in a pinch, Mattie. Can you do 'em for me? I gotta have 'em, that's all."

"Land's sake," she grumbled. "What do folks think I am anyway? Press this and clean that . . . Rush through an extra big wash for Mis' Sykes, just so she c'n put away every last thing clean, down to the last doily—and what the hell's it *matter*, I ask you? St. Peter's gonna have his hands plenty full checkin' 'em all in, without stoppin' to check their luggage and their linen closets, if you ask *me!*"

"How about this little job of mine?" Jim said patiently, ignoring all that.

"Well, Idaknow . . . I still gotta rush out an extra bunch of stuff for Hank and Jennie Calloway, account of they're *not* goin' up to the Hill at all but up to L. A. for all of next week if you please! At least, they think they are," she said, shooting a narrow look at Jim, which might have been in invitation to laugh, or shake the head over such foolhardy ones. "*They* put no stock in any of this stuff— so they say," she went on, mechanically picking up his coat and looking at it again. "But some others I could mention come slinking round last night—even after it was dark. One fella, he brought in the goldarnedest-looking rig I ever seen, like a sheet with slits for sleeves in it, that he said he wore once to a masquerade down to El Centro, something he called a *domino*, can you beat that? I thought dominoes was something to play a game with, didn't you?"

"Sure thing," said Jim amiably.

"Well, the men are going to be funnier than the women anyway," said Mattie with a touch of malicious satisfaction. "You hear what the Professor's goin' to wear?"

"Nope," Jim said, still humoring her, "what's the Prof going to spring?"

"Just a bran'-new set of underwear, that's all—and I mean all! Never been worn, he says. Long sleeves and long legs, white as the driven snow, sez he! And with that long white beard of his for a bib and collar—say, won't he be something to pin wings on?" said Mattie with a ribald cackle. But she had given Jim's coat a shake and laid it down on the ironing board and begun to smooth it into position for pressing, so Jim stood watching her, a shade uneasily, not wanting to say anything that would jar her out of her preoccupation. After a minute he thought of Alfred, having just passed him, so he offered him up for speculation.

"How about old Alfred? I bet he's got himself one of those things they wear when they sing in a choir—you know—surplices?"

"I wouldn't know nothing about any surpluses, I'm sure," said Mattie with an abrupt sniff, almost as though she'd caught a whiff of sulphur on the air. "That Alfred! Psalm-singing old s.o.b.—and if he thinks he's going to get up *there*" (it was plain that she didn't mean the Hill this time) "to pester the life out of his poor little wife again—though I guess that wouldn't be allowed any more!" She gave an evil little chuckle and another slanting glance up at Jim, without raising her head. "You know why he put in all that there concrete around his house?" she asked suddenly, and something about the way she said that made Jim shift from one foot to the other.

"Oh, I don't know. Something about not liking flowers or wanting to be bothered with them," he said offhandedly, to head her off. "Look, Mattie, about how long d'you think that—"

But she cut him off instead. "Well, I'll tell you why. His wife had the prettiest little garden up there, put it all in herself you know, because she just loved flowers—and you know damn well *he* never did a lick of work there in his life, made out like he was above such prettifying of the place. *He* was working on his goddamned soul!" said Mattie viciously, slamming down the iron and giving Jim's coat a jerk into another position, as if she was mad at it. But then she hushed her voice again, deliberately. "She was a delicate little thing, you know. Kind of mousey, but sweet, and sort of frail, and *he* said it was too much for her, workin' out there in the sun, see?"

Jim didn't see and didn't care, but Mattie was bent on putting across her point. "She loved that garden, I tell you, just loved to work in it, and I guess it did tire her out sometimes. So she was too tired for *him*," concluded Mattie pointedly, letting her iron pause for a minute while she looked straight at Jim, and he kept

hoping she'd move it before it scorched a place on that white coat—
and wishing he could get off this spot he seemed to be stuck in, too.
But she went right on. "So what does this big baboon do but go and
tear up the whole lot from fence to fence, and put down paving,
right up to the walls, like it's been ever since. Nearly broke her
heart, it did—poor little thing—and then he went around moaning
like his own was broken when she died. As if he hadn't just as good
as killed her himself," said Mattie darkly.

There was a very short silence, and then Jim said, as though he
hadn't heard her at all, "Look, Mattie, all I want to know is how
long it'll take you to do those things."

"You're in an awful hurry, aren't you?" She put her head on one
side and pushed out her lower lip, but she wasn't looking at him now.

"Well, I'd like to get them again by four o'clock if I could."

"Four A.M., I s'pose you mean," she said perversely.

"Four P.M.," he said firmly. "It's for a party, understand? Not
what you think."

"That's what they all say," she snapped back, reverting to her
earlier theme as if she were going to play the record all over again.
"I notice you come chasing round the last minute, though—same as
all the rest. Some party. Funny thing to me is," she added slyly, "how
few folks'll admit it, if they *are* going."

"So maybe they don't know. Maybe they haven't made up their
minds what it's all about. So *what?*" said Jim, getting impatient
finally.

"Well, it's a funny thing they wouldn't know by now. Whether
they're going up or *not* going. They've sure had plenty of time to
think it over." She stopped, and it seemed to be a full stop, and
then she added slowly and heavily, "Oh, Gawd, I guess nobody's
ever ready, Jim, when it comes to that."

He just stood there, watching her as she picked up his coat again
and reached for a hanger which she fitted in under the shoulders, and
hung it carefully on a hook nearby. She was turned partly away
from him by then, and seemed to be looking it over critically, passing one red hand down the pristine sweep of the lapel as she
muttered, "Me—and my dirty mouth . . . Me—washing up other

folks' dirty clothes . . . How d'ya like that?" And whether she was speaking to him now or someone else, he didn't know, but it seemed to him he had to find something to say.

"I like it fine," he got out finally, uncomfortably, trying to misunderstand her or at least pretend he did. "Looks all right to me. But how long will you be, with the rest of my stuff?"

"Oh, that." She sounded contemptuous now. "Fifteen, twenty minutes, I guess."

"Okay, I'll be back."

"Oh, give me half an hour, can't you?" she said peevishly. "I'm not going to be rushed off my rocker by every pipsqueak with a pair of pants to press . . ."

"Sure," Jim agreed. "Sure, that's okay. Thanks, Mattie."

He was glad to get away from her. She was a tough old buzzard, and no mistake. Though, for all he knew, she might be going to turn up with the rest of them—*just in case.* And all she'd need for white raiment would be a good-sized tent, and she probably had that stowed away too. Jim tried to get a laugh out of that, all by himself, but this whole joke had had the juice pretty well squeezed out of it by now, by the ones who still thought it was funny. He was sick of it himself; decided what he needed was a Coke, and maybe somebody like Bud to chew the fat with while he was waiting.

So he went along toward the general store, and on the way he spoke to Letty Finch, aged ten, who was doing a tight-wire act along the wooden curbing. She was a dainty little thing with brown curls, and brown eyes which she rolled at him as he passed. But when he said, "Hi, Lets," she didn't bother answering; that was too much trouble for a kid that age . . . Or it might be her attention was distracted by one of the Cummins twins, the one with the sun-bleached scraggly bob, who came tearing along down the side lane just then. He heard the exchange of conversation behind him as he strode away. Little Cummins was excited, all out of breath.

"Say, Letty—d'you know what? I just found out something."

"Well, what?" said Letty, trying to sound bored.

"D'you know the world's going to come to an end tomorrow?"

"Oh, it is *not,*" said Letty.

"It is so! I heard my mother and father talking about it."

" 'Tis not," said Letty.

" 'Tis *so!*" said little Cummins shrilly.

"Oh, pooh," said Letty. "I never heard anything so silly."

"It isn't silly—it's scary! Aren't you scared?"

"Of course not. Because it isn't so."

" '*Tis* so, I tell you. My father said—"

"I don't care what your father said," said Letty superciliously. "Because my mother says the world comes to an end when you die. That's all."

PART FOUR

*"The shadows of departing day
Creep on once more."*

CHAPTER 12

The day was moving on, and it was four-thirty. Four thirty-two, to be exact. For Roger, more than twelve hours had gone by. Twelve empty hours. He was sitting again in the comfortable chair facing the window, looking out at those nearby hills which ran together or crossed each other in outlines of varying shades of dull green, all shimmering slightly in the faint haze of a hot afternoon. It was quiet outside, and in the house behind him now—after that sudden violent argument across the patio a while ago, which he recalled as something already distant and unimportant. More quiet still since he had turned the radio off; the news program, the news, all bad, ever increasingly, cumulatively bad, bit by bit.

Now and then he could hear Miriam moving around in her room, humming a little—which was unusual—then quiet again. He set his mind deliberately to wonder why she was humming. He wondered, also, if he dared sneak another cigarette. He was well supplied again, since Alfred's trip that morning, and the cryptic message relayed about the hibiscus bush . . . But he didn't move, not so much for fear of Miriam's coming to the door, as because for one moment now he was caught in the spell of all that lovely silence outdoors. Suspended on it. It was as still as death might be, he thought, though full of sound—and life—if one tuned one's ear for it. That was not just a ringing in his own ears, it was the song of insects, thousands strong, filling the air, the small distant sounds of a child's voice or a dog's bark down in the village—shrill enough to be heard up here, yet only incidental notes against the great humming silence around him. All around him, under him, surging like a wave that he could rest upon. But not for long. Never for very long, before something closer still, not in the room or in the house but inside him, broke through to devil him again. Conscience. Worry. Even idle jealousy. Even the mere craving for a cigarette, God damn it . . .

Off in another corner of the house, Norma was dressing for the evening; she was, in fact, all ready (at least she hoped she was ready for what came next!), but she found herself lingering in her room, straightening things on her dressing table, deliberately puttering. She was also hoping that Joyce would come in soon because she wanted to talk to her before the others showed up. So for the moment, and then still another moment, she sat gazing out the window, thinking intently, and at the same time listening for the sound of arrivals out in the patio. Or any sounds at all, like those distant voices raised in bitter argument, earlier in the afternoon. Strange, how she had thought for an instant that they were Roger's and Miriam's voices. Perhaps she had only dreamed she heard them.

She had gone in to lie down for just a few minutes of relaxation, leaving her door ajar, as it was now, and of course she didn't know she'd been asleep at all until she discovered herself sitting stiffly upright, with that unmistakable note of passionate altercation ringing in her head. Yet there were no actual words or voices to be heard by then; they had stopped—or else they had not been real at all. So she had lain down once more, but not to go to sleep again. The earlier uneasiness, which had awakened her before dawn that day, had returned in full force, and her thoughts began darting back and forth between the morning which was behind them, and the evening which still loomed ahead. Back to the tensions so plainly building up between Roger and Miriam, and forward into an uncomfortable, almost embarrassed wonder as to whether those tensions might be hardening into something like a permanent animosity. Back to Bertha, in the kitchen, all but boiling over with her own emotional excitement, and to Joseph who had begun to wear a pinched and haunted look as the day wore on. Yes, and to Miss Amelia who had nearly driven her demented all the time she was fitting her blue silk suit, what with her painstaking care to get it exactly right, and the little hints that she kept dropping all the while to indicate to Norma that it was the white lace dress which she should have been working on. (Imagine going to heaven, or even to San Francisco, in a white lace dinner gown!) And there was Alfred, too, careening up and down the hill, in his condition of unholy abandon—for he had made three trips that morning, instead of one! And finally her own child arriving with that look of sweet complacence (and that very smoothly agreeable young man) and the very devil in her eye as soon as it lighted upon Jim.

Poor Jim. No wonder he hadn't wanted to come back again this afternoon—though no doubt he would be driving his grandmother up there when he found they were both definitely expected. And why on earth she'd ever invited Mrs. Mears for today, she didn't know, except that she had thought the Norbecks needed some fresh conversational contributions, and Mrs. Mears had been to some of the same far places they had known, though under very different conditions . . . And of course she'd forgotten that this would be the Appointed Day. Oh dear, oh damn, thought Norma. How did people ever get themselves so tangled up, in such involved—such delicately ridiculous—situations, and manage all the while to take them seriously? She was making far too much of all this herself, just because she had an uneasy houseful of temperaments staying, or coming and going, on her normally peaceful hillside. A few fanatics, who had lived too much alone, like Alfred and Amelia, and a brace of unhappy married couples, who had lived too much together, possibly. Yes, and an unmarried couple too, of course, if one counted in Joyce and Jim.

Joyce—and Jim . . . The fact was that she had come to think of the two that way: together—to see them as a pair, in spite of her reluctance to accept what that coupling stood for. She had been honest enough in what she'd said to Miriam that morning; had said more than she meant to, really. She *had* grown very fond of Jim, even while she'd gradually become aware of certain things that he lacked . . . and she didn't mean material things either, despite that slightly malicious crack of Miriam's. (She would have been a fine fool if she hadn't acknowledged that the lack of money, or the means to make a living, mattered.) But she could recognize now, the more clearly for having talked it out into the open with Miriam, the successive states of mind that she herself had passed through as she watched those two youngsters growing up, and growing ever closer to each other. So unconcerned, she had been, at first; just quietly, secretly entertained by the terrific friendship which they'd struck up at once. It was such wholesome child's play, and rather engaging to observe from the sidelines. She had even been glad that there was as nice a boy as Jim for the child to play with down here.

And then . . . the beginning of apprehension, the slight retraction (not quite withdrawal) of her indulgent approval, as she sensed a change, saw the thing was deepening. Not just this business of Going Steady, for that, as she'd told Miriam, was little more than a tribal custom nowadays; no more than a phrase to cover a temporary phase. But by the following summer, as she saw them spending every waking hour together, her first faint apprehensions had begun to grow into definite concern. They were so beatifically content, that she was almost ashamed to find how hard it was for her to watch. She kept telling herself that she mustn't spoil it for them. (You're only young once, she kept reiterating—only young once.) But they were so young. Too young—to talk about getting married! She could only hope they would get tired of each other pretty soon now. The sooner the better. And the more they saw of each other . . . perhaps that was the answer. It couldn't last much longer.

But it did. It had. And Norma's course had become more difficult by the day, and week and month. It sounded so simple to be clever about one's children: where and when—and when not—to guide them; how to regulate their speed if not always their direction. (So easy to see where other parents made mistakes!) But there was nothing simple about it, and in Norma's case there was no one to turn to in consultation. The time she had tried, very tentatively, to reach Mrs. Mears on the subject, it had been rather like trying to put through a long-distance call, when nobody answered. There was not even a responding click. Not that she disapproved of Joyce. "Such a nice child," she'd said vaguely. "Nice child . . ."

"Yes," Norma said smiling, "she *is* nice. But—as you say, a child still. I'm glad you agree."

"I?" The other appeared surprised, as if it had nothing whatever to do with her. "Oh well, that's Jim's affair, entirely. I don't urge, or, on the other hand, try to dissuade him from whatever course he may decide to take." There was a very short pause, and then she added, "Never."

"How wise," the younger woman murmured, but at the same time— How impossible, she thought wonderingly. How could you abrogate the responsibility, even if you wanted to? And could you *help* influencing the child, or young person who was so close to you, even by standing aside?

So she had continued by herself, very carefully—without ever letting them catch her at it—to drop small unobtrusive hints, like tiny weights to slow their pace, pulling back on the only emergency brake she could find at hand . . . Wait. Wait and see . . . Until you've finished college. Until Jim knows what he is going to do . . . Look around a bit more, both of you. See a little of the others, now and then. Just so you'll be sure, darling. You have to be able to compare him with the others and still be sure, you know . . . Only she never said it in quite those words—just tried to slip the idea in between the lines. Never let them think she was against them. Never seemed to take them too seriously. Though that was a pitfall too, as she'd been warned, for the moment always came when Making Light— of the most serious thing in life—became the one irretrievable parental offense . . . which would drive them away, far away, out of reach.

Like so many before her, Norma marveled in reluctant recognition of this endless phenomenon . . . the creation of a life which grew— and grew, in all dimensions, until almost without warning it had gone out of sight and out of range and quite beyond any conception of control. You bore a child, out of your own body; you cared for it in its ineffable helplessness, you watched it grow, trying according to your lights to nurture its mind and body so that it would grow sturdily and strong. You saw it stand alone—with love, and pride— and heard it thinking for itself . . . the most endearing and exasperating nonsense of course, with every now and then the most astonishing bit of wisdom thrown in. Something that you'd never taught it, had never even thought of for yourself! And suddenly you saw that it was running on its own momentum—running, not standing still, not walking—but *where*, you didn't know, and this was frightening.

And when you reached out or called out—softly or loudly, it didn't even matter which, because your voice was only a whisper in the roar of wind raised by the passage of the young. They went so fast; speed was the thing they loved, or was that only relative, because *you* were slow?—slowing down though you were hurrying, hurrying . . . calling, Wait! Only now it wasn't wait and see—it was wait for *me*. (Was that, if one were truthful, what one had meant all the while?) In any case, the whole thing was out of your hands; couldn't you get that into your head? It was gone, taking some of you with it, which could never be returned. But it might come back and see you now and then, just to see how you were doing on your own. Hoping you'd learn to stand alone . . . Why yes, that was the extraordinary, extraordinarily *funny* thing about it: you spent a lifetime, half a lifetime anyway, teaching and training it to stand by itself erect and strong, and then discovered that it was you who had to learn to stand alone, if not aloof, all over again. You, yourself, Norma Collins.

She came to, with the sort of jolt one gets from trying to catch one's self in mid-air before falling all the way off—to sleep—or somewhere. Or had she really been asleep this time? She was shaking slightly; she'd caught herself at it, sitting bolt upright again, so it must have been with silent laughter, because she remembered that there had been something very funny that she was dreaming about; but when she put her hand up to her face to brush away a strand of loose hair, her eyes were wet, and she knew she'd been crying also. What an unpleasant dream—if dream was what it was. In some way it had seemed more like a storm blowing through a long tunnel, with those two running figures seen dimly far ahead, though they still *felt* so very close to her. It was, she thought—sitting stock-still for a moment with a sense of shock—either a bad dream or a revelation.

Whatever it was, she was glad to come out into the daylight again. She shouldn't have let herself get started thinking about Joyce and Jim if she wanted to quiet her imagination, or even to doze off peacefully. She had never reached a quiet place, a plateau of simple acceptance, in her concern about those two. She could *not* feel happy about their marrying; not now, at any rate. Yet she was so truly fond of Jim by this time that here she was, having traveled all the way around to the point where she'd begun to feel a growing distress as she observed the symptoms developing between them these last six weeks (as if it were her ache, not theirs!) and finally a pang of real dismay when, arrived full circle, she had seen Joyce bring that Landis man in the front gate today.

Joyce's mother got up at last, decisively. There was no use in trying to rest any more. There was no comfort or relaxation left in her. She would go and have her shower. But standing under a hail of water did nothing to wash one's mind clear of what was already in it. Those two! And the stupid, destructive way they'd taken to break down the very thing which had been four years in building; almost as though they were trying to outdo each other in throwing rocks at that fragile structure. Perversely and stubbornly determined to provoke and even wound each other in the contest.

That perfectly uncalled-for greeting of Joyce's today, for instance, in front of the strange young man. Norma could have smacked her child with pleasure, and the same impulse returned to her again as she remembered Jim's look of grim dignity as he'd stood there, dirty, half dressed and drenched with perspiration; even his ears glowing red, poor boy, as they stood out from his head with the glare of the sun behind him. It was not what the girl had said that was important. Everybody bandied insults about nowadays, learned to give or take a few in stride. No, but her intent had been to goad, or possibly to anger him. That was plain. Didn't they know, the poor young dolts, that they could utterly destroy the most precious thing they would ever find in life? Was it up to *her* to tell them that? (Citing chapter and verse out of the book of experience?)

Oh *no*, thought Norma. No. She had come back into her room and was mechanically putting on her clothes, but then she paused and stood there in her pink nylon slip, with her eyes closed and her soul naked in the bitter wind which still swept over her sometimes in unprotected moments. (Though seldom, nowadays, because she was

143

a *sensible* woman—or so they said.) And being sensible, as she had tried to be for so many years, she opened her eyes again and went over to the chest of drawers to get a fresh pair of stockings, telling herself that there was no possible way for her to know whether the thing which Joyce and Jim had almost had was precious or not. It might be simply that they were at long last emerging from their private, self-enclosed young dream, finding that it was not made of stuff to survive the climate outside. And if so, it was up to them—not her—to find it out, and go about the business of living, unencumbered by the ties of loving until they were better fitted for them. It took so much longer to grow up than most people ever realized.

Meantime, this just meant that she would have Joyce for a while longer herself . . . until someone else came along, or even while the girl paused to consider Don Landis. But having, as it were, thus steadied the ground under her own feet, Norma stood transfixed in recognition of that last thought, seeing it quite clearly for what it was. No, she thought again—oh no! One could not deceive one's self to that extent, surely. Whatever Joyce really wanted, to make her happy, she wanted for her, at whatever cost to Norma Collins, and there was no argument to be had there, not even with herself.

So she went on dressing, and presently sat down before the mirror, though not quite facing into it, for she was all ready now, but gazing rather absently aside, her glance touching the footboard of her bed, the chest of drawers, the dressing table here in front of her: all solid, made of wood, but if the wood were vaporized there would be nothing there. Looking at the picture of Bart standing in its frame, a flimsy thing of silver and paper and glass—but he *was* there, and always would be—and not at all because of any resemblance to his transient self at the age of twenty-nine. And moving on again, her glance found the open window, and went through it into the very faint blue haze outside, where everything was alive, not just the growing things, but the seemingly empty air . . . where life was ending all the time, and going on again. And people talked about the end of the world, which was in fact always on its way, by one approach or another. And she was waiting passively now, though her ears were still alert. It was not until she heard the click of the patio gate and a murmur which was Joyce's voice, blended with a deeper one, that she thought—There! Taking a deep breath, conscious of her own breathing again; and, as an afterthought, she picked up a nail file and busied herself with it, just for appearances' sake.

CHAPTER **13**

The murmuring came nearer, and broke off with a laugh in duet, mezzo and baritone, as it approached the front door. Then they were in the living room, not far from her own open door, and she heard the man's step starting up the stairs, and a second later that stage whisper sounded behind her.

"Hi!" She turned, as if surprised to find the girl's head peering cautiously around the door.

"Hi, yourself," she said. "Did you have a good swim?"

"M-hm. It felt good. But I'm just as hot again now as I was before we went. This is a stinker for the end of March, Mom."

Norma smiled, watching her as she came on into the room, dressed only in her swim suit, with a long loose cotton shirt over it and flapping open.

"Yes, it is awfully hot—and still," Norma agreed, and then they both added together in ominously hushed tones, and a two-way smile of shared amusement, " '*Earthquake weather!*' " After a second, Joyce tacked on still another addition, idly but with an air of thoughtfulness. "*That* would be an Act of God too, wouldn't it?"

"What do you mean—'too'?" her mother countered.

"You know very well what I mean, Mrs. Collins," said the girl with cheerful severity. She had begun to wander round the room in a way she had: not restless or nervous, but in a sort of fluid motion, flowing here and there, stopping to touch something lightly as she passed, an ornament on top of the bookcase, the tip of a silk pillow, then moving on again. It was like a slow, non-rhythmic, completely unself-conscious dance, and Norma knew that she was thinking, all the while.

"I suppose that's what makes everybody so—contentious," Joyce said finally. "They say it always does, after all."

"Earthquake weather?" parried Norma.

"Yes . . . though it wouldn't matter much which kind of upheaval one was waiting for, would it?"

"No, I guess not." But she was wondering what it was that Joyce was mulling over. Her own quarrel with Jim? Or had she and this Landis man had some slight disagreement already?—an impish hope inquired quickly—but Norma pushed it away. No, more likely the child had overheard something; some words between the Norbecks possibly? "You know," the mother said, by way of sending up a trial balloon, "I had the most curious sensation this afternoon, after I came in here to rest. I think you and Don had already left for the beach. Anyway, I must have dozed off for a few minutes, and I dreamt I heard the most terrific argument going on, out in the patio or somewhere in the distance. It actually woke me up! But of course it wasn't anything at all. There wasn't a sound to be heard."

Joyce had come to a standstill now and was regarding her, still thoughtfully.

"You didn't dream it," she said.

"Oh, good heavens, Joyce, you mean they really were . . . ? Why, it sounded dreadful—really frightening, like a nightmare. What—happened?"

"Nothing, as far as I know. Don and I were just about to start off when it broke out, and it sounded so appalling, I didn't know what to do. I nearly came to get you. In fact I started back across the patio—and then it stopped."

"They weren't in the patio, then," said Norma—as if that mattered; though she supposed what she meant was that Joyce couldn't have actually seen what happened.

"Oh, no. They were in the kitchen."

"The *kitchen!*"

"Sure. Why not? They were still cleaning up after lunch, I guess. Or maybe doing something about dinner. I wouldn't know. I began to wonder if we'd be having any dinner," Joyce remarked, with a faint grin. "Though I didn't hear any dishes or metalware being hurled around."

Her mother was staring at her in a lingering disbelief, though she was trying hard to adjust her thoughts before Joyce finished speaking.

"You mean," she said at last, "that it was Bertha, and *Joseph*—shouting at each other like that?"

"That's right. And they were both speaking English, too, Mother."

"Well, they generally do, after a fashion."

But the girl shook her head vigorously, so that the wisp of ribbon holding back her hair flew off and her pony tail became a silky mane around her face instead.

"But that's what I mean! They were speaking *plain* English this time; none of that glub-a-dub stuff of Bertha's, and Joseph was speaking *fast* too, and talking more than she was. I mean, it wasn't just Bertha sounding off in one of her usual eruptions. No *accent* at all," Joyce insisted, and for a transient moment Norma reflected that maybe that was why she had thought of the Norbecks first, in that confused moment of awakening. But none of it made any sense.

"I don't understand it," she said. "I never heard them even bickering before. Oh well, I suppose it *is* just this crazy hysteria that's got on all their nerves. I'll be glad when this day is over and they get it out of their systems. And I hope we *will* get some dinner. By the way, I don't know if you took in that Mrs. Mears would be here. I had asked her for tea some time ago, and then thought we might as well have them stay on, since Bertha was bent on putting on a banquet." She had dropped in that reference to the Mearses, intentionally, not only to get away from these other diversions but to see what comment would grow out of the information. But there was none.

Joyce's expression was still noncommittal, and after a minute she went on, as if merely continuing her own story. "It was something Bertha was dead set on doing—that's about all I got—and Joseph was equally determined she wasn't going to do it. He sounded furious, and frantic. Really desperate, for him. We thought one of them was going to murder the other, for sure."

"And then you say it stopped—just like that? You don't think . . ."

"Oh no. I don't think the bodies are lying there in the kitchen. In fact, we saw Bertha taking a small paper bag out to the garbage pail (not big enough to hold Joseph, darling—and she hadn't had time to dismember him) as we started down the road. She had a hat on." And Joyce began to giggle.

"A *hat!* I never saw her wear a hat except on those very few times they went up to town. Not since they first came here!"

"I know. But I think this was one that Mrs. Mears gave her, once. It looked like it. I'll bet it was a Paris number about thirty-forty years ago. A straw hat, with a brim rolled up behind and down in front, and a cluster of climbing roses at the southeast corner."

"Do you suppose she was just trying it on—I mean, that it's to go with her—costume—tonight?" asked Norma.

"Well," Joyce considered the matter, doubtfully. "It was pink. Not white."

"Oh, Joey, you're making it up! You've made up this whole darned thing," said her mother, suddenly annoyed.

"No sir, I did not! Cross my heart and hope to—" Joyce giggled again. "No, I better not say that *today*, had I? But you can ask Don if you want to. I nearly fell out of the car looking back at her."

"You don't suppose she was trying to leave, without notice or something, and Joseph was restraining her?"

"Maybe. Or maybe she just wanted to go and pay a few calls before departing this earth. I don't suppose you could be sure just when you'd run across certain of your friends again."

"Oh well, I give up," said Norma. "I really give up."

"Okay," her daughter conceded lightly, stretching her arms above her head and letting them drop to her sides. "I just thought you might like to know, that's all. If you're harboring a couple of spies, f'r instance."

"Up on this hillside? A lot of valuable information they must have gathered up here in a couple of years!" They chuckled together.

"Well, criminals then, fugitives from justice," offered Joyce. But

148

Norma's smile grew slightly absent, as her thoughts returned to actualities.

"I'm glad it wasn't the others, anyway," she said, and added shamefacedly, "To tell the truth, the first thing that came into my mind—when that ruckus woke me up, I mean—was that it was Roger and Miriam having a set-to out there."

Joyce was looking down at her curiously, and a quizzical twinkle had come into her blue eyes.

"M-hm . . . I wondered if that's what was on your mind when you looked so bewildered about their being out in the kitchen. I never could get you to admit before that there was so much as a ghost of a bicker in the Norbeck cupboard."

Norma felt trapped, and her own wonder at the moment was, why she ever fancied she was fooling her little daughter for a moment.

"Well, I shouldn't have admitted it even now. But I guess we're both aware that there is some sort of tension there, even if they don't generally argue with the volume turned up. Rog and Miriam have been through a long and difficult period, dear. I only wish there were something more we could do to help them both relax. More to amuse them, perhaps."

"Yeah," said Joyce. "I think that's what she's looking for, all right." There was an odd little note in her voice, and Norma looked up at her quickly. She *had* noticed that faintly provocative thing in Miriam's manner at lunch time, then. It was nothing so obvious as a firefly gleam in her eye, or a seductive tone in her voice; it had been scarcely discernible, except by means of that alleged sixth sense which warned a woman when some other woman appeared to be—encroaching. And Joyce was a woman now. Though she had just dropped herself carelessly onto the chaise longue, and looked about fourteen, with her hair falling back from her face, like a long loose bob, and her long tan legs stretched out in front of her.

"You ought to get dressed, dear," said Norma automatically, and then, "By the way—are you *dry?*" she demanded, and Joyce felt her hips.

"Dry as an old bone. We aired ourselves on the beach before we started back. You don't think Don would let me use his nice plushy upholstery for a sponge, do you?" And she linked her hands behind her head, as though just settling down for a nice long chat. Which was what her mother had wanted all along, but something kept pulling them off on these tangents, and the time was short. It must be nearly five . . . and it wasn't the weather she wanted to talk to Joyce about, or Joseph and Bertha—or the Norbecks either. Or Don's upholstery!—though maybe Joyce meant that as a lead.

"I didn't see his car," said Norma.

"Nice job," said Joyce. "Dark green convertible, with an off-white top."

"That's nice," said Norma.

"*He* has a good job, too. D'you like him, Mom?" the girl asked suddenly. So there they were, all at once, arrived at the point: the small opening in the circle which they'd been going round and round, and Norma had to say something. But not too much, she warned herself. Not too much.

"Well, he's attractive . . . I don't know yet, dear—I've hardly had a chance to talk to him. Do *you?*"

"Of course I like him." Joyce gave her hair a toss, back from her face, but it was like a banner in the wind. "He's fun, you know. I wouldn't have asked him down if I didn't like him. Though I must say he almost asked himself!" She grinned, not smugly, but sharing the amusement with her mother. "He certainly piled on the attentions all week."

Norma appeared to consider a moment before she said, stepping carefully, "He has a nice manner. Seems very pleasant, in fact. And rather experienced, I daresay."

"M-hm," agreed Joyce again, the grin retreating to her eyes, where it lurked teasingly. "And that's just what I need, isn't it, Mom? A bit more experience. Variety, I mean." And when her mother didn't take that up, she said, with a touch of challenge, "After all, that's what you've been telling me for several years, isn't it? To see different ones, play the field, get more perspective . . ." She was smiling openly again, enjoying herself as she played back Norma's own theme song, which the latter had fondly thought she could put over without words. No, she hadn't fooled Joyce for a minute.

"Yes, that's quite true," she said soberly. "I even think it was a good idea. I still think so."

"And *I* think you're so right, Mother." For the life of her, Norma couldn't have said whether her precious brat was continuing to make fun of her or not (who was fooling whom around here, anyway?), for she went on with that same dead-pan expression, looking rather dreamily over her mother's head and out the window. "Take Don, now. He's older, and he's got quite a bit to offer, you know. Pretty sharp, Don is, and a go-getter—in more ways than one . . ." Again that fleeting touch of a smile at the corner of her mouth, and again, quite seriously, "I think he's going places—and seeing people. Interesting people. And he's *done* his stretch in the Army, too," said Joyce, coming to an abrupt period with what seemed rather an emphatic irrelevance. Norma felt cold for the first time that afternoon. Was this her doing? Did her child really mean any of that superficial stuff and nonsense? Couldn't she see the sort of man this Landis was?

But she said steadily, "Well, I'm glad you asked him down, dear. I think that was a good idea, too. And we'll all have a chance to get to know each other a little, if he stays on, over the week end. Or maybe he can stop off again on his way back from San Diego." And then she added urgently, "But, darling, you really must—"

"I know—I'm going right now!" The girl sat up, head and shoulders rising, feet coming to the floor lightly, all in one easy co-ordinated motion, the kind of simple physical thing that Norma found herself watching enviously nowadays . . . She moved *too* fast; and that was not what her mother had been trying to say that time, anyway.

"Yes," she put in hastily. "I know you've got to get dressed. It's almost five. But wait a minute, dear." Joyce was standing now, looking down at her. "Even if you have gone and fallen a little bit in love with—Don—" (The name came out with a little difficulty each time, over a lump in her throat, like the reversal of swallowing hard.)

"I didn't say that," said Joyce perversely.

"I know—I know! I'm not putting it right. All I meant was, even

151

if you have fallen a little bit *for* him, or even like him a great deal, and enjoy being with him—just for a change—don't forget, at least while the others are around, that . . . Well, Jim is still human, you know. He has feelings."

There was a moment's silence, before Joyce answered quietly, "Was I as bad as that?"

"It was—pretty uncalled for. That kind of teasing, before strangers, doesn't always sound the way one means it."

Another brief silence, and then Joyce said judiciously, "I'm sorry about that, Mom."

"Oh, it wasn't my feelings that you hurt."

"Well, I'm not going to apologize to Jim, if that's what you're asking me to do. He was just too ridiculous, skulking around over there in the weeds—just trying to be *earthy*, I suppose!" But she was not amused even by her own joke now, and her voice was like a thin hard shell. She was standing so close, now, and loomed so high there beside her, that Norma couldn't keep craning her neck to look up into her face. But Joyce had put her fingertips on her mother's shoulder, with a light touch that was a caress and an appeal at the same time. That was a way she had, too—very infrequently, of communicating further, beyond the words she spoke. And presently she added, "Mother, he's not getting anywhere. He's not even trying to."

"Is that what's wrong?" asked Norma, after a small pause.

"I—guess it is. He won't explain, if there's anything else. I've given him lots of chances to. And I wouldn't care, if he'd just do *something*—go back and finish college, or go ahead and enlist now, or even get a regular job until he *is* called up. But he won't move, Mom, except if we get married—as if that would settle any of the rest of it! He seems to be stalled, before he even starts— and I *can't* marry him if he's going to be like that all his life."

So that was it, thought Norma. But before she could find an answer, in fact before the words had died, Joyce herself broke in to contradict their soft despairing echo. "But I suppose I *would*, if I really loved him. So there you are!" she said, and her tone was light again, and even the pressure of her fingers had left her mother's shoulder. But Norma turned and looked up, and was puzzled by something new and speculative which she found in the blue eyes, still steadily regarding her. "I s'pose," Joyce repeated thoughtfully, "it's easier to be sure—once you've *been* married—isn't it? I mean, it must be easier to know for sure when something's wrong, that can't be changed. Or is it? I've wondered so many times about you, Mother."

"Me!"

"Well, of course! I'm not completely dumb—even though young," the girl threw in with that defensively satirical touch which was itself so young. "Did you think I didn't know that there were men who were interested in you, darling—since Daddy's death?"

Norma was used to her daughter's swift changes of direction, but this was such an unexpected turn that she found her mouth opening, and closing again, without having uttered a word.

"Why," Joyce went on swiftly, "I used to worry that it was *me*—hanging around your neck like an albatross or something—that kept you from marrying again." And at that Norma began to laugh in little silent gasps. At least, it appeared to be laughter.

"Oh, Joey, I never even dreamed . . . One just can't guess what a child will think of. Of course it wasn't you, my lamb. I didn't want to marry anybody, after your father."

"I know you didn't, at first. And I'd have hated it if you had. But later on—well, you should have," said Joyce firmly. "And you may not want to admit it—to me, anyway. But I think lately you have realized that, yourself."

"Realized what, for heaven's sake? That I ought to have snapped up somebody like that man Leslie Sanderson, for instance? Or old Mr. Buchanan—would you have liked old Mr. B. for a stepfather, darling?"

But Joyce ignored all that.

"Roger," she said. Norma looked at her, aghast, and when the echo found its voice in her throat it was a whisper. "*Roger . . .*"

"Before Miriam got him," the girl said calmly.

"I think you must be absolutely mad," said Norma finally. "Rog and I were never even . . . He was a lot younger than I was, in those days. I mean—he still is, of course . . . three or four years . . ."

"That wouldn't matter now . . ." Joyce put in shrewdly. "And you know, you *might* get a second chance one of these days, Mrs. Collins—from the look of things around here."

"Will you please go and get yourself dressed, you young monster?" said Norma, in a low voice, sternly. "I've had enough of your fooling, for once. And the others will be coming out any minute, and Mrs. Mears arriving—and—"

"I'm going! I'm going! Won't take me five minutes. See—I'm gone!"

And she was gone. But for a moment longer Norma sat there, a little too shaken to move. She was really angry with Joyce, but she was furious with herself for feeling shaken. Shocked, yes, that the child should ever have thought of such a thing, and more so, that she could speak of it so cold-bloodedly. But even so, *she* ought not to feel jolted to the foundations by a remark which was merely silly as well as callous. Certainly she had been fond of Roger—most of her grown-up life, it seemed—but not in that way. And that was certainly not the reason for her watching Rog and Miriam with such concern since they'd been up here. She wanted him to get well; she wanted him to be happier—of course she did! But couldn't one person ever have a clear, disinterested sympathy for another—yes, even of another sex? Oh dear, oh damn, thought Norma for the second time within the hour. Joyce had really put the cap on this unpleasant day, for her. And the evening—oh, dear *God*, the evening was still to come.

She got up from the bench in front of the dressing table where she'd been sitting all this time, without a glance at the mirror (she didn't even want to look and see if her face was red), and crossed the room to the door, and as she went out into the living room, she could hear Bertha singing again, not so loudly or vociferously as in the morning, but still with a sonorous determination. And she had changed hymns again—appropriately—to: "Now—the—day—ees oh-*ovare*, Night-ees draw-eeng nah-eee . . ."

Nighties drawing nigh, Norma thought, a shade hysterically, conjuring up the picture of all those white robes, marching . . . fixing her mind upon it as though upon something safer, and in the long run less grotesque that the things which had been occupying her thoughts for the last hour.

CHAPTER 14

She had scarcely set foot on the paved terrace outside the door, when in one of Bertha's sudden abstracted lulls, her ear caught another sound: the crunch of gravel under tires, and she thought, That would be Mrs. Mears, and Jim. And with a quick sense of relief, because she was no longer fleeing from something behind her but going forward to meet what lay ahead, she stepped out into the patio. She would go over to the gate to meet them. There was no time now to reconnoiter, anyway; only to take note as she crossed the grass that all was quiet in Miriam's and Roger's rooms, and that on the other side, Bertha's hymn had leveled off to a mere hum in minor key.

Meantime, beyond the wall and out of view, the motor hum had ceased and there was the sound of a car door slamming—but no voices, and it occurred to her that Jim might be sulking about having to come up here so soon again. If she had been Jim's age, or Joyce's . . . The fact was, however, that if she had been, she never would have mistaken the tone of a 1953 Nash for a 1937 Studebaker, and so would not have been surprised, when she was still some yards away, to see the head and shoulders of Mr. Bixby rising into view and turning toward the gate. A shy but beaming smile broke over his face as he saw her apparently hurrying to greet him.

"Hello, neighbor," she said cordially. "How nice to see you! I heard that you were down, but wasn't sure whether it was true. We don't often see you in the middle of the week." And that, she realized (wanting to laugh), sounded very much as though she'd been sitting up here wondering, engrossed with the comings and goings of Mr. Bixby! Steady, Norma . . . she wasn't getting off to a very good start for a woman who had a handful of very mixed guests to manage deftly for the next few hours. But she kept her smile steady and serene as the little man opened the gate and came toward her, still beaming.

"Ah, Mrs. Collins," he said. "It is good to see you—always. So good. I wasn't even sure whether I would have the—pleasure, this time. But I hoped!"

It sounded as though he were a little surprised to see her, too; though why, she couldn't imagine, since she lived there, after all. But no doubt he hadn't expected her to rush to the gate to greet him. She had always been friendly when he dropped in, but not quite that friendly! She liked him, and felt sorry for him. He was a funny little man, somehow, and she didn't know why he seemed a bit pathetic. Probably just because he was alone, and must be lonely, though he never gave any hint of that; never talked about himself at all. She was thinking rapidly now, as they shook hands, whether she might not ask him to stay on for dinner: that one more odd ingredient in the already assorted mixture, could hardly matter, one way or another. It struck her that Roger might even find him interesting, though she knew nothing about the man except that he was an agreeable and self-effacing neighbor . . . And that he had a firm, warm handclasp, not moist or squishy like that of some plump men . . . while today, his brown eyes, generally so melancholy, had a little twinkle in them that she had never noticed before. Not quite a merry or mischievous twinkle—more like a spark of hope, perhaps. And his smile, so round and enveloping, was in some way grateful. Though she saw that he carried under his left arm a bulky filing envelope of the accordion type, buff-colored and tied with cord of the same color, which made her wonder if he'd come to sell her something. It seemed a curious thing to take along when paying a social call.

"Come over and sit down," she said. "The others will be out presently. I have some visitors staying with me, whom I think you might rather like." And turning, she led the way back toward the sheltered part of the terrace, and as she did so, saw that Bertha was standing in the doorway over in the corner, waving—but not to attract her attention, it seemed, because whatever the gesture was, it ceased as soon as Norma turned her way. She had just caught the tail of it, apparently, like a rocket streaking out of sight, for the woman vanished immediately into the shadows beyond the doorway. And why, in the name of all that was mysterious, was Bertha waving at Mr. Bixby? The answer was, of course, that she couldn't have been. She must have just happened to look out to see who was arriving—must have been shooing away a fly, or something! And *she* must be quietly losing her mind like all the rest of them, thought Norma, almost resignedly.

They sat down in a couple of the comfortable redwood chairs, facing out toward the hills, Mr. Bixby sitting a little forward on his, since his legs were short. He had placed his large envelope, or whatever it was, on the grass beside him, with a sort of casual care, as if it were a hat or something equally unremarkable, but he wished to remember where he had put it. It probably took the place of a brief case with Mr. Bixby, and as such, would not be in the least out of character, for everything about him gave the impression of frugality. His suit was made of good cloth, but Norma had never seen him wearing any other but this black conservative business garb. On anyone else it would have seemed incongruous, down here in the country; on him, anything else would have seemed so. And his car, small and black and carefully groomed like himself, was far from new; in fact, he had mentioned picking it up second-hand some time ago.

They were speaking of the weather now, inevitably. A beautiful day. Rather warm, yes, for this time of year. Though not like summer, of course. It would get much hotter, later on? he inquired.

"Oh yes, *much* hotter. But I rather like it—it's so dry. And the nights are never bad, up here. Are you likely to stay on, do you think?" She asked idly, knowing he had taken the Weber house for only six months, though the owners expected to remain abroad for a full year.

"Yes—s," he said. "I think—I might. The truth is, I have been giving it much thought." He was smiling at her in that same hopeful, enveloping way. "My lease is just expiring on the first, you see." She couldn't see why that should be—no, not amusing exactly, but something to be smiled over companionably. In fact, his smile seemed to ask for some special, responsive comprehension, as though there were some element—warm, urbane—to be shared between them in this question of renewal or non-renewal of his lease. (Almost of sentiment!)

But nevertheless she said, "I see," and smiled back at him encouragingly. And then added, "It will be very nice if you decide to stay on a while longer."

"Thank you, Mrs. Collins," he said, as gratefully as though she had given him a present. She returned to the weather.

"No, I don't think you'd find it too hot. More of a relief from the city and the smog, I'd say. But then, I never liked the city very much, myself."

"You lived long, in Los Angeles?"

"About nine years," Norma answered. "We came out West only a year before my husband—died. Then, when he was gone, I had to get a job, of course. It was during the war—otherwise, I suppose I might not have been able to find work, without experience or any sort of training." She smiled ruefully, remembering her abysmal unpreparedness, but he was nodding with a solemn look of understanding.

"Nevertheless, I did manage to make a living for Joyce and myself, when we needed it," she went on, and stopped, as though to put a period to that. And then, making a deliberate effort to get away from this personal recital, yet without too abrupt transition, "It was during those years that I first knew Mr. Norbeck, the guest—that is, one of the guests I was speaking of a moment ago. That was while he was working as a cub reporter, but he became quite well known later on as a foreign correspondent."

"Yes," Mr. Bixby nodded. "I know the name—Norbeck. Roger Norbeck, is it?"

"That's right," said Norma, with unexpected eagerness. Unexpected to her. But she was listening critically to every word she uttered now, suspicious of herself. "He and his wife are spending a month up here with me. He had a very bad heart attack last fall. Somewhat better now, but not fully recovered."

"So?" said Mr. Bixby politely.

"I'm afraid he's not going to be able to go back . . ." But having begun that, Norma realized that she didn't want to go on about Roger either. And she was clearly aware that Mr. Bixby's attentiveness was, in some manner, suspended, waiting for her to finish this irrelevant topic and come back to her own life history? she thought ironically. Not likely! But his compassionate gaze (like that of an old spaniel) had not wavered from her face. She wished the Mears family would hurry up and come; it must be nearly five-thirty . . .

Having lost the thread of what she was saying, she let a pause grow up, and Mr. Bixby waited for a decent interval before changing the subject. "How old was the little girl then?" he inquired, while Norma stared at him, retracing her errant thoughts.

"Joyce, you mean? When Bart . . . she was not quite seven." She stopped again—and went on rapidly, to leave that moment, that date, even that little girl of six, far behind.

"Later on, much later on, when I was able to, I put her in school down in La Jolla, and I found this place—to wait for her, and try to put some roots down, for her as well as myself." Her glance traveled round it, seeing not what her caller did, but the little box it had been, with no garden at all—which she'd bought so cheaply. "I wanted Joyce to have something real for a home, something to come back to in vacations. And this, as it happens, is about halfway between the school she went to down there, for three years—and Occidental, where she has been for four more . . . It has been a good place for us," said Norma.

"Yes," he said. "You did well." But she hastened to correct what she guessed he was thinking.

"Oh, I didn't do it all on my commissions in the kitchenware department at Miller, King and Company. No, I had a very dear aunt in the East, whom I was devoted to. Her own husband died, later on, and she had no other family, and left me all she had. I was just lucky," she said simply. "And by that time, I had worked long enough to know *how* lucky, believe me. Fate has an odd, left-handed way of trying to even things up, I suppose . . ." She couldn't imagine why she had told him all that. There was no secret about any of it, but she didn't generally run on this way, about herself. Mr. Bixby was too good a listener.

"And now," he said, prompting her to go on, "she is back again."

"Back—? Oh yes, she came back today. But that was just from a little visit to some friends."

"I meant to say, she is finished at the college, and back at home—to stay? The little daughter is grown up," he said quietly. Norma looked at him, not knowing that her very look protested, Why bring that up? Dissecting her past, her present and now—it seemed—even her future, which depended upon Joyce herself. And suddenly a monstrous thought occurred to her: a reason for this persistent interest which she had been too obtuse to guess at before. Of course he had seen Joyce on occasion, several times probably, but Norma had been so concerned with the problems raised by Jim's devotion to her child—with young love, in fact—that it had never crossed her mind that old men sometimes liked young girls too.

"Oh yes, indeed," she answered hastily, once she'd caught up with this thought. "She's graduated, and quite grown up now, but she has granted me this little period of three months (no more!) to spend down here, before starting off on a career of her own."

"So?" said Mr. Bixby, still softly.

"Yes," Norma rushed on, brightly. "I'm not sure yet whether it will be a job up North somewhere or in the East" (Joyce would have been surprised by that!) "or marriage, almost at once—to one of these young men who are—well, very fond of her, to put it mildly! Jim Mears, for one." She didn't know why she threw Jim into the breach right there, but a definite name seemed a more solid brick for the wall she was quickly building to shut the older man out.

"Not the one they call 'Young Mears'?" he said, frowning, for the first time since he had come in the gate. No, he didn't like that! Well, so much the better, then.

"Oh yes," she said firmly. "Jim has been a very ardent suitor for several years. They choose their partners extremely young, these days, you know—and a good thing too, I daresay." (What *was* she saying?)

But Mr. Bixby ignored all that as if he hadn't even heard it, and very gently now he prodded, "And you? You will stay here? When the young daughter goes away to take for herself the job, or the husband?" And that was not what Norma had expected him to say next, and she was confused, as by some adroit maneuver. Quite suddenly at a loss, though of course that could be simply because she herself didn't *know* the answer to his question. She shrugged her shoulders. "I? Oh, I'm not sure. That is, yes—I think I'll always keep this place if I can. I have grown into it now myself, you see. Found many little things that can be done in the village—for people who are ill, or old, or very much alone. It doesn't sound like much, but I've grown—so fond of most of them." She broke off rather self-consciously, for she saw him nodding again in that sympathetic way. "And then of course I'd like to keep the place for Joyce to come back to—and bring her children." She smiled hardily, to show him that she wasn't such a poor weak thing as he evidently took her for, and Mr. Bixby once more enclosed her, protectively it seemed, in that round, beaming look of his—so like the moon coming up behind him, which was nearly full.

"You might—marry again, yourself," he suggested, with what seemed an odd, but very gentle insistence.

"I!" she exclaimed in a shocked tone. "Good heavens, no."

"No?"

"Certainly *not!*"

She knew she had spoken sharply, more sharply than she had intended, for she knew also that the man had not meant to be impertinent. In fact, he now looked so taken aback that she would have softened her rejoinder for the sake of civility, if it hadn't already escaped her. But she did not intend to correct it, for no one must think that she was one of these voracious females, these man-eating—no, man-*hungry* widows, just waiting for her child or children to be launched before setting off on another venture of her own. No one! Not a perfect stranger like this—not Joyce herself—not Miriam . . . or Roger. (Rog and Miriam least of all!)

It was what Joyce had said, of course, not fifteen minutes earlier, which had caused this instant and extreme reaction, before Norma could control and tone it down. She *was* shocked, as though by something offensive. That two people in quick succession should suggest . . . should really think she was such a fool—or possibly so calculating—as to be looking around already for prospects (even among her own well-married friends!). Oh, Norma, be yourself. Mr. Bixby meant nothing of the kind, knew nothing about her except what she had chosen to tell him. It was only what Joyce had said that had upset her, and he had merely set off a delayed emotional explosion, blasting out the wall she had built up in herself. But she was a little angry with him, nonetheless; just for sitting there and saying something so outrageous, flooding the second level of her consciousness with the very suspicion which made her angry with herself.

"I see," said Mr. Bixby finally. "Yes, I understand."

You don't understand anything, she thought, but aloud she said, "There's nothing to understand. I don't know why people so persistently imagine that a woman must always—invariably and perennially—want to marry again. The older she is, and the sillier the idea, the more they seem to foster it!"

And the more she said, the worse it sounded, she told herself, and the sillier she made herself look. So why didn't she stop it? She had no realization of how lovely she actually looked at that moment, her color a little higher than usual, her blue eyes wide open and sparkling, even if with annoyance. And Norma had a way of sitting very straight indeed when she was disturbed, her chin lifted a trifle so that she seemed to look over and beyond whatever had vexed her. While all the time, Mr. Bixby continued to regard her steadily, observing the woman before him, and the now inescapable fact that the view he saw—so clear, so close—was in truth a distant one and would remain so for him always. A mirage, no more. His round smile held firmly in place, though it was no longer full like the moon, but slowly emptying of the light it had contained . . . or merely reflected, for that matter, for was he not a dead world himself?

Norma's glance crossed his without engaging it, and saw beyond him that Roger's door was opening on the opposite side of the patio. Her quick relief was augmented by a sense of gladness—which quickened also, in spite of her, as she saw him coming toward her across the grass—and both in turn were checked by a warning to herself that she must take care, though it gave her a slightly strangled feeling of *caution*, which she had never had with Roger before. But at least his coming would put an end to this disconcerting tête-à-tête with her neighbor. And she noted thankfully too that Roger was looking well, for him, this evening; rested; his lips not so blue—even a little spring in his step as he approached them.

She introduced the two men and saw that they were estimating each other with the expertness of long habit and an automatic reaching for a common line of communication. But there was no time to wonder what they would think of each other, before the door from the living room opened briskly and young Mr. Landis came out to join them, and it occurred to Norma as the three men stood there, that she could hardly have collected three more different specimens if she had searched for them. Even when Joyce appeared a moment later, the three did not turn on one spring, with a single look of simple male appreciation, as one might have expected. Don Landis had that look—oh yes—and well he might, for Joyce looked extremely pretty: very pink and clean and shining, in a crisp pink cotton dress; very young and healthy, vital and lovable. But she saw that Roger's look was plainly avuncular, both fond and critical. As for Mr. Bixby—she watched him closely out of the corner of her eye— he was very polite. He was always polite. But his glance at the girl, as he bowed and spoke his stiff little greeting, was almost perfunctory; disinterested. Why, thought Norma, he didn't even look as interested as he had when he'd been looking at *her* so attentively a few minutes ago! And feeling less flattered than slightly ashamed of herself, she abruptly made mental amends for her earlier mistrust of him, by deciding once more to ask him to stay on for dinner.

As soon as a break in the conversation gave her an opening, she did so, and thought that he looked confused for a second. Pleased, but at the same time dismayed, as if not certain that he should accept. Norma, herself the one who was at ease now, said warmly, "Do stay. We're a rather haphazard lot, as you see—somebody always coming and going. There, that must be the Mearses now . . . She

163

looked up to catch Joyce's eye questioningly. "Isn't that the sound of their car? We really want you to. Besides—" She had almost said, Besides, this is an evening to be celebrated, you know!—and caught herself back in quick recoil from actually uttering the words, for she was still hoping *nobody* would bring up that subject of the End of the World. Not till after dinner anyway!

Fortunately, Mr. Bixby didn't seem to notice the single word she had left hanging in the air by itself. "It's very kind of you," he murmured. "I would—enjoy it."

So that would make eight, she figured hastily. And Mr. Bixby, odd little number though he was, might even help to balance the oddly assorted group . . . of which there was now a general rising and regathering to meet the latest arrivals who were approaching across the grass.

Two more dignified figures could not have been imagined than that of Mrs. Mears and her grandson, both tall and erect, the woman almost as tall as the six-foot-plus young man. She moved slowly and carried a cane, but used the latter more as a pointer for every other step rather than leaning on it; nor did she deign to take Jim's arm, though he kept careful pace with her. They were a strangely distinguished pair, thought Norma, as they came on, side by side, and the resemblance between them was very marked now; not only in height and general bearing, but carried out in the plain strong features—even to the outstanding ears of both, though the old lady's were slightly masked by the sweep of iron-gray hair drawn smoothly over the upper part of them. Imposing was the word for both of them at that moment. But it was the incongruity of their attire, for an evening like this, which caught Norma in the midriff, like a spasm of laughter hastily choked down—and they must have planned it, intentionally, though whether they had done it as a joke, or in all seriousness, she didn't know.

To be sure, Mrs. Mears did sometimes appear in clothes that she must obviously have owned for an appreciable period of time. But today she wore a dress of Chinese linen, beautifully embroidered, which she had probably bought about the year 1910. It must—even then—have been very expensive, for it was exquisitely made. It also had a high boned collar which reached almost to her ears on either side, and a skirt which reached exactly to her ankles. All starched, and pristine white. And over that, against the probable chill of the evening, she had put on a long silk sweater, finely knit—not by hand, but well made by machine, with a long tasseled sash of the same knitted silk, tied low around her waist, with the ends hanging free. Norma remembered having a sweater like that in powder blue when she was a very young girl, so the vintage of this must be the same. Only it also was all white, or very slightly creamed by the passage of approximately thirty years.

As for Jim, he was strictly up to date, impeccable in white tuxedo and black trousers, with bow tie to match. Norma couldn't remember ever having seen him dressed up, as for a formal party, before. But it was the contrast—the slapstick contrast against the morning, when he had stood there, almost on the same spot. *Why* had the silly boy done it? For now of course he looked absurd again, in equally extreme contrast to the easy sport coat and slacks which Roger wore, or young Landis' well-cut light gray flannel suit. She hardly dared to catch Joyce's eye now and fairly prayed the child wouldn't burst out laughing, or make another wisecrack much sharper than the one at noon, though she could hardly have blamed her if she did, this time. For Jim was really being childish.

It had taken only a few seconds, from the time the two had first appeared, to the greetings, gay or restrained, to the introductions and again the reshuffling and reseating in the semicircle of chairs which were all more or less facing out toward the open end of the patio and the hills beyond. And in spite of herself Norma *had* caught Joyce's eye, and it was sparkling, very bright, so that her mother's instant thought was that it might be with anger more than mischief this time, until she saw the girl blink quickly—just once—and realized what that glistening brightness was. So she was sorry for him now, was she? Well, there was no accounting for the young—or old; no, not for any of us, thought Norma.

She was doing a bit of literal accounting, on her fingers, as Joseph arrived with his battery of bottles to place alongside the tray of glasses already on the glass-topped table, and she murmured a word to him about putting on that extra place in the dining room. She wondered fleetingly whether he was ill; the poor man looked so gray, with that bleak glazed look in his eyes, like a skim of ice—or was it fright? She hadn't dreamed that *Joseph* would succumb to the contagion of the village, but one could never tell what fears lay ready as a breeding ground in anybody's soul, and she couldn't stop now to find out what was wrong with him. She was more puzzled at the moment, as to why her number wasn't yet even—who was missing?—until all at once there came that sharp slap of a door across the patio, like the clap of hands to command attention, and Miriam was coming out and across to join them. Swiftly, gracefully, like a white bird sailing low and easily over the ground, to make a perfect two-point landing. She was dressed in a white faille gown, the skirt opera-length and very, very full, the bodice close fitting and just barely covering the swell of her breasts, arms and shoulders entirely bare, of course; pearls in her ears, and a mere spiderweb of straps to hold the very high-heeled sandals on her feet. Quite an entrance, thought Norma, as the other murmured softly, shyly as a young girl, "*Am* I late? I'm sorry, dear . . ."

But at least things would begin to pick up and pull together now, the older woman reflected as she did the introductions over again, and looked round to make sure Joseph was distributing the right drinks to the right persons; saw also that Joyce was bending over Mrs. Mears, offering her Bertha's choicest canapés. Finally, and thankfully, Norma sat down again, beside Don Landis, as it happened. But for some reason the conversation didn't start up as easily and spontaneously as it should have. The attempts at small talk were still sporadic. Miriam had settled herself with a little swish beside young Jim, and was murmuring something to him with a hint of low-voiced laughter. Little Mr. Bixby looked rather lost beside Mrs. Mears, who was paying less attention to him than to the canapés. And Roger was just sitting now, looking into his glass, not making an effort to talk to anyone. Oh well, thought Norma again, they'll all perk up a bit when the drinks begin to work. For the moment even her own flow of chat, which usually came so easily, wouldn't seem to start. She felt too tired to bother; couldn't

166

even think of a reasonable opening line to get Don Landis going—perhaps because she saw that he was slightly bemused since Miriam's appearance. (And the same thing could be said for Jim, and maybe that was what was holding Mr. Bixby tongue-tied too!) But what earthly difference did it make, after all? Earthly . . . The word reminded her of the very thing which had made the whole day so tense and tiresome, trying to thread her way between a lot of buried psychological mines, and turning to Don, she remarked, for utter lack of other inspiration, "You know, I really think we ought to drink to the Occasion—just by way of starting off the evening in the proper spirit!"

"What's that?" he responded quickly, with a ready smile. "Somebody's birthday, or something?"

"Well, no—not exactly." She smiled back at him over her glass, reflecting that he must be the only one here who hadn't heard about it. Hardly fair to keep him in the dark all alone, was it? Might even be illuminating to see how he would react. She took another little sip, and said, " Perhaps you hadn't heard that tomorrow would be the end of the world?" She mentioned it with gentle matter-of-factness, like the weatherman's prediction for a sunny day, or a few light showers.

They all laughed then—at what she had said—or the way she'd said it—or at the look of polite astonishment on Don's face? In any case, there it was, and she'd done it herself, opened up the very topic which she had prayed nobody would mention. Just to get her old party going!

CHAPTER 15

The laughter had given Don his cue, so when his reply came, it was given with an air of mock caution, his expression still politely noncommittal as he regarded Norma intently.

"*What*—did you say, Mrs. Collins?"

"I said—" she began, and got no further, for she was stricken by a horrid wonder as to whether Joseph was still there, somewhere behind her, puttering at his impromptu bar. She couldn't imagine how she had come to be so thoughtless, just because she was sick and tired of the whole silly business. But by the time she'd moved her head unobtrusively, to glance one way and then the other and satisfy herself that he had really gone back into the house, Miriam had taken up the answer for her, caught it eagerly and carried it away. And they were all watching and listening in a spellbound fascination, as they would to any wonderfully good story, expertly told, whether or not they had heard it all before.

Yes, she told it well; not, perhaps, with the same joyous spontaneity that she had that morning when she was first announcing it to Roger, but with a more delicate edge of amusement, and the fine points sharpened. There was even a certain pity and perception in the retelling of her meeting with Miss Amelia, and a little indulgent shake of the head when she touched on Alfred, but throughout, she kept the very flavor of fun—and irony, on the tip of her tongue, so that each one listening could not help but savor it on his own private palate. They were all smiling now, in appreciation of this entertainment unexpectedly provided, with here and there a chuckle, or a ripple of general laughter. Norma, looking from one to the other, saw that Joyce, perched on the arm of Roger's chair, was watching Miriam with frank admiration, and Rog himself, with a broad grin, was enjoying the act his wife was putting on. Only Mr. Bixby was frowning, very slightly, as though puzzled by an idiom which he could not quite follow. And of course the explanation of this curious event was ostensibly for the benefit of Don Landis, so that, quite naturally, all the dark mischief in her eyes, the slight motion of her long hands, or the lift of one bare shoulder to accent the mocking lilt in her voice—was focused directly on him during the two or three minutes which she took for the performance. It wasn't more than that, but it was quite enough to take possession of her audience, and set the tone for the rest of the scene in which they all had some part.

"So you see—" she ended softly, her eyes wide and solemn, "how privileged you are, Mr. Landis, to have been invited up here for *this* particular evening!"

"That I do!" And he let out the laugh which had been gathering in him as he listened. "It's only the most amazing thing I ever heard of. How do people *get* that way?"

"It's not nearly so funny, though," said Norma, "when you *know* all these people, and see them getting so wrought up over nothing." But that was a sour note, and she wished she hadn't uttered it; let these others have their fun, after all, as long as it did nobody else any harm. She was surprised when Jim echoed her with an unexpected and emphatic, "You can say *that* again!"

He, for one, was wishing that Mom Collins hadn't brought this thing up at all, though he guessed probably it would have come out sooner or later during the evening. He didn't like these outsiders making sport of his village, and that was a fact. That Landis, for instance, and even the Norbecks. As for the little fat slob sitting over there beside his grandmother . . . it struck Jim suddenly that only those two, the elders of the whole group, had not laughed. The one, sitting straight as a spar in one of those wrought-iron chairs, holding a glass of tomato juice which had been scarcely touched— and the other, looking gravely smug and comfortable, settled down into the cushion of his own fat. Damned old crook, Jim thought. And then, more ominously, suppose that guy tried to get Gran's house away from her? Which could be the very thing he was hanging around here for; anything he could collect on his fat fingers, up to the last minute. And suppose—it seemed impossible, but somehow the impossible doubt crept up on Jim again—just suppose she did put some stock in this wild-eyed prophecy? After all, she'd never *said*, one way or another. And—again for the first time—it struck him smack between the eyes that she was dressed *all in white*. Good grief! thought Jim . . . Though Miriam Norbeck was in white too, for that matter; what there was of it. He was disturbingly conscious of her, so close beside him; of the smooth bare arms and back and shoulders, even of the faint perfume in his nostrils, and he took a quick gulp of his highball to steady his head, because this dame made him dizzy. The whole cockeyed setup made him dizzy. And it kept right on spinning.

Don Landis had just inquired of the company in general, "Where is this hill they're going to climb—to heaven, if I may be so bold to ask?"

"Right over there," said Norma, waving her hand with a proprietary air, since that was still her View, after all, and always had been. "I see three hills," said Don. "Or is it this drink? I've only had one," he added plaintively, and Norma said at once, "Why, of course you have—" and glanced around for Joseph. So Miriam stepped in once more to answer his question.

"Look," she said, her wave more imperative than Norma's, "it's *that* one, where the other crosses in front of it. It has that little tree on top, see?"

"Little tree on top," he murmured, squinting his eyes as though dazzled by the color, cast back upon those hills from the sunset; the afterglow reflected upon them so that they were already beginning to appear less like solid earth than like a painted picture of it— or like a memory of the earth, idealized as it might seem when one had left it.

"Look!" Miriam said again impatiently, though they were all looking now, with varying degrees of reflectiveness, out from the semicircle which formed a box seat for the daily panorama. "Come over here," she insisted, getting up and holding out a hand to him, so he arose (perforce, or willingly? Norma asked herself, noting that he had given Joyce a wink in passing) and took the hand which Miriam extended, as they stepped out of the circle to stand a few feet away. "Don't you see that little knob of a tree that stands out all by itself on the round summit of *that* hill?" she pursued, pointing a long red-tipped finger, while he stooped a little as though to sight along her bare arm.

"Oh—h—yes," he admitted finally. "I think I see now where you mean."

"Well, it couldn't be plainer," she said disdainfully, "even if it has such a short little trunk." And added fondly, "Like one of those little old short-handled umbrellas."

"I always thought it looked like a button," remarked Norma practically. "You know—the kind with a shank on the underside of it?"

"Or like a mushroom," said Don, considering it judicially. "Most like a mushroom, I think." But Miriam turned away from him at that.

"Don't even *say* that word!" she said sharply over one naked shoulder raised as though in defense. "I hate it!"

There was a slight wave of surprise which went over the faces in the semicircle: surprise caused by her vehemence as well as by the word association which had obviously caused it.

"Sorry," he said. "That does have an unpleasant connotation nowadays."

"I just won't have you calling my little tree a mushroom. *You* may call it a button, if you like, dear," she said graciously to Norma, coming back into the group and sitting down again. "I love that little stubby tree all by itself, on top of the world. I walked all the way up there this morning," she added dreamily, twirling the stem of her empty glass. "It's a gorgeous view from there."

"I'll bet it is," Don remarked carelessly, also taking his seat again. "I wouldn't mind taking a stroll up there myself—in the moonlight, preferably." And then he added, with a chuckle, "In fact, I'd admire to see that parade up there tonight, even if I have to join it!"

"Oh, me too!" said Miriam eagerly.

"You couldn't get into it, dressed like that," Joyce said to Don, and then she giggled. "Unless you wear your white swimming shorts!"

"M-*hm*," said Miriam approvingly, and—Gleeps! thought Jim, wouldn't you know he was the kind of guy'd go in for white trunks—white *satin* probably!

But Don replied urbanely, "Oh, I don't know. I think my swimming shorts might be the answer . . . If Mrs. Norbeck can join the parade in that—very becoming—outfit!"

Laughter, of course . . . Even Mrs. Mears conceded a small grim smile. But Miriam retorted loftily, "I'd have you know, *Mr.* Landis, that I have a gorgeous and *quite* enveloping white stole to complete my costume when the hour arrives!"

"Well, Don could use a big bath towel, couldn't he?" said Joyce.

"As to that," he returned with dignity equal to Miriam's, "*I have* a perfectly tailored dingus made of bath-toweling—call it terry cloth, don't you?"

"That's right," both girls agreed.

"Doubles for beach or bath—"

"And what could be more appropriate!" Miriam beamed at him. "Beach robe and swim shorts. To cross the Styx, you know, in case you rock the boat."

"Hey," he objected. "I thought this was a scheduled flight, not just a boat ride . . ."

How long, thought Norma, can they keep this up? Haven't they got anything else to talk about—any other topic in common among the whole seven of them? And *why* didn't Joseph come back to 'tend the drinks? She tried to catch Roger's eye, but he was reaching out to pick up the cue Don had left hanging there.

"Drown—or crash," he said, turning it over to examine it, "the end's the same, presumably."

"Ah, don't be heavy, darling," Miriam put in sweetly. "This is a party, remember?"

"That's right." He looked down at his glass, as though reminded of its purpose.

"And the drinks need freshening," Norma said quickly. "Rog, would you please—until Joseph comes back—?"

"Yes, certainly." He up-ended his glass now, and drained what was left there, preparatory to getting up. But then, forgetting what she'd asked, his mind still on the other thing, he looked across the half circle and said, as though directly to Norma, "You know, it's amazing. Simply amazing, what people will refuse to believe, when it's set right before them . . . and then the other stuff—like this— that they'll actually swallow."

"You referring to my bourbon?" Norma retorted. But it was Jim, now, who put in glumly, "I bet they have an awful stomach ache down in the village tomorrow morning."

"Ah, Jim!" Miriam's tone was reproachful as she leaned toward him and reached for his unoccupied hand. "Jim, don't be serious about it," she pleaded, for the second time. Don't let's any of us be serious tonight. Just think how absurd it all is, and how foolish it's going to seem to them, too, when they look back on it."

"Sure," said Jim. "Unless they find they've been swindled out of something more than just a pipe dream."

"You know what?" Miriam said gaily, ignoring that, gathering in her audience again with one urgent, sweeping glance. "I think they're having the time of their lives, literally! Having a lovely, foolish pipe dream, as you say—but which won't hurt anybody. It just gives them something to think about, probably, instead of their drab little, sad little lives."

"Escape?" said Joyce judicially. "Could be, you know. I never thought of it that way before, but it *fits*. Sort of an emotional jag to get-away-from-it-all, that's carried them right off their feet."

"You mean they think it will," Jim said shortly.

"Well do I remember the time I thought *I* could fly!" Don contributed with a reflective grin. "Absolutely sure of it. Tried to take off from a second-story balcony—landed in a clump of bushes, luckily for me . . ." Joyce giggled, but Miriam broke in, her voice rising a trifle.

"Let's drink to them, shall we? Come on, doesn't anybody want to propose a toast to all the sweet and simple—and believing souls still left in the world?" She lifted her glass and saw that it was empty. "I want to drink to them," she said wistfully, and flashed another glance around the curving group, an invitation to gaiety—even a supplication—which reached across to Mrs. Mears, and the fat man beside her, and came back quickly past Norma and Roger, to meet and join for a moment the look of understanding in Don's eyes.

"Eat, drink, and be merry," he said softly, but he left the rest unspoken, and his tone was so low that it might not have carried to the others.

"Well, for the third time," Norma put in firmly, making herself heard at last, "we can't drink to anybody with empty glasses. Rog, won't you please take over? I'm sorry, but Joseph must think one drink lasts forever."

"Oh, *I'm* sorry," Roger muttered, and got up finally, turning first to Mrs. Mears. "May I get you something, Mrs. Mears—" he began, and then broke off, seeing that she had practically a full glass of tomato juice in her hand. But she said unexpectedly, "Why, yes, thank you. Yes, Mr. Norbeck, you may. I believe I'd like to join in this. Will you make mine a Bloody Mary, please?" And handed him back her glass, as for correction.

So Gran had spoken finally, and Jim, in the act of swallowing, choked and gulped. But whether it was the faint incongruity of Mrs. Mears' firm request, or her decision to join hands with the spirit of the evening, something had eased the tempo, made the laughter more spontaneous. Roger, with his mind now on the business in hand, refilled the glasses, and they all began to talk more easily, and together, if not all at once. Norma was pleased to see that the party was at last running on its own momentum. Joyce was the only one, of course, who had had nothing but ginger ale, but needed nothing more, as she sat laughing over there, with Don leaning close to her; even Jim, though he was still cautiously nursing his first drink, appeared less hostile, more relaxed. By this time, also, Mrs. Mears was telling Roger, who had now taken a chair between her and his hostess, about the time she had had her first sip of vodka. And Miriam was flirting overtly with Mr. Bixby, who seemed in a somewhat dazed fashion to be enjoying that. And it was so nice and companionable—and natural—to have Rog there beside her; she could hardly recall now, why she had felt she should avoid him, earlier. To be sure, there was something hovering in the background, some cloudy problem still to be solved, or dissolved, but for the present it was quite enough to look around the little group she had gathered there and think comfortably, Yes, they're off, now. They're going to get on all right, and the party's on its way.

They were on their third round, and Joseph was once more hovering in the background, trying to announce dinner, when Norma's attention was caught by a sound outside the rim of this circle: the unmistakable click of the gate, opening and closing. It was virtually dark by now, except for the glimmer of light from the two shaded lamps which hung on the terrace, close to the house, one at the main entrance into the living room and the other over in the corner by the dining-room door, so that it was impossible to see clearly who might be coming in from the outside world. She felt a momentary flicker of resentment against any intrusion now, just when everything

174

was getting cozy, but watching the figure approaching, through the dusk, she could see only that it was a man—a spare, angular-looking shadow of a man.

Roger, who had been saying something to her, noticed her expression and paused to turn and look where she was looking, while Miriam stopped short in the very middle of a peal of laughter. But when the voice came solemnly, "*Good* evening, ma'am," Norma recognized at once—with a mixture of annoyance and relief—who it was.

"Oh, Alfred!" she exclaimed. "I couldn't see who you were . . ." And couldn't imagine why he'd come, either, as the shadow loomed now at the edge of the group. She wondered apprehensively if he were sober or even partly so, remembering that he had seemed to be well on his way as long ago as that morning; yet he had put on his deacon manner, for the moment at least; his unbending, holier-than-thou-or-anyone-else expression, and that sonorous voice which he used whenever he had something to say in the meeting house.

"*Good* evening, all," he intoned, and Joyce and Jim both spoke together, "Hello, Alfred." After which, a small silence like a cool breeze drifted over the little group that had been making so much chatter a couple of seconds ago.

"I *beg* pardon, for intruding," he said stiffly.

"You're not intruding, Alfred. Of course not . . . You know everyone here, I believe—oh yes, except Mr. Landis . . . And *you* all know Alfred," she added quickly, thinking as she said it, How ridiculous!—even as Miriam said in her best social manner, "Oh yes, *indeed*," and Roger added a careless "Hi, Alf!" Don Landis had started to rise but Alfred ignored him entirely.

"I did not come here to intrude, nor to be in-tro-duced, neither," he said loftily, as from some great height. "Only to bring one last message, ma'am, as one whom neither snow-nor rain-nor heat-nor gloom of night can stay from swift completion of his appoint-ed rounds."

"It doesn't look like snow, does it?" said Miriam in a whisper, and Norma saw that Joyce was beginning to shake with silent mirth, and wished she could laugh herself, but somehow didn't want to.

Meantime the uninvited guest had stepped forward into the middle of the group, extending his hand toward Norma, not by way of greeting, but offering her what appeared to be a piece of paper. "That was *all* there was, tonight," he finished sorrowfully, as though he would indeed have liked to bring her a batch of important documents, more befitting a night like this. Norma took what he handed her, could see in the dim light from behind her that it was a colored post card (of Las Vegas, was it?—yes, Rita Burns had written that they were going east that way) and felt even less like laughing but rather more like bursting into tears.

"Oh, *Alfred!*" she said. "You shouldn't have bothered to bring this all the way up, tonight."

"I am—proud—to do my last duty, ma'am. And may we all say the same," he finished, lifting his face to the dark sky, rather as though scanning it for rain. But Norma had an awful feeling that he might attempt to lead them all in prayer any minute.

"That was nice of you, Alfred, and I'm so glad to have this. But I wouldn't for the world have had you take all that trouble."

"Trouble—is all we can take with us, my good woman. *All*," he finished hollowly.

"Oh no! No, Alfred, I'm sure that isn't so."

"You may not—*think* so, Mrs. Collins. But you may not be fully prepared. It hardly looks to me like anybody was prepared around here," he said loudly, casting his bleak glance around the shadowy circle, punctuated regularly by hands, each one holding a highball or cocktail glass which clinked occasionally.

"Oh, I think we'll have time enough still," said Norma gently, helplessly. Why didn't somebody else help her out, for heaven's sake? This couldn't go on, and she *couldn't* in all conscience, offer the poor man a drink—and if she sent him out to Bertha at this juncture, it might be calamitous, for the dinner—if nothing worse. So she got to her feet, and held out her hand, and said firmly, "In any case, it was *very* nice of you to come up again, and I *do* appreciate it."

"You're welcome, I'm sure. You're very welcome." But somehow the tone was not so sonorous now, and he gripped her hand, as if for a last hold on something human.

"And we'll be seeing you, Alfred!" Joyce spoke up suddenly and cheerfully.

"That may be, Miss Joyce," said Alfred. "That may be . . ."

"Oh yes, Alfred!" said Miriam, also rising to the occasion, and quite literally too, taking a step toward him and stretching out her hand with a dazzling smile. "We'll all be there, you know. All of us." But he stiffened up and drew himself back—without actually taking a step—and he did not take her hand.

"I doubt that, ma'am," he said more loudly still, as though to make sure God—who was his witness—could hear him, however far away. "I doubt that, very much. And I won't detain you any longer. *Good* evening, all," he concluded, as he had begun, and made a half-turn toward the dark again, but found that Roger Norbeck was standing there beside him now.

"Well, anyway, some of us'll be there, old boy. You can be sure of that," he said kindly. "You and me, and a lot of others."

"You think so, Mr. Norbeck?" the man said hungrily.

"Why, I'm sure of it. Wherever it may be, old friends'll get together. We're great pals, Alfred and I," Rog said to the others, his hand across the man's shoulder. "Alfred's my *pal* all right!" And suddenly the two were chuckling together, though it was a rusty sound coming from Alfred's throat.

"By jiminy, that's right, ain't it?" he said. "Say, thank you, Mr. Norbeck."

"Thank *you*, Alfred!" Rog insisted, and the other said once more, rather huskily, "Thank you kindly—and I better be goin' now."

He went across the grass, blindly, but he was not staggering. He knew he was walking all right. And he knew just about where the gate was. He missed it by a couple of feet, and had to move along a little, sideways, till his hand found the top of it and then the latch. They couldn't see him though, not that far off. It was dark, and anyway they were drunk. They were drunker than *he* was, God damn it. He hadn't had a drink for hours . . . and oh, Jesus, how he needed it . . . how he *needed* it! He could have cried in his anguish. But nobody could see him now, if he did.

He was out of the gate, and lurching down the driveway, and then getting into his old car. And though he was crying like a baby now, the tears running down his face, he hardly knew it himself. His hand fell on some unfamiliar object on the seat—a small paper package, crumpled and stiff against his fingers. That old stale package of cigarettes he'd found in the house . . . and he picked it up and fumbled in it till he'd plucked one out and got it between his lips, and felt in his pocket for matches and had to strike several before he got the damn thing lit. Not that he wanted a cigarette anyway. What good was a twist of dry tobacco to him? He wanted a drink, and that was the only thing he wanted, and *they hadn't offered him one in there.* They'd sat around, all of them, with glasses in their hands—did they think he couldn't *see* them? And there were bottles right there on the table behind Mrs. Collins, a dozen bottles anyway. And they hadn't offered him one measly drop. All sitting there swilling it down, even that innocent young girl (if she *was* innocent!), that child—though her shape wasn't any child's any more. And that other Jezebel, practically naked to the waist . . . He hated them all.

No, that wasn't true, because he liked Mrs. Collins, no matter what. She was a nice lady and a good woman. And she'd always been good to him, before. Even if she hadn't given him a drink. And he liked that Mister Norbeck; he was his friend. He'd said so, himself! And that *was* true, because he'd helped him out, bringing him the cigarettes; poor devil, that was what *he* wanted—and them not letting him have any, just because they thought he might die or something. Didn't know they were all going up in smoke themselves, did they? (And serve 'em right for not offering their fellow man a drop in the desert.) He'd been glad to help that poor fella out, knowing his smoking wouldn't make a mite o' difference either way. Why shouldn't they have what they wanted now, what they *craved,* seeing as it was only for the last few times? Why couldn't he have a *drink?* Oh, God Almighty, why did you take away that last drink?

CHAPTER 16

The truth was that Alfred at that moment was the victim of his own earlier precautions. He had not intended to drink at all during that Last Day. He never intended to, for that matter. But his intentions regarding today had been more clear and cogent than ever: he meant to do each small duty to the last, even as he had run errands for Mrs. Collins and that Polish woman of hers all day long, right up to this last trip with one single card from that devil's resort (oh, he'd seen the picture right enough, but he hadn't read the message—that was one thing he'd never stooped to), and then when the final moment came, he would ascend to Abbie without the slightest taint of liquor on his breath.

But Alfred, in his painfully divided soul, knew very well that his intentions could not always be fulfilled. Sometimes he was sick, very sick; and sometimes he was afraid, because there was a chasm which opened at his feet between him and Abbie which he could not be sure of crossing over, and if he didn't—if he couldn't . . . It was not so far across, but when he looked down, it was an abyss so deep that he could not see the bottom. And then the Fear grew up in him until it filled him to the brim, and the only way he could get rid of it was by pouring in something else to take its place. So he had to have that ready, when he needed it. Like medicine on the shelf. And knowing that this day of hope and dread was relentlessly on its way, he had provided for it, and at the same time tried to protect himself. He was in the curious position (for a problem drinker) of being his own detective. If someone else, family or friend, had been there to try to watch and hold him back, he would have used all his cunning to deceive them, but since there was no one but himself to care what happened to his own immortal soul, he had to play two parts, with one constantly plotting to outwit the other.

So he had bought three bottles; that is, he'd paid for one—a mere fifth—and taken it home, but he'd had Larry put the other two aside, to be picked up when he wanted them. His favorite brand, not always to be had in the village, though there were all too many times when any rot-gut would do if he could get no other. Still, there was a feeling that this was a ceremonial occasion, and if there was any drinking to be done, it should be of the best. Though he was shrewd enough to realize that if there had been *three* bottles right at hand, reproachfully staring at him (pleading with him!), he might have felt he had to use them, not to let them go to waste. Alfred was frugal to the core. On the other hand, if he found he did need something on that Night-Before-the-Last, and got a little head start, just to help him on his way, he knew he might use them up too soon, all three of them, and get left *without* . . . Naturally, he did not care to buy a case this time, lest he be caught with part of it to be accounted for among his personal possessions. The rules said one must dispose of all one's most dearly valued personal property, and They would surely know that only such liquid assets were of any real value to Alfred now.

But he had not started during the night, though he'd suffered torments, and had been awake for hours at a time. He told himself that he had spent the night praying—though he had prayed to Abbie, not to God. Prayed to her to forgive him, to wait and watch for him that next morning, to help him get across that bottomless crevasse between earth and heaven, or heaven and hell, whichever it was; *not* to let him fall in, please, God—*please*, Abbie! And when he was once over there . . . He had gone on thinking about her then, because that seemed to fill his mind better than praying. Abbie was very sweet; very small and neatly made; a little faded by the time he got her, to be sure, but she was meek and compliant. Far more so than his first wife, though Bessie had given him three children: four, counting the one that was born dead. But he'd had nothing but trouble with *them*, trouble even feeding them all those first lean years; trouble with them all the way, though he'd done his best to bring them up straight. Beaten the fear of God into them, or tried to. But the boy had turned out not *honest* (a son of his!)— picked up for petty thieving of automobile parts on the streets, before he was fifteen. And the girls were sluts at heart, even earlier, "necking and petting" with the boys—as they called it then—at thirteen or fourteen years of age!

He was well rid of them; didn't know what had become of them by now. He didn't want to know. God knew that he had done his utmost with them while he could. Bessie had taken them all with her when she'd run off with a man that Alfred had never even seen. He would never divorce her of course, any more than he'd have let any action she might bring go uncontested; why would he, when the rights were all on his side? He'd been a good and strictly faithful husband; honest and upright to the letter, and to the last cent of providing for her rotten brood while he had still to call them his. Nobody could ever say otherwise. And if she preferred to live in sin, that was up to her, not up to *him* to give her the satisfaction of her legal freedom. Not up to him to condone her actual wantonness by making it respectable. It was, no doubt, God's own justice that she had died, in childbirth, some years after she had left Alfred.

Those years between had been bitter hard ones for him, for he was not a man to take his pleasure where he found it. He was not even a hard-drinking man, then. But he had *worked* with a kind of frenzy; sometimes night and day, so as not to have to get extra help for the bookkeeping and such; had built up his small grocery business until it was thriving enough to sell out at a good figure, when he came down south to get away from everyone he knew, himself included, and look around for something else to do. That was when he had met Abbie, and married her. And he'd been a good and faithful husband to her; nobody could ever say he'd even looked at another woman. Or if he looked, that was as far as he went, and few men could say as much. And he'd given her everything, within reason, that a woman like Abbie could wish for. Fortunately she was not one to care about clothes and fripperies.

She was a retiring little thing by nature, anyway, which was why they had found their way down to live in this back-hills spot; he had also found it was much cheaper to live here. And he'd built her a house, and given her the stuff to go in it, and fix it up; he'd even gotten all those rose bushes and bulbs and seedlings for her to plant around it . . . And it wasn't until the garden had begun to come between them—no fissure in the earth then, just a small level plot of ground—that he put his foot down. It wasn't so much that he felt she loved the garden, and the flowers, better than she did him (such a notion his brain could not have formulated), as that he suspected darkly that she was using it and them to circumvent him. She was not strong enough to do all that stooping and weeding and digging in the earth—outside of the housework, naturally—so it had to stop. And he had stopped it, effectively enough. But she grew no stronger, puttering around the house all day with the blinds drawn so that she couldn't see out any more; and she had died, anyway, not two years later, as if to spite him—and left him and his conscience alone together.

There was only the bottle to stand between them, on occasion. Not all the time, for Alfred knew that he had two antagonists now, and there were considerable periods when he managed to ignore the one in order to fight off the other. And again there were those moments when it, the insidious go-between, appeared to be his only friend.

It was just such a moment when he had waked that morning, and seen the sunlight which looked blacker than the darkness of the night before—during which he had still kept some tenuous grasp on hope, kept calling across to Abbie . . . But the impersonal sun, which he never doubted would *not* rise tomorrow, laid bare in ugliness the expanse of asphalt all around his house: from his bedroom window, when he got up to shut it—and the bathroom window when he went to wash his stubbly face—and the kitchen window when he went to boil himself a couple of eggs, and dump a spoon of powdered coffee into that same boiling water . . . All around it . . . And he could not deny, even to himself, the reason why Abbie had kept the blinds down for a year and seven months. So he had a drink. He had to have it to get started on this Dreadful Day. After that he'd be all right.

He had two stiff ones before he started off, but by then he knew that he could make it, look the world in the eye—even spit in it if

182

he felt called upon to do so—and take off from any old hilltop that was handy when the moment came. Meantime he felt a sort of fervor for completing any duty that presented itself, including of course the little errands which he was accustomed to perform for Mrs. Collins and several others. He even had a warm and altruistic feeling for them all, and certain ones in particular, like that fellow Norbeck who needed cigarettes, to get *him* through the day. Alfred made sure that he would get them, and get the message about them, once they'd been planted in their hiding place. And though he'd been a bit late in starting on his rounds, and kept stopping to greet people in the village cheerily because he felt so friendly to them all by then, the delay was of no moment. No, nor the fact that a few things were forgotten to begin with; the only important thing was that he deliver everything, no matter how many runs it took. In fact, the number of trips he made began to have a virtue in itself, showing how conscientious he was. So up the hill and down the lane and hither and yon he ran his ancient pickup truck, sometimes singing as he went (Bertha's hymns had given him that idea, and it seemed a good one, to practice for that night), stopping once at his house to have a little snifter because it was an unusually warm day, and after all, he was as steady as a judge. He could tell by the way he drove, with such *authority*. And by the time he had completed his third trip to Mrs. Collins', it was noon or after, so he just slipped the truck up onto his own parking lot—and thought how nice and neat it was not to have any damfool driveways to back in and out of.

He would just get himself a sandwich in his own kitchen (he had figured, at ten slices to the loaf, it cost him possibly four and a half cents—including whatever spread he used—against two bits down at Pete's) and then he'd slip along down again and pick up that brace of bottles from Larry. But meantime he might as well finish up the one he'd started, and then he had forgotten all about the sandwich, and must have dropped off for a little snooze . . . Because when he came to, it had the look of afternoon outdoors, that ominous look of the day which was more than half gone, and sliding faster on its downward descent.

He'd felt like hell then, and had some difficulty figuring things out, like a tough sum in arithmetic. But when he had, he wasted no more time, and walked on down into the village, straight to the store, scarcely noticing the people he passed—though there weren't many around, which was just as well, because he didn't feel at all friendly any more. And when he found the door not only closed, but locked, he couldn't understand it, and peered in through the window and knocked on the glass till his knuckles hurt, getting madder every second. And when he went into the post office next door and demanded of Miss Netta Bloom why the store was closed and where the hell was Larry, she looked severely at him down her sharp nose, and said, "I'm sure I wouldn't know, unless he's gone home."

So then he'd gone to Larry's house, and he had found Larry all right, with his little tight mouth closed up like his store. Wouldn't say anything, except to agree that it was shut up for the day. "Like a holiday, you mean?" asked Alfred cunningly, knowing he could catch him on that one.

"You c'n call it that, if you want to," said Larry.

"But California law doesn't close down on sales of liquor on holidays!" said Alfred triumphantly. "Not even on Sundays!" he thundered.

"How 'bout Election Day?" The query was succinct enough, though after a second's thought the other added, "Yep. Looks more like —*Election* Day to me."

That rocked Alfred on his feet; that is, he was swaying slightly —but it must be on account of the heat, which they weren't used to this early in the year. He was sweating hard. But he kept on prying at the clam which Larry had become—his old friend Larry, his *pal*. He put it on that basis finally: surely he'd do that much for a pal . . . When all was said and done, he'd *bought* that liquor several days ago. Oh no, he hadn't, Larry said; he hadn't paid for it. There was such a literal finality about those last words that Alfred knew he was licked as far as Larry was concerned. He'd sworn at him and turned and left him, muttering with a dark rage that suffused his whole body as he went plodding back through the village, seeing nobody now. In fact, there was nobody around to see.

So he kept on out toward his own place again, and from his desperation, a sort of inspiration was born. Or a memory. Or just the teasing, torturing tail end of a recollection . . . Because he wasn't sure, and he'd broken into a stumbling run as he came near his house—to find out, as soon as he could. The thing he *thought* he remembered was that he used to stow away an occasional bottle in those cupboards he'd built for Abbie's jellies and preserves. Not in the house, but around two sides of the lean-to shed which had been added as a garage for the truck. He'd built them himself, very strong and substantial, with doors to keep out the dust, and locks on them to keep out any prowlers. And it had occurred to him as a wonderful place to hide something from Abbie, because it was the one place she'd never think of looking! The only thing was, they might be locked, and then he'd have to stop and waste more time looking for the keys.

They were locked. He'd tried them all, wrenching and shaking the strong iron catches, like an angry dog. And then went into the house and searched, pulling out one drawer after another, looking in cardboard boxes—every hole or hiding place he could think of, and when he found a few keys he took them out and tried anything that was near the size. But nothing fitted. So he got some tools and tried to screw and pry and jimmy every rough edge or cranny he could find, but his hands were shaking so he couldn't get a purchase anywhere . . . And besides, he'd built those doors to last; put his honest artisan's skill into making them as solid as a vault. So he went back to renew his search in the house for extra keys, which *must* be some place. And the only thing he'd found was an old stale pack of cigarettes that he must have left there before he'd quit smoking. He'd never cared much about smoking anyway—didn't know why *anybody* minded giving that up! But he'd lit one feverishly, hoping it would help him—which it didn't—so he went on with his frantic, scrabbling search for those keys. And he must have spent two hours, all told, before he gave up, sobbing, with his face in his hands.

He'd gone out finally to look at the cupboards one last time. They faced him smugly, across the end wall, and along the right side wall too, clear back to the wide doorway. (He'd never bothered to put in a door on the shed itself.) He'd picked up a tool again, and dropped it after a minute, knowing his own work was impregnable, to himself . . . in his present state. Weak and sick as he was. Even if he got one door open, it might not be the one. He'd told himself he wasn't even sure that there was anything left in there at all. He couldn't remember anything about that first period after Abbie's death. Only the way people had looked at him. Yet some of them had been kind, and he began thinking now which ones—might be kind enough, again—to give a poor parched soul in the wilderness —a little drink . . .

That was when he'd gotten into the truck again and begun cruising around, fitfully, canvassing the village, as if to pay a few last friendly calls, like the self-appointed deacon which he had often fancied himself, in his stronger moments. A couple of times he went in and shook hands lugubriously all around, and said he'd see them up There later on. Once or twice he came to a stop outside a house, and didn't even go in, but after sitting there a minute suddenly started up again and shot off down the lane and around the corner, maybe . . . looking for somebody else. Once was when he thought of Hank Calloway—*good* old Hank, he didn't know why he hadn't gone up there right away. But when he got there, the house was all shut up, doors and windows too, and shades pulled down and he felt as if they'd done it on purpose. Shut the house right in his face. It was as he turned away from trying to peek in the one window on the porch where there was a little crack between sill and blind—the place was empty, all right—that he saw the Professor standing on the other side of his hedge next door, looking at him.

"They've gone away, you know," he called. "Up to Los Angeles for a week or two."

"Oh," said Alfred. "That's too bad. I wanted to see Hank." He felt bowed down, oppressed, that he hadn't seen Hank to say good-bye to him.

"Anything I can do for you?" asked the Prof, and Alfred had looked at him and his long whiskers and wondered if he could: if he had anything in that musty coop of his except books and stuff like that. He didn't know the Professor very well, to tell the truth —had always been a little afraid of his piercing eyes; didn't even know if he was a professor. They just called him that because he knew so much.

But Alfred looked back at him, his thirst clear in his eyes, and said doubtfully, "Well, I don't know. I don't—just know . . ." And the old man had taken him in the side door into the dark hole he called his den, and told him to sit down, and gone out the other door without saying another thing, and after a minute he'd come back and—bless his whiskers—handed Alfred a tumbler with—a drink in it. Not a very big drink, and not very strong . . . and that was all. No bottle any place around, and no offer of any more; the old man didn't even sit down, but stood there watching him thoughtfully as he gulped it down, and then he saw him out the side door again, as briskly as he'd called him in. But it had helped him on his way, wherever he was going next.

He didn't know what had made him think of the Collins place up here on the hill; he'd only been up three-four times already that day, and there wasn't any reason to go again, but it had come to him suddenly that there might have been some mail in that afternoon, and if so it would be the *last letter*, and he couldn't let Mrs. Collins down now. So he'd stopped once more on the main street, and again gone into the hole-in-the-wall which was the U. S. post office, just as Miss Netta was going to shut down her wicket. And sure enough, there was that single card for Mrs. Barton Collins; from Las Vegas of all unholy places. But just the same, he would do his duty to the end—and so he had. (There had been just about enough gas left to make it too, though he had frugally refrained from adding any that day.)

And now here he was, outside the gate. Shut out—in the dark, nothing to light up the blackness except the red gleam of a foul-tasting cigarette. Nevertheless, he stuck it back between his lips as he kicked the old starter with his foot, and wrenched the gear lever into low, and right on from low into high . . . And now he was coming down again—down the hill, leaving them laughing up there behind him, a glass in every hand—and nobody had even offered him a sip. Man's inhumanity to man, that's what it was. And the Professor's little snifter was only such a drop as to be blotted up in the dry caked soil—no, soul, which was Alfred. Like what they called a Trace of Rain, when the whole countryside was gasping and praying for a cloudburst. The only thing that thimbleful had done was to pick the heart up in him for a few minutes, set his rusty wheels rolling a little easier—the way his wheels were rolling now, *down* the hill, and *around* the bend, and down another slant a little faster—and it suddenly became a point of honor not to put on his brakes, but give his wheel a spin around another curve—and *down* again, for Alfred was quite aware that he had been driving with incredible skill all day, and he would show them just how good he was, by God. He missed the edge by inches a couple of times, and marveled at the accuracy of his own eye, the sweet responsiveness of his old tin can of a truck which shot down the last stretch toward the village—but not quite all the way, before it took the turn like a horse galloping into its own barn, except that it did it on a couple of wheels instead of hooves—right up the slight incline to the garage, and there with grand finality, Alfred slammed his foot down on the brake. Or something. It might have been the throttle instead, but it probably would not have mattered either way, because his eye, so uncannily accurate up to this very second, had missed by half an inch.

It was the right side of the doorway which caught the fender, but the truck plowed right along the wall and straight to the end before it stopped, perforce, with a crash of metal, and rending wood as well, as the cupboard doors gave way at last. Alfred sat there, gripping the wheel with all his strength to brace his body against the shock—but his brain took the shock instead, and ceased to function for a moment or two, as the noise of further rending continued behind him, one of the side cupboard doors torn off completely and crashing down on the truck body, which was only kindling in itself. And in front of him, on top of him, everywhere it seemed, there was a hail of jelly glasses, jars, preserves, some dropping with the thud of bullets, some breaking with smaller splintering crashes to join the parent crash, some oozing already, stickily, over

188

the hood, down the cracked windshield. Oddly enough, there was one light still going—one of the small side lights which modern cars no longer have—and for which Alfred now gave absent thanks, for through one unobstructed space still left on the windshield he could see, straight ahead of him, on a shelf even with his eyes, one flat pint of whiskey, *standing* there intact before him. It had been hedged in—carefully hidden by the front rows of jelly jars. Oh, Hallelujah, Heavenly Day!

He got out without much difficulty and went around to climb up on the crumpled hood till he could reach that perfect specimen, standing inviolate like a shrine. Then carefully getting down and backing away, cradling the treasure in his hands, he went along past the undamaged side of the car, taking no notice of the occasional jelly glass smashed into a curious sticky pie on the concrete floor, nor was he aware of what caused the peculiar squidge and squelching noise as he stepped on one here and there. He was vaguely annoyed when he had almost reached the doorway to find that one foot was loath to leave the pavement—stuck fast or something—but he solved the difficulty without even thinking about it, simply walking out of that shoe which, luckily, was old and loose. Nothing—*nothing*—could divert him now, and he hobbled up onto his front porch, where there was one old wooden chair against the wall, and he sat down on it, giving a powerful wrench at the screw cap on the bottle. Then, with an angry groan of frustration, he leaned over it, gripping the whole top of the bottle in his mouth, biting at the seal with his strong front teeth, gnawing around it like a dog on a bone, until he'd broken through the stiff plastic paper. Until with a deep grunt of effort he could unscrew the cap, and then—then, at last—raised the bottle to his lips to let a long, long swallow pour down his throat. Hallelujah . . . Hallelujah, oh, Lord.

He sat there, letting that soak in, and then another gulp, and another, and presently a measure of peace began seeping through him; peace and a grateful dullness, with the sharp edge of anguish moving off at a little distance. The dark world was not so black now; the moon was coming up, and though he could not see the lights of the village from here, he could feel that they were there and he was still a part of that world; even after a time began to feel more friendly to it again. Funny about that; but he couldn't stop to go into it right now. There was something that he must do in a minute, though he couldn't remember what that was, either. It was only when he heard a strange sound, thin and distant—so it couldn't be in his own head—growing clearer for a minute as a breath of air brought it up the draw between the hills (the sound of singing, that was it, singing hymns!), that he was reminded of what it was he was supposed to do. Something about changing his clothes—but *that* seemed altogether too much trouble—and besides, if he didn't start pretty quick, he'd never get there, because the others were on their way already. They might have waited for him, he thought resentfully, but he couldn't seem to stay mad, even about that, for more than a second. They were the only friends he had, when all was said and done. When all was said—and done.

He took another swig, and screwed the cap on, and clutched the bottle to him as he got up. Yes, he better get started. And as he went toward the edge of the porch again his dulled sensory equipment, which had lost the sound of singing now, picked up another kind of signal, strong and pungent. A strange, unpleasant smell, and for an instant he had one more stab of panic, sharp as pain . . . Couldn't be sulphur—already—that he smelled? Was he going to be left behind forever, and not catch up with the ones up on the hill? But he crawled carefully down the two porch steps holding onto the corner pillar with one hand and the bottle with the other, and once out on the flat asphalt in front of the garage, he saw that the fumes —yes, smoke, and plenty of it—were coming out of *there*. A burnt sweet smell, though he still could not identify it, nor had he the slightest recollection of the cigarette which had been jarred from his mouth onto the seat beside him when he had—so firmly and finally—put the car away. All he could take in was that his truck was well on the way to burning up, but he never thought of trying to get it out of there now, especially with those timbers from the door frame lying aslant across the crushed rear end of it.

The one thing further which worked its way through the clouded channels of his mind was a dim but definite recognition that Providence had exacted a relentless balance, disallowing his own secret quibbling about valuable possessions. That little old truck *was* of value to him, after all, and he had disposed of it now—in order to reach and find this bottle, held close to his heart. So that was fair enough, wasn't it? He had the bottle, and the truck was gone. The house was nothing to him; he was even rather glad that he'd never have to live in it again, with all its memories and reminders.

Though, for a moment, as he took one wavering step down the paved slope in the direction of the road, he thought that—maybe —he should try to save the house, because it was Abbie's house, and he had built it for her with the best there was in him. And there was another thought following after that one, like someone calling to him; another reminder, that he wasn't going to be living any place on earth after tonight. So maybe this was the better way to go, trying to save the symbol of something good, to bring to Abbie, for a peace offering. (Or so that he might rest in peace himself?)

He turned around again and looked at those rolls of smoke coming out thick and dark, but with a different texture from the other darkness, and thought he saw a lick of flame, and shuddered at the question which flared up inside him: what if he went back into this fire now, and did what he could to put it out—for Abbie's sake? Would he then be absolved from that other everlasting conflagration?

But they'd been *told* to climb that hill, the word had gone out, and how could he tell which directions to follow? It was all confused, and very confusing to a man as near the end of his rope as Alfred was. If he could just make the grade now, the long grade up that hill . . . But it was a hell of a long pull up, for a sick old man. Thank God there was a little bit still left in the bottle, which he would finish up in a minute now, and throw it away among the bushes, forever. And that would give him the strength to make it to the top or to make his *decision* as to which way—out—he would take.

PART FIVE

"... *nor think the battle long.*"

CHAPTER 17

Dinner was over, and on the whole it had gone off very well. Miriam and Joyce had both been very gay, and seemingly carefree, each in her own way. Roger had come out of himself, or back to himself once more, and when Rog was at his best, he was very good indeed, and Norma was grateful for it, noting how easily he had started Mrs. Mears talking about her travels of years and years ago. Even Mr. Bixby had chuckled once or twice, and she'd been grateful for that too, knowing quite well that she hadn't been very nice to him herself at the outset of the evening. (For no fault of his own, poor inoffensive little man!) It had never struck her before, how his round face, shaped for geniality, so often smiling, was nevertheless —yes, even when he appeared to be beaming sympathetically, it was a sad face. She'd felt, when his glance turned her way during dinner that it was anxious . . . apologetic, could it be?—and reminded herself to be especially nice to him later on.

In any case, dinner was over at last, successfully. And Bertha had surpassed herself. They had all exclaimed, or sighed, or groaned in reluctant ecstasy over the banquet—it was no less—which she had provided. So that was one more lap behind them: one more section of the "Day" clocked off. Morning, noon and afternoon; and here was evening—about which she had felt such foolish apprehension all day—already well on its way. Norma, moving toward the door once more, thought with satisfaction that it must be close to nine o'clock. And to Mrs. Mears, just in front of her, she said optimistically, "D'you know, I think it's nice enough for us to sit outside again for a while, don't you? Seems almost unbelievable, in March—but shall we try it, and see?"

The older woman assented, and Norma turned back for a second, as the others all filtered out to the terrace again, to ask Joseph to bring the coffee out there. It was when she emerged alone that she found Mr. Bixby standing beside the door, quite obviously waiting for her. She smiled warmly, noting that the look of anxiety was still there.

"It was so kind, so good, of you to include me," he began earnestly. "I wish to—thank you."

"But I'm so glad you could be with us, Mr. Bixby! And we've got a nice long evening still ahead of us. It isn't often that we can sit out after dinner is it, even in the summer? But no—I forgot, you haven't been here through the summer—not yet."

"No," he said gravely. "No, I am sorry. It would have been most pleasant, but—"

"But I thought you said—" she began, and paused, trying to think what it was that he had said, only a few minutes before the others had arrived . . . That he was considering renewing his lease, for another six months. That was it. So he couldn't have decided against that just during dinner! But he went on determinedly, ignoring her interruption.

"There is something else that I must say, Mrs. Collins. You've been so very kind. Always. Kind to a stranger. You must not think that I would—take advantage—of that . . ." He stumbled over some difficulty, and she looked at him, perplexed, not knowing what it could be.

"Why, of course not," she murmured, trying to pass it over.

"I did not mean—to be presumptuous," he said, and stopped. It was a full stop. That seemed to be the conclusion of what he was trying to say; she couldn't think what the poor man was talking about. But she said gently, "No, I'd never think that, Mr. Bixby."

"No?" His anxious eyes still questioned her. And then, "Thank you," he said gratefully. "I couldn't leave, without saying just that much. Well. That is all."

"But you're not leaving!" she protested.

"No. No, of course not." Suddenly he smiled all around the full beaming circumference of his face, and shrugged his shoulders and spread his hands. "First, I go beyond myself," he said. "And now —I am not even polite, making you think I eat, and run! But I shall not be coming any more to the little village. It is better so. And I thought I might not have the opportunity—later, among your good friends, to apologize for what I said in a foolish moment."

Oh really, Norma thought, this was getting a bit too much, and furthermore, it had no bearing on what had been said earlier. She had spoken sharply for a moment, shown her annoyance; yes, she realized that. But the fact that he couldn't possibly know *why* she had been cross—that was the very thing which had left her feeling slightly conscience-stricken about him. And here was he, apologizing . . . for what? He thought he had offended her; she thought she had offended him! Well, obviously she had, but this was getting silly. She remembered, only just in time, not to be cross with him again, if he was so abnormally sensitive.

"And now," she said firmly, "let's go and have our coffee."

"Yes," he agreed at once. "Yes, thank you. But first—I think I would like to go to the bathroom."

She almost burst out laughing then, not only at the unexpected shift of topic but at the way his matter-of-factness had exceeded her own. Not to be outdone she said, "Why certainly—" and led the way back to the living-room entrance and shooed him through the doorway ahead of her and to the left into her own room where the light was on, showing the bathroom door ajar beyond. And as she stepped back for him to pass by her, she noticed for the first time that he had that ridiculous pinkish filing envelope tucked under his arm. She had forgotten about it; wondered now if he had had it parked under his chair all during dinner, wondered if he slept with it under his pillow. She choked down her incipient mirth and turned back quickly toward the patio to hide her widening smile in the half-light.

The rest were all standing around out there, drifting for the moment like separate particles in a saturated solution which has been well shaken before settling down again, in slightly different formation. The chairs, in fact, had been shifted somewhat since before dinner. Joseph, assuming that the guests would not be sitting outdoors again that night, had returned the furniture to its daytime pattern, widening and flattening the intimacy of the semicircle, so

197

that it now appeared the setting for some other tableau, broader in scope, less personal perhaps. The moon was up now, nearly full, and spreading a diffused and cloudy radiance over everything outside the enclosed garden. The lamps beside each of the terrace doors were lighted also, and Norma saw that Joseph had the coffee tray arranged at the end of the glass-topped table, and was looking for her, so she went over to fulfill her final dinner rites.

She was intent upon these for the next few minutes, pouring the coffee—and into her best cups, too, she noted, the tiny eggshell ones which she almost never used, but Bertha patently regarded this as the one, and final, occasion for which they had been treasured all these years. Glancing up now and then, she saw that Mrs. Mears had in due course seated herself in one of the two large chairs with their backs toward the house and terrace. Absently, too, she heard Don still smacking his lips over the dinner which he had just consumed.

"Boy, oh *boy*, I never ate such a meal in my life! I'm not sure I can bend to sit down."

"Oh, that's the way we always feed people, just before they go to heaven, or you-know-where," Joyce said blithely. "Like the man in death row who gets his choice of favorite foods."

"Yeah," said Roger, "and you may not be fooling, my child! I know one thing—if I do sit down, I may never get up again." He gave a heavy grunt, suiting the action to his words, and Norma looked up quickly in momentary concern. She knew he wasn't supposed to eat such heavy meals, and hoped he hadn't overdone it . . . But, my goodness, she couldn't watch every forkful a person put into his mouth! Not even—Roger.

When she had finished pouring the coffee and taken her own cup over to join the others, she saw that they had all settled themselves by this time, and she dropped down into the other big chair beside Mrs. Mears—quickly and unobtrusively, so that the men wouldn't have to get up again—observing as she did so that Mr. Bixby had returned and was now sitting in one of the straight chairs, over next to Roger, while Jim had planted himself on the flat end of the chaise on Rog's other side, his knees spread wide, the cup and saucer held with awkward care in his big paws. Three men in a clump . . . Oh well, if they'd rather huddle and talk business or baseball—what difference did it make? The fourth man, she noted, was ensconced on the long swing over to her left, with Miriam and Joyce on either side of him. And which of them had engineered *that?* she wondered. Miriam, or Joyce—or Don himself? Ah well, Joyce ought to be able to take care of herself, and she did look delectable tonight in that pink thing. Her mother knew, if anyone did, that one had best not be lulled by that innocent apple-blossom look into thinking that the child was not alert and fully aware of what went on around her. Even a mite dangerous in her insight and her candor. But Norma didn't care to follow out that line of thought about her daughter . . . Any more than she wished to think about Rog—except as a pleasant guest, on a pleasant evening.

The lovely evening, which had been such a long time coming, and which would soon be gone. She and Mrs. Mears had the best place from which to contemplate it, as indeed they should: the two dowagers in their box seats, with a clear view across to the distant hills whose outlines grew more distinct as one's eyes became accustomed to the diffused dimness out there; a darkness permeated with a light so subtle that it was like faith, implicit yet invisible. There was another sort of light out there, too—off to the right a bit—a bare suggestion of it as though the dusk itself was faintly rose-colored; a trace of afterglow perhaps, though surely it was late for that. Norma thought idly of mentioning it, decided it was a trick of her own vision, and besides, she wanted to hold onto the stillness and the peace as long as she could. A sort of lull had fallen on her little party—but not, she hoped, the lull before the storm! They were all feeling the after-dinner letdown, no doubt; heavy, full of food, the exhilaration of the cocktails evaporated, no other sort of stimulant yet offered. (She thought belatedly of liqueurs, the only thing which Joseph had forgotten, but she made no move.)

It was that point when one didn't know whether they were all enjoying themselves, digesting in a state of pleasant torpor, or beginning to get bored, wondering when they could go home, or go to bed. Conversation started up here and there, but it was fitful, sporadic. They were not spaced widely enough to be actually detached, but for the present nothing joined the three groups together. One of those moments came when no one spoke at all. Over in the swing, the muffled giggling caused by some witticism of Don's had ceased, almost as though it had been hushed in readiness for what came next. Even the business talk between the two older men had idled to a stop, following a remark of Roger's, as impersonal as a growl of thunder as he muttered, "We know well enough what keeps the whole balance of the economy so precarious—or we ought to. And it's not installment buying, or the farm problem, or any other strictly internal problem." He hadn't said war, or possible war—or cold or hot—and Norma prayed that he wouldn't continue in that vein. He did not, and Mr. Bixby did not reply directly. She was even rather thankful when the latter addressed his next remark to Jim.

"You planning to go into business, young man?" he asked politely; an idle inquiry, surely. But Jim looked up at the older man, as if startled by the question. And he snapped his answer back, short and fast.

"No," he said. "I'm not making any plans."

The others had been only half listening until now, but it was Jim's curt reply which focused their attention suddenly upon him. And when he added, "I'm waiting to be called up, see? Letting the government do my planning for me—" there was no lessening of hostility in his tone.

"I see," said Mr. Bixby mildly. "I thought—" He looked perplexed, but evidently decided not to pursue the sentence he had begun.

Even then, the whole thing might well have rested there, and gone no farther, if Miriam had not spoken up in protest, impulsively, from the far end of the dusky ellipse.

"But, Jim!" she said, and stopped, as Mr. Bixby had. But having checked herself, she found that Jim had turned toward her and was waiting, and so were the others, for what she had been about to say, so that she had to go on in some fashion. "Oh well, you just mean you aren't saying what you're going to do, afterward." She dismissed it lightly, as if realizing that she had misunderstood his reply to Mr. Bixby. But Jim was obdurate.

"No, I mean I just don't see any use in laying plans two years ahead." Replying to Miriam instead of Bixby, the antagonism had gone out of his voice, which made it all the more plain that there was something about the older man which Jim mistrusted or resented. To Norma, it seemed best to head off any further inquiry from that source.

But when she put in casually, as a signal to detour—but not too abruptly, "Well, there'll be college to finish up first, won't there, Jim? Which will give you time to plan from there on," it did not accomplish what she had intended, and Jim looked over at her as if she too, Mom Collins, had joined the ranks of the inquisitors.

"Maybe," he said. "And then again, maybe not, if I don't go back to college. The whole point is, *I* don't know what kind of a setup I'm coming back to a couple years from now."

"Oh, Jim! You sound like *Rog!*" The exclamation had broken from Miriam before she could stop it that time—instinct with protest and a sort of distressed impatience. It was clear to everybody now, that that was what she had started to say before, and a shock of slightly startled surprise ran around the open circuit of the group.

"And that, my boy, is very bad," said Roger dryly, inviting them to laugh it off. But no one seemed to care to pick up something which might prove to be a very hot wire. So Rog himself went on, "My wife means that I've grown near-sighted, Jim. Can't see beyond tomorrow, like these poor devils that are going to climb that hill tonight. Can't see beyond my nose, perhaps . . . and my nose smells something sulphurous in the wind," he muttered. But no one laughed at that, either.

"What I mean, darling," said Miriam swiftly and smoothly now, "is that *your* horizon has been cut down, of necessity—foreshortened, shall we say?—by a special and temporary situation. But Jim's too *young* to feel that way. To wait for the future to come to him, instead of—oh, at least reaching for it, going out to meet it!"

"How right you are, my dear. That only the young have any license to reach for the future. But nowadays, even they . . . oh yes, I see Jim's point, perfectly."

"Of course you do!" she shot back. "You won't admit there *is* a future, for anybody. That's what I'm talking about—" But Norma cut her off. This had to stop.

"Surely we all know how hard it is for young people to make any long-range plans nowadays," she said firmly, trying to make the subject sound quite academic. "There are so many obstacles—aren't there?—before they can even get started. So much—uncertainty." And that, she thought, was sufficiently banal to make them drop it in sheer boredom. But it seemed to have given Miriam time to catch her breath, recover her control.

"Oh dear, yes, even I'm bright enough to see that!" she said coolly. "But I still think it's all wrong, at any age. Not to press ahead, regardless . . . not even plan or *look* ahead, just because you can't see all the way." She turned to toss away her last cigarette, concluding with the detachment of a slight disdain. "It's an attitude of complete negation, that's all."

"But I don't feel negative, Mrs. Norbeck," Jim said, and he sounded puzzled, now. He was confused by the cross-currents which he could feel moving back and forth but he still had the impression that they were eddying around *him*, and the personal question which old Bixby had first put to him. (The old fool ought to've known that nobody could plan anything these days, and then they wouldn't't've gotten into this rigmarole.) "I guess I'm just not in such a terrible hurry—about some things, that is—as some people think I ought to be. I've got certain immediate problems to work out," he added, with that curious dignity which had a way of rising up in him without his knowing it, like another presence, standing within, and taller than he was. "And seeing as I've got a couple years to put in first— well, trying to map out any route now seems kind of like trying to see around a corner forty-five miles away. Too much like a blind date, maybe."

"With the faceless future, eh?" remarked Don Landis unexpectedly.

"Sure," Jim agreed. "Oh, sure. No face—no shape—nobody can even tell you at second-hand what the gal looks like."

"Well, that's exactly what you've got, brother," said Don lazily. "A date with fate." It sounded much too glib, coming from him. But Roger had already taken hold of Don's phrase and given it his own inevitable twist.

"Haven't we all, in one way or another?" he asked.

"Oh, that's all very well," said Miriam impatiently. "But it's *not* what I was talking about."

"I'm not sure I know what we are talking about! Does anybody?" Norma tried again, on a rueful, humorous inflection. "Or how we ever got into it." And that was that, her tone seemed to say, dismissing the matter, and inviting anyone to begin a pleasanter word game, more suitable for a party. But she had reckoned without her own child.

"I think—we started with Mr. Bixby's asking Jim what his plans were." Joyce spoke for the first time, gravely, with an effect of judicial interest in the original topic.

"And I said I hadn't any," Jim put in.

"And Roger said he saw your viewpoint perfectly," flashed Miriam. "And *I* said—"

"Look," Jim insisted earnestly. "I haven't *got* any view. That's all I was trying to say, right from the start, so why make something else out of it?"

"Ex-actly." That, from Roger, was more of a punctuation mark than a comment. A flat period . . . But then he added, as if unable to let it stand alone, "No view. No outlook. No certainty to build on. No—security, at any age. Does anybody begin to get the idea yet?"

Miriam gave a long dramatic sigh, and sank back in the swing as though relinquishing, if not resigning, her erect position.

"Oh, dear heaven, here we go again. Give me a cigarette, Don. My case is empty."

Don turned attentively to do her bidding, while Roger gazed across at them, a somber gaze, and Jim looked from one to the other and then back at Norma, uneasily, seeing at last that this debate was no longer personal to him, and deciding to keep his mouth shut from here on.

It was Joyce, again, who broke the pause.

"What *is* security?" she asked, almost curiously.

"Why, there you are," said Roger to the night at large. "Our youngest member doesn't even know what it is."

"Well, people talk so much about it," the girl said in her thoughtful, candid voice. "Sometimes I wonder what they really mean by it."

"I think we chiefly mean—safety, don't we?" her mother hazarded, resigning herself at last to their choice of parlor games. If this was the way they wanted to spend the evening—why, so be it.

"But safety—from what?" persisted Joyce. "From everything that scares us? Surely we're not such sissies as all that!"

"I think, Miss Joyce," said Mr. Bixby gently, "that each one asks only to be safe from what he has learned to fear." He had for some minutes remained so quiet that that brief comment, so softly spoken, had the somewhat startling effect of an unexpected return to their midst. Roger threw him a quick look as if wondering where he had come from.

"That's right enough," he agreed. "And we could say the very conception of security takes different forms according to the period or place which has conditioned us. During the thirties, for most of *us*, it meant a job—and three square meals a day. While during the war, it meant—a night without bombs, say. But now . . . there isn't any at all."

"You mean there is no longer any such thing—as security?" asked Joyce. "Not anywhere?"

"There never was," said Mrs. Mears, and for an instant the sound and the surprise of this new voice seemed to hold them all spellbound. But Jim, who'd waited for that voice so long—waited for it to *say* something—felt let down.

"Aw, Gran," he protested. "Aren't you kind of forgetting? It was a pretty different setup when you were growing up, wasn't it?"

"Certainly," she replied crisply. "But there was no security. There were merely different things that people feared, in different places, as Mr. Norbeck has said. On different levels, if you like. There was far more poverty—more widespread, more unrelieved. There was always disease and death—and less knowledge to fight it off. There was insanity (and insanity was a hopeless horror, then) . . . There was crime . . ." She seemed to hesitate a fraction of a second. "And cruelty . . . Cruelty is not a new invention, you know. There was even war, now and then. Here and there," she finished, with a curious effect of detachment, born of the enormity of her final understatement.

"'Here and there,'" repeated Roger, seizing on it grimly. "And now and then! That's *it*. The wars were bloody enough, God knows, but they still had some limits of time and space. There *were* safe places, in other words, large areas where people could live without terror, as on bedrock."

"Not in California, they couldn't!" Don retorted in an audible aside to Miriam, but no one laughed, and no one was diverted.

"Nevertheless," said Roger doggedly, "we used to regard most of the earth's surface as solid ground to live—and build on."

"We used to think there was such a thing as a safe and sheltered life," Mrs. Mears stated. "But we were wrong."

"They do say some types of shelters . . ." Don suggested dreamily.

"No," said Mrs. Mears.

"No good?" he asked, with mock concern, and Norma heard Miriam give a stifled sound, just a breath of laughter, or sheer hysteria perhaps. At the same time, there was another sound, from somewhere off behind the swing—a quick, sharp interchange of voices which seemed for a moment to have broken out of nothing; to have broken rudely into the conversation here, so that Miriam turned her head with a startled jerk as though to see who had spoken over her shoulder. And Norma, herself alarmed by the unintelligible sounds of altercation, saw Joyce straighten up alertly and lift her hand to catch her mother's attention, while her look said plainly, There—that's what I was telling you about, this afternoon. But it was only a moment, a very few seconds, before the voices had ceased as suddenly as they'd begun, and if Mrs. Mears had heard them at all, she gave no sign, as she followed up Don's latest flippancy.

"Even if the concrete walls were ten feet thick—there might be someone in that shelter with you, young man," she said almost sternly. "Someone too close to get away from."

"Someone—oh yes—" said Miriam, and broke off, and there was no laughter in that breath. It seemed there had been no other voices either, except these, out here, pursuing their own preoccupation.

"You mean," Joyce said doubtfully to Mrs. Mears, "that the closer we are to someone else, the more vulnerable we can be, don't you? Or—one might even be all alone in the shelter, and still not safe—from what's inside you."

"Which brings us to the elementary proposition that 'four walls do not a prison make,' nor a fortress either," said Don, in a tone of such patent irony that Norma wondered once again why each of his remarks, even when they seemed to hit the mark, had that flat ring. He was not stupid, this young man, but there was something lacking. Sincerity, perhaps. He was not shallow—but empty. Full of quotations and clichés, but he didn't use them the way most people did who were given to such phrases, simply and trustingly because they believed them. There was no belief in him.

She looked at him searchingly, and said in quiet reproof, "Well, Don, this is a fairly elementary discussion, after all, no matter how we stumbled into it. And we don't pretend to be profound thinkers, any of us. At least, I don't suppose we do."

"Oh hell, who said we did?" Roger broke in roughly. "We're just a group of average, middling-intelligent people, trying to use our heads for a change, but we are talking about entirely different things."

"*Are* we?" said Mrs. Mears distantly. But distinctly.

"I think we are, Mrs. Mears. You're speaking of the psychological, personal security of the individual. I'm not. I'm talking about that person's whole world—everybody's world—and the insecurity, the complete uncertainty today, of its continued existence."

There was no answer to that, or if so, no one had an answer ready. The explosive force with which he'd spoken had knocked flat their game of words, momentarily. Until Jim reached out, gingerly, to pick one up, like a jackstraw. "There you are," he muttered. "That's the one. Uncertainty. That's where we started, anyway."

"Check," said Don. "That's where we came in. Or am I wrong?" he added politely, a little bored now, and Miriam laughed again, unexpectedly, though it was anything but a happy sound.

"Oh yes, you're right, Don. Both you and Jim. That's where we started, and that's as far as we ever get. It's so futile, this kind of talk—that's what I keep telling Rog, but he will keep trying to Face the Facts, as he calls it."

"Sorry," said Roger briefly.

"No, I'm sorry." Joyce spoke up in quick apology, as if it had all been her fault. "I got too serious—or too curious, I guess. It's something about this funny night, and those people all going up there, thinking they . . ." She stood up, suddenly, as if by putting the group into motion she would get the party going again. But no one else stirred.

"You gotta date or something? Where you going, child?" Don asked lazily, and Joyce looked down at him.

"I don't know," she admitted.

"Doesn't know where she's going," he said indulgently. "Well, no more do any of us. That much has been established in this conclave. By default. Sit down, woman, and enjoy the beautiful uncertainty of a moonlight night, can't you?" He reached to pull her back beside him, and Norma, across the way, felt her lips tightening, not at the possessive (or was it merely greedy?) gesture but the insidious methods that he used. Calling her "child" one moment, for example, and "woman" in the next breath! That man was dangerous, she thought.

But Miriam had just said, "I know where I'd like to go, tonight," softly, as though daring one to guess.

"Still want to go up that hill again, don't you?" Don responded indulgently—or, Norma thought, it might be with a certain shrewdness, for she saw Miriam nod smilingly.

"I'd like to go up there with all those other watchers of the night," she said dreamily. "I really would."

"To get away from it all, I presume," said Roger, in a grumpy tone.

"Well, you could go up, you know," Joyce offered practically. "Not to the top of *the* Hill necessarily, but around the path on the other ridge, over there—" She turned slightly where she stood, and her arm glimmered for a second in the light from the kitchen windows, as she pointed toward the bulky shadow of the nearest hill.

"Yes, I know," said Miriam quietly, with a suggestive mischief in her voice now which made her sound almost demure. "I walked over there this morning."

"I heard you the first time," Don retorted. "Just casing the joint, weren't you? My God, have I got to go mountain climbing with you girls, on top of that dinner, and this conversation? Come on, Joyce honey, sit down and quit rocking the boat, can't you?"

For he still had Joyce's hand, gently trying to draw her down on the swing again, while across the lawn Jim seethed, and his teeth were tightly clamped, and a few feet nearer Norma prayed, Oh, Joey—don't! Don't like that man too much . . . And don't let him play you off against a woman like Miriam . . .

CHAPTER 18

Joyce did not pull away from him, yet she did not sit down beside him either. She was still standing, in the same spot, her knee close to his, but she had turned her head from looking off at the dark hillside, a complete half-turn until she was looking past him toward the kitchen windows. And then her glance came back and circled the whole group, questioningly.

"D'you know, there's something similar," she said slowly, "between these two things—the end-of-the-world, as they see it coming . . . and as *we* fear it may. Don't any of you get what I mean?"

"Yes," her mother replied calmly. "The same idea struck me earlier today, though I admit it seemed a bit far-fetched."

"It's more than far-fetched," said Roger. "It's plain damn nonsense."

"*Rog!*" his wife protested.

"I beg your pardon, Norma—and Joyce, my dear . . . but if we're going to talk about these things at all, we'd better keep some clear distinction between reality and fantasy, hadn't we?"

"Of course, Rog," Norma said. "But there *is* something—an eerie sort of resemblance—more of a reminder, maybe."

"In one case," Roger said inexorably, "we are trying to estimate and face up to a terrible reality. In the other, these people have worked themselves up to a fever of hysteria over what is nothing more than superstitious make-believe, sheer self-delusion."

Joyce had sat down again at last, on the edge of the swing seat, and she had withdrawn her hand from Don's grasp and linked her fingers together around her knees.

"All that I was trying to bring out," she persisted, "was that there was just a faint family resemblance between *their* end of the world—and ours."

"And that we're all equally capable of building up delusions," put in Miriam, pointedly.

"Maybe theirs is more like a symbol," Norma suggested hesitantly. "Unconscious, you know, but expressing this world-wide fear of some very imminent end."

"Okay—okay, so maybe it *is* a psychological phenomenon. You will admit, however, that there is one slight difference between our village friends and the objective view which I assume we're trying for. They are rushing toward the end, you might say, as fast as they can get there. Whereas, if we have one coherent thought left among us, it is to prevent the end from arriving on this earth."

"In other words, they only want to get the hell out of here. Or off of here!" said Don, with a sardonic chuckle, but Norma, thinking of the different ones she knew, said softly, "I don't suppose any one of them has been very happy, here. They're tired of the struggle and of coping with this world, poor souls—so this is their way out."

"All right, all right!" said Roger. "But at least we're trying to stand and meet reality on its own terms, whatever they may be. Or are we?" His voice dropped on the question.

"Reality *is*—what one believes in," said Mrs. Mears austerely. "Whether it's the imminent possibility of leaving this earth before morning . . . or the looming probability of atomic destruction."

Roger shook his head, like a wet dog. "I'm sorry, Mrs. Mears, I suppose that's axiomatic today; what one thinks, *is*, and so on. But look at it, for God's sake! Just because fifty or a hundred-odd people, more or less, think they're going to walk off that hilltop into eternity—doesn't mean that any single one of them is not going to be here for breakfast tomorrow morning, now does it?"

A full second passed before the old lady replied stiffly, "That will be answered—tomorrow, Mr. Norbeck."

Jim felt a sudden horrid prickling in his hair, and took his head in his hands to quiet it, because for a minute there . . . but of course she didn't mean what the words might have meant. She didn't believe that stuff! She couldn't possibly.

"Meantime," Joyce said thoughtfully, "tonight *is* the end, to Bertha—and Miss Amelia—and poor old Alfred—so it's much more real to them than anything they've read or heard, about what might happen, say next year . . . or even next month—"

"Or tomorrow morning," Roger said, so matter-of-factly that it took a moment for the impact to reach home.

"*Tomorrow!*" Joyce said, catching her breath with a slight gasp.

"Why not?" he said, and left it there in a silence which began to hang there uncomfortably, until Don Landis broke it up.

"Br-rother! Am I glad I got invited up here for tonight! Your hillside's better than any bomb shelter they've got in town," he remarked to Norma appreciatively, and for that moment she was also rather glad that he was there, since he appeared to be the only person present capable of going Roger one better and making what he'd said more ridiculous than ominous.

"You wouldn't be forgetting, would you," the latter cut back dryly, "that radioactive particles could be sucked right down these canyons? Or the possible distance they estimate that blast alone can carry, now? Or that our water and power and communications would be—well, let's just say suspended?"

Norma saw Miriam's head twist convulsively toward Don; saw him reach to take her hand, and was really glad that he was close by to do so. As for herself, her spine had stiffened more with indignation than with fright, and she said sharply, "Roger—*really!* What do you think you're doing? Telling ghost stories to terrify the children?"

"All right, Norma." He accepted the rebuke quietly, but he did not apologize for his grim extravaganza, if indeed it could be called that. "Joyce seemed surprised and shocked that I should be thinking in literal terms of tomorrow, and I was simply trying to bring the thing into close enough focus to look at it—as an immediate possibility, which I believe it is . . . or could be. The eventual tomorrow comes, some day, you know."

No satire there. No dramatic impact. Just a quiet statement. The faintest shudder seemed to pass around the group, as though a chill damp draught had stirred among them, but the evening was still perfectly quiet, though a little darker now, for the moon had slipped down out of sight. Norma had almost a physical sense of trying to shake off that leaden cold which went to one's very marrow. Perhaps it was actually getting cool out here—not only in her imagination, and she turned toward Mrs. Mears, meaning to ask if she'd like a wrap or would rather move indoors. But her eye fell on her coffee cup which was still there on the flat chair-arm, and glancing across to the small table near Roger and Mr. Bixby, she could see the glimmering shapes of other cups and saucers, and for a moment she was sidetracked by the reflection that it was odd of Joseph to have forgotten to come back for them. Maybe she'd better gather them up herself and take them out . . . But the lead in her bones was heavy as well as cold. (As though paralyzed, Roger had said, earlier that day.) Yet it was dreadful of him to spoil the evening for everybody this way. Only Joyce—still Joyce!—hanging onto Rope and reason; undismayed, undefeated. Trying to hold her own against Roger's attitude, or what he represented.

"Look, Rog—you say the eventual tomorrow comes. But what you really mean is that the *event* scheduled for tomorrow is bound to come—isn't that it? And sometimes, scheduled events are postponed, or even called off."

"Accounta rain," drawled Don. "Look, child—were you on the debating team in your class, or something? Just the same, I think the gal has you there, Norbeck. Though of course," he ruminated solemnly, "there's always the little matter of a rain check." Was he still holding Miriam's hand, while he said that? Norma couldn't tell; she only saw that he was not holding Joyce's. And suddenly Roger exploded.

"Oh hell," he broke out, "I don't care what kind of a goddamn metaphor we use. This thing is real—horribly real—and possibly imminent. Can't any of you get that through your heads?"

211

"But is it, Rog?" Norma said, keeping her voice low, though she would really have liked to let go with a good loud scream—tell them all to go home—go to bed—and never come back here again. But apparently one just had to keep on arguing reasonably—to the end. "I know a great many people thought it was imminent a while ago, but that—"

"Well, let me say here, just to keep the record straight, that it was not the bird-brains who thought it was, Norma. Nor the easily panicked man-in-the-street. It was only the best brains in the world— that's all. The few great scientists, the few real statesmen—they're the ones who've been the most gravely troubled. The most fearful, if you like."

"But that was some time ago. Time moves so fast . . ." said Norma. "And things do change. The leaders themselves, their viewpoints and their methods—oh, everything, Rog!"

She knew she wasn't equipped to express herself in such matters, but for a moment he didn't answer and she hoped she'd stopped him at last. Then, almost inaudibly at first, he began muttering.

"Like something we dreamt last night. Last year. Just a nasty old nightmare." His voice rose oddly, not loudly, but in pitch. "A great big bugaboo—and isn't it a relief that it went away! We *told* you it would go away if you'd just pretend it wasn't there!" His abrupt falsetto was grotesque, but nobody even tittered. Norma gathered her breath and said—still forcing herself to say it steadily, "That isn't funny, Rog. And it ignores the almost superhuman effort that men have made to try to come together."

"I wasn't trying to be funny," he said. "I was crying out to heaven, in my own peculiar way. And I was *not* discounting the effort, so help me. Our people have been making a magnificent try— and I hope to God they'll keep on trying. Never quit trying. We can *never* quit trying!"

Suddenly he had thrust himself up from his chair and was standing over them, himself a looming shadow. Yet it was to get away from them rather than threaten them that he took a few strides past Jim, out to the open side of the dim circle of people. Norma thought, anxious for him now, that he should not be getting so excited; she shouldn't have contradicted him; they shouldn't have got into this at all, knowing what an obsession it was with Roger. But he had turned back halfway toward them, and spoke in a carefully measured way.

"Just because the others are more amiable, periodically, when it suits their purpose to be so . . . No, that doesn't convince me. Not overnight, or even in a few months' time, or a few years' . . . It will take many years to make sure—even of who's on our side. It's quite conceivable, you know, that the whole alignment will change also. As to people smiling, making large promises, and the sun peeping out coyly from under the black overcast . . . Though at the moment, of course, it's gone under again," he pointed out, with a detachment which was strangely flat in contrast to his roughness of a moment before. "Just another crisis, which at first seemed just a small black cloud, no bigger than a man's hand," he finished speculatively.

Joyce said in a rather small voice, "So—you think there could be—I mean, even this present crisis *might* be—the very one—" And she stopped also, finding there was nowhere to go beyond that word.

"My dear Joyce, I'm no prophet. *I* don't have premonitions. I'm not even a reporter any more. All I see is that this thing has gone on—and on—for more years than you can remember, my dear. Sometimes the tension is worse at some points while seemingly easier at others. And we've had repeated crises, over and over again. We may have many more. We've had waves of hope, too. But meantime the weapons on both sides have got bigger—no, I'll spare you the bigger-and-better line. Just more deadly."

"Oh, my God," breathed Miriam. "Can't someone stop him?" (Turning with a gesture of appeal—to Norma—back to Don—even looking over at Jim, as a last faint resort.) But Roger went plodding on, head down again, and standing still.

"So the danger is always there, as I see it. I believe it will be there as long as we live, Joyce—all of us here tonight. Even you and Jim. You kids . . . And one of these days—or years—somebody's likely to put his finger on the push-button, maybe intentionally, maybe just because he's nervous. Either way, it'll be sudden. And that's about the only thing we can count on. It won't even be as far ahead of us as tomorrow. Tonight—" His speech had come to an end without a period, so abruptly that it gave his listeners the feeling of being in a car, crashed to a sudden stop against an unyielding wall. Only Miriam kept on, like a flying body thrown clear, still crying out.

"But what earthly good does it do for *us* to beat our brains out now—tonight—against something that's beyond our comprehension? You've said yourself only the greatest minds can begin to grasp the possibilities, and there's nothing we can *do* about it."

"Well, that's a matter of opinion. There's such a thing as co-operation," Roger mentioned, "even if it's only by way of learning some of the elementary principles of self-preservation—if, and when. But that's too obvious to discuss."

"Many people," said Mrs. Mears, "are already engaged in the struggle for self-preservation, Mr. Norbeck. Mere survival—whether their battle is for the necessities of life—or against disease, or some other—mortal—infirmity. Had you thought of that? When someone has all he can do to keep his head above water, someone he loves from sinking too, it may be—any thought beyond the immediate urgent present becomes rather academic, don't you think?"

"And *meantime*," Miriam said, and there was pleading in her voice now, as well as desperation, "with all of us, all the while, we have to go on living somehow, Rog."

"We can *not* go on living in our sleep," said Roger sternly. "Unless we wish to wake up dead, some morning . . . Or continue . . . sleeping," he muttered, turning away from them all and walking out into the farther shadows of the patio, as though wading out into darker, deeper water. Norma had a quick impulse to call out after him, and choked it down. And then she looked back at Miriam, who had leaned her forehead on her hand, covering her eyes, and her voice was very low. But they all heard her.

"You see—that's what he believes," she said sadly. "He never used to be like that, when he was working. He used to go all out for the facts . . . report the evidence, as he called it. And analyze what he reported, of course. But he didn't try to drink up all the poison in it, personally."

Norma felt almost sickeningly sorry for them both; for Roger, living with that nightmare, day and night, and for Miriam, who had to live with it too. She saw that he had come back to the edge of the group, quietly, like one of the shadows out there, materializing, and she didn't know whether he had heard Miriam's last words or not.

"Well, I'm sorry, gang," he said. "I shouldn't have started sounding off like that. Spoiling your pleasant evening . . . But it's the ingenuous refusal of the average citizen to stop and think—and look a fact in the face, no matter how ugly its mug may be—that's what gets me. Makes me a little rabid, I guess."

Joyce broke in with the urgency of someone who had seen a strange light, suddenly.

"D'you know what, Rog? I think you *want* us to be scared!"

"Maybe I do," he answered calmly. "Though I assure you I wasn't consciously trying to frighten anybody, myself." He looked around as if to apologize to someone there, and then continued, "But now you bring it up—yes, I think a little fright is necessary, at this point. And perhaps always."

"Oh, Roger, no!" Norma exclaimed. "That's what we've done for far too long, already. Too many have lived in fear, and it's all wrong."

"I know. It would seem so. And yet, as Mr. Bixby pointed out, earlier, we live and learn, by fear. From the time we're infants. A little fear teaches us to respect hot things that burn—and sharp things that cut us—and falling off high places."

"That's caution," said Norma quickly. "Not terror. Not nameless dread, growing into panic."

"Nameless," Roger repeated. "Yes, that would be running beyond the scope of what is real, once more; like our neighbors from the village. But this thing has a name, and it is real. It is the atom bomb, my friends: the hydrogen bomb, in case anyone needs further reminding—whether delivered by plane or guided missile, or whatever. Nuclear warfare. And the only known deterrent which we have so far found is fear. A mutual, respectful fear—on both sides. That may still save us, you know. A little fear, squarely faced, may forestall that ultimate terror, and what follows after."

"And how are you going to keep a little fear from getting out of control?" demanded Miriam. "If everybody gets so frightened that they don't know which way to move—and strike out blindly—and hit that very push-button which you mentioned—"

"Yes," Norma said. "Or it could become a sort of—paralysis. Stopping us short, in dead center, afraid to move in any direction at all." She could feel herself saying that deliberately, hear the words as they came out, the particular word which he had used that morning, and she was shocked by her own ruthlessness in reminding him of it. But it was Jim's voice which answered, out of the pocket of quiet where he had stayed for so long that she'd almost forgotten he was there.

"You meant that—for me, didn't you, Mom Collins?"

"No, Jim. She meant it for me," Roger replied for her. "And I admit the reminder may be justified. Maybe there is no way of keeping fear in check, once it is conceived; of using it and not becoming its victim. But I don't know of any other prod which is sharp enough to keep us alert. All right, Norma," he said harshly, "maybe I am frozen into uselessness by my own fear that the future will make any present egotistical endeavor of mine—rather less than useless, shall we say? But if the rest of you were more afraid, I could be less so. I could sleep better at night, if others slept less easily, were not themselves lulled by this brand of fatalistic complaisance. I guess that's about the size of it, and you can think me a monster if you want to."

"Oh, look here, Norbeck, that's laying it on, you know. The government isn't being lulled any, to speak of. They're keeping their powder dry—and that's their business, incidentally."

Roger's head came up, to gaze the length of lawn between him and Don Landis, in something like surprise.

"Who's talking about the government?" he said. "I'm not. I'm talking about *us*. We still choose our government. So far."

"Oh, we're talking about choosing and voting now, are we?" said Don, and Roger repeated mildly, "I'm talking about us, as individuals. Not even We-the-People, as a mass, but all the separate persons, all over the country. Though if we're too lazy, or too preoccupied: if we're unwilling—or afraid—to learn to think for ourselves, there *are* those who are only too ready to do our thinking for us. We all know that. We've watched it taking place in one country after another, even if some of us have looked on from too long a distance to see it clearly." He paused broodingly. "What I'm contending is that there is some irreplaceable contribution made by every one of us who manages to keep awake, and aware—of what goes on. Of what could happen."

"But, Rog!" Joyce expostulated. "Whatever makes you think we're not aware of it? Why, there was even a poll a while ago that showed how large a proportion of people (and it *was* large, too) was very much aware . . . of what you're talking about. Goodness knows enough has been published and dinned into our ears. Too much, maybe—like the old 'wolf-wolf' fable!"

"Maybe so," Roger agreed. "Maybe they just don't believe what they've heard. Can't believe, and won't believe—and won't be bothered . . . until it's happened." His voice dropped off heavily.

Two or three seconds ticked by, and the others waited, wondering if he had finished finally, and apparently he had. But still the rest sat listening, as to the echo of what had been said, or for some new portentous sound which was not yet audible. What they actually heard was the sound of singing, far off and faint; some hymn, it seemed to be, a little off key. And it was at that same moment that the lights in the kitchen wing were switched off—all but one little glimmer in the pantry, and with the darkening of that row of windows, the patio itself was suddenly darker. So that as they looked at each other in surprise, to confirm whether someone else had heard what must be only in one's own head, they could not see each other's faces distinctly any more.

CHAPTER 19

Norma exclaimed involuntarily, "Oh *dear*—" and Miriam, startled, said sharply, "What's that?" Her back was toward that side of the house, and she was aware only of the extra blanket of shadow which had fallen without warning.

"Just—Bertha and Joseph, turning out the lights in the kitchen," Norma replied at once, to reassure her, and also to cover over her own inadvertent sense of shock.

"Oh . . ." the other said, a little blankly, and she attempted a laugh, which somehow fell short of its mark. "That was the weirdest effect coming when it did—those voices—and then that sudden shadow . . . Absolutely weird . . ." she repeated in a hushed voice, as though unable to shake off the spell of something inexplicable.

"Only the lights going off, again—all over the world," said Don. "Beginning in the kitchen. Must be some significance in that."

Miriam turned on him with a flash of uncalculated anger and reproach which forgot for a moment to be provocative. "Oh, *stop* it, Don!" she exclaimed. "You make a joke of everything, whether it's funny or not."

"Oh, no I don't," he said.

"Well, *why*, then—why do you talk that way? *You* think it's coming, too, don't you?" she challenged him.

He waited a second before replying, though she was sitting up straight and tense now, and there was an insistent pressure behind her words; a direct dare to say where he stood.

"I think it's—quite likely," he said, after that instant of deliberation. "Something's got to give, some place—some day."

Norma had a curious sensation as she heard him say that; not of surprise exactly, for though some instinct rejected his reply as *not* what he believed, it did not surprise her a bit that he would tip the truth one way or another if it suited his book to do so. What she felt was more an automatic wonder as to why he chose the defeatist line, for it was not in character. Strange, how well she had come to know that young man in these few hours, and without even talking to him very much, and one thing that she knew was that he was too tough—or possibly too callous—to be alarmed. She even saw, for a moment—as it were, distantly—that Don Landis with his all too patent faults might have, not so much a compensating virtue (everybody *had* at least one!) but some real value under certain circumstances. Yes, in time of war, for instance . . . the very conditions they were fearfully contemplating—that same tough fiber and insensitive nerve might well stand him, and others with him, in good stead. It divided her uncomfortably to recognize this. But it was Miriam who broke out in passionate protest.

"Oh, what's the *matter* with you all? You men, especially! You're fairly feeding fear in all of us! Calling for devastation and destruction—wishing it on us! *Asking* for it. Well, I'm not! And I don't believe in any of it, for one minute—you hear?" She threw the last two words out into the middle of the circle, but though in effect she was scornfully repudiating the defeatism of the others, it was actually, Norma thought, more like a defiance of the thunderbolt . . . Like superstition denying its own images. Miriam was refusing all these fearful conjectures, not because of any positive belief or evidence to refute them, but because she was herself afraid, terribly afraid that they were true. She had come to her feet suddenly (rather as she had that morning) as though she couldn't bear the topic any longer; wanted to get away from it—from all of them, in fact.

"I don't believe it either, Miriam," said Joyce, but in her level steadfast voice. No hysteria there. "I just don't believe that God will let us destroy His wonderful world," she added simply.

"Why not?" said Roger. "He lets men destroy one another. And themselves, too."

Miriam had glanced back, fleetingly, at Joyce—and over at Roger once more—and now moved swiftly across the circle, passing in front of Norma, to whom she said, "I am going—to get a wrap."

"And I"—Norma rose and picked up the cups which had been lying on the broad chair-arm between Mrs. Mears and her—"am going to take these out to the kitchen," she finished calmly, as in reply to Miriam's word of explanation, though the other was already out of earshot. Thank goodness for the mundane, the commonplace gesture to turn aside from a course which could not, must not be followed any farther in this company. But as she moved toward the small table between Roger and Mr. Bixby, where she had noticed those other empty cups, she heard Mrs. Mears saying coldly, "We can't blame God, I suppose, for everything we find we can't explain—in ourselves," and Roger answering readily, "Right! That would be only another refusal of our own responsibility, this time refusing to accept the blame where it lies: on ourselves."

"So . . ." said Mrs. Mears. "Doubtless our great lack—of security, or whatever we choose to call it, comes back to our lack of faith in God and in ourselves."

Norma had stopped short, a few feet from the table she'd been aiming for, but it was not that lonely voice which had halted her, nor even the realization that since her two hands were already full, she couldn't pick up the other cups and saucers—though there was a sort of dim baffled consciousness of this physical awkwardness confronting her. It was distress which caught at her, because this was one subject which she did not want and would not *have* bandied about on her hillside. She wanted to cry out at them to stop. Stop all this sophistical argument. Right now. (But try and do it! she thought, despairingly, for Roger was going on again.)

"That wasn't what I meant," he said, "though I know it's the fashion today to blame everything that's gone awry on our loss of religion."

"Well?" said Mrs. Mears, still distantly.

"I don't think we've lost it, that's all," he said, raising his head to gaze off into the dusk. "I'm not referring to thirty or forty years ago, when the scientific viewpoint seemed to be in disagreement with *belief*—as such. I wouldn't know about that. Maybe we— mislaid it for a time, in our confusion . . . Maybe we woke up and found what we were treasuring in our holiest places wasn't the real thing, and threw it away in revulsion." He paused, reflecting, though he seemed to be absently watching Joyce now, who had gotten up from the swing and gone to the glass-topped table, picking up the silver tray there and coming quickly and silently back across the circle to where her mother was standing.

"I'll take them," she whispered, and Norma looked down at the blurred silver oval, as though not quite comprehending what it was for. Her practical child. Her steadfast child. Her eyes came up again, to meet the girl's eyes, across two feet of dusky space, and she whispered, "Thank you, dear," in return, and put the cups she was holding carefully on the tray. And took another step to pick up the other two, lying on the table, to transfer them also to Joyce's waiting tray. And then straightened up, as though finally freed from what had held her, and said quietly, "Roger." He looked up at her at last, though not apparently in any surprise to find her there.

"Rog, old friend," she said, to make it softer, "I think we've talked about too many things tonight. Things that were really too big for us to tackle. And now, I think we've reached the one—that we should let alone."

"All right—" he said, but it was not a finished affirmative, with a period after it. In a way it was docile, like a corrected child, but it was reluctant too; not satisfied. He got slowly to his feet—in recognition of her authority here? Or was it mere belated acknowledgment of a woman, standing, while he was seated? "You're right, Norma. Religion is not a thing to be—debated. But look, will you just let me finish the thing that I was trying to say?" he asked, very courteously, with an intensity of purpose which could not be denied. What was there for her to reply? "No, you may not"? Ridiculous.

"Why—of course," she said, and moved back toward her former place, leaving the floor to him who would be so bold . . . But she did not settle down again; just paused, with a temporary look, seating herself on the chair-arm for the moment. And Roger did not begin at once on what he had seemed so anxious to say.

"I don't think that we ever lost religion. Though it may have seemed so, because so many strayed—or stayed—away from church. But what they were actually staying away from was the lack of those things which couldn't be found there. Or because of other things which had taken their place—fanatic—inflexible. Rigid. More like the corpse of God than the Holy Ghost," he muttered. Someone gave a slight gasp, a nearly inaudible exclamation. And Roger said rather sadly, "That shocks you, doesn't it? And if I said that there are some who never feel so far from God as they do in a church, that would also shock you. But did you know," he remarked, looking around the group in the manner of one making a general statement and inquiry, both at once, "that it is very hard to find anyone who doesn't believe in *something*? Doesn't turn—sometime—later if not sooner, to search for the source and center of his being?"

Joyce, who had been standing nearby, erect and large-eyed in the gloom, holding her tray in front of her, moved slowly away from him—but thoughtfully—taking what he had said with her, as if balancing it on the tray she carried . . . over toward the swing, and Don, who sat alone there now. The others watched her, thinking their own thoughts, until Mrs. Mears said with stiff asperity, "I think that what you call religion, Mr. Norbeck—" but he cut in before she could go further "—*is* religion, Mrs. Mears, believe me. In its most elementary, immaterial sense. It's the very root of it that lies in every man's soul, whether he knows what it is or not. You may not call it that. The church—any church—may not recognize it as such, but—"

He stopped, to take one full breath, and went on with extreme care, as though quite aware of treading on thinnest ice, yet personallly committed to proceed to the point he had set out for. "What I am trying to say is that whether you're Catholic or Jew—Baptist or Methodist—or Buddhist—or Mohammedan—or some guy groping his own lonely way through the dark, you have each got something of what every other one means by religion, whether he has light enough to see that, or honor enough to admit it."

Norma hoped that he was through. She saw with some thankfulness that Don had gotten up as Joyce approached the swing, picked up the remaining cups which had been parked casually on the grass, and taken the tray away from her, with an indulgent "Too heavy for a great big girl like you."

Jim saw that too, and swallowed a lump of mortification. (Why hadn't *he* had the gumption to do that, backwoods oaf that he was?) He wished again devoutly that he hadn't come up here, wished with all his heart that Gran would get up, say it was time to go . . . Wished Mr. Norbeck would quit all this religious talk which made everybody so uneasy and uncomfortable. People didn't *talk* about such stuff . . . It was *embarrassing*, even in the dark. But no one stopped him. Maybe no one could. Mrs. Collins said in an aside to Landis, "Just leave that on the table, Don. I want to take it out in a second." And he put the tray on the table as directed, and returned to the edge of the circle where he remained standing, with his hands in his pockets, quite at ease. (One knew they were not clenched inside his trousers pockets—as Roger's probably were.) And looking down the length of dark oval toward the other man, he was in a position to observe that Miriam had also returned, wrapped closely in a white shawl like a shroud which pinned her arms to her sides. In fact, she looked like some small armless mummy standing there, upright and still; so still that probably no one else was aware that she had come back.

"No doubt we should take great comfort from all this," said Mrs. Mears, her dryness more astringent now than ever.

"No comfort, Mrs. Mears. All I've been trying to say is that we can't explain our troubled state by any loss of religion, because in sum total, we haven't really lost it. And since each person takes his own inner course, comes nearer to his goal—or falls far short of it—by his own private route (no matter if or where he goes to church), I'm saying that our belief in God is actually contained in each individual concept, which by its very nature cannot and does not encompass all the other separate roads to the same end. So Joyce's simple—and rather lovely—faith does not comfort me in the very least. And my different conception, of an almighty force which permits—and perhaps *intends*—us to exercise a certain freedom of will, subject only to our own personal limitations—yes, even to the point of utterly destroying ourselves—is, I'm sure, entirely meaningless and empty to her."

There was blank silence when he stopped that time, as if no one there had understood a word of what he'd said, though he had put each word down with such agonizing precision, with an effort that seemed almost beyond his strength, for he sounded unutterably tired as he concluded, knowing that he had said nothing much after all. Only that people saw things differently. Life and death. Even God.

As Don Landis presently pointed out . . . (He *would*, thought Norma—this very glib young man.) He had pulled out a cigarette and lighted it with deliberation, and when he had it going to his satisfaction, he remarked cheerfully, "In short, everybody looks at every little thing a little differently—check?" No one bothered to answer that, and he added, playing it for a laugh, "Even the rapidly approaching end of everything—whether we're due to be vaporized, or take off into thin air from some given hillside, on a night like this, yes?" But the laugh did not materialize, and it was the silence which grew more palpable.

Until Jim said quite unexpectedly, "Or die in bed." They all turned to peer at him, and Norma said reproachfully, "Oh, *Jim.*" So he began explaining, a little awkwardly. "I was thinking about two kids I heard talking this afternoon—couple of the village kids. One of 'em had just heard about this end-of-the-world stuff, and swallowed it hook, line and sinker, but the other one said, Phooey, *her* mother said the end of the world was when you died . . . Simple as that. That's all I meant." But the short pause following his explanation felt awkward too; it seemed to Jim that every time he opened his trap tonight he jarred them in some way. He didn't realize that for the first time in all this long palaver, ranging from dreadful possibility to the grotesquely impossible, the subject had been put upon a personal footing which no one could avoid. It was as though he had said something indelicate, and this caused a general embarrassment.

"Well, of course," said someone vaguely, "that goes without saying . . ."

But Joyce exclaimed, "So maybe it doesn't matter!" As though quite cheered by this discovery. "I mean—it's death we're talking about, after all, isn't it? And as it comes sooner or later, and it's only a question of *when* . . . But that's the catch, isn't it?" And she stopped in a naïve surprise.

Roger muttered, "Yes, my dear Joyce, that is—the catch." And Norma, trying to think of something she could say—anything at all, could only think, They are too young, those two, to recognize it as anything personal to them . . . It's just a hypothetical phenomenon, in spite of their closeness to it if war should come . . . Or was it because of that very thing—that they, their age and kind, would be the first in inevitable participation—that they had grown up to speak so coolly and impersonally of this most personal thing? She didn't know.

And it was Miriam, now, who gave a sudden laugh, like someone reaching for a straw, any straw of absurdity, as she crossed back again to the swing.

"Anyway, the catch works both ways! I remember so well the first time I was going somewhere by plane. The mere thought used to terrify me," she interpolated, and went on quickly, almost gaily. "I got myself all prepared for the worst: made my will, and cleaned out all my bureau drawers and left all kinds of notes and instructions around the house—just in *case*, you know. But here I am, I'd hate to say how many years later!" She laughed again, briefly. "No, dear, you never can be sure, one way or the other."

"So the trick must be," Don said amiably, "to enjoy present company while we can, eh?" He seemed to direct a note of appreciation toward their hostess, though his head turned very slightly, from Joyce, toward Miriam, as he resumed his place between the two. And Miriam shivered again, but not with cold, inside her fleecy warm wool stole; there was a warmth pressing against her thigh too, on the side next to him.

"There is another way—or trick, or aphorism, if you like," said Mrs. Mears. "You all know it, I'm sure: to act as though we're going to live forever—and live as if each day would be our last."

"Well, I know one thing," Roger said abruptly. "If I thought this was to be *my* last, I wouldn't've talked so much." And he gave a short dry chuckle which sounded more like a derisive bark.

"You had something to say, Mr. Norbeck," said Mr. Bixby gravely.

"Yes . . ." Roger admitted. "I had a lot on my chest. I won't deny that. But the fact is, if one knew there was only a certain limited distance to carry the load, I think one would try to carry it that much farther, in a semblance of dignified silence . . . Or anyway—silence."

"Unless," Mrs. Mears inserted quietly, "it is one that passes on—" But he seemed not to hear that.

"It's the indefinite span ahead of us," he said heavily. "Whether it's long or short; the imponderables of weight, and time, and one's own factor of endurance—the incalculable stress and strain—" he broke off in disgust. "And here I am with my mouth wide open again. Dignified silence, my foot."

Norma got up quickly, for glancing sidewise she had seen that the small glimmer left in the pantry was now gone. Which meant that Joseph had finished putting away the glass and china, and she felt almost guilty at having missed the exact moment when that light went out. She murmured to Mrs. Mears, "Will you excuse me a moment? I—want to see Joseph, and I think they may be going—up there, you know, any time now." Mrs. Mears looked up at her and nodded slowly, several times.

"Yes," she said. "It must be—time to go."

CHAPTER 20

Norma's going had seemed abrupt (though she had delayed so long, praying for Roger to finish) and there was a small gap left behind her, which did not close up at once . . . as if the others were all waiting for her return before speaking again. That was not so, of course, though they were each in turn waiting for something. Jim had tensed his muscles, ready to spring up, awaiting the one more word from his grandmother for which he'd been hoping this last hour or so. But still she made no move. Her hands were laid flat, palms down on the arms of her chair, with just the ends of her long fingers turned over the edges of the wood in a prehensile grip, preparatory to pushing herself up, or possibly to hold tighter to the support they offered. Though Jim could not see that. He saw only that she had not followed up her preliminary gambit, after she'd said it was time to go, and he felt an almost morbid dread that somebody else would get the bit in his teeth and start off again. And he was right—and it was Gran, herself, who gave the whirligig another twirl, as though in the absence of her hostess she felt a certain obligation to keep it from coming to a complete halt. She tipped her head a little stiffly in Mr. Bixby's direction as she said, "You must find us a very peculiar population, back here in the hills, Mr. Bixby. What with the village prophecy on one side, and the rather grimly fanciful talk which we've all been indulging in up here this evening."

"No," said Mr. Bixby mildly. "No. People are much alike in every place, I think. So much alike, inside them."

"You know, I think it's been interesting," Joyce offered ingenuously. "People generally talk about such dull subjects after dinner. All about diets and golf and business!"

"Yes, Miss Joyce. I have found it very interesting too," said Mr. Bixby. He seemed to hesitate for a moment, so that when he continued again the words sounded less purposeful than tentative. "What I have wondered, however, many times—is—exactly where the whole idea started. And no one has thrown any light on that, as yet."

"This *is* where we came in, isn't it?" Don remarked in a clearly audible aside to Miriam.

"Nobody knows, I guess," said Joyce. "It just seemed to start from nothing."

"But that couldn't be," said Mr. Bixby. "There is a germ, a seed, from which such things grow . . . such rumors."

"That's right," said Roger, nodding in recognition of something he knew all too well.

"The process is quite familiar," Mr. Bixby pursued calmly. "Once the thought is sown, or possibly transplanted . . . But there are certain features of this affair, which show an eccentric sort of calculation, so one has to ask one's self, 'Who—might profit, in the end?' "

"Can't see any percentage in it myself," said Don.

"By Jove!" said Roger. "I believe you've got hold of perhaps the only real factor in the whole imaginary setup. To run it down to the underlying motive, we'd have to find out who heard it first, and where. Well, for instance, where did *you* first hear it, Joyce?"

"Why—I don't know," she said a little blankly. "I think it was going strong when I came back from school. You told me, didn't you, Jim?"

"Don't remember, I'm sure," growled Jim uncomfortably, not because he had any inkling of suspicion being aimed toward him, but because he *knew* . . . and he was *not* going to tell anybody about Miss Amelia's hallucination. Besides, Mr. Bixby's unbelievable gall in bringing up the question of *who would profit* had brought him close to the boiling point.

"Mother knew of it," said Joyce reflectively, "but she didn't say anything about it to me for a long time. And then I never thought to ask her where, because once you'd heard it, everybody else seemed to know about it too." She looked around vaguely, as if to see if her mother were coming back yet. "When did you hear of it, yourself?" she tossed back at Mr. Bixby, beginning to enjoy the quiz tinge the conversation had now taken.

"It was—since about five months, I think."

"Five *months*! Why, Mr. Bixby, you certainly do get around!" Joyce laughed out again, more in delight than disbelief. "*I* never heard of it until a month or two ago, myself."

"That's interesting," Roger commented. "That you," he said to the older man, "being down here only periodically as I understand it, should have picked it up so early. Do you remember at all where *you* first got it?"

"Very clearly," said Mr. Bixby. They were all watching him expectantly, but he still spoke with carefully measured precision. "I heard it from a hitchhiker," he said. "A young man I picked up on the road one evening, just outside the village. It was in the autumn, late October or very early November, to be exact, because I had only been coming down for a few weeks. I was starting back to Los Angeles, soon after dark . . . *You* remember the occasion, don't you?"

He had been sitting a little forward in his chair, huddled over his own linked hands, looking down at them, and though the others could see that he had lifted his head a trifle, his position had not changed in any other way, and they could not tell to whom he had addressed the question. They were, in fact, somewhat confused by the pronoun he had introduced without warning; Jim especially wondered what the guy was talking about now, even as he became aware of something like a surge of blood through his whole body, up into his chest so that it was suddenly hard to get a breath, up into his head so that it made him almost dizzy.

"You asking *me*?" he asked shortly.

"Yes. You remember, I'm sure—last fall, a Sunday evening it must have been. I daresay you were on your way back to college after the week end." said Mr. Bixby quietly.

"I don't know what you're talking about," Jim said.

"No? That's odd. You don't recall telling me—in a sense predicting that I would be hearing this story the next time I came down, and for some time to come—?"

"Why, you lying old horse thief! Of all the s-slimy d-dirty old crooks!" Jim had come to his feet in a spurt of pure white rage. "You—*bastard*, you!" he exploded. Even in the half-dark his six-foot-two shadow seemed to loom nine feet high over the quiet, huddled figure in the chair, and he stuttered, not for lack of words or for any inhibition in using what he could lay his tongue to, but in sheer inability to get out the sense of enormity, of outrage, which choked him. In the same moment, his grandmother had stiffened into rigid erectness in her chair, gripping the wooden arms, and there was only one word which she could get out: his name.

"*Jim!*" she said. Like a shot which went over his head, past his ear. But Joyce was as fast as she was, and like another shot she was up and across the few feet of grass and beside him, pulling at his arm.

"Jimmie-Jimmie-Jimmie," she was saying, not loudly but very rapidly, as though the urgency were to reach some point beyond mere hearing.

"Of all the *gall* I ever *heard!*" He was not stuttering that time, as he looked down to see what had fastened so tightly on the stiffened sinews of his wrist, above one clenched fist.

"Jim, you must be crazy," she said in a whisper, still close, still hanging on, and his eyes moved up to seek the white face near him, and he was partially diverted. Which is to say that his next explosion blazed out at her.

"*Me* crazy!" he almost shouted. "Well, at least I'm not a dirty crook fattening myself on human beings before they're even corpses . . . like an old vulture hanging over something that isn't quite *dead* yet . . ."

"You react violently, my friend," said Mr. Bixby. "You found— and didn't like that I was getting in your way, perhaps?"

"In *my* way!" Jim's voice broke almost as if he were sixteen, and he had to begin again. "You're suggesting *I* was trying the same game you've been playing, is that it?" He glared around the group in a rather desperate search for comprehension. "Don't any of you know what he's been up to?" he demanded. "And now, there he sits, trying to pin this whole stinking business on me! *I* told him about it—how d'ya like that! *I* told him five months ago—when I never heard a word about it myself until February. I never even saw this guy until about a month ago—fat, greasy little slug—" He turned back toward the bulky object of his fury, but found his vision blocked by another shadow, standing there.

"Some misunderstanding here," Roger said crisply. "Skip it, Jim. Cool off."

"But I'm telling you—"

"You've said enough, for now. Enough, hear me?"

"You should apologize to Mr. Bixby, and all of us," his grand-mother said, her words and tone as stiff as her backbone.

"*I will not*—"

"Then I must apologize for you. And I do," she said in that cold, frozen voice. "Abjectly."

Jim could have cried, at that moment, like a kid. Not because of the reprimand, but the blank disbelief, the shocked amazement which he felt all around him. And they were shocked by him, not by the man who should have turned their stomachs, if they'd only listened to what Jim had tried to tell them. But instead of crying he found himself doing something like laughing, helplessly, though it was a shaky sound and lasted for not more than a couple of seconds. "How d'ya like that?" he said again, but only to himself, shaking his head to free it of more than anger and confusion, at the same time shaking his arm free of Joyce's. And Mr. Bixby, who had not uttered a word since Jim's last outbreak (had sat there quietly, watching, listening, not cowering under the threat of that monstrous young black shadow, nor attempting any explanation or rebuttal on his own part), Mr. Bixby got up now, with the slight effort demanded of any fat man by the raising of his own bulk.

As though nothing untoward had occurred, he said pleasantly to

Joyce, "I have enjoyed this evening, Miss Joyce. It has been most interesting. But it is time that I should go. Will you—"

"Oh, but Mr. Bixby!" Joyce exclaimed quickly. "Mother will be out again in just a minute." (As if Mother could fix everything!)

"Yes, I know. But I have already said my farewells. Earlier. If you will just say again, for me, that I am—grateful. Mr. Norbeck, it has been a great pleasure. Mrs. Mears . . ." He turned to bow to the old lady, so formally that it seemed an obeisance, as she held out her hand and his head bent down over it.

"It was not Jim," she said, very low, during that instant that his ear was close enough to have heard a whisper. And as he straightened and turned toward the others, who had not heard, Joyce spoke up again in real distress.

"I—I wish you wouldn't go, so early," she said. She was so ashamed of Jim, so amazed, and at the same time felt so inadequate, herself; kept wishing her mother would come back. She threw a hasty glance over toward the house, and saw that Miriam had gotten up and was coming smoothly toward them, as though recognizing that Joyce needed her support.

"It *has* been nice, Mr. Bixby," she said easily and warmly. "And I'm sure we'll be seeing you again while we're here, won't we? Or if not here," she said mischievously, lowering her social voice, but not enough so that everyone couldn't hear quite clearly, "perhaps— up top?" (tilting her head ever so little in the direction of the Hill) "or over *there*, when we've all landed again!" He did not echo her gay little laugh, and he by-passed the question she had thrown in to start with, but he bowed and nodded over her hand, and answered genially, "Over there, I'm sure. I'll be looking forward to that, Mrs. Norbeck."

Joyce walked with him out across the grass, not sure whether that was quite the thing to do, yet still not willing to let him make such an abrupt departure. When they reached the gate, out of earshot of the others, he turned and proffered his hand once more. (He was the hand-shakingest little man, she thought.)

"Thank you, Miss Joyce. It has been a privilege, knowing you and your lovely mother."

"But we've loved having you with us tonight!" she protested. "And you must come up for dinner again, soon. We don't always have such—peculiar evenings, you know!" She tried to laugh (gaily, like Miriam) but it came out embarrassingly, rather like a burp. It surely wasn't up to her to apologize for Jim, and besides, Mrs. Mears had already done that. Nevertheless, she found herself going right on. "I'm so awfully sorry about Jim's busting loose that way. I just don't understand—what got *into* him!" And then, more slowly, as if in some way compelled, "But, Mr. Bixby, Jim was not down here during all of October. Or in November either, until Thanksgiving. I know, you see—because we were together every day."

"So . . ." said Mr. Bixby. "I have been wrong." And he added unexpectedly, "I am very glad." Joyce thought for a second that he was going back—to apologize, himself, perhaps—and hoped he wouldn't. Oh no, don't, she prayed, for there was no telling what Jim would say next. But it was more as though the older man were listening to something, though the voices of the others were indistinguishable now, from where they stood. "Yes," he said musingly, "I recall, at dinner time, when the young man was laughing once or twice—and again, a moment ago . . . The laugh was different. Quite different. And a laugh comes too suddenly to be altered."

He seemed to be explaining something to her, and she felt very dense not to know what it was. He seemed also to be gazing earnestly at her, through the dark which was so thick out here that they could barely see each other's faces. He had kept her hand in his own plump one; not in any sticky way, but as if to retain her attention a little longer. And now, he put his other hand over hers, making a sandwich of it, but still with no insinuating pressure, just holding it very firmly. "May I say this, Miss Joyce—that I hope you will be very, very happy? I had . . . a little girl . . . who would be just your age, and I could have asked no more than to have her grow up—like you. Sincere, and loyal, and not afraid to think."

"Why—why, Mr. Bixby!" She was taken aback, to the point of stammering. "I don't deserve that, you know." And then, still helplessly, "I—didn't know you had a family."

"I had a family, yes." He had repeated her same words, yet thereby

232

corrected them in some sense which she did not immediately catch. "My wife. My mother. And my little girl," he said in a very still and level voice, and released her hand with the quick pressure of finality. "Good-bye, Miss Joyce. And will you say to your mother . . . No, nothing. She will understand."

She heard him fumbling with the gate latch for a second, and saw the dark blot of his figure pass through and blend into the outer dark, while the gravel crunched under his feet. And that was all she heard. She could not hear him repeating to himself an unspoken echo. I had a family, yes . . . A dear wife. A brave mother. A little girl, not yet ten.

A man did not say to a girl like this young Joyce, that his mother had lost her mind, at last, though not in any process of senility. That while he was shut away from them all, penned in like a dangerous animal, his wife and child had lost their very lives. (Together? Separately? He would never know. Of exposure, he'd been told—but not officially. It was the only, and possibly the kindest, word he had ever learned.) No, he didn't say these things aloud, tried not to think of them—uselessly—until some phrase set an old dead nerve twanging with pain again. One did not tell young girls too much of life (let them learn, or die, before they were quite ten years old); didn't risk talking of anything, much, even to a man like Norbeck, with his quick ear and keen eye, with a memory like a file of old letters, doubtless. Not even when he had asked in casual friendliness, if Bixby had been born in this country.

Oh no. It had sufficed to say that he'd come over at the age of fourteen, with an uncle; had gone to school a while longer and into business here. That was enough. Why mention that he'd gone back in middle age . . . to see his mother . . . to find the wife he'd never found before . . . to do quite well over there in business too, because of the contacts he had built up here . . . Though only for a limited time—for time was already running out in the early thirties. There was no connection between any of that—and this. There was no permanent place for him here, on this hillside; a rented house for a few months away from the city, that was what he'd come for. How could he have been so foolish at his age to think otherwise, even for a minute? To make that fumbling and inept suggestion to Mrs. Collins that *she* might wish to marry again (which she, so rightly, had struck away, like a stranger's hand on her arm).

For it didn't matter, not even as long as a minute. There was no new life here or anywhere, for him—and nothing was permanent—not even pain. Only a purpose; the work to be done, the money to be made. More money. Conscience money, in a way. Yes. (And in a way he was more dangerous now than he had ever been when they penned him up. He hoped he was.) And this small job here, this little foolish business in the back country, so unimportant despite its persistent and compelling undertone of reminder, of planted rumor, which was what had first caught his own acutely sensitive ear—that minor self-assignment was already accomplished, to all intents and purposes. So Mr. Bixby rolled his all too sturdy and enduring body into his car and under the steering wheel, and switched on the headlights which were to serve him for eyes again.

PART SIX

"*Watchman, tell us of the night.*"

CHAPTER 21

When Norma reached the door leading from the terrace into the dining room, she had paused for a moment, holding the tray which she'd picked up in passing, and wondering stupidly how she was going to turn the knob. But then she saw that the screen door had been left unlatched and was standing an inch or more ajar, and with her toe she swung it wider and went on into the room without so much as the click of a latch to announce her coming. That was, undoubtedly, why Joseph did not hear her, and just at first she didn't see him either, for the only light came from the small candle-shaped bulbs in the wall brackets. She was about to go straight past the dining table toward the pantry door, but on the way she suddenly caught that image in the corner of her eye, and turned her head, surprised to find him standing motionless, over on the other side of the room, his back to her as he faced the sideboard, with the top silver drawer pulled open in front of him. Yet he did not seem to be doing anything at all, just standing there, like a gnarled old tree bent with many years of weather, resembling the figure of a man by mere accident.

She stopped short with the feeling that she mustn't speak too suddenly, as one was warned not to shock a sleepwalker into an abrupt awakening. She put the tray down on the table, gently, yet making a certain distinct sound as the metal made contact with the wood. And still he didn't turn and didn't move, and she said tentatively, "Joseph?" And even then it seemed to be a full second or two before his hands pushed the drawer slowly shut. His arms fell to his sides and he turned slowly around, in the same spot, as though on a turntable, not moved by his own volition. She spoke gently again, though trying to make herself sound as every-day as her words were.

237

"I expect you've finished everything outside now, haven't you?" she said, and was about to continue that she would rinse the cups and leave them out there—before he could notice them and begin to apologize for having forgotten them. But she saw that he was not aware at all of the tray lying there on the table, and in fact did not seem to have heard what she said. He was staring in front of him as though he didn't even see her.

"Joseph," she said once more. "What—is it?" She went around the table toward him, still with that conscious sense of caution lest she should frighten the poor soul still more. For she felt a growing certainty that it was the grip of fear which had closed down on him so that he could not move, could neither hear nor speak. But as she drew closer she saw that he had begun to chew his lips, spasmodically, first the lower teeth closing over his upper lip and then the upper ones clenching down on the lower lip—and then clamping his mouth together with the thin lips turned all the way in, like a child trying not to cry. And then of course she realized that was exactly it, for as she said again, "Joseph," and added softly, "My dear man, what *is* the trouble?"—she saw that his eyes had filled with tears, and overflowed, running down his face, finding their way into the seams like rivulets, each coursing down some old eroded gully.

"Can you tell me what it is?" she asked again, and laid her hand on his sleeve. He moved his head stiffly from one side to the other, but whether it was in refusal or inability to speak, she couldn't tell. So she said at last, "Is it—this end-of-the-world thing, Joseph?" And that did seem to bring his eyes, still blurred as they were, back to some sort of focus on her.

"End otheworld. 'Tsright," he muttered, and the words were slurred also, in a kind of careless mumble, unlike his always precise diction.

"Joseph, you know that isn't so. It's just an idea, a sort of feverish notion that a few people have built up in their imaginations. It has nothing to do with the real world we're living in."

"I hope it *is* so!" he burst out with something like a last flicker of emotion, for it died away in another mumble, something that sounded like " 'Tsonly hope left." And this time she was more aware of the contrast between his usual prim articulation and this mumbling indistinctness: a sort of *native* indistinctness, however, without any barrier of accent.

"I don't understand, Joseph. Why don't you want to go on—living? Haven't you been happy up here? I thought you were." But at that, his eyes filled up again, and his mouth, which that last mumble had left hanging loose, a little open, began to tremble. He was abject, revolting, and piteous.

"Yes," he gulped finally. "We have been happy . . . madam." He got that out with an obvious effort of will, of recalling something. But it was too much of an effort, or not worth it, for he let it go again. "But I'm seventy-four years old, almost—and I can't keep beginning over and over . . . I can't begin all over again," he reiterated.

"But you won't have to. We'll just go on as we have been. Tomorrow will be like any other day. We'll make the work easier for you, though. You should have told me." She had never known how old he was; he was that ageless kind, who might have looked wizened at forty or fifty, and could be taken for almost any age above that, now.

"No," he said. "That's not it."

"What is it, then?" she asked patiently. "What *is* it—that you think is going to happen?"

"It's already happened, Mrs. Collins. It's done."

It occurred to her then, and she wondered why she hadn't been quick enough to think of it before, that something about the strain of dealing with today's exhilaration and apprehension (Bertha's? Alfred's?)—or worse yet, something that he'd overheard her own group saying when they were holding forth out there about the danger and devastation of more war—had thrown this poor tired man into a state of shock which had taken him back to the horror he had lived through—before they ever came here, which he and Bertha never talked about.

"Joseph," she said slowly, putting out her hand again to touch his forearm, which felt like a wooden stick inside his coat sleeve, "I realize that you have been through so much already, so much more than any of us can ever conceive, that you can perhaps never feel quite sure that such things do not happen here. They cannot happen here, as long as we—" (Oh no? She heard some alien doubt, some voice—was it Roger's?—jeering at her. But it was not that which stopped her.) Joseph had turned aside, as if to move past her, almost as if to brush her aside, though he had gone only a couple of feet when he came to a stop again, his head hanging forward and down, like an old horse who cannot go another step. "I can't go on with that any more, either," he said.

"I don't know what you mean, Joseph."

"That D.P. business," he said very low. "We aren't D.P.'s, Mrs. Collins. We never were."

"You aren't?"

"I was born in Martinsville, Nebraska," he said explicitly, "and Bertha in a little town about thirty miles away. We've never even been outside the country, neither one of us." She waited, and he went on. "Grew up there, got married, worked there all my younger days. Until we came out West after the first war." He turned back to face her doggedly. "You'll never know, the shame I've felt, to be deceiving you all this time."

"But why?" she said simply. "Why did you?" And waited again until he was able to go on.

"I was a clerk in a bank," he said dully. "Didn't make much, but we did all right, those first years. Had some self-respect, anyway. Put away something in savings. Even when the market crash came, I thought we were all right, because I never gambled on those kind of things . . . Until the banks closed," he said as though in conclusion: as in a logical and complete conclusion of all he had been saying.

"You lost all those savings," Norma said gently. "Ah, Joseph . . . Even when the banks opened again—didn't you get something back?"

"My bank didn't open again," he said. "It was one of those . . . And never paid but a few cents on the dollar. We lost it all. And my job was gone too. And I was in my fifties by then."

She let him go on. And as she listened, she knew how much more logical this was than the other story, the untold story, half hinted at and carefully covered over, which she had been led to believe before. The other had never been convincing, she realized now, though she'd supposed that was because she was unable to conceive what the real displaced persons had gone through—and they were emotionally unable to talk about it. But *this* was true. The little bank clerk, careful, saving, a dogged worker no doubt. Caught in his fifties without savings and without a job. The depression. That was the thing which had scarred this man.

He went on and on, now. Didn't know how they'd ever gotten through those years. Odd jobs. Bertha taking in washing. No work at all for either of them. Part time—weeding and watering somebody's garden Dishwashing. Messenger boy—at sixty, Joseph added bitterly. And after that again, no work, because by the time business got better again, he'd gotten older, and nobody'd give a man in his sixties a decent job. He'd never had a chance to do his own kind of work, in a bank, again. When the war came it was better for a while, but after the war—with the young fellows coming back . . . "You don't know what it's like, ma'am. Not knowing what you're going to live on, or which way to turn, and with somebody else depending on you, too." His voice had that faint tinge of reproach, not consciously blaming her, yet carrying the invariable implication that those who had not been there—on that particular spot—knew nothing much about life.

Nobody knows—nobody knows . . . Norma's thought echoed the everlasting inner cry of everyone, who never knows the whole story about anyone . . . But she did know how it felt to be alone, and frightened, and have nowhere to turn, with someone utterly dependent on her. (Someone who could walk, and talk, and feed and dress herself, but not much more.) And beyond all that, the ghost of her own possible responsibility walking with her; a presence which Joseph never could have known. Yet she had been lucky in so many ways: in the times themselves, and in the fact that she was still young then. For someone like this man before her, getting older—always getting older, the fright had never ended; not with the war or with the new prosperity.

Joseph's recital had come to a partial halt now, or a slowing down, with a difficult pause as he gathered himself for that last hurdle. It was Bertha's idea, he admitted finally. They'd seemed to be heading toward the brink of nothing again, three years ago. There just wasn't any way to start in all over, to get back to where they'd once been, or anywhere near it. It was just as if—in one way, at least, they *were* displaced persons, like those they'd been reading about. And that was how they'd come to work it out, to figure how they could come in on the tide of sympathy—with inexperience of this kind of work, with age, with suffering implied. Cash in on the compassion for people who'd suffered things *they* never had. Joseph didn't say this, but it was all there, in his lowered voice, the shrinking with which he all but made the admission.

Well, that was all. Bertha was a wonderful cook, and she—well, she had another kind of talent too; she could have been an actress, Joseph said, though he did not sound proud of that, either. She got a kind of kick out of the whole thing, Norma gathered. But Joseph didn't. He did what he was told, and learned to be a house-man, and never said a word more than he had to. And that was all.

"Why didn't you tell me?" Norma said. "After a while, I mean, when you knew me better. Wouldn't it have been easier, all around, than the strain of keeping up that pretense, all this time?"

He shook his head, speechless, until at last, "I guess it was my pride," he said humbly. "I couldn't, that's all. And I wasn't sure how you'd feel, after we'd deceived you once. I couldn't lose this last—refuge. But even the pride's gone now. The Lord knows I've got nothing to be proud of any more."

"You've done a good, conscientious job," Norma said slowly, feeling her way.

"And what have I got for it?" he muttered back. "Nothing."

She was silent for a moment, her pity withdrawing, as his self-pity seemed to rise—as pity always does. Besides, there was the little matter of what she'd paid them both for these three years, which was not inconsiderable. So her tone held a faint reminder as she said, "Nothing, Joseph?"

"Nothing but three more years laid on my back, Mrs. Collins. You know what you've paid us all the time we've been here—and we've hardly spent any out of it. We had some savings again," he said, raising his head and looking at her straight, like a man who could face the world again; and then dropped his eyes, remembering. "But not in the bank. We—never trusted any bank again. I've cashed your checks, and kept the money right here. You can guess about how much it would be by now. And Bertha gave it to that man."

Norma felt as if she had been running along in one direction, only to find they were going somewhere else altogether.

"*What*—man?" she asked, after a second of trying to reorient herself.

"The fat one, that calls himself Bixby," Joseph said. And added, in a sort of mournful reproach, which yet had more sorrow than accusation in it, "You invited him for dinner, *tonight*, ma'am."

"I don't know what you mean, Joseph. In the first place, he dropped in to make a neighborly call—if that's what you're referring to, though I can't see that that has anything to do with you, or even with what we're talking about."

"I guess *she* telephoned him, then. I might've known. I caught her with her hat on this afternoon, just going to walk down there. We had it out, all right. I never thought she'd do it after what I said . . . But this thing's set her crazy, some way. The woman has gone daft. I tried to watch her all the time—but I had too many other things to do—and no place I could hide it from her."

"Joseph, I still don't know what you're talking about. I'm sorry." She was trying to be very patient, very kind. "Are you telling me that Bertha has given Mr. Bixby all your cash savings for these last three years?" He nodded dumbly. "But why? What for?" Norma exclaimed, in growing exasperation with such senseless talk, as though Joseph were in fact fabricating the whole ridiculous story—as indeed he might, after the act they had put on for her benefit for those same three years. What sense could one make out of such people?

"It's because of this thing, ma'am—this thing they've prophesied. About the world coming to an end."

"I really don't see the connection," she said crisply.

"Maybe you don't know"—it was Joseph speaking patiently now, as if overlooking some stupidity—"that that was part of it? Anybody who believed in it was to get rid of whatever was most—valuable to him. You *can't* take it with you," he said bitterly. "Well, she's seen to that."

Norma took another brief moment to digest this. Mr. *Bixby*, of all people . . . and Bertha had had her hat on (why, that's what Joyce had told her too!), but Joseph had stopped her—and then *she* must have telephoned—to Mr. Bixby, did he mean? Oh *yes*—and she'd waved at him! Norma remembered suddenly that oddity which she'd dismissed as too improbable to believe . . . So that's why he'd seemed surprised and a little embarrassed by her own very cordial greeting. He hadn't come to call on the family at all.

"But why Mr. *Bixby*?" she said finally, in utter bafflement. "Was he going to invest it for you both?"

"No, Mrs. Collins, I'm afraid not. Mr. Bixby's been collecting some of the things people wanted to get rid of."

Even after all the confused preamble, which had already said the same thing several times, Norma was incredulous.

"I can't believe that, Joseph. It's just all of a piece with this whole crazy business. It's people's own fault for being so—so gullible," she said indignantly.

"That may be, but it doesn't change what's happened."

"But he couldn't—just take a sum of money like that—for nothing!"

Joseph was silent, and Norma thought of something else, and pounced on it. "Besides, you say it was tonight that she gave it to him and he's been sitting outside there with us (or in here at dinner) ever since he arrived. So you see, Joseph, I think your own apprehension has gone ahead of the true facts."

"It was after dinner," he said drearily. "While I was outside serving coffee. I didn't see he wasn't with the rest of you at first . . . but he was in the house—I don't know how long, but it was long enough for Her."

"In the *house*?" Norma repeated wonderingly, and then she remembered. Yes, of course. She'd shown him in, herself. But that—well, yes, she supposed he *could* have gone along through the living room, or even through the dining room, if Bertha was on the lookout

244

for him. And then returned again, and come out of the living-room door onto the terrace, unobtrusively. She had no idea how long he'd been in there. But she stared at Joseph now with the beginning of an unpleasant conviction.

"If this is true, we will do something about it," she said. "He is still here."

"Bertha gave it to him," Joseph said. "She *gave* it to him, don't you understand, Mrs. Collins? You can't set the law on somebody for taking what somebody gives you of her own free will."

"Maybe not, but—oh, something can be done, I'm sure! If it's really true, what you think. I'm still almost certain that there's been some extraordinary misunderstanding. But we must clear it up at once, before he leaves here. Joseph—" she said compellingly, "it will be all right, I promise you. You must believe me. You *don't* believe me, though!" she broke off, seeing his face.

"I don't believe in anything, now. You can't, that's all. Not when your own wife can do a thing like that to you, after forty-five years."

"So you'd—rather believe—it's the end of the world, wouldn't you?" said Norma softly, yet trying to reach through to his common sense, to make the words real to him, in their enormity, and absurdity.

"I hope it is," he repeated, as he had started out. "If not—well, there are other ways of ending it," he said grimly. "I always hung on before, on account of Her. But I'm not bound to her any more. Not any more." He moved his head stiffly back and forth, back and forth, from side to side.

"You'll always be bound to her, Joseph, by those same forty-five years you just spoke of. You know that, as well as I do. But I want you to know, and remember—something else. If"—she conceded that one small two-letter word to those who believed differently, but that was all—"if the world doesn't come to an end tonight, or any other night, by whatever means, and if we don't get the money back—you will always have a home here, Joseph, as long as I have a home myself. Now, do you believe *that*?"

She held his glance in hers, so firmly that it could not turn aside, and after a second she saw that his bleak old eyes had begun to blur again, as they had earlier, but now it was like the glaze of water over ice beginning to thaw.

"Yes," he said finally, not much above a whisper, "I do—believe you mean that, ma'am. Thank you."

"Oh, don't," she said quickly. "Don't thank me, just hang on, the way you said you've always done before. It's all we can *do*, Joseph, no matter how many times our own particular world falls to pieces."

She turned away from him before the watery blur in his eyes could brim over a second time. But as she went, murmuring that she must go back outside before Mr. Bixby even thought of leaving, she thought, What was she—God?—that she could say what she had, and even compel belief from one in Joseph's extremity? . . . Well yes, perhaps, in a sense she was, as anybody was, potentially, by proxy. And what she had said, or had been spoken through her, she would have to carry out. (So help me, God, she prayed.)

And then coming out onto the terrace, the wings which had carried her for a few feet set her down on the earth again, and she was not so sure. This was going to be very difficult. First, of course, the small mechanical matter of adjusting her eyes to the different light . . . It had not been bright in the dining room, but it was so much more dim out here that for a moment the figures were indistinguishable. They seemed to be standing now, several of them, so if they were breaking up, she hadn't come a moment too soon. Jim and Don and Miriam, together over *here*, cutting off her view of the others as she approached, and then she saw Joyce standing over near Roger, her back this way, still protesting or arguing about something, hanging on like a pup to a root, as Bart used to say . . . (Poor baby, she had yet to learn that it did no good to argue with life, or about it.) Mrs. Mears and Roger seemed to be the only ones still seated, and Norma's eyes searched that space between those two, which appeared to be just a dark blank now. And before she knew what she was going to say, she heard her own voice speaking out so loudly that it even startled herself.

"*Where is Mr. Bixby?*"

"He just left, a few minutes ago, Mother," Joyce replied, turning all the way around to face her. "He said he'd already told you good-bye—just asked me to say again that he'd—oh, you know, enjoyed the evening and so forth . . ." Norma did not take time to note that there was a certain constraint in the way Joyce had answered, rather faltering at the finish.

"We must get him back," she said. "There's something—some misunderstanding, I'm sure, but we must get it cleared up, right away."

"Why, Mother, what do you mean?"

"I don't know what I mean—exactly," Norma said. "That's what we've got to get straightened out. The whole thing's a little crazy but—" She had been speaking rapidly, but now she stopped herself with an effort of will; this wouldn't do; she would have to make it clear. "It seems," she continued, "that Bertha has given him quite a sum of money. Their savings, which they had kept up here, in cash."

"There you are!" said Jim. Norma looked at him, but went right on.

"According to Joseph, there's something connected with this end-of-the-world nonsense which I hadn't heard of. Part of the warning, or prediction was to—well, apparently to dispose of all their valuables, or most valuable property, before they went up there tonight . . . At least, that's all I could make out of it."

"That's right," Jim broke in again. "That's what I've been trying to *tell* you all!"

"You have?" said Norma, looking at him again.

"It happened while you were in the house," Joyce said quickly.

"But nobody would listen to me—they all thought *I* had hydrophobia or something—"

"Never mind that now," Roger cut in. "The point is, you say the man has taken Bertha's money?"

"She *gave* it to him," Norma said. "Joseph made that quite clear. But apparently he took it—yes."

"He's been taking everything they'd give him, I tell you. That's what he's been down here for."

"Oh, the poor damn suckers," said Don Landis, more in wonder at the simplicity of those, it seemed, than at the complicity of others.

"You mean you think Mr. Bixby started this whole thing—the

rumor—and the ridiculous rules—and then sat back to gather in all their poor little possessions . . . No! I can't believe it," Norma exclaimed. "There's something we just don't understand here. That's why—"

"I don't believe that man is a crook," said Roger slowly.

"But we've got to get him back here, to clear it up," Norma insisted.

"Okay." Jim was right with her. "I'll go down after him."

"Good," she said. "And then we can try to unravel—" But Mrs. Mears' voice cut across hers like a warning bell.

"No, Jim!"

And Roger said, "No. I don't think that would be wise, under the circumstances. Better let me—if someone will be so good as to drive the car."

"Oh, don't worry. I'm cooled off. Now that the rest of you are coming *to*," snapped Jim, and Miriam put in automatically, "Oh no, Rog—that might be a bit too much for you, now, you know." And Norma looked from one to the other impatiently, her sense of urgency overriding these meaningless delays.

"Please go, Jim," she said. "Right away. Don't let's waste any more time." And then, feeling the pressure of resistance and anxiety still around her, though the other pressure of immediacy was stronger, she added, "I'll come with you." She couldn't wait to talk the others around; they had done nothing but talk, talk, talk all evening long, until they had lost the power of action, but this time there was something to be done. She started across the grass before anyone could throw more obstacles in the way, leaving Jim to follow her—which he did, his long stride catching up with her within a couple of yards.

The others were left behind once more, and each time their number was less: by one, by two, and now by three. They stood or sat where they were, rather like figures in the old children's game; frozen in the attitudes in which the command "Still Pond—no more moving!" had caught them. They looked at each other, and listened to a car door slam, and then another, and the sound of the engine starting and rapidly fading, not dying but simply dropping away, swallowed up by one curve of the hill below.

Joyce said at last, tentatively, glancing in Mrs. Mears' direction, "I guess they're both all right, as long as they're together."

"Oh sure. Sure," Don replied cheerily. "They'll bring him back alive. Don't worry."

"I don't get this thing," said Roger. "I don't get it at all. There's something about that fellow that keeps nagging at my memory, but I can't get hold of it. Reminds me of somebody, probably, though it seems to be more than that."

"We don't know anything about him," Joyce said hesitantly. "I never knew he had a family, until he mentioned them a few minutes ago, in such an odd tone, too. 'My wife, my mother, and my little girl—' that's what he said, though I think the little girl had died, from the way he spoke. And he didn't say anything more *about* them."

Roger was watching her attentively.

"Bixby—" he said, trying the sound of it. "No, it isn't the name. And whatever it is, it doesn't seem to fit in this framework."

"Obviously, he doesn't fit out here in the country," Miriam threw in. "In those dark city clothes—"

"I don't think he *has* another suit," said Joyce suddenly. "I've never seen him wear any other. Or else they're all alike."

"I don't mean out in the country," Roger corrected. "I mean, in *this* country."

"Oh—" said Miriam, arrested by that. "He has no accent, Rog."

"No, but he is foreign-born. He told me himself that he came to the United States when he was a boy of thirteen or fourteen."

"Still, I suppose that could account for some little strangeness that we feel in him. He's so nearly like an American—like us, I mean—but not *quite*," Miriam meditated, and Roger continued thoughtfully, "Another strange thing is: why Norma—and you too, Joyce—had never heard of this property angle of the village prophecy. Unless there was something being covered up, deliberately."

For that moment or two, he and Miriam were like a team, each accustomed to the other's way of thinking, exchanging thoughts as they occurred. But Don picked up that last one, deftly.

"That's not too hard to answer. Did you ever hear of anybody who was willing to tell even his close friends what his own income was? So—by the same token, people keep pretty mum about what they're going to do with their own precious property—if—and when."

"Perhaps you're right, at that," said Roger, and dropped it there. He looked at Miriam again, but their exchange was broken, and he could not read her expression through the thick dusk; could only see that she was moving restlessly, as though to break up the shrunken circle itself.

"If and when—if and when!" she repeated with a half-smothered, barely stifled impatience. "Why do we keep coming back to that same thing over and over again tonight?"

"Because," Don said reasonably, "that is the question before the House tonight, isn't it? If—and when . . ." There was a certain calculated irony in the way he said that, quite audibly for all to hear, though in the last few words there was a muted overtone which carried only the two or three feet between him and Miriam, who knew exactly what he meant. But Joyce did not.

"Oh dear," she sighed. "I suppose they are all up there now, asking themselves just that. I'd almost forgotten. What an evening!" She sounded a trifle plaintive now, and Miriam seemed to echo the same note.

"It has been—a rather long one," she admitted, "though I daresay it isn't even very late."

"Not too late," Don murmured, on that same muted note, with his hand over his mouth, holding his cigarette as he took a drag at it.

But Joyce turned toward him, thoughtfully. "Look," she said. "Why don't you two start out toward the Hill—I mean, where you can look over and see what's going on."

"Oh no!" protested Miriam quickly.

"But you wanted to see the show up there, and after all, this other thing doesn't concern you two, and—"

"Well, why not?" Don said a second time, but in his normal voice, picking up the suggestion with a careless air of turning it over and handing it to Miriam to consider.

"But we were all going, weren't we? That is, you—and Jim—and—" She broke off.

"Oh, we'll come along presently," Joyce said. "When they come back with Mr. Bixby. I'm sure Mother will have all that ironed out and fixed up practically as soon as they get back," she added, more confidently than she felt. "And then whoever else wants to come along up and join you, can."

"Well, I don't know . . ." Miriam still hesitated. "Of course, if you think it's better not to have a regular audience, when they do come back to explain things . . . What do *you* think, Rog?"

"Go ahead," said Roger evenly, and Don addressed him directly, "Think there'll be any need for reinforcements? I mean, I could hang around on the outskirts, so to speak—"

"I hardly think that's necessary, Landis," Roger replied dryly. "The whole thing's undoubtedly a matter of misunderstanding, as Norma said. Not of apprehending a criminal."

"We—ell," said Miriam, still with that show of reluctance, letting it weaken very gradually. (Or could it be that she was watching herself weakening, imperceptibly?)

"Well?" Don repeated, looking at her. "How about your shoes?"

"I changed them when I went in to get this stole," she said demurely.

He threw his head back and laughed—it might have been exult-antly—and quickly checked himself. "I wondered why you looked so small, all of a sudden."

And Joyce said, "Oh go along, children. We grownups'll come up and chaperon you after a while."

So then there were only three left in the patio, Mrs. Mears still sitting stiff and silent as a stone image, and Roger leaning forward with elbows on knees, not looking after the merry couple, whose laughter could be heard trailing after them as they went out the gate, but at the ground between his feet, which was too dark to see. Joyce glanced from one to the other, uncertainly, aware now that her maneuver had been fairly crude. She had seen Roger look up at her once, as if to say, What the hell was she up to, or did she know what she was up to? Well, he had told them himself to go ahead, so that was that. But she wished once more that her mother (and Jim) would come back, with or without Mr. Bixby, so they could get that straightened out too. Joyce was young, and she hated waiting.

"I wish they'd hurry up," she said, and Roger raised his head again.

"Who?" he said.

"Mother and Jim, of course." But something in his voice that time struck into her like a sharp point, like a sliver of guilt . . . and she looked off in the direction of the gate which the others had already passed through a full minute ago. And then another thought came to her, quite irrelevantly, and she seized on it. Her mother had asked her to check Don's room to see if the bed linen had been changed and made up; things had been so haywire round the house all day, Mom'd been afraid it might have been overlooked. And now Joyce had forgotten all about it until this minute.

"Gleeps," she murmured. "I forgot something Mother told me to do. Will you excuse me a minute while I go and see about it?" she said to Mrs. Mears and Roger. Actually, she was relieved to have something like this to keep her busy until the others got back. Jim and Mom, that is . . .

CHAPTER 22

"Mr. Norbeck, may I talk to you?" said Mrs. Mears, out of the pause which had followed Joyce's departure.

"Why, certainly. Of course." He'd raised his head again, to look at her with attention, for it was clear that she was not inquiring whether she might interrupt his meditation with a little small talk.

"I find," she said slowly, as if each word were a difficult step to take, "that I must talk to somebody. You said, earlier this evening, that if we knew we were near the end of our road, we would prefer to carry our respective loads that much farther—in silence."

"Yes, I guess I said that."

"I find," she repeated, "that there is one burden which I cannot carry out of this world. I will have to leave it with someone. Though —I'm sorry—to lay it on your shoulders."

Roger said kindly, despite some inner apprehension now, "I don't know what it is, Mrs. Mears, but if there is anything I can do to help you . . ."

"No, you can't help me. But you seem to have a deep sense of conscience, which goes far beyond the merely personal twinges which most of us feel. It may be, later on, that you can make the decision which I'm—unable to make. Cowardly of me," she muttered, while he waited for her to go on. Finally she lifted her hawklike old head and seemed—if it were possible—to sit more rigidly erect than before, gripping her hands together on her knees and gazing straight in front of her, not at Roger at all.

"I had a son, Mr. Norbeck. Philip, Jim's father, and my only child. I don't know how to tell you this, leaving out the nonessentials, yet giving you the truth. I loved him very much—which I daresay should go without saying. My husband was much older than I, and he died when Philip was small and I was still a relatively young woman. We were together a great deal as he grew up, traveling or at home. He was not—the mama's boy type, I don't mean to imply that. Not at all. But I daresay—I spoiled him. Perhaps he had some inherited defect, which would have been there in any case." She stopped, as if she needed to rest, in the midst of a long climb; to gather strength before she could go on again.

"You can't blame yourself for every quality inherited by a child, from all the different strains which go to make him up," said Roger, adding cautiously, "if that is what you are doing." He wasn't sure what she was leading up to; was only trying to give her a helping hand.

"No," she said reasonably. "And by the time one wonders where to lay the blame for what has gone wrong—it's much too late . . . At any rate, Phil was likable, and clever. He could do things rather well—that is, anything he cared to make an effort about . . . like shooting, or golf—playing the drums. Trap drums, are they called? He had a remarkable sense of rhythm—and a—I think you'd call it a peculiar sense of humor," she said thoughtfully. "He was not a good student, ever, and he had a weakness for girls. He was—let out—of school, three different schools," she said explicitly, and went straight on without further explanation. "When he married, it was because he had to. In fact, I made him do so, because I also had a sense of conscience. Though perhaps it was misplaced. I certainly had no feeling for the girl—except the one which is quite usual, I believe, for mothers of sons to hold. I felt that she had trapped him in the usual way. She was pretty, of course, but cheap. Common. I never doubted that she was—a harlot—by instinct, even if she was too young to have gone far on her course. As far as I *knew*, Philip was the first. So I made him marry her."

The evening had grown distinctly cooler by now, but Roger had begun to sweat slightly with the discomfort of listening to all this. Why, in God's name, she had picked *him* to tell her very personal story to, he could not see, nor what connection it had with any rudiments of conscience or responsibility which he (Roger Norbeck) might have. But there was nothing to do but sit, and wait, and listen.

"Jim is the son of that marriage," said Mrs. Mears. "It was an unsuccessful marriage, naturally. It could hardly have been otherwise, even if it had been more—compatible as to their relative backgrounds. I did not help it," she said, with ruthless honesty, "though I insisted upon their staying together, for a dozen years or more. Perhaps I wanted to rub his nose in it. Perhaps I wanted her to reap the fruit of her early indiscretion by suffering over his inevitable later ones. I don't know. We use our moral attitudes too often to disguise our own real emotions from ourselves . . . I do know now that I was a snob. I wasn't nice to the girl. Correct, you understand, but not nice. She *was* common, if one wants to speak in those terms. But I believe now that she was decent, before and after she married Philip. And of course, of the two, he was the one who amused himself, outside. They were divorced finally, and she remarried after a time. Jim was not happy with either of them then, and came to spend more and more of his vacations with me . . . while Philip, meantime, went his way. It was an expensive way, Mr. Norbeck. I had to help him out again and again. My husband left me a good deal of money when he died," she said candidly, looking over at Roger for the first time. "I have very little left now. Whatever there is, will go to Jim."

"I believe I was told that your son was killed in Korea," Roger said, hoping this would help her along on whatever remained for her to tell, and finish it up.

"Yes, I have no doubt that you were told that. That is what I have told—everyone, until this minute."

"You mean, he isn't dead?" Roger asked, beginning to see, or think he saw, a faint glimmer of light down the long dark corridor which they were following, he being led unwillingly by this strange old lady whom he had never seen before tonight.

"Yes, he is dead. Now. But he was not killed in Korea. He never went to Korea. He was not in the Armed Services at all."

"I see," said Roger, seeing nothing, and she looked at him gratefully—just for that.

"He went his way, as I said. There were times when I almost lost track of him. Until he would need some money again. He gambled too," she said, rather by-the-way, as though that were almost to be expected. "I mean—that, in time, became his other chief diversion. Along with women. He never married again. In fact . . ." There was another rather longish pause, and when she started again Roger knew from her level voice, held steady with the utmost effort, that this was going to be It. "He was very careful, I believe, never to let himself become entangled in that way, again. But there was a woman, finally, who . . . Oh, the details are not necessary," said Mrs. Mears abruptly. "But this one did not care to be shaken off, like the rest, when he was tired of her. She threatened him: threatened to sue him, even to kill him—or herself. So he said. There must have been exceedingly unpleasant quarrels," the voice observed, in what to Roger seemed a stony classic of understatement. "And once, at least, he struck her, or as *he* said, pushed her so that she fell— against something . . . He killed her," the old lady went on rapidly, after a moment's pause. "He was apprehended, and tried, but because there was the evidence of a rather violently worded letter from her, or perhaps because—I'm afraid I really don't understand about these things," she said with an accent of faint apology, coupled with extreme distaste. "But it was something like that. Some possible question of self-defense, or else showing that it was not premeditated. Nevertheless he was convicted. And sentenced—for life.

255

The only good thing that Philip ever did," his mother said, "was to keep his real identity a secret. He had already been living with this woman under another name for quite a long while; had in fact used it elsewhere from time to time, when he found it convenient, I suppose—and somehow, by the grace of God—they never discovered that he had another one. Another name, I mean," she added grimly.

"How did you learn, then, what had happened?" Roger asked.

"A clipping, very soiled, and already several months old, was sent to me in the mail. Addressed only to my post-office box number, printed in pencil. No name. It was obviously the final account of when he was sentenced, with a brief résumé of the case. You know the way some newspaper writers go in for a sort of—chop-licking description of such scenes?" she said, with something like detachment now, as though she were slowly moving away from the scene. "What the prisoner looked like, whether he was pale, whether he smiled or flinched when the sentence was read . . . ? The details of this description fitted too well for me to be left in any doubt. Besides, I had heard the dead woman's name . . . before. I don't think he told me how the clipping came into his hands or how he had hidden it. He just said he had given it, later, to some 'friend' who was coming out on parole, with instructions to mail it—"

"He *said*?" Roger repeated.

"My son escaped," Mrs. Mears stated calmly, "about five months ago. I don't know how; only that he made his way this far without being detected. He came home, to his mother—once more, for protection," she said, in a voice which was even, thin, and wrung with suffering. "And I—sent him away. Jim was at college, but he might so easily have come down for that very week end, as he sometimes did. I made Phil go away, that same evening, and promise —never—to come back. He said he would never let them take him again, alive, and he didn't. He was caught, late that night—shot, and killed as he tried to get away. I read that in my own newspaper, the next day."

There was nothing that Roger could think of to say, and he didn't try. To a fellow who had done his stint of police reporting 'way back, this was old, old stuff. But to hear it told by a woman like this one, was something even he had never met before. She had leaned back in her chair at last, as if the iron in her old spine had finally crumbled, her head dropped forward, and there was no perceptible emotion left in her voice when she went on again, presently.

"Now, there is Jim. Only Jim. He looks like his father, speaks like him too, his voice, that is—but not his laugh," she put in absently, which seemed curiously irrelevant to Roger. "Certain mannerisms are similar too. But I do not think he is like . . . in other ways."

"Jim's a good kid," Roger said gruffly. "I'd bank on that."

"Jim," she said, "is more like his mother . . . thank God. A sort of common earthly quality. Good earth, not dirt. Dependable. But for a minute there, tonight—"

"Oh, he reacted as any kid would—put on the defensive," Roger said quickly. "He'd heard a lot of this gossip in the village, and didn't know what Bixby was getting at."

"*You* know, though, now. Don't you?"

Roger looked at her for a moment, realizing all at once that he hadn't gotten round to filling in the gap toward which she was pointing.

"It was Philip whom he picked up that night along the road, not Jim. There was that strong resemblance still, in spite of the difference in years. And it was dark," she said. "It was Philip who told Mr. Bixby that story—or prediction—about the end of the world."

"But why should he—where did *he* get it, do you suppose?"

"I think he made it up."

"I don't get it," Roger said. "Why—?"

"I told you . . . that he had—a peculiar sense of humor."

"Good Christ," Roger said, under his breath, "even at a time like that!"

"Yes," she said simply.

"Practical joker, eh? Well, I don't suppose he thought anybody would be fool enough to believe it."

"He might have thought someone would be smart enough to use it," she remarked slowly. "And I'm afraid that would have amused him, too. Of course he may have had some other motive which fitted in with his sense of the—ridiculous. Something we shall never know, now."

"But you're inclined to think, then, that Bixby is the one who has carefully spread and fostered this fantasy?"

"I don't know," she said. "I wish they would come back."

"Oh, I think they're talking it all over," Roger said, wishing he felt as sure of that as he sounded. "Just trying to make head or tail out of it as we are. Mrs. Collins can keep any situation under control."

"Possibly, if anyone can. Though even Mrs. Collins is"—she seemed to hesitate for just a breath—"quite human," she finished delicately. "And I doubt if she knows very much about Mr. Bixby, or even about Jim. We never know quite enough about anyone else, to keep from making mistakes. The sad thing is that each one knows only a part of the *whole* story. And I don't mean just this little fable—for the simple-minded, but the entire plot of this business of life and death. Do you understand why I have told you all this, Mr. Norbeck?"

He thought a moment and then said, "No, not altogether. I'm not sure that I do."

"Because of Jim, of course. And Joyce. I have done everything— *everything*," she repeated distinctly, "to save Jim from knowing that last sordid chapter of his father's life. He—disliked his father, or at the least, distrusted him, from the time he was a fairly small boy, and he hates the bare reminder that he resembles him in any way. I'm not quite sure what this knowledge would do to him . . . But you see, I am not morally sure whether the likeness goes deeper than *I* care to admit, myself. Or whether Joyce should know—what there is to know. Or her mother. I have not been able to bring myself to speak of it, to either of them. It might wreck two young lives, quite unnecessarily."

"Yes, I see that," said Roger. And he thought, So you want me to take the responsibility of advising or sharing this decision with you. Oh no, he thought. "Well, I'm not a criminologist, Mrs. Mears. I have no knowledge of such things. Only the loose ideas that anyone hears being batted about, as to the possibility of—inheriting some criminal tendency. And in this case it would seem to have been more a matter of an amoral inclination, not sufficiently disciplined." He wondered, as he said that, what it meant—but she agreed nevertheless.

"Yes . . . But with Jim . . . No, I have *not* spoiled Jim. I have leaned backward until it almost broke my spine to avoid that . . . My heart, at least. The boy has no notion of how much I—love him." It was hard for her even to pronounce that word, Roger observed. "Though in a way, I think he has a feeling for me, too. It may be only that he feels bound to me, in some way. And that is wrong, too . . . All wrong. Whatever one does for a child is wrong," she said bitterly. "Now, you see, whatever I've given or withheld from him, the effect has been utterly negative, and I have left him in a vacuum of indecision. Immobility may be the truer word. He is standing still, Mr. Norbeck, at the age of twenty-one —seemingly incapable of making a definite move in any direction. Waiting to *be* moved—by the Army—or some girl, who may or may not be Joyce, after all . . . or by some gust of wind—or rage—like that flare-up tonight."

Roger was silent for a moment, considering what she had said, and much besides. Finally he said, "No, I don't think so, Mrs. Mears. Jim is a good kid. A very good kid—I'm sure of it."

"Thank you," she said coolly, as if in civil acknowledgment of his effort to reassure her. And realizing that she thought he was merely trying to make her feel better, it occurred to him conjointly, almost incidentally, that this, his ability to size people up, was probably the only thing he was still good for. So he tried again.

"I mean it, Mrs. Mears. You see, I've had a lot of practice in listening to men talk—men and boys; listening through the talk, to what they mean. And I say again . . . Mr. Bixby is no crook, and your Jim is no potential criminal. Jim's all *right!*" he reiterated. "Just give him time to find his feet. That is, of course—" He fell abruptly silent as the brisk sound of a door opening and closing came from behind them. But Mrs. Mears went on quietly, ". . . if there *is* yet time. That's what you were about to say, isn't it? And I can't give him time, any more than I can take away his inheritance. . . . But I can set him free—to a certain extent. Though I shan't be here to see what he makes of it."

"Oh, sure you will!" He meant that to be gentle, but it came out gruffly. And the warning sound of Joyce's heels clicking on the paved terrace had ceased as she came out onto the grass to join them.

"For goodness' sake, aren't those two back yet?" she exclaimed, her anxiety making the words a trifle shrill, and irritable, as with children who have overstayed some permissible excursion.

"Nope, not yet," said Roger, taking pains to sound careless about it. "They're probably having another cosy little seminar on the end of the world. Forgetting that we'd like to know the conclusion too. And it isn't as long as it seems, Joyce. Probably not half an hour since they went off."

"I suppose that's right. It just *seems* like a couple of hours. I didn't even look at the clock when I was in the house, so I don't actually know what time it is."

"In any case, it is time to go," Mrs. Mears announced. And though it took an obvious effort, she gradually pushed herself up until she was standing, a tall gaunt shadow beside Joyce, who looked at her in dismay.

"Oh, but—aren't you going to wait for Jim?"

"No, my dear."

"Well, of course I'll run you down, then. Our car's still here."

"That won't be necessary, thank you, Joyce. I am not going down. I'm going up—with the rest of them."

Joyce stared at her, completely speechless for a moment, and Roger, who had stood up, also with something of an effort, had nothing to say either, which was no help.

"So you see, I don't need a car, my dear," the older woman added, with a combination of graciousness and pride. Yes, she sounded proud, thought Joyce, like someone who knew her own strength. But of course she *didn't*—because she'd never be able to make it. And it was all so silly, so unlike Jim's grandmother.

"But—but Jim wouldn't like it, you know," Joyce protested, just to gain time, "if you went up ahead of him."

"Ah—well, we all have to get used to that," said Mrs. Mears.

"Still, I think Joyce is right." Roger spoke up firmly now, ignoring what he knew she meant. "Jim would certainly want you to wait till he gets back. It's a long climb, I gather, from what they tell me."

"Yes, it's a long climb," she conceded. "I have planned for that." Which, to Joyce, made no sense whatsoever, but Roger was beginning to understand rather too well.

"Does Jim know you're planning to go up there?" he inquired pointedly.

"No, Mr. Norbeck, he does not." And then she added with delicate emphasis, "And you remember my saying that Jim and I have never interfered with each other, or tried to influence the other, in any way." She turned to pick up her cane, which had been leaning against her chair, and when she straightened and turned back, she was ready to go.

"Good-bye, Mr. Norbeck," she said formally, but he did not reply.

He saw, however, that Joyce had straightened too, with the stiffening of determination, and as Mrs. Mears moved away, the girl moved with her.

Watching them go, with compunction for Joyce, Roger reflected that it was a cold-blooded thing that the old lady was doing, and the kid didn't have a chance against that iron purpose. Nor would he, if he had taken a stronger stand. And just what did he mean by a strong stand, anyway? he asked himself derisively. If it had come to a wrastle with the old girl, *he* couldn't have held her back himself, big strong he-man that he was! But nevertheless she had picked him to carry her burden for her; that was plain enough. The load which she was unwilling, or unable, or afraid to carry up that hill with her. The decision which she had left for him to make . . . Though he could see clearly, as though it were bright day, that—as Joyce had no chance against Mrs. Mears' will tonight, the latter would have had none against the girl, if she should choose to marry Jim. Nothing would stop that youngster, not even that grisly story and all its implications. So there was no decision. But the burden of the older woman's grief and sense of guilt-in-responsibility remained, and she had gone out there to lay it down. And tomorrow morning, he would be the only one who knew why she had done it.

He was horribly tired, himself, and would have liked to go to bed. Just bed. But there was still this business of Bixby, and Norma's absence; Norma and Jim, who must have been gone at least an hour despite what he had said to allay Joyce's anxiety. He knew quite well that they were not down at Bixby's house all this time. He knew almost to a certainty that they had not found the man there, and had tried to follow him out to the coast; to intercept him before he reached the coast highway, that is. Norma should have known better than to do a foolhardy thing like that. And *he*, Norbeck, should have known better than to let her go off with Jim at all, no matter how convinced the inner Norbeck was that Bixby was decent, harmless, and just another victim of the assorted phobias which had taken possession of those idiots in the village. The fact remained that Bixby was an unknown quantity. (As who was not? Even when you'd known them for years, they could still surprise you sometimes, for better and sometimes worse. Better or worse . . . in sickness and in health. Even your wife? Good God, couldn't he get that out of his head? He must be going batty with all the rest of this gang— and he was the guy who was so sure, five minutes ago, one minute ago, that he could appraise another man: two men—and a girl. But not his wife!)

Well, better wait a few minutes more, since he didn't actually know how long it had been since Norma and Jim had gone . . . Or Miriam and Landis. He made his way over to the edge of the terrace where there was just enough light from the lamp by the door to see the face of his watch. And then he sat down to wait, his glance moving restlessly back and forth across the patio. But all he saw was a pair of faintly gleaming eyes about ten inches from the ground, bearing down on him from the outer shadows. No, you don't, old girl, he thought; just because the party has gone, you needn't think you can come and cozy up to me. "Keep going, Cleo," he said aloud as the eyes lost their glow and the cat took shape, approaching him. Oh, this was the night for a prowl, all right. Cat on the prowl—everybody on the prowl. But Cleo passed by loftily, with

262

her tail straight up as if she'd neither seen nor heard him, in fact. She proceeded purposefully toward the swing seat, as though that had been her intended goal all the time, and sprang up on it and with complacent deliberation turned around a couple of times and settled down into a fur mound, flat and circular. Oddly, the tactile memory of its softness and its warmth came back to Roger.

He held his wrist out to squint at his watch again. He'd give them another couple of minutes anyway. Or was it himself he was giving those minutes to, because he wasn't quick on decisions any more, as he used to be? Yet the fact was that he could not make himself believe that any of this—nor any of these people—was quite real . . . Mim was real, yes—but she was just off taking a stroll (as he'd encouraged her to, dammit!) not aiming for eternity . . . But all the rest of it was a little too ridiculous. He found himself suddenly wanting to laugh, aloud and loudly, at this silly farce which somebody had contrived, very badly it seemed. Bad construction, unreal characters and situations . . . no self-respecting producer would have considered for a minute putting such a thing on the stage. And nobody but a lunatic could laugh alone, anyway. Laughter was one thing which had to be shared. It was at that precise instant that Norbeck discerned, without any warning, but with a sense of shock at his own stupidity (for it had been all too plain to see), that Mim had gone off now on that fool's excursion for a little fun and mirth, which he'd refused to share. Worse than that, there was a kind of shame in this apperception that he had somewhere lost his sense of humor, which some people called a sense of proportion. The one thing which no one will admit he never possessed. Mortified, he couldn't explain to himself how or where he had let this happen, and he would damn well have to do something about that. Beginning tomorrow.

Tomorrow. But meantime there was this everlasting night to get through; the surrounding night in which he appeared to be marooned, alone with a cat. It was all silent now; no sound of singing in the distance; no sound of dishes or of argument in the house nearby; no sound of anything, only the faint throb of his own blood in his ears. Or was it—more than that? He sat forward listening intently, more suspicious of his imagination now than of his heartbeat, and only when he was finally sure that the vibration was real, mechanical and coming rapidly closer, did he begin to relax and realize that this wait had been something of a strain, and he was very, very tired now.

So he continued to sit there, listening, to the slew of tires as they came to a stop out there; to the motor abruptly cut off, and to the voices: someone calling hello (that was Norma) and some other woman's voice answering, but farther off so he couldn't tell who— was it Mim? Couldn't even be sure of that . . . And a male voice too, which sounded like Jim's. So they were back, all right. They'd be coming in here in another second, Roger thought, and he might as well stay right where he was, waiting for them. Waiting.

CHAPTER 23

Joyce had been on her way back to the house, when, crossing the roadway below, she thought she heard Jim's old motor grinding up the grade, and stopped hopefully to listen. Yes—oh, thank goodness they were coming back. So she waited for them, and though she had moved well away to the side of the road, their lights caught her as Jim swung around the last curve and up into the driveway, and she heard her mother exclaim, going past her. And again, Jim had no sooner thrown on the brakes than the car doors on both sides swung open and Norma called back, "Joyce! What *is* it, dear?"

"I was just watching for you," Joyce said simply, coming up to join them. "Oh, Mother, I'm so glad you're back!"

"Darling, did we make you anxious? I'm sorry. I suppose we were gone longer than we realized. But it gave *me* quite a turn when I saw you standing out there in the middle of the road!"

She wasn't in the middle of the road, Joyce thought mechanically, but that wasn't worth correcting. It was this other thing she'd have to explain: to Jim, of course, but it seemed easier right now to do it through her mother.

"Well, I'm sorry too, Mom. I didn't mean to scare you, but you see, I was just coming across the road from the trail when I heard the car, so I waited—"

But that didn't seem to register somehow, for Norma went on quickly, "Thank heaven *you're* all right, anyway . . . What an evening! Horrible. Poor old Alfred . . ." she finished, and that wholly unexpected tangent diverted Joyce from the thing which she was trying to tell them.

"*Alfred!*" she exclaimed, as one shocked by such inconsequence.

"Alfred's house is burned practically to the ground," Jim said.

"Just smoking there in the middle of that awful pavement," Norma continued. "Though I suppose the pavement is what saved it from spreading, even on a windless night like this. The whole village might have gone before they knew it."

"Holy smokes!" Joyce murmured in an awed tone, supremely unaware of the ineptness of the words she had used. And then, "Where was Alfred himself?"

"We—don't know, actually," her mother replied.

"We think he's probably in there," Jim said bluntly.

"You see, dear, we couldn't do anything to find out. He had some kind of roofing that didn't burn as much as the rest—just smoldered and fell in, or down, on top of everything. It's like—a great big dilapidated hat, all charred around the edges, with bits of porch or foundation showing underneath—like a person's hat and shoes, and the person himself gone," she added with a slight shudder. "But his truck is there, in the ruins. What's left of it. I'm very much afraid," Norma said sadly, "that poor Alfred set—and lighted—his own funeral pyre."

"Oh golly, Mom—how awful."

"It's a mess," Jim said, with feeling. "That's why we were gone so long. Trying to put it out, though it was pretty well down to smoke and embers when we got there. Nobody else around of course—whole crazy population gone up the Hill, I guess."

Joyce swallowed; decided that was hardly the cue for her to give him her news, and asked hesitantly, "What—about Mr. Bixby?"

"He was gone," her mother said.

265

"Car, and all? Did you try to get into the house?"

"Yes. When there was no light or sound, or sign of anybody—or of the car either—Jim forced one of the windows. We wanted to see if he'd left anything, but he hadn't. Not so much as a toothbrush. I should have expected that," Norma said wearily, "because Mattie had told me once that he kept nothing down here, not even an extra suit or pair of shoes. You know Mattie and her gossip . . . but she cleaned the house for him once a week, and I daresay she knew what she was talking about, this time. Well—that doesn't matter, does it?" Her voice dropped off. Joyce saw that her mother was so tired that it was hard for her to keep anything in sequence now. "At any rate, it was when we didn't find Mr. Bixby at the house, and were standing out on the step discussing what to do next, that we saw this smoky haze from somewhere below and behind the hill. So we went down to investigate."

"You and Jim—make quite a team," Joyce said, softly now, and fondly, too; even a shade wistfully.

"Sure do," said Jim. "She's got what it takes to back a guy up." And whether he said it in admiration of her mother, or with a tinge of personal arrogance, to Joyce's ear there was something more: comparison—and the thing which had begun to thaw and melt under her breastbone froze up again.

Norma said, "Thank you, partner. But I for one am through playing cops and robbers—and fireman too, for tonight anyway. If you children have any other ideas, please let me know. But I'm going in."

She had left them there in the dark, and it was the first time they had been alone together since Joyce returned that day, at noon. They could not really see each other now, yet they were not so far apart in inches that Jim couldn't have reached her if he had stretched out his long arms to put them round her. (Why didn't he? . . . Joyce waited, knowing she must tell him about his grandmother, but thinking—if he did, it would be easier; and if he did, that little hard cold lump inside her might begin to thaw again and disappear. But he didn't, and though they could each feel the other's presence, like an almost intolerable physical ache, neither one moved an inch.) Neither one knew what to say—which wouldn't give the other some slight edge; some small advantage, over him—or her. And neither one could give that much.

Eventually, of course, they took mutual refuge in the matter-of-fact talking of the impersonal incidents which had been happening around them, but had nothing to do with their two selves. Jim went on about the fire down at Alfred's place, and it was only natural—she told herself—that he should still be preoccupied with such a melodramatic event; so she took to questioning him very practically about how he'd ever managed to do anything about putting it out when the house was so detached from the rest of the village. And he explained that he had a shovel in his car (Joyce knew that, but he reflected that that was the kind of thing a girl wouldn't remember) and then he'd gone over to the Petries' place—nobody around of course—and got a bucket out of the shed, and a length of hose to attach to Alfred's outside pipe which they'd once used for the garden . . . He explained again that it was only smoldering by that time, or they couldn't even have got near enough to damp down the charred fringes or smother them with sand, to keep it from starting up again.

All very noncommittal and impersonal, and quite typical of their habitual matter-of-factness together; but this time the tone of naturalness served as a bridge over the gap of misunderstanding or mistrust which lay between them. They discussed it earnestly, and perhaps also with relief in finding something to share again, though not too intimately. But what they were sharing was, after all, only the gruesome mystery of Alfred's end; mulling it over with a kind of shocked fascination, since it touched neither of them closely. Jim, in spite of his seeming preoccupation, didn't really want to go on this way, but there was nothing else he could say to her tonight.

And Joyce was intensely aware of what she ought to be telling him, and had so far failed to do. It was a chilly undercurrent running through her mind all the time they stood there; an uneasy trickle, like a tap left running in another room; something she would have to tell him to go and fix, sooner or later . . . But she kept putting it off because she also knew he couldn't fix it, and her own concern, approaching dread, of how he would react, was mixed up with an unreasonable sense of guilt as well, though she didn't know why. She just didn't know how he would take it. So far, it apparently had not occurred to him to ask where his grandmother was, so he must assume that she was still up there in the patio, with Roger, and her mother too, now. Or else he simply hadn't got around to thinking about anything except Alfred and his melodramatic demise.

"I keep thinking about the old guy," he said once. "And whether he did it on purpose. Sure was one way of disposing of all *his* valuables."

"Oh, Jim, he couldn't have. It's too grim, nobody could—" But she stopped suddenly, thinking of that other gaunt figure, proceeding relentlessly around a hillside trail, with flashlight poked in front of her. (Mrs. Mears had certainly brought that along, on purpose, in her white handbag!)

"Well, it was a clean sweep, anyway," Jim said briefly. "That's for sure. House and truck and contents."

"What makes you so sure he was in there himself? He may be up on the Hill this minute," Joyce said reasonably. "You know, with all the rest of them."

"No."

"Why not?"

"Well, if you must know . . . I didn't tell your mother this, and didn't think she'd seen it until she said that about the shoes—and maybe it was just a figure of speech, anyway, I dunno. But—when I got up fairly close to the garage part of the shack . . . Well," he began again, "one of the old boy's shoes was there, lying kind of under where the doorway had been—only, of course, all those beams and stuff had fallen across the end of the truck. I could just see the shoe sticking out a bit from under the rest. Couldn't even make out what it was at first, even with my flashlight."

"Oh, Jim," she said faintly.

"It was—all by itself," he explained, with an awkward attempt at delicacy. "I mean, just lying there sort of scorched and shriveled. But I couldn't see in under the debris beyond it, and it was still 'way too hot to get at anything, with the equipment I had . . . Nobody could have lived in there, that's all," he finished definitely.

268

"Oh, Jim," she said again. "It seems so horrible, and useless. I never liked the queer old thing, and I'm not going to pretend I did." She paused, and added honestly, "He gave me the creeps sometimes, the way he looked at me. But that doesn't make it seem any less grim, and sort of pitiful, now."

"You know what?" Jim said, rather suddenly. "I've had the feeling right along that—somebody was doing to die, tonight."

For a long second she said nothing at all, and then, "So have I," she acknowledged.

"I don't get hunches, generally. Heck, I'm not psychic or anything," he said a little defensively. "But when that kid this afternoon—you know, I was telling the gang about it up in the patio tonight—when Letty said the end of the world was when you died, I thought, Why, sure! That's *it*. For everybody."

"With or without premonitions," Joyce said soberly.

"That's right. Of course, if a guy *plans* to do it—it's no premonition."

"No," she said miserably, for this was getting no easier and she was getting no closer to the point she had to reach. "No . . . And I don't know how anybody *could* plan to do it!"

"Scared of something, I guess. Or sick. Or just bored. Tired of it all, maybe." That last he had begun to say by way of being funny, or at least less morbid, for Joyce was sounding pretty upset.

"I know," she murmured, and she was not thinking of Alfred either, but was still pushing on in that other direction. "Oh, *Jim*—" it burst from her like a cry, though spoken very low. "I don't know how to tell you something. And I *must* tell you—I've been trying to, but I don't know how to start." (How to describe that image which she could still see more clearly than she could him—plodding up the hill beside her—and then ahead of her as the trail grew narrower—and then away from her as the old lady had turned her back implacably upon the world she was leaving behind. She seemed so close to Joyce still, like a specter with its arms around her . . . instead of Jim's.)

Even now he didn't reach out to touch her, and didn't speak for quite a while, so that in the thick dark she'd almost have thought

269

he wasn't there, except for the dim white hulk which was his dinner coat. Though it, too, seemed like something bodiless, hung there against a black backdrop, several feet from the ground. Until at length he said, heavily, "It's not about Alfred, though, is it?"

"Oh no—no, not about Alfred."

Well, he'd known all the time that she was half thinking about something else, but he'd had a blind feeling that if they could just get by this dark spot where they couldn't see very well, keep themselves busy talking and pondering the other peculiar manifestations of human nature, which didn't really matter a damn to either of them—oh well, he'd just thought maybe they might get by, until they could reach each other again. But if she had to tell him, why that was that.

"Okay. Why not just tell me?" he said.

"I don't know how you're going to take it." She sounded uncertain still, almost timid. (*Joyce*, of all people!) "Because maybe I've got it all wrong, myself. I may be making too much of it. It took me so terribly by surprise, you see."

"I guess I can take it," he said steadily. "I guess maybe—I know it already."

"You *do*? You knew she was going up there, all the time? Oh, Jim, I felt so absolutely awful about it, with you not here."

That threw him. That left him dangling absolutely nowhere.

"Going where? Who?" he demanded. "Miriam? Have she and Landis gone over to the Hill together?"

"Yes—yes! Of course they have—I *sent* them off together," she threw back impatiently. (So that was it. He'd been half wondering where the others were, but now he got it: she'd deliberately gotten rid of them and waited for him here, so she could get this over. He felt sad, and very old, as if he were looking back on his youth, a long, long way back—from his fortieth birthday, say—to the only girl he'd ever loved in a long and pointless life . . . That is, if he didn't get knocked off somewhere in Asia or the Middle East, maybe.)

But meantime the love of his youth was saying, "They've got nothing to do with it! What's the matter with you, anyway?" She sounded almost cross, the way she always did when she was 'way ahead of him.

270

"Well, you said something about Miriam going up there—"

"I did *not* say anything about Miriam going up there until you *asked* about her, just now! I'm talking about your grandmother."

"Gran?" He knew he sounded exceedingly stupid, but he had to make some readjustment here. "Gosh, I kind of forgot she was still here, what with everything else going on."

"She's not *here*, Jim. Not now." She made a slow and careful statement of it.

"Well, where—oh, you took her down, did you? I don't see why we didn't see you then, on the road."

"Listen, Jim. Your grandmother has gone *up* the hill. Up to the *Hill*, with all the others. No, I don't mean Miriam and Don, but all those others like Bertha and Joseph and the ones from the village. Now do you understand?"

He stared through the gloom for several seconds, before he asked, "How? How did she go?"

"She walked, with her cane. She took the upper path from here, of course."

"But that still leaves a long way around the shoulder of Sage Hill —and then down across the gap and up again," he said, quite reasonably, with an almost cautious detachment. "That last is a steep climb up from this side, even if it isn't so long."

"I know," Joyce said.

"She can't possibly make it." His voice was still quite unemotional, still exploring the simple basic facts. When Joyce made no answer to that last, he said, evenly, "Why did you let her go?"

"I tried to stop her."

"Well, look," he said—still controlled. "She's an old lady, you know, Joyce. She can't go climbing mountains. Surely you could have done something—"

"I tried my best to keep her from going. But she was absolutely determined to go. I knew there wasn't any use talking, Jim, even while I was trying to argue with her. And then I went along with her for a little way, thinking I could persuade her after a bit, when she saw how difficult it was going to be. Or even help her a little. But I couldn't do either one. She made me come back. Just stopped in her tracks and told me to go home. As if I were a little dog,"

Joyce said reflectively. "That's why I was standing in the road, waiting for you."

"I think you must be nuts," he said, the reaction beginning to rise in him at last. "Absolutely *nuts*. I wasn't here—your mother wasn't here—it was up to *you*. 'Tried to stop her . . . Tried to persuade her . . . Went along with her a little way . . .' Haven't you got any sense at *all*?" His voice was rising too, but Joyce's tone was level as she replied, "Have you ever tried—to stop your grandmother—from doing any single thing she was set on doing? I'd like to see you try it."

"Well, that's exactly what you're going to see, right now!" His voice was curt, and from the direction it came, she knew he'd wheeled away from her; was already several feet away, and then he must have stopped again or spoken over his shoulder. "How long ago did she start?"

"Oh, I don't know, Jim! It seems so long—but it may be only fifteen or twenty minutes."

"My *God!*" he said, and angry as the tone was, it was still farther away, several yards now perhaps.

"It was only a few minutes from the time she turned me back that you and Mother came," Joyce said, but he didn't answer that and she could hear his steps crunching loudly down the gravel to the road. Suddenly she heard herself calling after him, on some impulse of desperation—accusation—reproach (she didn't know what made her say it, but she couldn't seem to hold it back), "At least *she* took her flashlight, so she can see where she's going!" But though she could still hear him crashing along out there, there was no response to that either, and she didn't expect any.

Jim had in fact heard the word flashlight, and knew very well it would have made more sense for him to stop, go back and get his own from the car, even if it lost him a minute or so. But it was partly his anger with Joyce which kept him from acknowledging her suggestion by so much as a moment's pause, as well as this feeling of frantic haste: to catch up with his grandmother, and stop her before it was too late. He had no time to identify either feeling, as he went lunging on across the road and up the bank into the wide

272

mouth of the trail. He knew it all so well he could have found it in his sleep or with his eyes shut, and as it was, there was starlight of a sort—dim yet clear enough to eyes accustomed now for minutes past to no other illumination.

But as he went, it was not only his feet pounding along the path, nor his breath coming faster, nor even his blood pumping harder to carry him along, but that surge of alternating emotions, anger with the girl he'd loved, and anxiety—almost an anguished tenderness, for the older woman—which like a pulse, piston-like, drove him on his way. He had no way of knowing why his wrath with Joyce had flared so high and bitterly, though at first he kept repeating half-whispered phrases to himself . . . "Damned little fool" . . . "Crazy idiot, standing yakking about *Alfred!*" But it was not blaming Joyce so much for Mrs. Mears' departure, or even for letting her go, as possibly reproaching her in his heart for not understanding what he felt about his grandmother—and why. He had already forgotten how difficult Joyce had found it, even to tell him that she'd gone.

As for Gran, he had no idea why she had done this thing; not any—for she couldn't have gone right off the beam with all the rest of those lunatics, and she couldn't possibly think she'd make the grade (literally) with that heart of hers and at her age. All he could guess was that he must have failed her in some way, and that he must catch up with her, must stop her. But it was harder to see, once he'd gone around that first wide shoulder of the hill: more brush closing in on the narrowing path, more unevenness of sand and occasional small rocks, and naturally his black dress shoes with their slick soles were not exactly regulation attire for such an expedition. He stumbled off the path entirely at one point and snagged the cuff of his white coat on the stiff sharp finger of some blasted bush. He was swearing now, and panting slightly, and praying silently, leaving his rage with Joyce behind him, as in extremity one jettisons any unnecessary freight. He was concentrating only on Gran, and getting there. (And how she'd ever gotten this far herself, he didn't know).

It was the little blob of light which he saw first, some distance ahead—not even sure it was a light until he saw it moving, flickering, disappearing farther on. He called out sharply, *"Gran!"* and then hearing how harsh his voice had sounded, called again, urgently, throwing it after her, but with a lift of questioning hopefulness, like a cajoling echo of his first shout. "Gra-an . . . ?" She didn't respond and the light kept going, and so did Jim, pounding harder, so that he was aware that he sounded like a herd of elephants, or buffalo— or both . . . Anybody could hear him in this outer silence, so he saved his breath as he gained rapidly on the light which seemed now to be scarcely moving. Until he was close enough to speak without calling, in an almost normal tone.

"Hey, Gran—*wait* for me, can't you?"

They were going slightly downgrade now, toward the gap between the hills, and as he slithered a trifle on the sandy path in his haste to overtake her, he could finally see her tall shadow ahead of him, a dark silhouette in that faint aura of light, which had come to a stop—just before his feet went out from under him and he sat down flat in the path. The light slewed around to point at him, and he got up and dusted himself off—knowing remotely that this was funny, but he had no breath, no nothing left to laugh with, though he tried for a carefully humorous inflection as he demanded, "What's the idea anyway—going off without me?" Finding as he said it that he had to speak carefully to keep his voice from shaking. Only then did he know fully what a scare she'd given him. And only then did she snap off the flashlight in her hand.

"I didn't need company, Jim," she said.

"Well, heck, you might have told me you were coming up here, so I could have been prepared, myself!" He sounded aggrieved that time, and she could take it for a joke or not.

"I thought this journey was one that everybody should decide on—by himself."

"Gran, you're not going all the way," he said gently, a little worried again by the flat seriousness with which she spoke. He'd been so sure that he had only to catch up with her, let her know he was *with* her, to bring her back again.

"Yes, Jim, I am."

"But *why*, for Pete's sake? You don't believe—what the others do about tonight. You know you don't, Gran!" (Trying nervously to kid her out of it now.) "Come clean, now, this is an act—but it's no joke if you overplay it."

"Act," she said. "Act of God? No." She seemed to raise that question only to put it aside again, but all so distantly that his nervousness was chilled into dread.

"I don't *get* it, Gran."

"What I believe—is not necessary for you to understand, Jim. You and I have never tried to influence or coerce each other, have we?" she reminded him, and added sternly, "You shouldn't have come after me."

"But my gosh, I couldn't let you go off that way! That's a big climb ahead, and you're not so—well, I mean you're—"

"I'm doing very well, don't you think?" Her voice was even, her breathing was no more labored now than he had often heard it, but the fact was he couldn't tell how she was doing, for he knew she was quite capable of covering up—until her last breath. And he began to realize what he had always known, the strength of will in that old frame which he had never really battled with before.

"I think you're doing swell, this far," he conceded. "But there's no sense in overdoing it. We're going back now," he said flatly, trying the masterful line. "While the going's good."

"You are going back," she said. "I—am not."

"Well, then, I'll go along with you." Feeling like a weak fool as he reversed himself, not knowing that Joyce had said exactly the same thing.

"No," his grandmother said. Adamant. And Jim's own sense of helplessnes grew, engulfing him. He wondered if he could pick her up and carry her back. Might. If it hadn't been for the dark, the unevenness up and down, the distance . . . he must have come half a mile, maybe more. And she was a big woman, almost as tall as he. Still, he might try . . . But there was something else; a final indignity, if he had done so: spiritual, not physical. Insuperable, between them.

"Gran, you'll never make it," he said simply.

275

"Yes, I think I shall. And now"—politely, wishing to be detained no longer—"I'd like to go on again. Alone. But thank you, my dear, for offering to come."

"Look, you can't *do* this! Come on, toots—" the ridiculous name he called her on very special occasions, which generally made her chuckle; his throat fairly closed up on it this time, and there was no answering chuckle, and when he groped to get his arm around her bony shoulders, they were rigid, unyielding.

"Jim, can't you let me *go?*" she said at last, her voice attenuated, sapped of all emotion. But she was asking for release. That was plain to him, now. Finally. To his stubborn heart and stupid head. He dropped his arm.

"Okay," he said. He stood aside, and she snapped on the flashlight, focusing its circle on the ground. "Good luck." He made himself say it. "I'll see you—"

"Of course . . . Good night, dear." And for one second she raised the flashlight to point it full at his face, and then returned it to light the path. He couldn't understand why she had done that, but it had dazzled him momentarily so that he couldn't even see her shadow moving away from him; only hear her slow steps and the slightly different sound, a curious stubby noise which her cane made on the ground, periodically.

He was so stunned that he continued to stand where he was for a few minutes. So numb he couldn't quite take in what had happened. That he had come up here to stop her, and *had* stopped her, and let her go on again. He couldn't think it through; the only thing he seemed capable of grasping was that she had made up her mind to go up there tonight, and once Gran had set her mind on any line, there was no changing it.

But that started his own brain turning over, slowly, recalling different things . . . His grandmother's dislike for his mother, as far back as he could remember. No, that had never changed. Her unyielding championship of his father, even when he had hurt her to the marrow. Her indomitable silent battle against shrinking financial resources, lessening vitality—increasing age; never admitting that she had lost so much as an inch, or even a millimeter, against

276

the Adversary, whatever it might be. That very thing she had said here only a few minutes ago . . . It must have been a kind of religion with her, Jim thought. Never to try to change anybody else's mind, and never to let anybody change hers. He didn't even know that he was seeing it in terms of "have been" until the thought had gone past him, like a ghost on the path. And then without any warning at all, he saw himself standing out on the hillside in the dark alone, like some silly fool who walks in his sleep and suddenly wakes up wondering where he is.

What am I doing, hanging around here? he demanded—it might have been aloud, or silently, it didn't matter which. What the hell am I waiting for? I thought she needed me, some way. So where does that leave me? Standing out here on a hillside in the middle of the night—in a dinner coat, yet! (With the clear chanting of hymns in his ears, now.)

He continued to jeer at himself as he started walking back. Wasn't even as though he had a girl out for a midnight stroll, for there wasn't any girl. (No girl.) He wasn't mad at Joyce any more now; not in the same way, for it was evident to him, a trifle belatedly, that she couldn't have stopped the old girl either . . . Old Girl: he'd never called her that before—belittling, patronizing or whatever. So don't start now, he told himself. Just because you find you aren't as important to her as you thought. Or to the girl you left behind you. For after all—even with the anger gone—there was still that guy that Joyce had brought down here to wave in his face like a red flag. Yes, he'd reacted in his usual bull-headed way, but it was perfectly clear to Jim that she was through with him; that like his grandmother, she had had enough.

He didn't know how he'd ever messed things up so badly. Making himself believe that because it had nearly killed Gran when his father went off that way and got himself killed so unnecessarily, it might make it easier for her, old as she was and everything, if he stuck around, himself, as long as he could. And thinking that he and Joyce would get things fixed up right—and tied up tight—if they had more time to work it out. But maybe he wasn't thinking at all; maybe he'd been only stalling, figuring it was somebody's else's move, not his. Gran's—or Joyce's—or the Draft Board's—or just the Three Old Fates, maybe. He didn't know why he'd ever doped it out that way. But whatever he'd thought, it had been one hundred per cent wrong, and that went a long way to clear his head out, now. There was no longer any question about what he was going to do next.

He'd started back slowly, just slogging along, but he was walking faster again. Stumbling more than he had going out, because his instinct for the path did not seem so acute, sharpened by fear. And possibly because he wasn't concentrating on every step he took, but thinking several steps and miles and hours ahead . . . If he started right now, that is, as fast as he reached the car . . . of course he'd have to stop a coupla minutes at the house and change into some decent human clothes again . . . and then go right on . . . Even in that old crate he'd get up to town before morning, be at the recruiting office before it even opened up. Might catch on this next quota—though it could be as long as a month to wait, if that was already filled. Close to the end of the month right now, of course, but volunteering would put him in ahead of the draftees. Notices generally came out about the fifth, he'd been told. He'd have plenty of time to Put His Affairs in Order (as they called it), before he had to go back for his physical. When he was signed up, he'd come on down again, later in the day. Today . . . What there would be to do when he returned, Jim didn't know and refused to think of. He did know that he was not going to wait around here until the morning to find out; not after his grandmother had gone off the way she did. That was her business now, and he had his.

Seemed a long way back to the road, but he kept going at a pretty steady clip, and finally made it, with something of a sense of relief as his feet struck the black-top: like coming back to the beginnings of civilization after a prowl in some unnatural or supernatural world. But he didn't pause for thought or breath now, just hit right up the gravel of the Collins parking place, and headed for the old Studebaker, guided by the shadowy white hulk of Landis' car beside it. And he wasted no further reflection on that guy— or any of the rest of them. Jim had had enough too, and knew when

278

he was through, and knew where he was going now and kept his mind on that. He fumbled for the door handle, was in under the wheel, kicked the old starter and closed the door again, all in one motion. He had the brake off and the lights on as the engine started, and slipping down the driveway to the road again, he was on his way.

CHAPTER 24

The lights had not caught Joyce this time, for she was seated on the low wall, out of their range. She hadn't moved when she heard him coming; just sat there waiting. Waiting, to give him comfort, and comprehension maybe, when he came back, defeated. For she knew from the slam-bang pace of those footsteps that Mrs. Mears was not with him. And she knew that he'd be perplexed and perhaps still angry—but not so much with *her*, now—and very much alone, and possibly in need of sympathy, as one in sorrow. So Joyce was there to give him whatever she could that he might need, and that was why she had waited outside for the last half hour; walking up and down, standing still and listening, and finally sitting on the wall, hugging her short pink sweater close around herself, though she was not cold, only awfully anxious . . . She had nearly gone on into the house when he left, in a rebound of anger as high as his own; it was so *unfair* of him to blame her as he had, or even take it out on her. And it was so much the last straw, after the way he'd behaved all day. She'd even gone as far as the gate and put her hand out, groping for the latch.

And then she'd turned back, and waited. She didn't know just what she'd expected him to do when he came up into the driveway. Perhaps she thought he'd stop there, showing his uncertainty, or go over to the gate himself—at least give some sign that he was looking for her, thinking of her, sorry for the way he'd spoken, or something . . . But he hadn't so much as paused. Just hurled himself into the car, and gone off like one of these jets from a standing start.

Couldn't get away fast enough. Disappeared into the dark, hell-bent, while Joyce was watching—eyes strained wide, but dry.

She was not a weeper, though she thought she would have liked to cry then, if she could have. She *hurt* so. But there was no use in waiting out here any longer. She certainly wasn't going to wait for Miriam and Don. She didn't give two hoots—or whistles!—about Don Landis, the old wolf. She'd known he was just that when she invited him down, no matter what she'd tried to put over on her mother. It didn't even surprise her much now to look back and recall that his seeming interest in her had deepened markedly after she had, in some casual connection, mentioned that the Roger Norbecks were spending a month or two with her mother. Mm-hm. She realized candidly that she had been deftly maneuvered by this Old Master of thirty-two, and her pride should be deeply hurt. Would be, probably, if it weren't otherwise preoccupied. The laugh was on her, that was all. And the most excruciating part of the joke was that she'd been trying to throw a scare into her mother, as well as Jim. Make her mother appreciate Jim more, not just treat him like an engaging puppy! Oh dear—why couldn't she laugh at that now? She didn't know—and didn't care. She didn't *care* any more, she told herself fiercely.

So there was nothing to do but go in and go to bed. She went over to the gate at last, which was standing open as her mother must have left it for her when she had gone in, expecting her to follow. And as she went on through, she realized in surprise that Norma and Roger were still out there in the patio, talking, for her ear was caught by the intermittent murmur of their voices. She could even see them dimly, not sitting but standing—over at the edge of the terrace, though they were partly in the shadow of the big oleander bush, halfway between the living- and dining-room doors. They were standing close together; so close, indeed, that they made one shadow with the oleander, and if her eyes had not been young and keen she could not have been so sure of what she saw, for they had suddenly stopped talking. Joyce moved quickly and quietly over the grass, and kept well over toward the far side of the house. She was sure they had not seen her, for neither one was looking her way.

She wasn't so dumb, after all, and she hadn't been so wrong

about what she'd suggested to her mother that afternoon; only about her own affairs—hers and Jim's—that's where she'd been wrong, all the time. All these years. And it seemed very queer that she and Jim, who were young, and free, and so ready for each other (they had thought), were the ones whose love had gone far off the track . . . while out on the hillside Miriam and Don (those two old pros)— and here in the patio the prosaic middle-aged—were finding comfort and even, possibly, some sort of fulfillment in each other. Very queer. But that was the way things went, Joyce thought, and this —*this*—was growing up. And moving softly, she slipped past the point where they could have seen her, and on into the house behind them.

She had not glanced back again; had had only that one glimpse of momentary tableau, and saw no more of what followed than of what preceded it. They had been sitting in those two chairs nearby, for some little time. Norma had told him first of the fire at Alfred's and then of what she and Jim had found at Mr. Bixby's house— which was, of course, nothing. And Roger and she had talked with somber speculation of both men: Alfred and Bixby. Both puzzles in character, as yet undecoded, though Alfred's was easier to guess at, and his story appeared to be concluded. As to the other man . . .

"I'll never understand it," Norma said, at length. "Never. How any human being could do such a contemptible thing to people who've been decent and friendly to him! Quite aside from the elementary point of honesty."

"I know. It's pretty hard to figure—why he'd even take the trouble . . . But you know," Roger interrupted his own ruminations, "I have a kind of hunch that the explanation here may be a very simple one. Possibly just too simple for us to grasp."

"Like—simple goodness, you mean? I wish you were right," she said, almost wistfully. "You said at first you didn't think he was a crook."

"I didn't. I'm not sure I do, even now."

"But—he's gone," she reminded him. "With the loot. Unless you think Joseph was lying, and all the rumors Jim had heard are baseless, too?"

"No. Not that. But you remember I told you earlier that there was something about him that bothered me, from the start? Some resemblance or recollection."

"You mean you've remembered what it is?"

"No," he said again. "Not yet. I can't quite get hold of it. It isn't his name, because that doesn't even ring a bell. Names are easy enough to change, anyway—even by anglicizing a foreign one. It isn't his face, either, unless that's very much changed, also."

"Don't you think he just reminds you of somebody?" Norma asked reasonably. "I know I often have that feeling, when I first meet a person, and then afterwards wonder why I ever saw any resemblance."

"That's very possible, of course. And my faculties are not as sharp as they once were," he admitted wryly. "I couldn't place Landis at all, for instance, though we evidently met him within the last year or so."

"Oh!" Norma exclaimed involuntarily. "I'd almost forgotten about *that* one . . . Where—?" She paused, suddenly conscious that she was moving in the dark.

"Oh, they went on up the hill a while ago—he and Mim—to see what they could see," Roger answered, with such elaborate carelessness that she said merely, "Oh. Oh yes—of course. I forgot they were all talking about going up to see the show over there. Silly ghouls," she added rather irritably, "as if there weren't more important things going on right under their noses! I suppose Joyce and Jim have gone up too, now. I thought they'd be coming in, right after me—" She broke off, and Roger let that all pass by, continuing as if she had not brought in this diversion.

"If I ever saw this man—Bixby—it was longer ago, when I was sharper. I can tell you that much, because this feeling I have about him goes deeper. It's—almost certainty. I'll remember it presently. I'll dredge it up somehow, I promise you. In the morning, maybe. After I've slept on it. I find I'm—rather tired, now."

"Oh, Rog, of course you are," she said apologetically. "It's been a horrible evening, and so long. It must be very late."

"Well, I think I'll turn in, if you don't mind. I don't see that there's anything practical to be done about this thing until morning anyway, and we find out what he really has gotten away with—if he has—and if there's anybody else who can throw any light on it. Meantime . . . I hardly think it's worth waiting for the Watchers of the Night to return," he added.

"They'll all be dead too when they come back," she said, and then realizing the word she'd used, corrected herself hastily, "I mean they'll be dead-tired after all this to-do."

He reflected that the first word might be the true one, when it came time to count the living, and those missing, the next day. Not only Alfred, but Mrs. Mears might well be among the latter. It was plain that Norma hadn't even noticed that her eldest guest had departed in her absence; perhaps Joyce had already told her when they met outside, though if so she would certainly have been enough concerned to mention it. No, very likely she had just assumed that Joyce had taken her home. In any case, he saw no reason for his giving her one more item to worry about at this time of night. Norma had risen and taken a step or two toward the house, but that seemed to remind her of something and she stopped again.

"Did Joseph and Bertha go, do you know?"

"Not out this way," he said gravely. "Cleo and I have been right here, on guard."

"I expect they went out the back door, poor dears," she said, with some obscure regret that Bertha and Joseph should have felt obliged to go that way. "They must have gone, by now," she murmured. "Well, I must go in and see about things in the kitchen . . . Do go and get some sleep, Rog."

"Yes, I will." But as she took a step away from him, he added with a flicker of curiosity, "What—are you going to do in there, at this time of night?"

She turned her head and answered casually, "Oh, just go out and line things up a little for breakfast. Bertha has a way of putting things in places where I can't find them easily," she explained practically. "Changes them all around every so often. Puts the knives where the cooky cutters and muffin tins used to be. Hides the oatmeal from me. I think it's a game with her . . . Well, good night, Rog."

He didn't answer; stood still, watching her move away. But suddenly he spoke after her again.

"Norma."

"Yes?" She did pause then, to look around.

"Tell me something, will you?"

"Of course. If I can."

"Suppose, for the sake of argument," he said slowly, "that this really was the end. Tonight."

Oh dear, she thought. Not *that* again. But she said patiently, "Well?"

"I mean, suppose you believed that, saw no good reason to doubt it. Would you still go out to the kitchen, to—get things lined up ahead, as you say—for breakfast the next morning?"

There was a moment's silence while she considered the question, and then she said, "Why, yes. I think I would. Of course."

"Of course?"

"Well, I mean, just in case day does come again—and somebody is hungry," she said simply.

"Just in case," he repeated softly, thinking it over. And then he was taking a couple of steps after her, and she wondered why, what more there was to be said; but she stood waiting, on her guard.

"Norma, my dear," he said, and still she waited, though she found her hands tightening into fists by her sides, her nails sharp against her palms. She took a deep breath to override—and rise above—the apprehension which was rising in her. But she had given him the only answer there was, and she stood her ground as he closed the small space which had opened up between them. He put his hands on both her shoulders, and held them firmly, looking into the shadows of her eyes, and she was thankful that there was not light enough for him to see any more. For a moment, it was something like panic that she felt—and that, more of herself than Roger, though his fingers had tightened also, gripping her arms.

"Hold it—" he said, very low, so that the two words were almost toneless. "Here they come—now."

"Where?" she whispered back, and then a little wildly, "*Who?*"

for he had drawn her back into the shadow of the oleander at the edge of the terrace where they now stood, and she turned her head expecting to see Miriam—and Don, no doubt, approaching from the outer dusk. She'd thought there was a little sound over there a minute ago but she'd been too engrossed to pay attention, and now—oh, what a *fool* she was to have let even the appearance of anything like this overtake them! But there was no one there— that she could see—until, her gaze circling wider to the right, and then back, left, toward the kitchen wing, she saw what Roger, facing that way, had observed at once.

Two shrouded figures issuing cautiously from the kitchen door out onto the terrace, though in the dead quiet they apparently assumed that everyone else had gone. The big, billowy figure came first, boldly leading the way, while the smaller one followed doggedly, a few feet behind. They were crossing silently, on a diagonal line over toward the gate, when suddenly the woman turned (to check up and make sure *he* was coming?) and stopped, and went back to him. Roger and Norma stood frozen in the privacy of their own shadow, feeling like eavesdroppers, though not a word had been said. And then they saw that Bertha was only fussing with Joseph's robe, something about the neck or collar of it, pulling and tugging at it— to get the proper hang, no doubt, while he stood and suffered these last ministrations.

Norma began to shake with uncontrollable mirth which caught her off-balance and unaware; at least it felt like mirth, though what she wanted was to cry, but Roger murmured, "Steady, old girl— steady," and put his big hand gently over her mouth. So then she turned blindly toward him, still shaking, but stifling the little gasps she was making, against his chest, leaning on him now, his arms around her. While he, looking over her bent head, could see that those other two were going on again, somewhat closer together. Maybe Bertha was leading him by the hand. Roger couldn't tell. The two shapeless bulks blurred together out toward the gate, and presently the click of the latch told that they had gone on through. And Norma must have heard it too, for her shoulders were quiet again under his hands.

She stood that way for one long unmeasured second; not more

than that, really, though it was long enough to tell her all she needed to know. To remind her of the comfort, long denied her (even if it was she who had denied herself), of leaning on someone; the more-than-physical support of having someone's arms around her. To give her warning (for it was that, late as it might be) that Joyce had been partly—yes, very nearly right about her mother's feeling for Roger Norbeck. But only partly.

This was not the kind of love she had known before. This was a lonely kind of love, never to be shared. It was made up of one part pity—her very great pity for this old friend—and one part yearning, her own yearning for the cloak (sheer warmth) of affection, and still another part which was a fondness for this particular man with all his likable faults and exasperating virtues—for she knew very well that one loved a person in spite of, and not because of, either. There might even have been—in fact there might *be*, now, but dormant— the pulse of life beating between them . . . but she was too old for continuing life, and he—but it didn't matter because, strangely, that would have come last, not first, with them. If . . . And there was no "if"; only the recognition that there was much that she and Roger could have given each other, even now. But Roger had a wife, whom he still loved. *Roger had a wife!* So no matter what Joyce had said or surmised about those two in her young detachment, or whether it were true—or what might happen with them still— that was *all* that mattered now.

Norma raised her head, and stepped back, away from him.

"Sorry," she said, and there was only a rueful note to be detected in her voice. "That must have been hysterics, I guess. I never had them before."

"Kind of shook you up, didn't it?" he said sympathetically. "Two grown people playing ghosts. Unbelievable! It was weird enough and funny enough to make anybody come a bit unstrung."

"It was—coming on top of everything else," said Norma evenly. "This whole ghastly evening. Well, anyway, thanks for stopping me from breaking out in maniacal laughter."

"And I was going to say the same to you, before that apparition."

"The same . . . ?" she repeated slowly.

286

"That's right . . . Thanks."

"What for?" she asked, in some wonder.

"Why, for showing me, in the simplest way possible, that it doesn't matter a damn whether I have time to finish my still unwritten book, any more than it matters if that breakfast of yours is eventually consumed. Just so one gets on with the preparation of it. In case, as you said, there may yet be another day—and somebody left alive. To eat, or read, or take some kind of nourishment."

So that was what he had been going to say, a few minutes ago, if only she had had the wits to guess it! And when he added, "It's a cinch that one can't finish what one hasn't started, isn't it?"—she said in a small voice, "Yes, I suppose it is. But you knew that all the time. I didn't show you."

"Oh well . . ." It was a long sigh that he had given. "I guess some of us are myopic, and some of us try to look too far ahead. In any case, thank you. For being what you are, and everything you've done for Miriam and me. And for the offer of your quiet hillside too, because I think I'll be taking further advantage of all this now. For a while longer, anyway—if I may. While I get started on that job. The book, I mean. Beginning tomorrow morning . . . As God and Norma Collins are my witnesses."

"Oh, *Rog*—" she exclaimed distressedly, for that was the kind of thing which shocked—no, more offended her, in its flat irreverence. Yet even as she protested, she knew that to Roger there was no blasphemy in what he had said. She made herself go back a step, a word or two, and accept it. "I'm glad. I'm very glad," she said thankfully. And then went on a step, as she added, "*This* morning, now." Though that seemed rather inconsequent, even as she pointed it out.

"That's right. It must be." And suddenly he laughed again, un-expectedly to them both; a small chuckle but this time it was real, without bitterness. "Remember the guy who was giving out with all that high-flown stuff last night—something about the eventual tomorrow comes? I guess we'd really better go and get some shut-eye, hadn't we? To be in shape to carry on with the eventual today . . . Good night, old dear."

For a second she felt an irrepressible flicker of resentment, not at his seeming abruptness, but because he kept calling her *old* girl, and *old* dear. And thinking sadly, Oh dear, how petty can I get?— she answered softly, " 'Night, Rog."

This time, she was the one who watched him walking away, toward the other side of the house. Then her eyes turned blankly, more in momentary blindness than in simple darkness, over toward the patio wall and the spot where she knew the gate to be, and the Hill out beyond, where people were climbing around and singing hymns and disporting themselves in one way or another. For her part, all she wanted was to go to bed.

CHAPTER 25

By the time she had made that last stop in the kitchen, arranging things so she could put her hand on them at once in the morning, no matter how dead sleepy she might be, then; fixing Roger's tray in the pantry, putting the coffee pot and the tin of coffee (which Bertha had *not* hidden, thank heaven) on the table right beside each other . . . By the time she had found the oatmeal, which had been perversely placed—for eternity, no doubt—in a certain topmost cupboard, where it had *never* been before, Norma felt she could have lain right down on the kitchen floor and gone to sleep there. When she reached her own room, she thought she was ready to fall into bed, and sleep forever, possibly.

But it seemed that the day just past was one of those which not only took a lot of weary living through—but now, inexorably demanded that one live it through again. Hour by hour, though not in chronological order. Turning the clock backward and then forward again, from one person to another (Mr. Bixby, Joseph—yes, and poor repulsive old Alfred); pointing the minute hand back to her talk with Miriam at breakfast, and with Roger later in the morning, and again, so many hours later still.

Well, now at last he would be able to write his book, and Norma found herself wondering what kind of book Roger would write, after all; whether she would even like it when it was done. It was a relief to feel so detached about him, but it was strange too; reaction, of course, from the near panic of apprehension which had gripped her for a while, lest she were becoming inextricably involved in his life— and Miriam's—or in some deep-rooted emotion of her own which had pushed almost to the surface without her knowing it. It would have been so mortally humiliating to have had either one of those things happen, at her age. But because she had drawn back in time, turned away before she had in any sense given herself away, she had built herself a stronghold from which she could look out dispassionately at the other two, hoping they would solve their own problems. Could even look back on her own panic and see that it was partly cowardice, born of her unwilling recognition that she would so soon lose Joyce.

Joyce. She wished the child would come in. Though of course there was no harm in their all staying out there if they wanted to. She was glad at least that they were all together now, as they must be. That hillside path must have been something of a public highway tonight, with people coming and going, some in robes and some in evening dress! She was glad that it was Miriam who had started out with Don . . . no, no, she didn't *mean* that—what she meant was that she was glad it was *not* Joyce who had gone off with him alone in the beginning. Even so, she couldn't fathom why they didn't come back, for the whole performance must be getting rather tedious by now. Norma flopped over impatiently. She didn't usually lie awake and listen for her little girl. She didn't usually lie awake . . . but this seemed to have become a pernicious habit in the course of twenty-four hours. She'd been doing it all day—lying and listening, sitting and thinking, waiting—for what?

She got up finally and went across to her door, which she had left a little open, so that there was a faint vertical bar of light to guide her in the dark. She went through and stood listening again at the foot of the stairs, but there was no sound at all, indoors or out. She looked through the dusk of the living room into which a little light was filtered from the terrace lamps outside, her eyes as clear as a cat's from her long vigil in the dark, and saw that the door to the den where Joyce had been sleeping during the Norbecks' visit was slightly open, as her own had been. They always left their doors open at night. But without formulating the thought which had come to her, that she would rather it were closed—while others were staying in the house, she crossed the length of the room to the den, looked in (just to make sure, though she knew the child wasn't in), and though the den was darker so she couldn't see now, she had a definite feeling that someone was there. She moved carefully so as not to disturb her, if . . . And Joyce was there! Had come in quietly long ago, apparently, and was sleeping sweetly. Dreaming of— whom? her mother wondered.

But she retreated quickly, so that not even the sense of her presence should penetrate that quiet sleep—feeling like something of a fool, if the truth were known—and closed the door with care. She couldn't understand why she hadn't heard them come in, and as she went back across the living room, it seemed odd to her, too, that Joyce had not turned off the patio lamps. Unless, indeed, she was not the last one to return . . . But Norma, reaching the living-room door again, pausing to listen to the utter silence of the house, which seemed to be dreaming also, snapped off the switch, so that everything was suddenly darker outdoors and in here as well. And if anyone was still out roaming, she thought—she really didn't care.

She went back into her own room, closing that door too, and felt her way across to the bathroom, where she turned on the light for a moment to get a drink of water, and glanced at her watch before she turned it off again. It was after three. Well, she could go to sleep now, she thought, for a few hours at least. Just knowing that Joyce was in had brought her a measure of peace, and when she was back in bed again it began to seep through her like a grateful sedative. She had almost drifted off, but not quite—for she knew she had not been asleep this time, had been listening right along, in spite of herself. And she knew there had been a sound, almost too faint to hear, but *something*. Probably a step on the stairs just the other side of her bedroom wall, though he was certainly being careful not to disturb her or anyone else. In fact, it seemed unnatural to

Norma that any man, especially a young unmarried man, should be that careful. Well, perhaps she was wrong and there was no one there at all. And then again she was sure, for that was a step, careful but with the heaviness of weight, pressing on that first tread which had a giveaway creak to anyone familiar with every inanimate board in her own house. But if that were so, then how could she have heard it a second before? Unless there were two, in single file, one going first—as light as breath—and then another following . . . Oh Norma, Norma, be yourself, she thought in stern admonishment. She was ashamed of her jumpy imagination, but more ashamed of her suspicion.

This wouldn't do, and she must go to sleep, or she would be dead to the world when it was time to get up again. To get breakfast for the others, since Bertha and Joseph would certainly not be on deck until late, that day, nor did she expect them to be. That was her job, her only responsibility in this house now. The practical mechanics of living. Somebody had to look after those, after all. So she lay still; perfectly still, and began at last, to drift—again.

Nearly an hour went by, and it was four o'clock once more, and Roger was sitting on the side of his bed, his feet on the floor, though he made no effort to get up. He was rubbing his hands over his face, stupidly, with a dull wonder as to what could have waked him up this time, when he was so drugged with sleep, so dead for more of it. He was uncomfortable in some way, but it wasn't just that . . . No, something else. He had a feeling of great oppression, not unfamiliar to him these days, but it seemed heavier than usual, and though he was not conscious of having been dreaming, it was almost like waking up in another time and place, away back among those days before and after the war, during his last assignment in Europe: days vivid with interest as they passed, but darkened by long shadows of the things seen and heard in their course. It was as though he'd been thinking of them in his sleep, and, wakening, was now continuing without a break along the same line of thought.

It was a line which he avoided in the daytime, knowing from much travel to and fro that it was a dead-end road, leading nowhere.

Knowing also that if it had not been for this long period of illness and waiting to get well, he would never have spent those hours of shuttling back and forth among those dead reflections; he would have been going somewhere, leaving the past behind as any healthy person did. You had to, if you were going to keep any detachment in which to do your job. Even when you were writing up the hideous stuff that came in after the war, which had to be told, to be gotten across to the people at home, you had to do it with your head. Another thing too, there were so many stories, incredibly grim, that they'd become one endless epic of collective suffering, often too much alike in their repeated patterns of tragedy to stand out singly, as belonging to separate persons. (Indeed, many of the latter had lost the individual personality of sanity.)

Yet Roger had learned that occasionally a voice left some indelible record on his brain when he had no surrounding substance of detail which he could call up consciously to place beside it. And he found now that he was thinking of a voice, like a symphonic theme or phrase repeating itself in his head, silently, tauntingly, while he kept trying to identify it. Curiously enough, he had no ear for music; only for voices. And this one he had heard not long ago: a quiet tone without resonance, like a radio turned down very low. Deliberately hushed—that was it, as if someone might be listening. The same thing he'd been aware of more than once when talking to some poor devil over there, somebody who no longer had reason to fear ears in the walls—or outside, say, around a corner, or in a shadowed doorway—but speaking like that still, from habit. Only, *this* was more recent, very recent. Last night, in fact . . . So it had gone to bed with him.

He knew now why he had waked up thinking of those things. Two lines of consciousness had joined together in his sleep. Now also he knew what had been gnawing at him all last evening. It was *not* that he remembered Bixby. He'd probably never laid eyes on the man before. The face was not familiar, and he'd known that all along; neither shape nor coloring nor any personal quirk of feature. But it was the *look* of the man, which was like that of many men, and women too, the look behind the eyes, of suffering—but something more, too: the watchful careful look, unsleeping, though it appeared not to be watching at all. Oh, God, yes, it was that, coupled with the muted voice which saved its breath with equal care, made certain no unintended ear should overhear.

Roger dropped his head into his hands, not trying to remember any more. So Bixby was one of those. A refugee from hell. He should have recognized it at once—not the man, but the fact: that look as of the inside man retreated, withdrawn to a great distance. Even the look of considerable age, though the face was plump and not much wrinkled. Why, this man probably wasn't much over sixty, though he had seemed so very much older than—Mrs. Mears, for instance. Or Joseph, who was a phony, and he had recognized that easily enough . . . And now the passing but mildly astringent irony of that perception came through to him as well: that Bixby should turn out to be what Joseph and Bertha had said they were—when they were not. A curious counterpoint, that, which Roger, taking note of it with his nonmusical ear, could nevertheless appreciate more than most people.

But, as for Bixby . . . why, certainly, Bixby had said last night that he had come over to the United States when he was a boy. But he'd left it there, omitted mentioning that he might have gone back sometime later on. That was one thing which had thrown Roger off the track. And he couldn't have said now whether the fellow was a Czech, or a Pole—or an Austrian, maybe? He could have been any one of those, for any accent he might have had must have been obliterated over here in his youth. He could very well have come from one of those countries which had been taken over first by the Nazis and next by the Communists, its people caught in one riptide—earlier, before the war—and then in another sweeping in reverse, a Red Sea at high tide.

But Roger was sure of only one thing, and it scarcely occurred to him that he had no proof of that. He had awakened, knowing this thing, and the conviction was so strong that it left no room for doubt in him. He pulled his head up out of his hands, a half-formed notion in it that he ought to go and tell Norma about it, and then remembered that this hour of the night was no time to tell her anything. Besides, there was something else nagging at his confounded memory. If it weren't for this oppression nearly smothering him, he could think better; this dreadful depression weighing him down, anchoring him to the roots and bowels of the earth . . . (And who the hell was *he* to be depressed, who'd been through nothing, compared to a man like that—who'd sat there at the dinner table smiling, quiet . . . and out there in the patio later on, more quiet still, listening to all that everlasting twaddle, of which he—Norbeck— had uttered more than his share.)

But what was bothering him now was . . . he almost had it, and it slipped away again and he made another grab to reach it . . . something about the village and those damn fools giving away their worldly goods. Why would a man like this, who seemed such a decent sort, try to take advantage of people like those? Why would he even take the trouble to hang around, like somebody at a give-away program? For there was a certain authority about Bixby, despite his seemingly deferential reserve. He had the look of success, of the kind that has no need to proclaim itself in outward trappings, expensive clothes and cars and houses, which were for the womenfolk, after all, of which Bixby seemingly had none. One suit—or two, of the same material, and a rented house and a second-hand car were doubtless sufficient for his purpose, whatever that might be.

Whatever that might be. Was it possible that what the man had been through (which Roger didn't even pause to question now) had turned a normal acquisitiveness into some devious and strangely crooked channel? Or had he actually been so put to it to gain a foothold back here in this country, to make the barest living for himself alone, that he would go to any extreme, even to this extremity —this tiny village in the back hills and the few odd bits of change that he could pick up in his own two hands, by any means at all? Of course, he might even figure that people who have been so fortunate as to live here in peace and relative comfort and comparative safety—and don't appreciate it—have no real right to any of it.

Or was there an even more obsessive purpose in this little man, such as acquiring every dollar he could lay his hands on and sending it back to that place from which he'd come, to those who could make it easier for others to escape and set up life elsewhere? To make good for other families what—just possibly—he had not been able to do for his own. Yes, that was possible, though it seemed hardly credible, as Roger turned the thing back and forth, that a good purpose could become such an obsession that a man would do anything at all, even lend himself to a petty cold-blooded business like this, to gain another nickel. Yet obsessions were queer things, and Roger knew that a mind possessed could rationalize practically anything.

He also knew that people who had undergone great suffering in any form were sometimes hardened by it until they had great strength themselves but could become quite merciless toward their fellows (indifferent or blandly patronizing toward what anyone else might suffer), while others were not so much toughened as tempered into fineness. It was strange that the conditions of ordeal often seemed to bring men and women to one extreme or the other. The war had taught him that. Though he found it more difficult to believe in simple goodness (that was the phrase Norma had used, wasn't it?) than in any of the varieties of evil. So when it came right down to it, there was nothing he could tell her about Mr. Bixby, after all—nothing to relieve her mind in the middle of the night. That the man had been through hell, and back, was no assurance that it might not amuse him to let others endure a bit of purgatory.

So all that Roger had dredged up in his sleep could certainly wait till morning. He heaved himself up from the side of the bed and began the ritual of wrapper and slippers and stumbling over to the closet door to dig up a pack of cigarettes. The other packages, which Alfred had brought that morning, he had carefully distributed in other strategic places. One of these days, he supposed, Miriam would run across one of them and there would be recriminations and hell-to-pay, generally. Meanwhile he would have his furtive smokes, as many as he could get in, and enjoy them while he might. Alfred had secreted two cartons among the thick leaves of the hibiscus bush, so he had a good supply for the moment. Good old Alf . . . And suddenly he remembered the gruesome news about Alfred, which he had quite forgotten. It gave him a rather painful shock, centered entirely in the problem of how he would renew his hidden stores when these ran out. Maybe he could prevail on Jim to do a little smuggling. Maybe he should start rationing himself on these, to make them last a little longer. But it would do to think of that tomorrow, and for the moment he lit one eagerly, though he frowned disapprovingly to note that his hand was shaking. Like an old soak thirsting for the first long pull from the bottle—or the weed. Like Alfred.

He plodded over to the window and stood there looking out between the curtains, rather shamed by his reflections of the last minute. He was a cheat, too—though he was cheating only himself in the long run. And wasn't that exactly what they all did, in the end? Alfred with his craving, which he no doubt excused to himself in his own way; Bixby, in whatever way he took to explain his mode of robbing Peter to pay Paul; each human being who fell short by so much (more or less) of the way he meant to live. Yes, fully intended to live, given another chance, another day, another lease on life, no matter how short. He had been cheating himself, especially these last months, as he delayed day by day in beginning on the book, no matter how honest his uncertainty, nor how imminent and overwhelming his reasons had appeared to be. He had wanted to be sure where they were all heading before he took his eye off the horizon and buried his nose in his own admittedly self-centered work. And then, of course, he'd wanted to be sure it was worth doing, and that he'd have plenty of time to finish it—yes, that especially—and when he did finish, that it would still have some meaning, and that there would still be someone left around to read what he had written.

The recollection mocked him now, though he had felt such enormous relief when he had come into his room here, a few hours ago. Almost the peace of accomplishment, though there was nothing accomplished except the decision. A sense of exhilaration and release, now the brakes were off, the way was clear, and he was ready to go. Even the painful dread about Miriam had dissipated, because she had so wanted him to start writing, to *work* back toward a more

296

normal life. So that would be all right and they would be happy again, together.

It had taken him some little time to get off to sleep; fact was, he might have had a bit of indigestion because he wasn't used to eating like that any more. Bertha and her banquet! Superb—but enough to floor a farm hand . . . Now here he was, a few hours later, awake again, and the surge of exhilaration, like one more wave in the ocean, had rolled by and flattened out. The peace he had felt earlier did not seem to have outlasted his sleep. Nor any excitement, either. He was going to work in the morning, oh yes, but that was merely a stern and conscious determination. His high tide had leaked away. In place of that serene sureness there was only this sense of deep unease. This oppression. He wasn't certain if it was physical or mental. He looked down at his big chair, but could visualize no comfort there. He might feel more comfortable if he moved around a bit. So he started prowling once again.

Past the door to Miriam's room, which had for some reason been left halfway open; wider than usual, as though it might have been forgotten. He hadn't heard her come in up to the time he went off; had been half listening for her, until he'd told himself that those four might easily make a night of it over there on the hill, wherever they were—watching the Watchers—wisecracking to keep themselves awake. Perhaps he hadn't really believed that, but it had sufficed at the time. He did believe that he had never been a jealous man. Miriam was an alluring woman and had her little ways of coquetting now and then, but they were no more than social gestures. His pride in her, even if it had something to do with the male pride of possession, had been not only in her attractiveness, but in her ability to attract. Beyond all that, he'd always had utter faith in her. Why, even last night, in his lonely fear of losing her true love, he had been able to brush aside as preposterous any thought of physical faithlessness on her part.

But he must have come a long way, in twenty-four hours, when he could stand here, having to remind himself that after all there were *four* of them out there together! And then, going one obscene step farther and telling himself that Miriam was *not* the woman

297

to make love under hedgerows, or to lie down in a thicket on a hill-side. She might or might not be fastidious about her men, but as to time and place, she would be. That he did know. Well, hadn't he been married to her for eight years? And wasn't *that* a fine thing to be reduced to? An ignominious last stand. No wonder his marriage was going to pot, if that was the material of which his trust was made. Not a jealous man? Why, you self-deceiving fool, you're only the insanely jealous type, and didn't know it! He shouted at himself, in silence, to come back from that borderline before it was too late.

He had hesitated near her door for a second, but did not go over to glance in, as he would have done on any night but this. Some-how, he made it a point of honor not to go to that door, but rather to accept on faith (yes, faith—in goodness, and his wife) the fact that she was in there, deep and comfortable in sleep, as he wished he were. And he would not disturb her even with his yearning. He would go out and get some air. That's what he needed, for some-how the room seemed stifling tonight. After the warm day, doubt-less. He opened his outer door softly, and turning right, walked over toward the patio wall. Stood for a moment, thinking he heard that far-off singing again; decided he didn't, and turned around, not noticing that a dark shape had jumped down from the wall without so much as a gentle thud, and was following after him, close to the ground, stalking his footsteps silently. He paced back along beside the house, passing his own room, and Miriam's outer door, which was closed; glanced up momentarily at the second story where a darker gap showed the French doors there, opened wide onto the small balcony; headed without any particular purpose toward the corner near the living-room door, where he would turn around.

But just as he had almost reached that point, he heard—not quite distinguishable, a little like a sleepy bird in its nest, inquiring if the night were waning—a small sound. And then another—oh, unmistakable now: a little breath of laughter, low and intimate, which he knew too well—coming from above. He stopped short to look up, found he was too close under the balcony to see the open

door and took one sharp step back. He knew even as his foot came
down that it had struck or brushed something, but he was not
prepared for the sudden howl of anguish and offense, behind him.
He swore, and caught himself from falling, as the shape streaked
away, but the discomfort which had been lurking in him ever since he
wakened surged through him now, all through his body, through his
whole being, though whether it was pain or shock or sheer emotion,
Roger could not know. It was like an explosion, but nothing like a
bomb which he could estimate as to distance, nearby or far away.
This was an explosion of the universe, but not the one he had
been waiting for, warning of . . . There was indeed the blinding
flash, but that was inside. There was no blast, no deafening noise
in his ears. While above, there was complete, unstirring silence.

In the corner, downstairs, a light had gone on, and he knew almost
at once that the sound of fumbling at the living-room door a
second later would be Norma. But he was so suffocated with this
surging rage—if that was what it was, this feeling of suffusion which
was worse than any pain, that he couldn't move or speak, until her
voice said anxiously, "What *is* it? Who's out there?" And then he
managed to gasp, still fighting for control, "Sorry, Norma—it was
that goddamn cat—" But already the shock of that fearsome howl
so close behind him had been engulfed in the other shock, and it
was not even control that he was fighting for but something else
more desperate, more necessary. Air to breathe . . .

"Oh, Rog, I'm so sorry! Wait a minute till I find the light
here . . ."

"No!" he said in a harsh whisper. "No—don't—come out—"
It was important, it was imperative (though he didn't know why)
that she should not come out. But it was more important that he
get back to his room, and he couldn't wait to argue. He didn't have
the pills in the pocket of this damn wrapper. They were by his bed.
If he could just make it that far . . . But she was speaking again
from the dark doorway, softly but urgently.

"But, Rog, are you all right? Can't I do something—"

"No—no—no—I don't . . . don't *want* you . . ." What he meant to
say was, I don't want you to come out, but he had no breath to spare

to finish it. This was a battle for breath now, his own personal battle, which no one else could fight for him or with him, and nothing—nothing else mattered at all—upstairs or anywhere on earth . . . Only air. There must be some *air* left somewhere in this world. Or if not this one, then . . . But he was nearly there now, the door to his room standing open as he'd left it. And Norma hadn't followed him. Thank God.

It was what he had said, and left unfinished for lack of breath, that stopped her in the door. He had said, "I don't *want* you," and one couldn't force one's self on any person in the face of such desperate urgency. She could hear him going back and knew when he had reached his door, and she turned back into her own room and presently, as if to relieve some fear he might yet have of her following, she turned out her bedroom light again. But she stood motionless in the middle of the darkened room, waiting, though she was not sure what she was waiting for. Perhaps, in a moment, she could go quietly along to Miriam's room and rouse her, if she hadn't already heard, so *she* could make sure that Roger was all right. She was still gripped with fear, and the frustration of not going out to do—or see—what must be done. It was that awful cat's yowl, of course, which had wakened her with such a sense of fright, but it was his voice also, which had sounded more—more stricken than with any mere anger or alarm that Cleo might have caused. And only then did it come to Norma that he might have seen or heard something else out there where he was standing, and that Miriam was *not* in her room. So it would do no good to go there. What she must do, what he wanted her to do was to stay here, and pretend she didn't know. Was that it?

She moved over toward her dressing table and felt for the bench which she could not see, and sat down there as she had that afternoon, her arm on the edge of the table, looking out through the open window toward the hills which she could not see either. A minute—or two—went by as she waited; it might have been several minutes; she couldn't tell, for the clock—all the clocks in the world—seemed to have stopped. And then she heard, quite distinctly, for she had again left her door ajar into the living room, the stir of silk against the wall as someone came down those stairs. And Norma bent her head in her hand, to cover her eyes even in the dark, in grief that this should happen here.

It was only a matter of seconds however, possibly adding up to another minute—but no more, this time, when there came a piercing wail from the patio—or from one of the rooms farther along, and her head jerked back again, sharply, as Miriam's voice cried out, "Oh, Norma—*Norma!* Nor—ma, please come . . ."

PART SEVEN

"Prophecy will fade away,
Melting in the light of day."

CHAPTER 26

The sun was shining brightly, and the day promised to be even more beautiful than the one before. There was not that oppressive stillness hanging over the earth as there had been, for the hills were drawing a faint current of air up the canyons between them, like someone breathing softly and easily. Nor was it quite so hot this morning, though the sun had been up for several hours. Norma herself had been up, it seemed, almost as long as she could remember. Ever since that terrifying cry had sliced through the dark. Hours—and hours—which went by relentlessly and had to be lived through patiently, one by one. There was nothing one could do to help them move a little faster, as each painfully dragged itself upright and prepared to march after its predecessors.

Even when she had reached Roger's door, a few seconds after Miriam's anguished calling of her name, there was nothing to be done. He had fallen so that the upper part of his body was lying across the bed, his knees and feet still trailing on the floor, and Miriam was kneeling too, her arm across his shoulders and her head down beside his. She was making little moaning sounds, which stopped when Norma opened the screen door. Her arm seemed to tighten around Roger, and for a moment she didn't move or speak. Then, when Norma had leaned over to feel his wrist, the younger woman slipped back onto her heels, looking up, pitifully.

"Can't you do something?" she'd whispered, refusing to believe what she already knew, until Norma had said it aloud, as kindly as she could. And then she just sat there crumpled on the floor, both hands over her face. She was in that bare-shouldered dress, the stiff skirt billowed around her, her hair disheveled, and though Norma could not bring herself to touch the bare shoulder, she did put her fingers gingerly on the soft, rumpled hair. It was only after another moment or two that she remembered that they must still call a doctor.

"Dr. Leslie is the only one around here," she explained. "He's rather old and not very . . ." But her thought went on that he was still modern enough to sign a certificate confirming a fact as old as man himself, and undeniable here. Aloud, she continued, ". . . but of course he'll come. He would not be up on the Hill with those others, I'm sure of that."

"All right." Miriam had acknowledged the necessity and slowly got to her feet, stumbling a little on the fullness of her skirt. And there was more than hesitance in her voice—it was piteously humble as she added, "Couldn't we move him—so he'll be—more comfortable?"

"Of course," said Norma, though there her thought had flashed back to that primary instruction of First Aid: Don't move the patient till the doctor comes . . . And there was another elementary rule too, not medical but legal—when murder had been done, nothing must be touched before the arrival of the police . . . But of course, neither admonition had any bearing here. Of course not. It was only as she went to the door a few minutes later, that she had paused with her hand on the knob, looking back at the other woman, and said, "You'd better go and put on something else, Miriam."

"Yes. All right," the latter acquiesced. Still humbly.

There had been no further reference, then, to what had happened earlier, or why, or how. And Norma had gone out into the patio and along to the living-room door in a dusk which was (inappropriately, it seemed) growing less black and a little grayer, moment by moment. Nevertheless, she'd turned on the light indoors with that sense of something like abandon which one feels in knowing that the person who might have been disturbed by such irregularities as lights going on and off, and people moving to and fro, would never be disturbed again. And the others didn't matter. She'd had some thought as she crossed the room that she would go in and speak to Joyce when she had called the doctor, but it was while she was still at the telephone that she heard steps coming down the stairs once more, and then saw a figure standing over there in the corner, waiting for her to finish . . . and she decided abruptly not to waken Joyce until later.

When she went toward him presently, having of necessity to pass him on her way out into the patio, Don Landis had said, "Mrs. Collins, I couldn't help hearing what you said on the telephone just now. Is there—anything I can do?"

She'd drawn in a full breath, and let it out with care before she'd answered, "Yes. You can leave. Immediately."

"Very well," he said evenly. There was a tiny interval as they looked at each other, since he was—in effect, though not intentionally—blocking her way to the door. "I needn't say how sorry—" he began, but she had cut him off.

"You needn't say anything."

He'd made no answer then, except to open the outer door for her, as she was obviously going out that way, and she went past him without further word or glance. A short time later, when she was again with Miriam in Roger's room, there had been the brief sound of a motor starting up outside, and she didn't know if Miriam had noticed it or not. If she wished to see that man again, no doubt she could and would. But not here. Meantime she'd given no sign, and Norma did not have to say what had been almost on her tongue: "No, that is *not* the doctor's car . . ."

And when the latter did come, some few minutes after that, Miriam was ready for him; not merely having wrapped herself in that enveloping, gray, nunlike robe, but starkly composed, ready with her immediate decisions. Somehow the fewest necesssary explanations of Roger's previous illness had been made; the wishes—or instructions—given about taking him up to Los Angeles. That day, if possible. And when that drew an instinctive protest from Norma, with her offer to have the services right here—though of course it was for Miriam to do what she preferred—the younger woman had thanked her gravely and said that was what she did prefer. To go at once, that morning. (Nor linger on the order of your going, Norma thought. Well, perhaps that was best all around.)

So she had shown the doctor into the living room to telephone Dan Biggs, who attended to such things in the village. For it was broad daylight in the patio by then, though Norma's hillside still lay in the shadow of another hill. And while they were in there talking, Joyce had come out of the den, wide-eyed though half awake, and had had to be told of Roger's death. Her eyes had filled with tears, bless her heart . . . Joyce was the only one who could cry, and her mother had felt obscurely grateful to her for shedding those natural, decent tears for their old friend.

At some point in the period of waiting which followed, Norma had thought to go into the kitchen and make some coffee for the doctor, and take a cup in to Miriam, who sat motionless in the corner of Roger's room, in the chair where he had often sat looking out—but she had turned it facing inward, so that she could look at him. And though it seemed a long time, it had not been too long really, before Dan Biggs and his assistant had arrived—and left again, eventually, when the sun having made its preliminary climb was just high enough to throw its first beams over the nearest hill. Norma had scarcely noticed that the day had come, and had quite forgotten how she'd longed, one day ago, to see the sun rise again in its customary fashion, and hear the birds singing in accompaniment. She was aware of all that only as part of some curiously mechanical performance: day and night, life and death, and the routine which belonged to those alternating cycles—almost businesslike in its automatic progression. So quickly organized and carried out, with little to say in the intervals between one chore and the next.

There had been that moment or two of colloquy with Joyce, before Norma had gone back to help Miriam with the packing of Roger's clothes. Pausing on her way, she'd said, "You'd better dress, dear, in case there may be some errand to do. And as soon as you think the Mearses will be up and around, you'd better telephone Jim—no, better go down there—and ask him if he'll take Miriam over to the junction in time for the eleven-twenty bus. She's determined to go that way, apparently." Almost without a pause, she added smoothly, "Don Landis has left, you know."

Joyce hadn't batted an eye at that. Had said, practically, "That's good. Then he won't be in the way." And added, as if faintly surprised—but only faintly, "I hadn't really noticed." Her mother took thankful note of that as she turned away, and some automatic mental process was already beginning to register its corollary, that Jim had somehow maintained his place after all, when the girl had stopped her.

"Mom. I'd rather not—go down there this morning. Anyway, why shouldn't I drive Miriam over?"

"Because I'd rather that you didn't," Norma said slowly. She could not explain exactly why, to Joyce, or to herself. She didn't mean to tell the girl any more about the cause of Roger's death than she already had, in calling it a heart attack, which in itself was true. And she did not mean to risk the chance of letting those two talk alone together; she did not want Joyce to be with Miriam any more. Unreasonable, perhaps, but the feeling was born full grown and very strong in her.

"But there's no reason why I shouldn't take her over, or drive her all the way up to town, as far as that goes—is there?"

"I don't think she wishes that, any more than she wants me to take her," Norma said, and knew that that was also true. "So please go down as I suggested. We'll have to tell the Mearses about this anyway, among the first, and it would be kinder to her to go than to telephone."

"But, Mother, I don't *want* to go down there," Joyce said, with a stubbornness which seemed to have a certain dread as well as obstinacy about it. And Norma thought, So she and Jim have not patched things up, after all, and she felt no flicker of thankfulness now, only of weary exasperation that the child should take this moment to make this other dreadful business one jot more difficult.

"Joyce, I don't think that this is a time when purely personal wishes should be given consideration, do you?" She looked straight into her daughter's eyes, which were troubled and perplexed in some way which she couldn't understand—but this was no *time* to go into anything more, as she had just said.

"But, Mother, you just don't understand—"

"I understand that you're making a small matter much more difficult, when I have other things to cope with, Joyce. I want you to do this one thing as I asked you to. Do I make myself clear?" And though her voice was stern with controlled emotion, it was the undertone of sorrow which came through to Joyce's ear, rather than that of patience overtried.

"All right." Her eyes dropped away from her mother's, and Norma heard a little sigh as she left her to go back to join Miriam in Roger's empty room.

That had not taken very long—an hour perhaps, or less—for Miriam to sort and Norma to fold and pack the clothes as directed; to put aside the other homely, heartbreaking things like shaving soap and toothbrush, to be thrown away . . . But neither one gave any indication to the other that these were anything but the in-animate objects which they appeared to be. They talked, when necessary, in normal everyday tones, giving their practical impersonal consideration to what should be discarded, what put in this suitcase or that to give away. It was the only way to get the thing done. And when that part of it was finished, and Norma had offered, with that special politeness due from one stranger to another, to help Miriam with her own bags, the other shook her head. It wouldn't take her very long, she said, and besides . . . Besides, Norma thought, she needed a while alone, before that hard glaze of composure reached the cracking point. She had herself been thankful to leave her and go back to her own room to dress.

Joyce had evidently gone down to the village now, and her mother saw that it was after eight o'clock. She also saw that her child had first taken time to make her bed for her, and tidy up the room. That was nice, she thought dully. Everything tidy and in its place. Except for some extraneous object over there on the desk, which she half saw out of the corner of her eye and knew did not belong there—without really noticing what it was, as she crossed over to the bath-room. It was while she was mechanically washing her face and brushing her teeth that she had begun to wonder what that thing was . . . because it couldn't possibly be what her memory, or her fancy, was suggesting. Nevertheless, when she came back into the bedroom she went directly over to the desk to check up, and saw that it was—exactly—what she'd thought it was: a bulky, pinkish object made of cardboard and tied around its middle with cord, and she stood gazing at it in fascinated disbelief, asking herself how it could *get* there . . . Until she recalled that she had shown Mr. Bixby in this way last evening; that he had in fact had the run of the place, for a matter of five or ten minutes, possibly. But why had he left his filing case behind, when he had clung to it so faithfully before and after dinner? Why leave it *here*? She wanted to believe that he had forgotten or mislaid it, but there was her own name staring at her from that piece of paper tucked inside the tape which held it together.

She seated herself, as though she felt she might need support, but still she didn't touch the thing, just sat looking at it askance for another moment. Telling herself to open it, see what it was, since it was so plainly labeled with her name. (Odd sort of package, for a going-away present! Oh, go on, look at it, you fool! You can't just leave it lying here on your desk. Besides, it might be important.) But she untied the cord reluctantly, and when she had the paper in her fingers—a folded piece of her own writing paper, it proved to be, with a couple of paragraphs of the same very neat small writing inside—her eyes refused to focus, to break it up into words. She had to shake her head (rather as one shakes a recalcitrant clock to get it started) and make a determined effort of will to read the thing at all. It was headed simply: "Dear Lady." And when she had read it through, she returned to the beginning and went right through it again, trying to fasten her attention on the few salient points, putting aside a reference here and there, for future unraveling.

It wasn't the writing which confused her; that was quite legible. And the English itself was entirely clear, with only that occasional unexpected twist of idiom which she had noted in Mr. Bixby's speech, and thought a little quaint, but quite in keeping with his personality. Even the meaning was clear, theoretically, but she found it impossible to grasp all at once. The events of the evening before had grown remote, in the light of what had happened since. Unreal. All that business—like stage business—of people climbing hills, preparing for the End . . . But of course that part of it was not unreal: Bertha's giving away their savings and Mr. Bixby's departure; that had actually happened, and this was what he had left behind, a sort of testament for her to execute . . . The first point, of course, was that he *had* taken all those things which the village people had offered him. However unwillingly, she had to accept that as unreservedly as he had accepted whatever they had pressed upon him. For that was the second point: that he had, you might say, appointed himself a—receiver. Yes, that's what it amounted to, in a quite literal sense.

But the next thing to be grasped was that this was not a confession; there was not a single note of repentance or apology in it. It was not a testament after all, but a mission which he was turning over to *her*, if you please! To return all property herewith enclosed . . . "or otherwise noted on receipts, for those large articles stored elsewhere . . ." Well, of course, thought Norma in parenthetical annoyance, it never occurred to us that he might have put things away deliberately in a locked storeroom and just left them there in the house! That was too easy for even her facile imagination to jump at. But here were the two keys, as the letter said, to the house and the cupboard, both tied together and filed away quite logically under the letter "K." Oh, perfectly logical, all of it, once one accepted the basic premise. But that was what she couldn't do. The whole thing was too implausible. Impossible. It was too simple to believe, that was her trouble. For what he wished her to believe was simply that he had taken charge of everything those poor deluded dupes had handed over to him, in order to keep them from throwing away everything they had or valued most; that he had held them in safekeeping until the day of hysteria should be past, and now asked her to return them. Because, he said, he could trust no other with this responsibility . . . and it seemed best that he should not come back again.

That's what it said here, if one could only believe it. (But why shouldn't he come back, for heaven's sake? He spoke as if there was some personal reason which she would understand, but certainly she couldn't be expected to be clairvoyant about his personal life. As far as she knew he didn't have any; just existed in a sort of human void.) As for the rest, it still did not seem in the least credible. That money, for instance, which Bertha was supposed to have given him: she didn't suppose for one minute, did she, Norma demanded sternly of herself, that that was actually stowed away right there under her hand, in that ridiculous thing that looked like an accordion lolling on her desk top? With the tape removed, it had begun to expand like a fat man with his belt undone, and after a few seconds, her fingers, almost of their own volition, felt their way cautiously along the alphabetical index until they found the letter for Joseph's surname—that is, the name by which she'd always known those two. She reached into the depths of that compartment and took out a separate envelope, compactly stuffed, held together by an elastic band, with the two names and the amount written clearly on the outside. The amount which Joseph, his deepest instinct reaching for one last shred of reticence, had told her she could easily guess at—and her guess had not been far off. She removed the elastic with shaky fingers and counted the hundred-dollar bills, and sighed deeply when she found they were all there. And when she had put them back again, she held the envelope in her hands for a moment, like something too valuable to put down, unable to think beyond a sense of awe, which was not thought, exactly.

Presently, as if in further test of her own eyesight, or perhaps by now it was just primitive, unconscious curiosity, she put her hand at random into another deep slit of the file, and studied the single piece of paper which she brought forth. This was plainly a receipt, for something stored away in the locked cupboard, no doubt. It said "Two"—oh no, it couldn't be what it looked like, that was too silly! But the writing was still perfectly clear. "Two quilted bedspreads." That's what it *said*. And the name was Mary Dennis, and Norma's memory nudged sharply at her incomprehension, as at a backward child. Why yes, those must be the heirlooms she had heard about so many times; the pride of old Mary's life. Of course. Her hand plunged in again, nervously, as if driven by some involuntary reflex, into first one deep crevasse and then another, bringing up strange assorted treasure from the bottomless past.

A rather lumpy envelope, containing an old-fashioned gold brooch, thick with seed pearls, and long dangling earrings to match . . . A

313

small box which she opened gingerly, discovering a star-shaped medal marked Military Order Loyal Legion of the United States, with the date, 1865—and she closed the box again, as hastily as though it had been a door lettered Private. Not even glancing to see who might have treasured that—for ninety-odd years! . . . And then, her fingers pulling with spasmodic impatience at the drawstring of a very small soiled bag of bleached muslin (which for a moment she thought a mere scrap of rag), she drew forth one of the most beautiful old rings she had ever laid eyes on, an emerald set around with diamonds, which she regarded dazedly. Every kind of thing was here, it seemed, from utter, absolute junk to something like this, of which she was afraid to guess the value.

She again picked up his note to her and scanned it until she came to the sentence which had puzzled her most, but which she now saw must contain his central meaning, if she could only reach through and find it . . .

". . . I do not want you should mistake what I do here for the 'good deed,' as you might call it. All I do is an expiation—or maybe a small revenge on forces whose real nature I learned to know too late. So you will see I am not too good or charitable a man—but you will please to understand that my concern here has been lest some unprincipled person take advantage of these ignorant or foolish people, for it looks to me that this strange game has been initiated by someone with no conscience or mercy. Believe me, I do not like such stupid, even willful ignorance, which invites invasion like any other vacuum, but it is necessary, I think, to protect it from the greater evil which plans to prey on it."

When she'd first read that bit, it had seemed too high-flown to be sincere in any way. Besides, she had been so confused that those appeared merely words to confuse her further. But now it seemed that his meaning had been as precise as his little note, as every step he'd taken along this curious route. That *was* what he'd been afraid of, all along: that someone was trying to victimize them all by exploiting their most primitive fears. And he'd taken all that trouble, all that *bother* . . . a busy man who came down here for a day or two at a time, as a brief retreat into rest and peace. While we were mean enough, thought Norma, to suspect him of all kinds of sinister motives.

The quiet care with which he must have made it known that he was willing to go to hell with his hands full—the meticulous pains he'd taken to file and label every item here (why, anybody who meant to get away with such fantastic loot would have obliterated every trace of where it came from!) seemed as quaint, as out-of-this-world as any part of it. And finally, the absolute and implicit trust he had put in her, to finish what he had begun . . . She dropped the small parcel and the other papers back in place, brushing her hand across her eyes, which were a little moist for the first time that morning. Something in her heart had begun to thaw, and yet her brain still seemed quite frozen, held fast in some rut of her own thinking, unable to break out of it. She couldn't understand.

With her elbows on the desk and her two hands holding her head, now bent between them, Norma gave herself up to a long moment, not so much of prayer (though it was nearly that) as to the painful effort to think this thing out. For there was something here which she did not grasp. What had made this revelation of Mr. Bixby's mission in the village seem so deceptive and preposterous was, she perceived, her difficulty in believing that anyone could have such impersonal compassion—for fools and simpletons. Such kindness, for people whom he scarcely knew; whom, moreover, he frankly considered stupid, since he had even called them willfully ignorant. While now, on top of this, or set against it in another column to balance it, was this possibility which he suggested (something that she herself had never dreamed of) that the whole affair had been a deliberate hoax upon the village, actually planned by some malevolent individual for some personal material gain, or even for the cruel enjoyment of a practical joke . . .

Yet even that was not the point that she was reaching for. It was . . . that Mr. Bixby, believing men and women capable of such stupidity plus such calculated evil . . . could yet contain within himself—the opposite ideal. Yes! That was it. She dropped her hands and sat looking straight ahead of her, trying to see further . . . further. Everybody knew—except the poor insane—that good and bad were there, on either side. She brushed that aside impatiently as if someone were trying to argue with her just to impede her progress.

But it did seem—almost—that any honest recognition of the dreadfulness of man, to the extent that one accepted it as inevitable, was apt to cripple, by just so much, one's ability to credit his potential for ultimate good. Each one's thinking was colored according to the light one grew in, nearer one end of the spectrum or the other: it could not encompass the whole range without distortion. And in the middle half-light where most of us lived, one could scarcely conceive the black depth—or blaze of glory at either extreme.

The remembrance of last night's debate out in the patio came back to her suddenly, in fragments. Joyce's trustful, confident "God won't let us destroy His lovely world." And on the other hand, there was Roger's overpowering conviction, amounting to a grim belief in the irresistible forces of destruction. But here was Mr. Bixby, an anomaly, containing in one person the accepted knowledge, even the dispassionate expectation of any man's depravity—or stupidity . . . and a still surviving belief that he was worth saving, worth protecting. He was neither a realist nor an idealist; not even alternately. He was both at once, taking practical steps to deal with life and man as they were, all the way through. That, at last, was the thing which had seemed incompatible, impossible—or so nearly impossible that she had not recognized it at first.

It was that for which she had been straining the very gates of her comprehension to make them wide enough to admit the recognition of what this little fat man *meant*, as a person. (Not merely in what he had said.) What he meant to her, in this solitary moment of perception, which she might never attain again. Such slender pinnacles of understanding were too arduous to reach, too sharp to stand upon for more than a second or two. She might even tell herself, some day later on, that she had deduced far too much from the few words he had written here—from the recollection of the few commonplace remarks he'd made—or even the curious collection of oddments which lay there on the desk. Certainly what he had done or said was in no way heroic. Just trying to prevent a few befuddled people from parting uselessly from things they loved (which held their bodies or their souls together), to put his kindness as a shield between them and someone who was trying to hurt them. No use in magnifying it. He himself disclaimed so much as a good deed . . . Yet there was something special about this thing that Mr. Bixby represented.

Where there were opportunities for heroism, there were issues large enough and clear enough to be unmistakable. Was a life to be saved, one had the courage—or had not. There was no question of whether the doing was worth doing, nor any niggling argument about the way it might be done. Sometimes, Norma thought, people will rise to actions greater than they are themselves, to sudden sacrifice, say, when they would not take the painstaking, piffling *bother* of doing some little thing . . . like this, which at first glance had appeared mere foolishness. Quixotic. So nearly incomprehensible that it had seemed there must even be some sinister motive behind it. *He* called it expiation and revenge. But whatever terms he used, she had begun to see it for what it clearly was: pity. Practical. Comprehensive. There was something else he had said at the very end of his letter, and she did not so much read the whole thing through again as let her glance settle slowly, from force of gravity, toward the foot of the page, and his final words . . . "One has such painful pity for any who throw away what precious things they have. This I think you also feel, Dear Lady. So I can trust to leave them in your hands."

Well, he was wrong. *His* pity was compassion, but hers at best had been a sort of pitying indulgence toward the whims and weaknesses of others. In some ways, she had been more impatient than indulgent. She'd felt sorry for Roger, yes, truly and terribly sorry for him, but that was because he was tied up with her feelings; he was *her* friend. But how smug she had been in her appraisal of all the others; how sensible and stable and even compassionate she'd fancied herself to be, standing in their midst, with hysteria on the one side and grim despair on the other, and the lightnings of young love striking somewhere in between. While even now she, who—of them all—should have felt that most painful pity for Miriam, did not and could not feel anything except this coldness lying at the bottom of her heart, which she did not wish to lift up or disturb in any way, for it was better left there. She already knew too much of what must be going on in the other's tortured mind at this moment, but there was no forgiveness in her; no brotherly love—for a sister.

She knew too much, yet still not enough for true compassion, Norma thought sadly. How strange that one could live, and live, and think that one had learned a lot, and then discover all over again that it was too little. Perhaps if she knew the whole story, even the whole of her own story, she could do better. But not only did one have no access to the answers at the back of the book; there were pages sealed together, whole chapters hidden away; buried . . . (Yes, buried.) That made the task of learning what was true, and assimilating mercy from it, much more difficult. Strange way to gain an education, but that's the way it was. Sometimes it seemed impossible, and her mind fell back from it now, dulled with fatigue from the effort she had been making, simply to understand.

As for Mr. Bixby, he was gone, for some reason that she could not yet divine, though that might come to her, eventually. But Norma felt certain that she would never really know any more about him than she did right now. Only this tacit evidence of a rare species of humanity which he had left behind in the shape of the pinkish cardboard object lying between her hands, though still a little beyond her actual grasp. It might be that Roger had had the real key to that, in what he had been trying to remember. He had come nearer to being right about the little man than anyone else. She wished that she could tell Rog that.

A simple, errant wish, quite unexpected. But it came upon her without warning, rushing into her emptiness so overwhelmingly that it went through her like pain, and left her shaken. It seemed so *unreasonable* that she couldn't let Rog know about that before he got too far away. Why, it was only yesterday morning that they'd sat out there talking together in the patio, after Miriam had gone for her walk. Norma could almost feel the sunlight which had flooded over them, as though that warmth were not yet cold; even with her eyes wide open she could see him sitting there (the rough hair, the heavy hands), leaning forward in his chair, studying the grass; almost, she could hear his voice thoughtfully repeating those words ". . . miles to go before I sleep. Miles to go . . ." That was only yesterday morning—*less* than twenty-four hours, right now—and he'd had a lifetime ahead of him still. A book to write; an urgent mission of his own to accomplish. So many things to do—in a day.

The wrongness of it, the sense of a predictable but irretrievable *mistake* struck into her now even more sharply than the first re-cognition that he was dead. It penetrated the numb layer of shock which had enclosed her throughout these last hours. It was the old rebellion: mortality crying out for life, and against its everlasting uncertainty of tenure, which was the only certain thing about it. And with this agony of revolt, a surge of anger even more than grief came welling up from the deep springs of inner conviction, which she had tried blindly to leave there, undisturbed. Unrecog-nized. It hardened into chilling certitude: that this death at this time had been unnecessary. It was the same cold awareness which had enclosed her like a sheath of ice, even as the sun grew warm outside, and held her rigidly apart from Miriam while they worked together, with something crying silently within her that it might have been, it could have been avoided! This waste of life unlived; of many things undone, unsaid, unlearned.

And it had all happened before. Not once but many times. Every day; could happen to any of them, at any given time. She'd *learned* that already, so many yesterdays ago. But here was today, and some part of it which she had not yet mastered in all these years or even while she sat here, thinking through it all once more. She was conscious of a penetrating sense of cleavage, as between two thoughts trying to gain possession of her; not just claiming her attention, but her final allegiance, though she was not quite certain of their exact identity. Only that there were these two incompatible, irreconcilable things struggling against each other, refusing to be entertained simultaneously. And when she got to her feet at last, it was not because she had resolved anything between them, but only to put them both aside while she went resolutely about her business. The

319

chill of bitterness was still lying deep within her, and at the same time, this odd sense of—gratefulness—was that what it was?—to Mr. Bixby; and the two would not lie down together.

CHAPTER 27

She had to finish dressing, having made such a hasty and haphazard job of it, earlier. But when she had done her hair again, and put on stockings (for no matter how it dated her, she was never *dressed* without stockings, even up here in the back country), Norma went out through the patio and stopped at Miriam's door to say that she would have breakfast ready in a quarter of an hour. And then she went along to the kitchen, carrying Mr. Bixby's filing case with her, recalling as she did so how he had hugged it to him everywhere he went. No wonder, now she knew what was in it.

She put it down on the splashboard by the sink, yet stood with her hands still cradling it as she looked absently out the window, wondering just how she was going to manage to put all these things back into the rightful hands, tactfully, kindly, without causing some ugly emotional backwash. It was going to take some doing. Joseph and Bertha were the logical ones to start with, of course, and possibly the most important ones to reassure, as well. On that reflection she untied the tape once more and took out their envelope, laying it on top of the other big one, as though to have it ready, at first sound of their waking.

It was unheard of for them to sleep this late, but they must have been very, very tired, poor old souls, after that vigil on the hill. She had no idea when they had come in, though it was probably not until the night was nearly over. Perhaps just long enough ahead of those hideous sounds in the patio for them to have fallen dead asleep in their exhaustion, and heard nothing from that far side of the house. She could even picture their shamefaced, furtive return, not coming in through the patio at all, but by the kitchen door, where she had purposely left the outside light burning for them last night. That was now turned off, so she knew they were in, and she had also noticed that the door from the pantry passage into their own room was firmly closed.

She went about making a fresh pot of coffee, began taking eggs and butter and cream out of the refrigerator, and as she did so, she also began wishing that Joseph and Bertha would sleep on until after Miriam had left. It shouldn't be too long before she was ready now, and Joyce would be back any minute, bringing Jim with her, possibly. In fact, Norma didn't see why she wasn't back already, and hoped belatedly that she hadn't given the child too unpleasant an errand. Never pleasant to break such news, especially to an older person waiting for his or her own summons, and it was plain last night that Mrs. Mears had been quite drawn to Roger, despite their lively disagreements. As it was all too plain this morning that Joyce did not want to talk to Jim, to ask any favors—or even see him, apparently. Poor youngsters—if they had really reached the point of no return to understanding between them. Poor blind babies . . . But she had made her own stern decision not to put out so much as a finger, not to try to *steer* any more, even by leaning ever so slightly one way or the other. Curiously though, it seemed to her now that they had been friendlier, talking quite naturally together out there at the gate, when she and Jim had returned and found Joyce waiting for them. He had lingered on out there with Joyce, instead of coming in to get his grandmother, when Norma came in herself.

It was only then that she remembered, with a sort of delayed shock, that Mrs. Mears had not been there in the patio with Roger, when she came in. Of course not! It was late by then and she would have gone home. Joyce must have taken her home, when she, Norma, and Jim had been so slow in coming back . . . But that was odd, too— Norma thought, pausing with the frying pan in her hand—because they would have had to go right past Alfred's place while she and Jim were there. There was a hiatus here, which her thought could not quite cross, since there was no other place where the old lady could have been. Unless she'd gone up on the Hill, to take off with all the others, which was sheer nonsense. Nonsense. She found she

321

didn't care to think about Mrs. Mears at the moment. So she proceeded to load the tea wagon with what she needed for the setting of three places on the glass-topped table outside, and promptly went back to thinking of Joseph again, and the careful labor which he always made of this operation. Ah well, she knew the reason for his inadeptness now. And all at once, quite arbitrarily, she reversed herself into wishing that they *would* both wake up. Right away. Somehow, the picture of their sleeping so soundly, which had been comforting up to this point, took on an unaccountable faint shadow in her mind.

She went out onto the terrace, into the sun again, and quickly set the table, listening with one ear for the sound of Joyce's return in the car, bringing her a report on Mrs. Mears. And when she returned to the kitchen, she found that she was listening, still, for some sign or sound of life from Bertha's and Joseph's quarters. She'd just like to know they were all right, that was all. Old people had no business climbing hills, especially at night. Especially Mrs. Mears, who might be ten years older than Joseph. But she didn't *know* that Mrs. Mears had gone up there, so why was she borrowing trouble from that source? Surely there was enough, already. Enough, her mind protested, coming closer now to prayer.

Nevertheless, when she had done every possible thing that she could do ahead of time, and was still waiting (for Miriam, for Joyce, for any murmur or sound of movement from that room across the pantry passage), her uneasiness had crept up closer too, like someone breathing stealthily behind her. She stopped once more at the kitchen window, by the sink, and again picked up that business-sized envelope, its well-filled compactness giving her subtle reassurance, even as she wished it had been thin enough to slip under their door so they would see it the first moment either of them opened their eyes. Without it, their awakening would be desolate. They wouldn't even want to get up and face another day. *They might not get up!* And suddenly her uneasiness became a rampant, full-grown dread. Joseph had said there were other ways of ending it. He might have— they might already—oh, but surely not. Those things one read in the paper, suicide pacts, and other desperate endings . . . couldn't happen here on this hillside.

But worse than that had happened, as no one knew better than Norma. And there was Alfred and his grisly finish, down the hill . . . and this unformulated but growing apprehension about Mrs. Mears. It all began to seem like some subtle blight—of self-destruction, could it be? Slowly spreading, like a disease, with the seeds of human extinction contained within each individual, as unsuspected and malignant as cancer cells, in turn destroying healthy tissue. Was *this* the way the larger world, made up of little people, would finally destroy itself? Each separate seed of fear, of cruelty or dominating selfishness—yes, of *evil* whether ignorant or calculated—growing relentlessly until it was beyond all control? The very question was unthinkable, and it was quite senseless too. So much had happened in these past few hours that it seemed her own imagination was coming unhinged or something. The *"sensible* Mrs. Collins" indeed. Standing at her kitchen window in broad daylight, waiting to serve breakfast to someone who didn't want it, waiting for others to wake up, who had no wish to waken. With the tray which she had set for Roger, last night, still lying on the pantry counter.

If she could only reassure herself about Bertha and Joseph, somehow. Perhaps—the thought came hesitantly—if she just listened at their door a moment, they might soon be moving about, or she might hear one or the other of them snoring. That would quite simply put these vague wild notions of her own to sleep. So on that impulse she turned quickly and went across the narrow hallway, and stood outside the door, her palm laid gently against the panel as her head bent closer, to listen more acutely. But the sound she heard was the soft metallic whisper of the latch giving way, and she found to her alarmed embarrassment that the door itself had yielded to the faint pressure of her hand. It had not been tightly latched, as it appeared, and for a moment she was so startled and aghast that she could hear nothing but the thudding of her own heart.

And then—thank God—another sound established itself, regular and rhythmic, measured against the silence, now that her inward clamor was subsiding. An almost syncopated rhythm, between one slightly stertorous breath, and another which was softer, but a little faster, persistently holding its own. Norma gave a sigh of thankfulness, and recovering from that moment of suspended fright, reached carefully for the doorknob. It was only then that she realized with a new and separate surprise, that through that four-inch opening, she was looking directly at the chest of drawers at right angles to the doorway and close beside it, with the mirror above reflecting the other side of the room which was actually screened from her by the door between. She had been concentrating so intently with her ears that she had scarcely registered the visual angle straight across to the two beds against the opposite wall.

But now she saw that one was empty, and the two old people were huddled together in the other, as for warmth, or comfort; Joseph's waxen face turned up to the ceiling like the effigy on a tomb—but *breathing*, oh, indubitably breathing, with that small stertorous whuffling sound—while Bertha's graying frowsy head was burrowed down somewhere close to his shoulder, one plump hand and forearm thrown out across his chest, and something (it looked like a wad of damp Kleenex) lying on the blanket where her inert fingers had released it.

Curiously, as Norma stood there for that extra second, she had no longer any sense of intrusion. Her first reaction of discomfiture over her unwarranted opening of that door, had wholly disappeared, for she was gazing not at Bertha and Joseph themselves, but only at a reflection, and that reflection itself distilled from something as simple as it was universal.

Her right hand closed gently on the doorknob, and putting out her left to brace and cushion the door as it came near the frame, she found that the envelope which she was clutching was in her way. Without further thought or hesitation, she slipped it through the still-open gap and laid it on the dresser, so close by; it took only the extra reach of her arm to do it—and that was the proper place for it, right beside Joseph's shabby old tie, where he would be sure to see it almost at once when he got up. And then she drew the door softly to and released the knob with care, and let go another small sigh of thanks. Of thanks, and something else which might be envy, though it had not the caustic quality of envy; only the sadness of longing for what she no longer had. Poor, silly old dears, she thought, as she turned away. They don't know how lucky they are. Or perhaps they did, after all. They had lived long enough to learn.

She crossed the hall back to the pantry, and as she did so, thought she heard Joyce's voice outside, and went to the patio door to see if she was right—and she was. The girl was heading straight toward that door as if she'd been told just where to find her, but she didn't call out, and Norma waited anxiously until she was nearer. And then what she said was not what her mother was waiting for.

"I was putting Miriam's bags in the car," she explained calmly, and for the moment Norma couldn't even think why that was not what she had expected.

"What about Mrs. Mears?" she asked at once. But Joyce was wearing her most noncommittal expression; her poker look, Norma had always called it, even when she was a child and put it on when-ever she was puzzled. It was an odd, unchildlike look this morning: still, and protective. She was perplexed, but she was also very much on guard, as she countered, "What about her?"

"Well, is she all right, dear?"

"She seems to be."

"But you did find her there at the house?" Norma pursued, hardly realizing what a strange inquiry that was, to make about an old lady at this time of day, until she found that her daughter had stopped on the doorstep to stare at her.

"You mean, you *knew*, all the time, that she'd gone up there on the Hill last night?"

"Oh no!" said Norma quickly, and then to save time and bridge over the confusion of explaining, "Yes, I suppose I did, when I began to *think* this morning, after you'd gone down there. Though I didn't see how it was physically possible."

"Neither did I," admitted Joyce. She put her hand out to the screen door which her mother had been holding open, and together they moved mechanically, rather absently, on into the small pantry where they paused again, as if agreed that this was the better place to talk.

"I tried to stop her, Mom—before you and Jim came back. But I couldn't. She just wouldn't pay any attention to me."

"Or to Jim, either?" Norma asked, as though it were a foregone conclusion that he had gone after her. There was an instant's hesitation, and then Joyce answered briefly, "No. I guess not."

"I see," said Norma, though she did not. "And you mean to say, she actually got all the way up there, last night—and back again?"

"Apparently. But I can tell you, I was scared to death when I went down there this morning."

"I'm so sorry, dear. I never should have made you—"

"Well, when I saw you didn't know about her going, I decided it was up to me to find out, before giving you any more to—worry about," Joyce said simply. "I was scared, though, even to ask anybody about her. And when I went up to the front door and found it standing open, and not a sound inside . . ." The girl shook her head and passed over that. "And then when I went on in and saw her lying there on the sitting-room couch, still dressed in that incredible white outfit of last night . . . But she was just dozing, I guess, and opened her eyes sort of vaguely when she heard me. She looked kind of white and tired, but no different otherwise."

"It's unbelievable," said Norma.

"I think she was as surprised as anyone, to be there. I mean, still *here*."

"I should think she might have been," her mother retorted, a little tartly now, in her relief. "She ought to be ashamed of herself for doing anything so foolhardy."

"Well, if she was—ashamed, or shamefaced about anything, I'd say it was about coming back at all. I don't think she meant to come back, Mother."

"I don't see how she could have gone off like that, leaving Jim—while she still *had* him . . ." Norma stopped short, but with the mention of Jim's name, there was another tight little silence on Joyce's part.

"Well, she did," the girl said definitely, after a moment. "And I'll tell you this much too: that it was the news about Roger that set her back more than anything else. *That* really shook her, and you know she'd never set eyes on him before last night."

"That was natural though, dear. Anybody would be—shocked."

"But I don't mean shocked exactly. Not as I was shocked, for instance. It was more as if she couldn't understand why *he* had died, when she hadn't. That was what floored her. It really was."

"I see," Norma said, once more.

"Well, if you do, it's more than I could, then or now! Especially when she kept muttering something about trying to hand on a burden to somebody else. It was—very peculiar. She looked at me for quite a long minute, as though she was going to tell *me* something . . . And then she shook her head and said, 'No, my dear, it seems we're not permitted to share our load. Or lay it down.' And yet she was perfectly rational, you know. I'd swear she was."

"Yes," said Norma softly. "I don't doubt it." And she wondered what it could have been that Mrs. Mears had told Rog while they were sitting outside last night. Whatever it was, she was thankful without knowing why, that the old lady had not told Joyce, this morning.

"Oh yes," Joyce added suddenly. "And there was something else, equally peculiar, only in a different way. She said once, kind of in the middle of all this and not apropos of anything, 'I think you ought to meet Jim's mother sometime, Joyce.' As if it had just occurred to her! As if *we* didn't know she's always acted as if Jim's mother didn't exist . . . As if he'd hatched out of an egg or something!" The girl broke off, with a little quaver in her voice.

"And where was Jim all this time?" Norma inquired. The blue eyes met hers in a clear blank stare, and the reply bounced back, off-handedly.

"Oh, Jim's gone."

"Gone where?"

"Up to L.A. To enlist."

"Oh," said Norma. "Oh—h . . ." And then, gently, "That was what you wanted, wasn't it, dear? For him to make some decision, and act on it."

"Yes. Oh yes, I think it's a good thing."

"Was his grandmother upset, over that?"

"Not a bit. Just said, 'I think it's time, don't you?' And that was all, believe it or not!"

"When did he go?" Norma asked, as if reminded by the word "time."

"Last night, I guess."

"You—*guess*. Didn't he tell you what he was going to do?"

"Nope. Not a word." Still very lightly. But that was it, thought Norma; that was why the child was hurt. (Oh, darling, darling, don't be hurt! They do such unaccountable things sometimes.) Aloud, she asked, "Did he leave some word for his grandmother?"

"No, Mom. He just *went*. French leave—like Mr. Bixby." (Mr. Bixby! The reference startled Norma, for of course—the child was thinking of someone who had left, taking all one had, with him . . . But she couldn't stop and correct that now.)

"Then *how* do you know—" she began, and Joyce answered patiently, before the question was even finished.

"Because he telephoned, Mother. While I was down there. She asked me to answer the phone. So I did. He must have started off last night in a blazing hurry, to be the first in line at the recruiting office when it opened up this morning. He was already there, and *in*. Signed up, I mean. But I suppose he was worrying all the time —about his grandmother, that is. You see, he'd expected to come right back again today. They always get a few days before they get their notice to report for the physical. But he got stuck." She grinned at her mother, suddenly and widely, like someone forced to appreciate some absurdity in spite of herself.

"What do you mean, stuck?"

"Just that the grandmother of jalopies broke down, that's what! And I really mean broke down. Had to be towed to the nearest gas station. He says he doesn't know yet if it's even worth fixing again, or if so, how long it'll take."

"Oh, poor Jim." Such anticlimax, Norma thought sympathetically —after his big decisive gesture.

"Wait. You haven't heard it all! The great big goofball went off without practically any money. He thought he had plenty to get up there and back, but he'd had the tank filled again before he started back, and then he had to pay for getting towed, so he had just about enough left for a telephone call. Oh yes, and I forgot to say that he's got himself a job washing cars at this gas station, until he earns enough for his bus fare to come down, or fix up the crate."

She added that last in a tone of detachment, but when her mother murmured again, "Poor Jim—" a sparkle came into the girl's eyes, like the rekindling of something which had been carefully damped down; but it was not sympathy.

"Oh yes, I'm sure he was really worried about his grandmother, by then. And hearing *me* answer the phone down there, this early in the day, gave him an extra scare, I guess. But I was able to reassure him about her, of course," she concluded. Quite formally, as though winding up her report. There was a moment's pause.

"You didn't, by any chance, offer to drive up for him, yourself?"

"I certainly didn't. Not by *any* chance! Why should I, for Pete's sake, when he— Oh no, it's impossible, it's no good any more. It's no *use*, Mother!" The spark had kindled to a flash, and guttered out. (Or been stamped out, for good and all.) She turned her head aside to look up and then down the row of glassed-in shelves on her right, with an impersonal interest in the stacked rows of china, as though they were a new acquisition which she had not seen before. She was standing with her back to the pantry window, her elbows braced on each side of the counter where she had been leaning, and Norma gazed sadly at her child.

She longed to say, of *course* it was no use—if they were both going to be so stubborn and so touchy; let themselves be hurt, and hurt each other by every silly thing they said or did. Far better not to marry, if they couldn't grow up that much, first. But she had learned at last, and promised in her own heart, not to interfere; not to try to steer, to push or pull back. Just let go. Let go, completely . . . And after all, how was she to know whether Joyce was right when she said it was no use? The only thing she could find to say was, "I'm so very sorry, dear. Sorry that I sent you down there this morning. It was the wrong time, in every way."

"Oh well . . . Somebody had to tell Mrs. Mears, and find out how she was, anyway." Joyce shrugged, and brought her abstracted gaze back from its study of the china cupboard. "I got her some coffee and breakfast, too, which was a good thing, I guess."

329

"That's why you were gone so long. I wondered."

"Well, I figured if I could get her to eat something it would take her mind off other things. She even got started telling me about the doings up on the Hill, and how it all got funnier and funnier as the night went on." Joyce gave forth a sound that was half gulp and half giggle. "Really, Mom, you know how *dry* she can be when she starts to take somebody off—and the story she's working up on that is just a *howl* . . . even to finding Alfred as they all came down again."

"Oh, Joyce—*no!*" Norma broke in, appalled.

"But, darling, Alfred isn't dead. I forgot you didn't know."

"No. I didn't . . . know. How did he ever get out of there? Oh, Joyce, are you *sure?*"

"He wasn't even in the house, or anywhere near it when it burned. Somebody found him on the way down, I tell you, lying in the ditch beside the trail. Comfortably drunk and sound asleep. In fact, he was quite annoyed when they insisted on disturbing him, especially when he found the show was over. Apparently he'd started up there, but hadn't gotten very far."

"Oh, Joyce, stop. It's just too . . . too . . . I can't take in any more, that's all." Norma had put her hands up to her face, and Joyce came across the narrow space between them to put her arms around her.

"I know. It isn't very funny, darling, but the way she told it, it was. I guess that was her way of picking herself up again. And after all, we can't cry over old Alfred. D'you know what he said when they got down to his house—I mean where his house had been?" The girl stood back at arm's length, with her hands still resting on the other's shoulders, but her head cocked sidewise at a quizzical tilt.

"All right, what did he say?" said Norma weakly, in a sort of resignation to anything that anyone might say or do, from here on.

"He said, 'Good riddance.'" Joyce paused and repeated the phrase in imitation of Alfred's sonorous inflection. "*Goo-ood* riddance. He said it was the Lord's doing, and seemed quite relieved the house was gone."

330

"I see." Norma repeated those two words conclusively, for the third time in the last quarter of an hour, though she knew she saw no more than she had at first. She must be very stupid.

"What's more," continued Joyce, "I met him for a minute myself, as I came out to get in the car after I'd left Mrs. Mears—so I—oh, you know, just tried to say something decent, that I was sorry about the fire and so on."

Her mother nodded several times, as if, once started, she couldn't stop, like one of these little mandarin images; then said irrelevantly, "How did he look?"

"Like death standing up," said Joyce. "But he told me solemnly, right then and there, that he was going to put up a gas station on the site. Thinks it's a natural, apparently, with the whole place already paved. Maybe he's right. Planning on putting Joe out of business, I guess . . . Well, there you are, and nothing happened after all." She had straightened up and dropped her hands, and though she'd taken half a turn away, she stood irresolute as though not sure where she was going next. And then lifting her chin and tossing back her hair, she added with a small suggestion of bravado, "The world didn't come to an end, for anybody, did it?" Norma knew very well what the child was thinking, though she was no longer quite child enough to put that supreme egoism into words. "Not for anybody!" she reiterated, as if confirming that, and with it her own resolution. Until, stricken suddenly by the recollection which canceled and wiped out what she had just said, she finished almost in a whisper, "Except—for Rog."

"Except for Rog," Norma repeated. The girl's eyes were searching hers now, but the question in them was neither asked nor answered, and after the slightest pause, Joyce went on quickly, striving to sound as impersonal as she had when speaking of Alfred a moment before.

"I told Miriam I'd take her over to the junction. You don't object to that still, do you, Mom?" Her mother shook her head, letting it pass. "Do you want to go with us?"

"No. I have—a great deal to do," Norma replied, rousing herself at last. "But please, put on a dress, dear—or at least a skirt."

Joyce looked down at her shorts and started to protest, then let that go by, also.

"Oh, all right."

"And do tell Miriam that breakfast is ready. She *must* eat something before she goes. And you, too."

"I had mine with Mrs. Mears. I don't want anything more, honestly. But I'll tell Miriam. She seemed to be just puttering around in there, half dressed, as if she didn't know what to do—though she said she didn't want any help."

"I know. I offered to pack her bags, too."

"Well, I'll go and change. There isn't too much time now before we ought to start if she's set on making that particular bus."

Joyce went, as quickly as always, and Norma was left facing the pantry window, confronted by that tray which she had fixed for Roger; still there, on the counter where Joyce had been leaning with her back to it and half concealing it. She would put away the silver and china now, as she should have done much earlier, instead of avoiding it . . . Remembering, as she folded the tray cloth and slipped the tray into its groove in the lower cupboard, how he had said to her last night, "If you believed that this really was the end— tonight—would you still go out to the kitchen to get things lined up for tomorrow's breakfast?" And she had said she would.

CHAPTER 28

Within five minutes she had wheeled the wagon out to the terrace again. But she returned once more to get Mr. Bixby's filing case, and brought it back and stood it on the grass by her chair, and then sat down in her usual place at the glass-topped table, facing out toward the hills. She waited for Miriam, as she had waited the morning before, a glass of orange juice at each place, the coffee waiting to be poured. (And the sun was shining brightly, the day still promising to be another gorgeous one; even more beautiful than the day before.) When finally she heard a door opening across the patio, she looked up to see Miriam coming toward her, and knew that all those long dragging hours since dawn had been a sort of temporal anteroom, where she had had to wait for this ordeal to arrive, and pass again. Like a doctor's waiting room, where others came and went, whose cases were important, or irrelevant, or both. But she had still to undergo her own test.

Miriam was dressed for the city, in blouse and suit skirt of oxford gray, with a small hat of the same color set severely straight on her dark hair, and she was carrying the jacket, with gloves and handbag, so it was plain that she did not intend to return to the room she had just left. (Nor would she ever return to this house, or this hillside, Norma thought with certainty; not even if she herself were to beg her to come.) Her lips had been carefully done, and she never wore rouge, but today her dark warm skin had lost its darkness as well as its underlying warmth; it was a yellow white and looked tight over the cheekbones. Her eyelids were not red but almost black—a dark unwholesome brown, and a little puffy. The eyes themselves looked old, and it occurred to Norma, distantly, rather as though it were a comment made by someone else than a thought of her own, that this woman would never look really young again, though yesterday it had been youth itself to which she had been clinging, the ebb of youth from whose frightening undertow she had been struggling to free herself, perhaps.

As she approached, her eyes held no expression whatsoever, but Norma made an effort to smile slightly—with her face, at least, and said, "Everything's ready." Rather pointlessly, to be sure. But when the younger woman had almost reached the table, she stopped a foot or two short of it, and looked down into the other's face.

"Can you—bring yourself to sit at the same table with me?" she asked.

"Oh, Miriam, Miriam—don't say such things! Sit down and . . ." Norma made a helpless gesture toward the glass of orange juice and the coffee pot, trying to speak naturally. "You must have something to eat, you know, before you start." But that, she knew, would not suffice. "You mustn't even think such things," she said.

Miriam laid her coat on the third chair, and seated herself at her usual place, and as she spread the napkin over her lap, she said—for it was not really a question—"How can I help it." And when Norma handed her her cup of coffee, she added, "Thank you." Politely, like a child. Stiffly, like a guest in a strange house, one who has not been invited. Norma passed her the toast, looking at her with an earnest intensity, as if appealing for some tacit agreement that they need not talk about this. But Miriam did not meet her eyes, and Norma accepted the thought, unwillingly, that it would have to be talked over, after all. It was an obligation laid on her . . . like the burden which Mrs. Mears had carried, maybe—or Alfred—who had each tried to pass it on. Miriam at least had made no attempt at pretense or excuse. She knew that Norma knew, in effect, what had happened last night. And Norma further realized that there was probably no one else on earth to whom the other woman would ever be able to talk. (And no one else who knew—what she had learned.) So she said, reservedly, "It's no use blaming yourself, Miriam, for what's happened."

"No use," the other agreed, but it was plain that she meant only, it could not bring Roger back.

"What I mean is, you are going to have to live with yourself. There's no use in building up some enlarged or overmagnified picture."

"Pretty picture, isn't it?" Miriam said, very low. "A lovely creature to be chained to, for the rest of one's life."

Norma sat silent, still arguing with herself, beseeching herself to leave the whole thing as it was. It couldn't be helped, now, or altered. But she lost that argument, as she had known she would, and took up the one which had been assigned to her. Counsel—for the defense.

"You're talking," she said slowly, "as though it were your sole responsibility."

"Well." That was all, the single word accepting the premise.

"Well, we both know that there were—many things which could, and probably did, combine to bring on that attack. We all knew it could happen, and it might have happened without any reason we could put our finger on. And there were certain things—his smoking, for instance—" She left that without a period, but Miriam didn't answer for the space of a long breath.

"You found those packages of cigarettes too, then."

"Yes," said Norma quietly, and a crack opened momentarily in Miriam's enameled composure.

"Oh, Norma, they are such children, aren't they?" It broke from her, the endlessly recurring cry of women, about their men. "He *knew* that was one of the things the doctors were most insistent about. And there he was, hiding them all over the place—from *me*! I don't know now how much he was smoking. I don't even know where he got them."

"I think it may have been from Alfred," Norma offered, in thoughtful speculation.

"I thought he was drunk and silly, that was all."

"So did I, at first. But I did see Roger go out to prowl around that hibiscus bush later on, after I'd given him the message. I was in the house, and just happened to look out . . ."

"And last night, he said that Alfred was his friend," Miriam recalled. "Made quite a point of it. Fine friend, I must say." But Norma pursued the line she had begun.

"Well, last night there was also that enormous rich dinner, and I'm afraid Rog ate far too heavily. So one *could* blame Bertha, and her mad determination to go out in a blaze—of culinary glory, I suppose one could call it. Or me—for not checking her vanity, for I knew perfectly well that it was out of all proportion."

"Yes, he did eat too much." The other picked that up tentatively. "And he wasn't quite comfortable afterward. I do know that. Though of course they say mere indigestion doesn't—"

"And afterward," said Norma doggedly, "all that talk. I'm sure he got too much worked up about it, arguing so long and so intensely. I was a little worried about it at the time, afraid it might be more excitement than he was used to. And the evening dragged on so, first one thing and then another. He got much too tired."

"Yes." Miriam again made acknowledgment in that one level word, as though she were the one on the judge's bench and must give that other one—in the dock—every possible chance.

"And then that dreadful cat," said Norma suddenly. "That was enough to give anyone an awful fright. A shock like that might— so even Cleo was in some degree responsible." But that sounded, as she said it, too far-fetched—even if perfectly possible—so that there was an echo of mockery in it which she had not at all intended. And Miriam, whose eyes had taken on some faint refraction of distant light, not of hope so much as reaching for a reasonable doubt, went blank again.

"Do you believe that, Norma?"

Did she believe that? Norma asked herself. It was a fair question. It was *the* question. She had set out to be scrupulously fair—to Miriam. To bring in all the evidence, without distortion. But it must be honest to be of any value, as Miriam's own question indicated. This was no time for polite or soothing excuses. And to be honest with Miriam, she had of course to be strictly truthful with herself. So after a moment she replied to the question, looking off at the hills, as though they were her Bible, and her hand was on it.

"I believe those are all true facts, Miriam. I haven't manufactured any of them. I don't know what part they may have had . . . But I'm saying that they might have combined, in a proportion that we can't judge . . . to overwhelm the slight physical resistance that Roger had left."

"Possibly," said Miriam. "Possibly . . ."

She had scarcely touched the things before her, but now she took a small sip of coffee. And then, abruptly, she put the cup down in the saucer with a small jarring clatter, and threw up her head, with her eyes half closed. "Even so!" she exclaimed. "Even if all those things are true—separately—they're got nothing to do with the truth. Nothing to do with me, no excuse for *me*. There isn't any. I don't know myself, how—or *why* . . . Oh, Norma, I could never explain —what happened to me." She had covered her face with her hands now, her elbows on the table, and the two women sat silent through a moment that was painful beyond imagining. (Such painful pity— painful pity; it was there inside her, not buried, but alive in the very words which Norma had read, somewhere—so recently.) And the sheath of ice which had separated her from Miriam earlier, and protected herself from the pain of seeing, knowing, feeling once again what the other was feeling, had in some way melted, leaving only coldness.

"You don't have to explain to me, Miriam. What happened—had begun to happen some time ago, hadn't it? Not just yesterday. I knew from what I heard you both say, yesterday. And from that conversation out here last night."

"That everlasting talk!" Miriam's voice was still quiet, as though to stifle the vehemence which broke through in spite of it. "I thought he'd never stop, never let go. Such a gay, *happy* evening—or it might have been—but he was making a nightmare of it. And it wasn't anything new—you're right about that, so I shouldn't have let it get me. He was like that every time the subject came up, and it was constantly in his mind. Constantly!"

"I know," said Norma. "I realized that too, more than I ever had before. It was like something that possessed him, though it wasn't fear so much as a sort of all-inclusive anxiety, wasn't it?"

"Oh, he wasn't afraid, himself. *For* himself. But he created fear, Norma. At least—in me, he did. The way he'd talk sometimes, the things he'd read aloud to me, and try to explain—it terrified me. I suppose I'm just a horrible coward, but I had to get away from it, somehow. Sometime."

"He drove you away from him, didn't he?" said Norma simply. "Poor Rog. It was an obsession, I can see that now. He said yesterday when we were talking, that it was like a kind of paralysis—that sense of imminence of destruction, that made everything seem futile. That's what kept him from writing, Miriam."

"I know, I know. And it was a vicious circle, because if he could have started work, it would have kept him from brooding so much."

"And from frightening you, when he really wanted to protect you."

"I—suppose so."

"He loved you very much, my dear."

"I know . . . I *know* . . . And I—loved him. Oh, Norma, can you believe me? You must know I did. I always will. But I wanted to live, too—not just sit cowering, waiting for the end to come . . . And so I—brought the end—on myself. On him. Oh, Rog. Oh, Rog."

337

"Perhaps he brought it about more than you did, Miriam. It was like fire, or something that got out of control, anybody's control. Someone said last night that a little fear is necessary. But he let it get away from him."

"But he was right!" said Miriam. "You and I know he was right. And when *it* comes now, I'll have to face it without him. I'll be alone."

"I don't think that matters, Miriam. 'We die alone' must be the oldest platitude on earth. Maybe that's what we have to keep in mind in order to keep our single fear from growing into general panic. From paralyzing us, or stopping us in dead center, unable to move. Or from running away, blindly."

"Like me," said Miriam, and Norma was silent. She knew that nothing she could say would help Miriam very much this morning. Not much would even register in her mind, and of that little, she would believe even less. (As when she had said, a minute ago, "Do you *believe* that, Norma?") But at some later time, she might remember one thing or another, and if what had been said were true, then it might help. The strange thing was that she had not known she was going to say any of this; she hadn't known until the words were out, that she believed exactly what she was saying. Now, she went back a step, in order to go on.

"No, I don't think Rog was right, Miriam. Or if he was, it was only up to a certain point—and he went too far beyond that. I don't know if he went beyond reality, or whether it was just beyond our comprehension. Do you?" But Miriam said nothing, sitting straight in her chair, her head bent and her eyelids down like blinds. "He was right—of course he was—about our having to face facts, but I think he took the furthest possibility as *fact*, didn't he? And nothing that hasn't happened yet *is* fact . . ." Norma stopped, and found Miriam's eyes, wide and dark with the blinds up, staring at her.

"As Roger's death—yesterday, was not yet a fact?" she said.

"Yes," Norma admitted, though the single word was extraordinarily difficult to utter. "Only a—potential fact. And that's what we live with all our lives, isn't it? The possibility that anything can happen, today—or tonight—or tomorrow."

338

"Anything," Miriam murmured, like a small desolate echo. "And it's always when we least expect it, and not what we were warned about."

"Of course," said Norma. "That's what we have to live with; not only in our separate lives. I suppose it's what we have to learn, and grow up to live with as a people. Or a world. Nothing is sure—but nothing is impossible."

"Except to bring back the dead," said Miriam, and Norma looked back at her.

"That's right," she said. And knew how cold it sounded. Cold comfort . . . But there was no comfort to be had, in that relentless conclusion. And it was harder to forgive someone whose fault bore even a faint distorted resemblance to one's own, than it was to forgive anyone else. No comfort to be given here. Only compassion, like Mr. Bixby's painful pity; not merely a soft sorriness for someone, not kindly tolerance or indulgence—not even sympathy . . . And certainly not condonation of faults, or facts, which were both irretrievable, no matter what one said. True compassion was an *informed* pity, containing in it the knowledge and the pain which enabled one to share what the other was suffering. Well, this was it, then, Norma thought.

"Miriam . . . I have to tell you this. I know more than you may think, of what you're going through."

"Oh, Norma, *please* . . . I know you lost Bart suddenly, but don't let's start pretending—"

Norma did not look at the face which turned sharply away almost as in revulsion, and she paid no heed to the interruption, except to acknowledge the one phrase.

"Yes. More suddenly than Roger. He went off to work one morning, and never came back." She drew in her breath, and held it, as if she were going down into deep water, for she had heard the small telltale clap of that living-room door, and knew that Joyce was coming out. But the fingers of her right hand were propped against her brow, screening that side of the terrace from her view, and she did not move them or raise her head, but let out the long breath which she'd been holding, and went on steadily. "Bart was an

339

excellent driver, you know. Everybody said so. Careful of his car and—well, careful. He wasn't a speeder. In fact, he never drove too fast, unless he was very angry. I've known him then to push down on the throttle—as though it was the anger itself that was driving him—and the car too."

She stopped. Why couldn't she get *through* this? Say it in one sentence . . . "We'd had an argument that morning at breakfast.' A silly fight, over nothing. Some stupid thing that didn't really matter. But I was hurt, and sore—and he thought I was quite unreasonable. I think I had been spoiled, in those days, by more love—than I had ever earned . . . I was offended, and I built it up," Norma said. "I was—pettish. And he went off, angry."

She knew that Miriam was looking at her now, her eyes burning into her, waiting for her to go on; she also knew that Joyce was standing there, only a few feet away, so she did not look up. When Miriam realized that she had finished, that she was quite, quite through, she said urgently, "But it was a collision, wasn't it? So the other may have lost control—it may have had nothing at all to do with what you've just told me."

"Oh yes, I know," said Norma. "There was only the driver in each car, and both were killed. So it could have been caused by any one of a number of things." She raised her eyes to meet Miriam's squarely, though she still did not look beyond her. "But one point that they were able to establish was that Bart was driving—much too fast. That's all I know, Miriam. All I've ever known, no matter how many things I've raked up and gone over in my own mind. I nearly drove myself mad in those first few weeks."

"And I always thought," said Miriam, "that you were the sanest and most sensible woman I knew."

"The Sensible Mrs. Collins!" Norma repeated bitterly, and then with a flash of something close to passion, "I *had* to be sensible, don't you understand what I'm telling you? For Joyce's sake, and my own—because we have to go on living if we're not utter cowards—and it's no use living in an asylum . . ."

There was no use in going on with this either, now that she had said what she had to say. Norma sat quietly, looking at her plump

340

hands (rather small pretty hands) folded in front of her on the table top, and Miriam at her right was motionless too, and off there a few feet farther, there was a corner of blue skirt which Norma was aware of at the edge of her vision. And then Miriam said harshly, "Even so, there's no comparison! None at all."

"I was not comparing—what you have done, Miriam—with what I did, or didn't do. That's a matter of our own separate moralities, and I do not condone yours, so don't ever think I do," Norma said sternly. "What I am trying to say is that you are not—a criminal, in the sense that you may think you are, this morning. As for what you may, or may not, have contributed to Roger's death, that is what you will never know, and you will have to learn to live with that uncertainty, behind you, as well as all the uncertainties ahead. I'm only telling you that I understand that—and it can be done."

She looked at Miriam's face with infinite sadness, as the other whispered, "Why, why can't we ever learn, in time?"

"I don't know . . . I don't *know*! Maybe that's all we're here for, to get an education, and most of us learn the hard way. I don't suppose there's anybody on earth who has nothing to reproach himself with. For hurting somebody, in some way that he can't undo—can never, never make up for tomorrow. Or even leaving something undone he'll never get another chance to do . . . 'those things that we ought to have done,' " she muttered. She was looking off at the far Hill, and her tone grew more abstracted. "Remember the old saying, 'How goes the enemy?' Meaning time—because it goes too fast, I suppose . . . But it's not the enemy! Because at least time gives us another chance, with every day." Her hands had tightened in their grip together, and she began speaking very fast.

"That's what Rog himself was trying to get across, wasn't it? Trying to tell us that we've *got* to learn what could happen before it is too late. To be everlastingly—vigilant, to keep our whole world intact."

"So he was right," said Miriam.

"But not about himself, was he? That's what he couldn't see. Though he knew so well that the individual—yes, every individual— every single one of us, is so important. And I *don't* mean just to ourselves!" Norma's soft fist was pounding on the table top now, though she was not aware of it at all. "Oh, Miriam, Miriam—everybody talks about our being so much further ahead in science than any other way, and how we've left ourselves 'way behind in all the rest of it—you know what I mean—politics and economics and all that . . ."

"Yes, I know," said Miriam almost indifferently.

"They've said it so often that we're sick and tired of hearing it. They talk about the atom as though *it* were the one worst terrible menace in our lives—but it isn't!" Norma cried, and Miriam's voice was toneless now as she said, "Just death."

"No. No—it's this thing in *us*, this horribly human thing in every one of us, which can go off any minute and destroy the world. Our own world. Death isn't the adversary either, don't you see? So it's fear with some—and anger with others, and greed—and sex—and pride, and all the other forms it takes . . Talk about a push-button to set off the final explosion . . ." Norma discovered what her fist was doing, and stopped it, and her eyes came back to Miriam and her hand went up, still clenched, to press against her chest. "It's right in here," she said, and her look was pitiful, as of someone who had found the cause of her own mortal pain. At the same time, she saw that Miriam's eyes were wet at last, before the blinds went down again, and finally she looked up to meet her daughter's gaze, which also held a strange shining, and she wasn't sure whether it was the glistening of tears or not. But Joyce spoke quickly, as though she had been only waiting for a chance.

"Mother, I think—if you don't mind, I'll drive Miriam all the way up to Los Angeles."

"Oh no—no!" Miriam exclaimed, her head moving back and forth in unseeing protest. "I don't *want* you to do that, Joyce. I'd rather not."

But the girl was looking past her, as though not hearing.

"I would like," she said to her mother, "to pick Jim up, and bring him down this afternoon." Norma frowned slightly in the effort to reorient herself. Taking note that Joyce was now wearing a crisp blue cotton dress, which was suitable enough . . . No, there was something else which was inconsistent; contradictory.

342

"Do you know where to find him?" she asked.

"Oh yes, I took down the street address of this gas station, and the name of the owner." (But she had been so definite, a short time before, about not going up. Ah yes, that was it.)

"Are you *sure* you want to do that, dear?" her mother asked.

"Absolutely sure, Mother. I was being—pettish," Joyce said, and Norma knew that she had never heard her use that word before.

"We'd better be starting then," Miriam said quietly, accepting the exchange which had passed back and forth over her head, and she got up from the table.

Norma walked to the gate with them, and stood with Miriam for a minute as Joyce backed the car around. Miriam had put on her suit coat, and now she was drawing on her gloves, which looked very odd, Norma thought, up here on a hill in the back country. But then she saw that it was a gesture, deftly prolonged, so that she—Norma—would not have to shake hands or embrace her. And it was true that a while ago she had found it most difficult even to look at her, almost impossible to touch her, but now as Joyce swung the car door open, Norma reached out to put her own hands on Miriam's shoulders and leaned forward to touch her cheek with her lips, and found it was not impossible at all; not even difficult. Just painful—as Mr. Bixby had said. But the ice had gone out, at last. Miriam turned wordlessly and got into the car, and closed the door. And only then she said, "Thank you—Norma—" and looked up into the other's eyes, a foot or two away, and shook her head slightly because there was no more to say, then turned it straight ahead, waiting for the car to move.

" 'Bye, darling," Joyce said softly. "We'll be back before dinner." (Not even noticing that she'd used that pronoun, which was not meant to include Miriam.) She lifted one hand and the fingers fluttered like a small signal flag, whose code her mother understood, and the car started slowly down the driveway, around the sharp bend into the road, and out of sight. Hope and despair traveling together, each to meet her lover. But hope was in the driver's seat once more, thought Norma. (Drive carefully, dear . . .)

And continuing to stand there, watching, after the car had moved out from under her eyes, she found she was looking across at the

343

same view of hills which she had known as intimately as faces. The same smooth round outline against the bright sky, with one small tree on top: the little stunted oak which looked so much like a short-handled parasol, or a cup-shaped button on a shank. Or—oh, very well, like a mushroom, if you insist. For she knew that she would never see it now without having to admit its faint incongruous similarity to the budlike fungus which had become a symbol. But even as her eyes made acknowledgment of what she saw in the distance, she was gradually becoming aware of sounds—and voices, somewhere behind her. From the patio—the house—oh yes, the kitchen, emerging into the patio no doubt. For jubilantly a voice broke out. Not hymns, this morning, but greetings with a new songlike lilt.

"Oh, Mee—sis *Coll*—eens!" And then . . . Correction. "Mis' Col—lins?" The same voice, undressed and a little uncertain. Plaintive. And Norma Collins, turning back, said quietly, though her tone could not have carried more than a few feet, "Yes, Bertha, I'm coming."

ABOUT THE AUTHOR

H. H. LYNDE was born in Spokane, Washington, where she went to school, grew up, and continued to live for most of her adult life, until ten years ago when she moved to Southern California, which has since been her home. She began to travel at the age of two, and early developed a love for the trains which then took four days and four nights to cross the continent. In the years following, she has rolled up a considerable mileage, though, as she points out, it has not been accumulated by much investigating of far lands, but largely by shuttling back and forth across this one.

Her writing career also began early, like that of most writers—in the schoolroom. At thirteen and fourteen, she was inclined to consider herself a poetess (though she dabbled in other media as well, such as short stories and what are known as Character Sketches); at seventeen or thereabouts, she wrote, co-produced and acted in a play—title now happily forgotten—which was viewed with mortification by the school's headmistress. The headmistress later demanded why the playwright had ever thought that she could write . . . adding that the desire to write was probably the commonest aspiration in the world. She concluded with the admonition to go home, put away everything she'd ever written for at least five years —and then see if she still thought she could write.

This no doubt excellent but ominous advice so jolted the incipient writer that she followed it literally, even bettering it to the extent of eight years or more—and then began all over again to learn her trade. Since then, abjuring both poetry and playwriting, she has had three novels published: *Remember Matt Boyer, The Slender Reed* and *Which Grain Will Grow.*